THE SHADOW SIDE

"*The Shadow Side* is exhilarating romantic suspense . . . never slows down until the final moment. Read this thriller."
—*Midwest Book Review*

"Stunning. A masterpiece of suspense polished off with a raw romance. This book, the best romantic suspense I've ever read, knocked me out. The characters were hot, the story was downright chilling . . . but so compelling. The pace constantly keeps you on the edge . . . giving you twists and turns and never giving you any clues as to what's going to happen next . . . until the very last minute! Don't miss this thriller; you'll be sorry if you do. They don't come any better than this." —*Romance and Friends*

"Ms. Castillo digs deep to reveal the darker side of passion and greed in this gripping novel."
—*Rouse's Romance Readers Group*

THE PERFECT VICTIM

"Castillo has a winner! I couldn't stop turning the pages!"
—Kat Martin, *New York Times* bestselling author of *The Fire Inside*

"*The Perfect Victim* is a gripping page-turner. Peopled with fascinating characters and intricately plotted . . . compelling suspense that never lets up. A first-class reading experience!"
—Katherine Sutcliffe, bestselling author of *Darkling, I Listen*

"Intense action . . . sizzling sex . . . a thrilling climax . . . the reader is carried along on the ride."
—Lynn Erickson, author of *On Thin Ice*

"Linda Castillo delivers a powerhouse punch."
—Merline Lovelace

continued . . .

Titles by Linda Castillo

THE PERFECT VICTIM
THE SHADOW SIDE
FADE TO RED

Fade to
RED

Linda Castillo

BERKLEY SENSATION, NEW YORK

FADE TO RED

A Berkley Sensation Book / published by arrangement with the author

PRINTING HISTORY
Berkley Sensation edition / May 2004

ISBN: 0-425-19657-7

BERKLEY SENSATION™
Berkley Sensation Books are published by The Berkley Publishing Group, a division of Penguin Group (USA) Inc.,
375 Hudson Street, New York, New York 10014.
BERKLEY SENSATION and the "B" design
are trademarks belonging to Penguin Group (USA) Inc.

PRINTED IN THE UNITED STATES OF AMERICA

10 9 8 7 6 5 4 3 2 1

"There is a Reaper, whose name is Death . . ."

—*Henry Wadsworth Longfellow*

prologue

DEATH TERRIFIED HER. SOMEHOW, SHE'D ALWAYS known hers would be violent. That it would come early in life. That it would be terrible and grueling, and in the end she would beg for it.

This was worse than terrible. Worse than anything she'd ever imagined even in her nightmares. Not even the lavender haze of the drug could dull the sharp bite of the knife. She felt every injury to her flesh with a thousand screaming nerve endings. Every second that ticked by like a death knell.

She struggled against her binds, twisting and straining until the wire scraped against the exposed ulna, causing agonizing pain in her wrists. But she knew it was useless. They had been as careful as she had been careless. Now she was going to pay the ultimate price.

The realization sent a surge of hopelessness through her, followed by a sickening rise of panic that pooled inside her like vomit.

This was it. The end. They were going to kill her and

there wasn't anything she could do to save herself.

The reality that fate could be so merciless filled her with outrage. After everything she'd been through, everything she'd overcome, everything she had endured in a life that had been far from easy, the last thing she would ever see was this dank warehouse and her own blood under the bright glare of the lights.

Goddamn them all.

She didn't care. Hadn't cared for a long time. About life. About death. She just wanted it to be over. Quickly and without all the humiliations of dying. As far as she was concerned she had died a long time ago.

She drifted toward the darkness, reaching and straining for it with her mind, wishing desperately it would swallow her whole, like a giant, ravenous beast that would devour her so she would simply cease to exist.

Another vivid flash of pain wrenched a scream from her, long and shrill and animalistic. She bit down on the gag and screamed a second time in outrage and fury, cursing them with every cell of her body. She rode the agony, felt it tear through her like a thousand tiny blades wakening every nerve with a ferocity that left her breathless. She tried to deny the horror of what was happening. Tried to convince herself that the God she'd always known would never be so cruel. But the pain was hellish and relentless and a thousand times worse than death.

She looked at her tormentor through the wet hair that hung in her face, and hatred welled inside her. The mask he wore should have terrified her, but it didn't. She understood all too well why he wore the mask, and she hated it. Hated him. Hated all of them.

She tried to speak through the gag, but it was impossible. With her last dying breath, she wanted to tell him she had betrayed him. That she'd left something behind that would destroy him. She wanted him to know she'd won one last tiny battle, if only for a fleeting instant of satisfaction before he killed her. That was all she had left, but it wasn't enough to save her life.

I'll see you in hell, she thought, and a maniacal sound bubbled up from her throat.

The eyes within the mask darted to hers. Within his gaze she saw the light of his exhilaration, the depth of his cruelty. And in that moment, she accepted her death. Accepted that it would happen here and now and there wasn't a damn thing she could do about it.

Except die.

Oh, but she didn't know how. Didn't know how to take her last breath. Didn't know when to close her eyes. When to let her muscles go slack. She didn't know how to stop living.

Dear God, she hadn't wanted to die alone.

She thought of her sister, and grief stabbed through her with the same hot vengeance as the knife. Regret stung her heart, but she knew there would be no reckoning, no righting of wrongs, no last good-byes.

Don't cry for me, she thought.

And when she closed her eyes, the world faded to red.

chapter
1

LINDSEY METCALF WOKE TO HER OWN SCREAM. IT
was a terrible sound in the stark silence of her apartment.
She sat bolt upright, the sheets bunched in her fists, her
heart beating out a maniacal rhythm. For several moments,
she sat there listening to her labored breathing, trembling
and disoriented and more frightened than she'd been in a
very long time.

Slowly, the nightmare receded and she became aware of
her surroundings. The dim light from the streetlamp slanting in through her bedroom window. The sound of sleet
hitting the glass. The tick of the wall clock from the living
room. The hum of the ceiling fan above her bed.

Shoving back the down comforter, she got up and
padded into the bathroom. She ran the tap into a glass and
drank it down without stopping.

She rarely dreamed and never had nightmares. Not even
as a child. But for the fourth time in as many nights, the
nightmare had wrenched her from sleep. She'd wakened
with a scream in her throat, her heart pounding, and her

body bathed in cold sweat. Afterward, all she could recall was a man in a mask and the utter certainty that something unspeakable was going to happen.

Struggling to get out from under the dark press of the dream, she returned to the bedroom, yanked her robe from the foot of the bed, and jammed her arms into the sleeves. A look at the alarm clock told her it was nearly three A.M.

Midnight in Seattle, she thought, and a now-familiar shudder of worry went through her. She'd been trying to reach her younger sister for almost two days. For whatever reason Traci hadn't returned her calls, and Lindsey's initial irritation had grown into concern.

Knowing sleep would not come again, she went into the kitchen, poured a glass of milk, and carried it to the living room. At the bar she looked down at the answering machine and felt another low-grade flutter of anxiety. She knew listening to the message again would only feed her worry. But suddenly she needed to hear her sister's voice— even if that voice was shaking with fear.

She punched the PLAY button and listened. "Lindsey, it's Traci. If you're there, pick up." A snowy hiss when she paused. "Lindsey, please. I really screwed up this time. I think I'm in trouble. Call me, damn it." A muttered curse and then an abrupt "click" as the line disconnected.

It was the dozenth time she'd listened to the message, and each time it brought gooseflesh to her arms. Traci rarely called. If not for Lindsey's determination to stay in contact with her, they would have fallen out of touch years ago. She wondered what had prompted Traci to break protocol, what had her so spooked.

I think I'm in trouble.

In all the years Traci had been in Seattle—even when she'd first run away at the age of fourteen—Lindsey had never heard her voice quiver like that. The only time she'd ever heard Traci scared was when they'd been children. Back then, they'd both had very good reason to be frightened.

Shoving thoughts of her childhood to the back of her mind, Lindsey snatched up the phone and dialed her sister's number. Four rings and Traci's answering machine picked up. "Hi guys. It's Traci. You know what to do if you want me to call you back." Beep.

"Traci, it's Lindsey. If you're there pick up the phone." She paused, aware that her heart was beating too fast and that it was suddenly vastly important that she speak to her sister. "I'm at home, Traci. Give me a call, okay, Sweetie?"

For a moment she just stood there, holding the phone, trying hard to shake off the uneasiness that had settled over her. Traci might only be twenty-four years old—four years younger than Lindsey—but she had good instincts and she'd always known how to take care of herself. She was probably going to get a good laugh out of this once she realized her overprotective older sister had been so worried.

But deep inside Lindsey knew good instincts were no guarantee against harm. In the early morning silence of her apartment, that knowledge made the hairs at the back of her neck stand on end.

Separated by miles and years, Lindsey and her sister didn't talk as often as they once had, but Lindsey still felt close to Traci. She sensed something was wrong. She felt it with the same intensity she had when they'd been kids and their stepfather had gone to Traci's room instead of hers.

They'd never discussed Jerry Thorpe or the havoc he'd wreaked on their lives, but it was a connection she and her sister shared. An undeniable link between two girls who'd grown up in nightmarish conditions. That connection may have frayed over the years, but it was still there. Tonight, Lindsey felt it as strongly as she ever had.

Realizing there was nothing she could do—at least not until morning—she replaced the receiver. "Go back to bed," she muttered to herself. "Traci's fine."

But as she walked down the hall toward her bedroom, she couldn't quite make herself believe it.

* * *

By noon the next day, Lindsey was pacing her apartment. She'd left two additional messages for her sister, but had yet to receive a call back. She told herself she was over-reacting. After all, Traci wasn't the most responsible young woman; this wasn't the first time she'd dropped out of sight for a couple of days. More than likely, she was out partying with her friends and hadn't bothered to check her answering machine. That would be so like live-for-the-moment Traci.

But no matter how hard she tried, Lindsey couldn't shake the worry churning inside her. At one o'clock, she called her best friend and business partner, Carissa Ross.

"Still no word from Traci?" Carissa asked.

"I'm really beginning to get worried."

"It's still early in Seattle, Linds."

"It's been three days now, Carissa. She's not picking up her messages."

Lindsey had met Carissa four years earlier while taking a class at Ohio State University. At the time, both women had been stuck in go-nowhere jobs and attending college part time in the hope of landing better careers. Over coffee one evening, Lindsey had mentioned her dream of opening her own catering business. A degreed pastry chef, she had the food service expertise but lacked the business experience and capital. Carissa, on the other hand, was a certified public accountant and had been looking to start her own firm. While she had the expertise and capital, she simply wasn't passionate about her chosen vocation.

Lindsey's enthusiasm had made an impression on Carissa, and over the following weeks the idea for Spice of Life Catering was born. They rented a postage stamp-size space just off of High Street not far from the university. After a rocky first year, Spice was in the black and earning a reputation both women were proud of.

In the three years it had taken to transform the fledgling

idea into a thriving business, their professional relationship had blossomed into a friendship that was more akin to sisterhood.

"Hmm . . . maybe she's out with some hunky new boyfriend," Carissa offered. "You know how Traci is. Maybe they're holed up in some fancy hotel having mind-blowing sex. Maybe they're—"

"Okay, I get the picture," Lindsey cut in.

"Like you have any idea what it's like to have mind-blowing sex."

"The kind of sex I have is none of your business."

Carissa snickered. "That's because you don't *have* sex, dearie. You give a whole new meaning to the word *celibate*."

"We're not going to have one of those you-need-to-get-out-more discussions, are we?"

"Come on, Linds, your idea of a night on the town is Chinese take-out and a trip to Blockbuster."

"So I like movies."

Carissa made a sound of exasperation. "That's not the point. I'm talking about men."

Trying to decide if she was amused or annoyed by her friend's good-intentioned meddling, Lindsey sighed. "Look, Carissa, I like men as much as the next girl."

"You certainly had me fooled. Exactly when is the last time you had a date with one?"

"I'm not keeping track."

"Let me refresh your memory, girlfriend. The last guy you went out with was that CPA I set you up with, and that was over a year ago."

"Oh. Him." Remembering, Lindsey winced.

"Mark Beck is hot, Linds. He's ambitious and attractive and—"

"And he spent a hundred bucks on some fancy dinner I couldn't pronounce, and then he expected me to have sex with him in the backseat of his Volvo."

"The backseat? *Really?*" Carissa burst out laughing. "Did you—"

"No!" Lindsey chuckled despite the fact that she didn't want to have this conversation.

"I can't believe he did that."

"The point is that I just don't need a man in my life in order to be happy."

"A girl doesn't need chocolate to be happy, either, but it sure makes her life a little sweeter."

"I'll keep that in mind next time I have a craving." Lindsey looked down at the answering machine and sobered. "We're getting off topic."

"Sorry. Have you tried calling the restaurant where she works?"

"I tried earlier, but there was no one there yet."

"What about her neighbors?"

"I don't know their names." Lindsey thought about it for a moment. "I'm going to call the police."

A pause ensued, then Carissa's voice softened. "Hey, are you okay?"

For the first time, Lindsey realized just how concerned she had become. "There was something in her voice, Carissa. I listened to her message a dozen times, and I swear she sounded scared."

"Is there anything I can do?"

"Thanks, but no."

After promising to keep her posted, Lindsey disconnected then looked up the number for Club Tribeca, the upscale restaurant where Traci worked as a waitress. She dialed, and a shrill female voice answered on the first ring with a rapid-fire utterance of "Club Tribeca!"

"I'm trying to reach Traci Metcalf."

"She's not here right now. Can I take a message?"

"This is her sister." She could hear the blare of rock and roll in the background. The din of voices. The clatter of dishes. "It's important that I speak to her. Do you know when she'll be in?"

"Hold on while I check the schedule." A click sounded, as she was put on hold.

"Sure," Lindsey muttered as two thousand miles of fiber optic cable hissed in her ear. In the back of her mind, she imagined Traci jumping down her throat for calling her place of work and checking up on her. If Lindsey had learned anything about her younger sister in the last few years it was that Traci didn't like people digging into her personal business.

A moment later, the shrill voice came back on the line. "She's supposed to work tomorrow evening."

"Did she work yesterday?"

"Um . . . let's see. Looks like she was supposed to, but didn't show." A beat of silence. "Oh, yeah, now I remember. Jamie filled in for her."

The words *didn't show* echoed hollowly in Lindsey's ears. "Wait a minute. Traci didn't show up for work yesterday? Are you sure about that?"

"That's what it says right here. Someone scratched her off the schedule and penciled in Jamie's name."

"Do you know why she didn't come in?"

"I don't know, lady. Stuff like that happens, you know? Things come up. The rest of us just figured she had something going on and covered for her. No big deal."

But Lindsey was beginning to think it was a big deal and asked to speak with the manager. A few minutes later an authoritative male voice with a hint of an accent came on the line. "This is Mason Treece, may I help you?"

"This is Lindsey Metcalf, Traci's sister. I haven't been able to reach her and was told she didn't show up for work yesterday."

An instant of silence. "I'd be happy to take a message and have her call you . . ."

"I've already left messages. She hasn't returned my calls."

"You've tried her at home?"

"Of course I have." Lindsey struggled for patience that was beginning to wear thin. "Isn't it unusual for her to not show up for work? I mean, did anyone check on her to make sure she's all right?"

"We assumed something came up. One of the other girls filled in. It wasn't a problem."

"Mr. Treece, I've been trying to reach her for three days, and she hasn't returned my calls. Frankly, I'm beginning to think there *is* a problem."

"I'm not sure how I can help, Ms. Metcalf."

"Do you know if any of your employees have spoken to her? Or maybe called her to see if she's okay?"

"I don't know off the top of my head. But I'm more than happy to check. Honestly, I don't believe her missing a day of work is cause for alarm."

"Normally, I would agree. But she left a strange voice message a couple of days ago. She sounded upset."

"Hmm. All right. I'll check with my other employees to see if anyone has heard from her. How about if I call you back at the end of the shift?"

"That would be great." Lindsey rattled off her home and cell phone numbers, then disconnected. Without putting down the phone, she dialed Seattle information and asked for the nonemergency number for the police department. She punched in the numbers, and a male voice answered with a curt, "Seattle PD."

Quickly, she explained the situation and asked him if there was any way the police could help.

"We can do a routine welfare concern check, ma'am. If you'll give me the phone number, address, description of the homeowner, and her vehicle description, we can send an officer by her residence to make sure she hasn't had an accident or met with foul play."

Relieved, Lindsey gave him the information.

"I can run the name through the computer while I have

you on the phone," he said. "See if we come up with any-thing,"

She heard computer keys clicking, then a decidedly un-happy "Hmm."

"What is it?" she asked.

"Looks like Ms. Metcalf has a warrant."

"A warrant?" It took a moment for the word to register. "You mean for her arrest? What on earth for?"

"Can't tell from this computer system. But it's an active warrant."

Lindsey was speechless. "Could it be for a hot check or something? Maybe she didn't pay a traffic ticket?"

"Maybe. Can't tell from here."

"You'll still do the welfare concern check, though, won't you?"

"Sure. I'll send an officer out there right away," he said.

But from the change in his tone, Lindsey got the distinct impression that, perhaps, he thought Traci might have skipped town to avoid the aforementioned warrant. "You'll let me know what you find?"

"Yes, ma'am."

"Thanks," she muttered and dropped the phone into its cradle. "A warrant. Wonderful."

Leaning back into the sofa cushions, she closed her eyes and tried to make sense of the warrant. As far as she knew, Traci had never been in serious trouble before. Sure, she'd shoplifted a couple of times as a teenager. She'd experi-mented with alcohol. Maybe even marijuana. But she'd never been in trouble as an adult.

She tried to convince herself she was overreacting. Traci was a grown woman. Maybe she'd decided to take a trip. Maybe it was like Carissa had suggested, and she'd found someone she cared for and was in some fancy hotel making mad, passionate love, and Lindsey was a complete idiot for letting her imagination get the best of her.

Or maybe the nightmares were a premonition and something unspeakable had happened. . . .

It was nearly five P.M. when the police called back. "This is Officer Bunger from the Seattle PD. I wanted to let you know an officer drove by the residence, ma'am. There's no vehicle in the garage or driveway. The house is secure. Front porch light is on. There was no sign of any problems. We did a walk around the perimeter and left."

Lindsey tried hard to be relieved by the news, but it did little to remove the stone of worry that had dropped into her gut. "Thank you. I appreciate the phone call."

"Sure thing."

She hung up and sagged against the back of the sofa, the officer's words replaying in her head. *The house is secure. There was no sign of any problems.*

Except my sister is missing, she thought.

Lindsey knew it was crazy, but she wasn't going to be able to let his go. She'd never be able to live with herself if Traci was in some kind of trouble and she did nothing to help. It had been almost three years since she'd been to Seattle to see her. A long time, considering Traci was the only family she had left. What would it hurt to take a few days off and fly out for a visit?

Mentally, she tallied everything she had planned for the coming week and realized Carissa could handle most of it. The rest could be canceled.

Chances were, Traci was fine and they were going to spend the next few days getting caught up on things, watching sappy movies, shopping at the Pike Street Market, and arguing over whether to have healthy food or junk food for dinner, the way they had the last time Lindsey had flown out to see her. If Traci wasn't all right . . .

Lindsey banked the thought before it could materialize. She wasn't going to go down that road. Not yet. Everything was going to be fine, she assured herself. Just fine.

chapter
2

RAIN FELL IN SHEETS FROM A TURBULENT SKY. Thunderheads hulked like brooding ghosts, obscuring the tops of buildings and slithering low to wrap the city in a cold and murky embrace. Lindsey turned the windshield wipers of her rented Taurus on high and wondered if the natives ever grew tired of the incessant storms. Tuning the radio to a local rock station, she left Seattle-Tacoma International Airport and took the 405 Loop north toward Bellevue where Traci rented a bungalow.

She'd tried to reach her sister several times throughout the day. Once in the predawn hours before she'd left Columbus. Again during her layover at the Minneapolis-St. Paul International Airport. And a third time once she'd arrived at Sea-Tac and was waiting for her suitcase to make it to the baggage claim.

Her messages had gone unanswered.

At just before seven that morning, Lindsey had called Carissa and told her she was heading to the airport and would be spending the next few days in Seattle. Considering

Carissa was not a morning person, she'd been a good sport about being roused from sleep and asked to take care of the week's engagements. She'd even agreed to water Lindsey's plants if she wasn't home by the weekend. Lindsey assured her she'd be back by then.

The wipers waged a losing war against the driving rain as she left the freeway and entered Bellevue. The neighborhood was upscale and composed of older, well-kept homes, with lush landscaping and towering trees. To her left, she could see the gray-blue water of Lake Washington reflecting an angry sky.

Five minutes later she turned left onto Calimesa and parked curbside. Traci's bungalow was an older home with a composite roof, small front porch, and mullioned windows. The brick had been painted an attractive dove gray, the shutters a glossy black that contrasted nicely. Dark green ivy shrouded the front of the house, giving it a rich, European look.

It was a classy place for a waitress. Traci had always explained the disparity between her profession and the high-rent neighborhood by telling Lindsey Club Tribeca catered to an upwardly mobile crowd and that a good waitress could make as much in tips as their salaried executive clientele down in the financial district. Lindsey hadn't questioned that. Now, as she sat in her rented car and studied the house through the rain-streaked windshield, she wondered if maybe she should have.

Since her umbrella was in her suitcase, Lindsey decided to brave the rain. Swinging open the car door, she grabbed her purse and hightailed it up the pavestone walkway toward the front door. Once on the porch, she used the brass knocker and waited.

"Please be home," she grumbled.

When no one answered, she cupped her hands and peered through the beveled side light. The foyer stood in shadows. She saw a console table with a Tiffany lamp. A mirror framed in intricate gold leaf. An imposing grandfather clock. Beyond, she could see the leather sofa and a large-screen TV in the living room. She used the knocker again, then tried her knuckles on the side light glass. When neither roused her sister, she turned up the collar of her leather jacket and proceeded to the rear of the house.

At the side yard, she found the gate locked. "Great," she muttered and peered between two cedar planks of the privacy fence. She caught a glimpse of a nicely landscaped yard, a wooden deck replete with Adirondack furniture, a hot tub, and a bed of winter-dead flowers.

Aware that her hair and jacket were getting wet, annoyed because she hadn't foreseen the need for a key, Lindsey spotted a large empty clay pot next to the foundation and dragged it over to the gate. Thunder rumbled in the distance as she turned the pot upside down and stepped onto it. Swinging her leg over the top of the gate, she used her arms to heave herself up and over. She landed on the other side in four inches of water that soaked her jeans to her knees.

"Traci, if you so much as crack a smile, I'm going to strangle you," she said under her breath.

Blinking rain from her eyes, Lindsay sloshed down the tiled path, ducking reflexively when a spear of lightning flashed overhead. She stepped onto the wooden deck and crossed to the set of double French doors at the rear of the house. There were no lights on inside and no sign of Traci.

Because she couldn't think of anything else to do, she tapped on the glass with her keys, then tried one of the doors. To her utter amazement, it opened. Stunned, Lindsey stood there for several long seconds, trying to decide if that was good or bad. When she'd called the cops for a welfare concern check, they'd told her the place was secure. If that was the case, then why was the door unlocked? Hadn't the cops checked? Or had someone else been there *after* the police had done their check?

Lindsey stepped into the house and shook the rain from her jacket. "Traci?"

The first thing she noticed was the music. Techno-rock blared from an intricate-looking stereo on the other side of the room. The house smelled as if it had been closed up for a long time. Lindsey closed the door behind her and looked around.

"Helloooo? Traci?" Slowly, her eyes adjusted to the semidarkness. "Are you here? It's Linny."

Crossing to the stereo, she located the power button and turned it off. The ensuing silence was deafening. "Is anyone home?" She tried hard to justify the quiver of unease in her voice. She'd just traveled twenty-three hundred miles, scaled a six-foot fence and broken into her sister's house. She was a little rattled, a little perturbed, and a whole lot worried. That was enough to make anyone's voice quiver, wasn't it?

The living room stood in disarray. One of the sofa cushions had been tossed haphazardly to the floor. Magazines and pillows and several expensive-looking curios littered the floor. An empty bottle of imported beer peeked at her from beneath the sofa. Traci had never been neat, but she wasn't a slob, either. What the hell was going on?

Puzzled by the mess, Lindsey stepped over a fallen Oriental vase and started toward the kitchen, her leather boots clicking smartly against the hardwood floor. At the doorway she switched on the light and for an instant just stood there, too shocked to move. Drawers had been yanked out and upended. Others stood open as if they'd been rifled through. Canisters lay open on the floor, flour and sugar and coffee beans spilling onto glossy Mexican tile. The refrigerator door stood open, and the motor wheezed like an asthmatic on a high pollen day. The coffeemaker lay on its side on the counter, black dregs leaking onto the granite countertop. The trash compactor bag had been ripped from its nest and turned upside down. The reek of old garbage hung in the air.

Lindsey's heart rolled into a rapid-fire staccato as she surveyed the chaos. This was the moment when Traci was supposed to jump out and surprise her with news that she'd just gotten back into town. Lindsey would quickly forgive her for worrying the dickens out of her, and they'd spend the next half hour or so cutting up and laughing this off.

But Traci didn't appear, and Lindsey didn't feel at all like laughing. All she could think was that this was not the result of one of Traci's wild parties. Someone had ransacked the place.

The hairs at her nape prickled when she realized the perpetrator could still be in the house. That her younger sister, who'd already been hurt so much in her short life, could be lying upstairs injured or unconscious—or worse. That Lindsey herself could be in danger.

Spotting the phone on the wall, she snatched it up and punched 911. A noise behind her made her gasp. She spun, gripping the phone like a weapon only to see a big Siamese cat hiss at her, then scamper across the living room.

"911, what's your emergency?" came a female voice.

Lindsey jerked her attention to the phone, but she didn't turn her back to the living room. "I'm at my sister's house. I—I think someone broke in."

She could barely hear the computer keys clicking on the other end of the line over the rush of blood through her veins. "Are you located at 353 Calimesa?" the voice asked.

"Yes."

"Are you alone, ma'am?"

The hairs at her nape prickled again. Lindsey squinted into the dimly lit living room, listening, wondering if she was totally insane for standing there holding the phone when there was a very real possibility that whomever had done this was still in the house. "I don't know," she said, her voice dropping to a whisper. "I don't see anyone, but I haven't checked the upstairs."

"There's a unit in the vicinity. You can either stay on the

line with me, or if you think you're in danger walk outside and meet the responding officer in front of the residence."

Lindsey thought about it for a moment, realizing if someone came down the stairs, they would be able to block her escape to the French doors. "I'll meet the cops out front."

"Okay. Ma'am, I've got an officer en route. ETA about two minutes."

Hanging up the phone, she walked to the French doors and turned to face the living room. She stood there a moment, listening. The pounding rain outside magnified the silence. Lindsey wasn't easily frightened; she'd faced plenty of monsters in her lifetime. But she was scared now.

Slipping out the door, she tried not to think about why.

Fifteen minutes later, Lindsey stood in the kitchen with Officer Wong, a trim Asian-American man with short-cropped hair and intelligent brown eyes. He'd arrived on the scene within minutes of her call. He'd immediately checked the upstairs bedrooms, assuring her there was no intruder lurking in the shadows—and no sign of Traci.

Lindsey trailed him as he walked from room to room and surveyed the scene. He spoke several times into the radio at his shoulder and scribbled notes on a small pad. He was kneeling at the French doors, examining the lock when a female voice chirped over the radio. He barked out a few cryptic numbers in response, then stood and turned to Lindsey. "Ma'am, what's your relationship to the homeowner?"

"I'm her sister." Lindsey approached him from across the room. "What do you think happened?"

"There's no sign of forced entry. The condition of the house isn't indicative of foul play."

"How do you explain the mess in the kitchen?"

"We've been called to this address several times in the last couple of months for disturbances. There have been a lot of parties here. Noise complaints. Loud music mostly."

He looked down at his notebook. "Last time an intoxicated male took his clothes off in the front yard and started playing his guitar."

Lindsey might have smiled if she hadn't been so worried. "I don't think this looks like the result of a party."

"If someone had come in to vandalize or burglarize the place, they wouldn't have stopped with the kitchen. The rest of the house looks to be in order. There's expensive-looking jewelry in plain sight in the master bedroom." He glanced over at the television. "That TV would have been one of the first things to go."

Lindsey stared at him, trying hard not to acknowledge the sinking feeling in the pit of her stomach. "Maybe I interrupted him before he could finish."

"Did you see anyone?"

"Well . . . no."

"Look, there's no sign the premises was broken into. There are no broken windows or jimmied locks. Your sister has a history of having parties here that tend to get out of hand. She serves plenty of alcohol, and I think that could explain the condition of the kitchen."

"But she's missing. I've been trying to reach her for four days now."

He frowned at her. "Are you aware that there's a warrant out for your sister?"

Lindsey tried to suppress the sharp kick of anger, but she couldn't keep it out of her voice. "So if a woman has a warrant, you cops don't concern yourselves with her personal safety?"

"All I'm saying is that a warrant can be pretty good motivation to skip town if someone doesn't feel like going to jail."

"She didn't skip, damn it."

"I'm not saying she did, ma'am. Just that it's a possibility you might want to consider at this point."

"What's the warrant for? An unpaid parking ticket? Bad check? Jaywalking? Noise pollution? What?"

"All I can tell you is that it's a felony warrant. We don't get the details over the radio."

"Felony?" She was so taken aback by the word, she could barely spit it out. "There's got to be some kind of mistake."

He didn't look convinced. "If I were you, ma'am, I'd call some of her friends and try to persuade her to turn herself in." His radio crackled, and he tilted his head and spoke into the mike. "2052 clear."

Lindsey knew enough about cop jargon to surmise he wasn't going to stick around to help her figure this out. "Is there anything I can do? Maybe I could file a missing person report, or something?"

"You would have to do that at police headquarters." He looked around. "Do you know what kind of car your sister drives?"

She had to think about that for a moment. "A BMW. Red. A couple of years old."

"Are you aware that there's no vehicle in the garage?"

"Maybe someone stole it."

Sighing, he strolled back toward the kitchen and motioned toward a single sheet of paper clipped to the refrigerator door. "Did you see this?"

Lindsey plucked the paper from the clip, realizing immediately that it was an itinerary from an on-line travel broker. It showed a flight departing Sea-Tac the day before and traveling to LAX with an open return. She hadn't noticed it before and for the first time felt a quiver of doubt. "Why on earth would she go to Los Angeles?"

"With all due respect, ma'am, if I were you, I'd concentrate on getting her back here and try to talk her into turning herself in. Things will be easier for her if she comes in voluntarily to straighten things out."

She looked down at the itinerary and tried hard not to feel foolish. But the seed of doubt had been planted. Maybe Traci *had* left town to avoid getting arrested. Maybe she'd planned to call later and get whatever mess she was in straightened out. Lindsey knew it was plausible. Probable, even. It would explain the message Traci had left for her. Maybe the warrant was the trouble she'd been referring to.

But none of those things explained why Lindsey felt so strongly that something was wrong. That something terrible had happened. It didn't explain the nightmares. Or the prickly sensation she kept getting at the back of her neck. She knew how crazy that sounded. But she'd learned a long time ago to listen to her instincts.

At the moment those instincts were telling her all was not well with her sister.

Three hours later Lindsey paced the lobby of the Seattle Justice Center and waited for the detective from the Missing Persons Division to meet her. She was damp from the rain, chilled to the bone, and trying like hell to ignore the low-grade anxiety that had been pressing down on her since she'd arrived. She hadn't eaten since her layover in Minneapolis some six hours ago, and her stomach was churning pure battery acid. To top things off, a headache was beginning to pound just behind her left temple.

After Officer Wong left the bungalow, she'd called several locksmiths, finally locating one who could squeeze her into his schedule. He'd been an hour late and hadn't spoken a word of English, but she'd gotten new locks installed on both the front and rear doors. If Traci showed up now and couldn't get inside, she'd just have to deal with it.

"Ms. Metcalf?"

Lindsey spun to see an African-American man approach her. He was the size of a woolly mammoth with hawkish eyes and salt-and-pepper hair cropped close to his scalp.

"I'm Detective Renner," he said.

She stuck out her hand and tried hard not to be intimidated. He shook her hand with an amazingly gentle grip, then motioned toward the bank of elevators. "Right this way."

The elevator whisked them to the seventh floor. The doors opened to a wide hall with gray carpet and institutional blue paint. He motioned right, and they passed through double doors marked HOMICIDE and into a large room dissected by cubicles. Half of the cubes were occupied. Lindsey counted five men and one woman, felt their suspicious cop gazes on her as she and Detective Renner walked toward a small, nondescript interview room situated between a row of beat-up file cabinets and the coffee station.

She knew her dislike of cops was irrational. But her stepfather had been a cop. Jerry Thorpe had worn a uniform and taught her at a formative age that not all cops were good. She'd come a long way since then, but she still couldn't look at a blue uniform without remembering all the things he'd done to her and her sister.

The interview room contained a wooden table and three plastic chairs. It was small and cold and as sterile as a hospital room. Renner settled his large frame into one of the chairs and motioned for her to sit opposite him. "I ran her name through the computer after you called," he began. "You know about the warrant, right?"

She nodded. "What's it for?"

"She got busted with two grams of heroin during a routine traffic stop. She compounded the situation by failing to appear for her court date."

Disbelief rose up inside her, followed by a quick jab of denial. "There's got to be some kind of mistake."

He looked at her with patient brown eyes that told her he'd heard it all a hundred times before.

"I mean it," she said. "She doesn't do drugs."

"Look," the detective said, "whether she does or does not do drugs is irrelevant at this point. What *is* relevant is that she's missing and didn't show up at court to get things straightened out. Okay?"

Lindsey didn't know what to say, didn't know what to make of any of this. There were so many questions churning in her brain she didn't know where to start. At the beginning, maybe. If she could figure out where that was.

"If she was arrested, why isn't she in jail?" she asked.

"She made bail."

"Who paid her bail? I mean, did she use a bail bonding company? What?"

He looked down at the report in his hand. "Mason Treece posted her bond."

Mason Treece. The manager of the restaurant where Traci worked. Lindsey had talked to him the day before and the bastard hadn't seen fit to mention that her sister had been arrested. She almost couldn't believe it. Almost.

"In order to get this missing person report filed, I'm going to need to get some vital statistics from you," the detective said. "Physical description. Vehicle description. Her place of work. Friends. Family. Boyfriends. Everything will be entered into the NCIC."

"NCIC?"

"National Crime Information Center. It's a national database that can be accessed by law enforcement anywhere in the country."

He left to retrieve a laptop, and for the next ten minutes he fired off questions. She answered to the best of her ability, but soon realized there was a lot she didn't know about Traci.

"If it's any consolation, I can tell you there's a high probability that your sister skipped town because of the warrant," he said without looking away from the keyboard.

"I don't believe that's what happened. She would have called me."

"Is there something specific that makes you think she's in trouble?"

For a crazy instant, she considered telling him about the dreams she'd been having. About the man in the mask and the blood and the knife. About her uncanny ability to know when her sister was in trouble. But she caught herself just in time. There was no way this detective was going to buy in to the psychic connection theory. Lindsey wasn't even sure *she* bought in to it. The way her luck was going, he'd probably arrest her for being a fruitcake.

Instead she told him about Traci's message, that she hadn't shown up for work, that the back door of her house had been unlocked, even though the police had done a welfare concern check, that the kitchen had been ransacked.

"I know the warrant looks bad," she said. "But I know my sister. I know she wouldn't call me to tell me she's in trouble and then skip town without letting me know."

"Any idea where she might be? Friends she might be with? Boyfriend maybe?"

"She'd mentioned a new boyfriend a couple of times. His first name is Brandon."

"Last name?"

She shook her head. "All I know is that she met him at Club Tribeca."

He stopped typing, looked at her over the top of his glasses. "Club Tribeca?"

"The restaurant where she works. She's a waitress."

"A waitress?" He made a sound that was part sigh, part groan. "Is that what she told you?"

Something new and uneasy niggled at her. "What else would she tell me?"

"Ms. Metcalf, it's probably not my place to tell you this, but since your sister is missing I think you should know that Club Tribeca is not a restaurant. It's a nightclub."

She stared at him, her mind racing through the implications of his words. "I don't see how that would have any bearing on her being missing."

He had the good grace to look uncomfortable. "Club

Tribeca is a topless club. It's upscale. Live . . . entertainment. A lot of local bands play there. They don't serve food."

Lindsey wanted to dispute that, but she saw the truth in his eyes. And she suddenly knew there was a hell of a lot more to her little sister's job than waiting tables.

"Anything else you can tell me that might help us find her?" he asked.

Remembering the photo in her wallet, she dug it out and handed it to him. "It's a couple of years old."

"Pretty girl," he said. "Mind if I keep this?"

"Sure. It's a copy."

He slid the photo into a thin manila folder. "The warrant isn't necessarily a bad thing at this point," he said. "If she gets stopped for any reason—traffic, whatever—the officer will run her tags and she'll be brought in. She may not like it, but at least we'll know where she is."

That wasn't the way Lindsey wanted her sister found, but at this point she figured she didn't have a choice. They could get the rest straightened out once she was home safe and sound.

It was dark by the time Lindsey parked the rental car in Traci's driveway and shut down the engine. She sat in the car for a moment, looking at the darkened windows of the bungalow, telling herself she hadn't been hoping to find the lights on and her sister's red BMW parked outside.

She popped the trunk latch and unloaded her suitcase. The rain had slowed to a drizzle, but the temperature had dropped throughout the afternoon. Shivering, she rolled her suitcase to the front door and let herself inside. The house was eerily silent and as dark as a cave. Turning on lights as she went, she lugged her suitcase up the stairs.

The guest room was small and furnished with Shaker style furniture. A queen-size bed, dressed in a green, crushed-velvet quilt, dominated the room. Two night tables punctuated either side of the slatted headboard. A single dresser and mirror encompassed the opposite wall. She set her suitcase on the bed and mechanically unpacked her clothes. She changed into a pair of drawstring pants and an Ohio State University sweatshirt and went downstairs.

She located a package of deli ham and some decent bread in the fridge and made a sandwich. The food eased her headache, but didn't do a damn thing for the most pressing problem: how to find Traci. There was no way she was going to sit back and wait for the cops to find her, when Lindsey was more than capable of doing some of the legwork herself. She just needed to figure out where to start.

She spent twenty minutes straightening and cleaning the wrecked kitchen. Remembering the cat, she found some dry food in the pantry and filled a bowl with kibble. She brewed coffee then moved on to the living room where she began going through the mail and papers strewn atop the dining room table. She found utility bills. Phone bills. A past-due notice from a dentist in Tacoma. She opened a certified letter from the City of Seattle Police Department, notifying Traci Irene Metcalf of her court date.

Finding nothing in the living room or kitchen, she moved her search upstairs. The master bedroom was large and elegantly furnished with heavy mahogany furniture, custom draperies, and oil reproductions set in velvet mats and framed in gold leaf. She didn't remember the furniture or art from her last visit, and tried not to wonder how her sister had been able to afford it.

The king-size sleigh bed donned a velour animal print spread, silk sheets, and an array of fringed throw pillows. A Salvador Dali reproduction brooded above the massive headboard. Adjacent to the bed, an entertainment center opened to reveal a flat screen television and an array of electronic wizardry.

Lindsey stood at the door for several seconds, a little stunned by the sheer beauty of the room. But then Traci

had always had a taste for the extravagant. Even when they'd
been kids, she'd wanted the pricey toys. As a teen, she'd
moved on to designer clothes and accessories. Things they
hadn't been able to afford, but the lack of money had never
kept her from wanting. Or even stealing on occasion. She'd
gotten into trouble in high school for stealing a pair of gold
earrings from Uhlman's Department Store. Luckily, Mr.
Hampton hadn't pressed charges. But Traci had paid the
price later at home . . .

Shaking off the memory, Lindsey stepped into the
room, wondering where to start. She didn't like the idea of
invading her sister's privacy. She knew that was the one
thing that would upset her. Traci was obsessive about her
privacy. But Lindsey figured the situation had moved beyond propriety.

Trying not to feel like a snoop, she opened the top drawer
of the night table and began to rummage. She found several
paperback best-sellers, dozens of bottles of nail polish, hand
lotion, and a pack of Virginia Slims cigarettes. A box of
personal checks and a checkbook register. She opened the
second drawer. A bottle of Midol. Prescription sleeping
pills. A tapestry manicure case. A box of condoms—half
full. Coconut-flavored personal lubricant. Frowning, she
picked up a small oblong box only to unearth a pair of
chrome handcuffs tucked beneath it. Refusing to ponder
why her sister kept handcuffs next to her bed, she opened the
box and was stunned to see a flesh-colored dildo and matching vibrator set into black velvet.

Embarrassed even though she was alone, Lindsey felt
the heat of a blush on her cheeks. "Jesus, Trace, that's way
more than I need to know about you."

She wasn't a prude, but she didn't like thinking of her
younger sister in terms of her sex life. Especially if that sex
life included handcuffs and dildos.

Snapping the box closed, she replaced it and continued

searching. She lifted a recent copy of *Cosmopolitan* magazine and found herself staring down at a pistol. It was small
and black with a wooden grip. It looked like a toy, but
Lindsey knew it wasn't. She didn't have anything against
guns, but couldn't help but wonder why Traci felt the need
to keep one next to her bed.

Closing the drawer, she moved on to the closet. The
smell of perfume mingled with cedar and a hint of dry
cleaning chemicals. Not exactly sure what she was looking
for, she began going through the jackets and slacks and
blouses hung neatly on plastic hangers. By the time she
reached the back wall, she was grinding her teeth in frustration.

Then she spotted the luggage.

It was a relatively new set with a designer label that was
arranged neatly next to a rack of shoes. Lindsey stared at
the four pieces, realizing that if Traci had taken a trip—
even a day trip—the one thing she wouldn't have left behind was luggage.

Trying not to jump to conclusions, she left the bedroom
and went downstairs to the study. It was an elegant room
paneled in dark wood. Built-in bookcases comprised the
wall to her left. Most of the books were popular fiction,
with a few classics and antiques scattered in. She saw
leather bindings, gold embossed titles, and paper dustcov-
ers. She hadn't known her sister liked books.

A carved rosewood desk sat in front of the single Palla-
dian window. A sleek black computer and desk lamp rested
upon its glossy surface. The blinking message light on the
phone caught her attention. Curious, Lindsey hit the PLAY
button. A message from Jamie at Club Tribeca asking Traci
to call her. Realizing the messages could be helpful, Lindsey yanked open the pencil drawer, found a Mont Blanc
pen and a pink legal pad, and scribbled down the name.
Her own voice sounded next, and she thought it seemed

like a lifetime ago that she'd called her sister from the shop. There was a message from the landscaper. Her massage therapist. An acupuncturist from Renton.

The next message gave her pause. "It's Striker. What's up?" A deep male voice. Authoritative. No-nonsense. "Call me, damn it. I'm at the office." Click.

She wrote down the name, found herself irritated that he hadn't left a number. Setting the pad aside, she turned on the computer, then began going through drawers as the system booted. She found a Seattle phone book and Yellow Pages directory. Stamps. Envelopes. Expensive stationery. Address labels. Bills that had been bound with a rubber band. She closed the last drawer and scanned the desktop. A gold message holder in the shape of a paperclip held two scraps of paper. She plucked them from the holder and read quickly. The first was a number with no name. On impulse, Lindsey dialed the number, got an after-hours recording for a dentist, and hung up. The second sheet of paper held a name in Traci's scrawling handwriting: *Striker*.

She didn't recall Traci ever mentioning that name. Who was he? Why had he called her? She glanced down at the leather blotter, spotted the corner of the business card sticking out from beneath it, and plucked it out. *Michael Striker, private investigator. Eighteen years of law enforcement experience. Criminal Investigations. Surveillance. Missing persons. Legal. Domestic. Washington License #535246. Results oriented.*

Why on earth had Traci been in contact with a private detective? Was he a friend? Or had she called him about a problem? Did it have something to do with the warrant?

Call me, damn it.

That wasn't the kind of message a private detective left for a client. Unless he was familiar with the client. Or maybe Traci wasn't a client at all. Maybe their relationship was more personal in nature. . . .

The phone jangled, and Lindsey nearly jumped out of her

skin. Pressing her hand to her chest, wondering who would be calling Traci so late, she picked up the phone. "Hello?"

An open line hissed at her.

Lindsey held her breath, listening, sensing someone on the other end. "Hello? Is someone there?"

Silence.

Gooseflesh rippled down her arms. "Traci?" she whispered.

The line went dead. Troubled by the hang up, she replaced the receiver. "What the hell is going on?"

From the foyer, the grandfather clock answered with a solitary chime.

chapter
3

MICHAEL STRIKER SEPARATED HIS DAYS INTO TWO
categories. Bad days, which were the days when he woke
to a hangover and it took every bit of discipline he possessed just to get his sorry ass out of bed. And the *really*
bad days. The *clusterfucks,* he called them for lack of a
better term. The days when he didn't have to get up in the
morning because he hadn't gotten to sleep the night before.
Days when the last thing he wanted to do was come to this
dank little office, or talk to another human being, or even
look at himself in the goddamn mirror because he didn't
like what was coming back at him. Those were the days
when he wondered what the hell he was still doing on this
earth when he could have saved himself and a whole lot of
other people a shitload of trouble if he'd had the guts to
pull the trigger.

But while Striker was a lot of things he wasn't proud of,
he'd never been a coward. He'd never been one to take the
easy way out. At this point in his life, he wasn't sure if that
was good or bad.

If it hadn't been for his ten o'clock appointment, he wouldn't have bothered coming in to the office. Even if he was sick to death of staring at the walls of his empty loft. He preferred the solitude over some long-suffering bastard who wanted him to take pictures of his wife walking into the Alexis Hotel with his business partner. But then such was the life of a private detective.

Shaking the rain from his trench coat, he hung it on the rack just inside the front door and crossed the closet-size reception area to his interior office. Sixty years ago Worthington Tower had been grand with tall windows, glossy hardwood floors, and high-ceilinged office suites. But time and circumstance had taken a heavy toll on the building, and over the decades the three story structure had fallen to near ruin. The once-proud façade was now humbled by graffiti and crumbling concrete. The tall windows inside the suites sweated like dirty sauna doors and offered a dismal view of a neighborhood that had been on the decline for twenty years.

Striker shared the building with Ming's, a Korean take-out restaurant, and a bail bonding agency office across the hall. The place smelled perpetually like a combination of sweet and sour pork, nervous felons, and soggy sheetrock.

But for all its shortcomings, Worthington Tower suited Striker to a T. The bonding company was low key and sent a steady stream of clientele his way. Ming put out decent beef short ribs and the occasional free meal. As an added bonus, the Red-Eye Saloon was only a block away, so he didn't have to go far to find anonymity and the temporary reprieve of a bottle of scotch. The arrangement was just what the doctor ordered for an ex-cop with a felony assault charge and ten-year prison term hanging over his head.

Four months earlier he'd been a homicide detective with the Seattle PD. He'd had a spotless record and one of the highest solve rates in the department. Then along came a killer by the name of Norman Schroeder, a legal system gone haywire, a fateful moment of bad judgment, and Striker's illustrious career got sucked down the drain like dirty water in a tub.

Striker had ended up in the muck at the bottom of the heap with the rest of the scum he'd spent the last eighteen years getting off the street. A hell of a fate for a man who'd once prided himself on being a good cop.

Talk about a clusterfuck.

He might have put Schroeder in jail, but he'd sold his soul to do it. For the life of him he couldn't decide if it had been worth the cost. He supposed he'd get his answer in two weeks when he went to trial and twelve of his peers decided how he would be spending the next ten years of his life.

Striker had just sat down at his desk when he heard the scrape of wood against wood as the outer door chugged open. He looked up from his laptop to see his ten o'clock appointment come through the door. A young woman with reddish-brown hair, a pale complexion, and large, dark eyes stepped into the reception area, as if she were venturing into a place that wasn't quite safe. He guessed her to be in her late twenties. A little too thin. A little too serious. Attractive, but not quite pretty.

Intrigued, he leaned back in his chair and watched her close the door behind her. She was of average height, with shoulder-length hair that was more curly than straight. She wore a black leather jacket, clunky leather boots, and bell-bottom jeans that were snug in all the right places. No body piercing's or tattoos—that he could see, anyway. A navy turtleneck swept over a narrow waist and smallish breasts. No jewelry except for the small hoops at her lobes. Not visibly wealthy, but she looked like she paid her bills. A plus, since most of his clients were as hard up as he was.

The day was definitely looking up.

Her name was Lindsey Johnson, if he remembered correctly. She'd called his answering service at eight that morning to set up an appointment. She'd been vague as far as why she needed a private detective, but a lot of his clients were reticent at first.

He wondered why she needed a private detective.

She paused in the reception area, then glanced through the open door of his office, and made eye contact with him. Striker felt that contact like a low-grade electrical charge that ran the length of his body then doubled back and did it again.

He stared at her, aware that she was walking toward him, that her hips were nicely curved. His eyes swept the length of her, then went back to a face that should have been ordinary, but wasn't. Her features were nicely put together. Small nose. High cheekbones. Wide mouth. But it was her eyes that made her face unforgettable. They were the color of top-shelf Caribbean rum. The kind that went down like hot silk, then knocked you on your ass when you were least expecting it.

She pushed open the door, and Striker had to steel himself against a sexual tug low in his gut. He knew better than to get sucked in by tight jeans or pretty eyes. But the knowledge didn't deter the hot jump of male interest, even though he knew he wasn't going to do anything about it. His life might be a clusterfuck, but he'd learned the hard way that things could always get worse, especially if you added a woman to the mix.

He sensed her sizing him up, but her scrutiny didn't bother him. He'd long since given up on the notion of trying to please. With the direction his life was going, he didn't give a good damn what she thought of him one way or another.

She hesitated, then stepped into his office. "I'm looking for Michael Striker."

He didn't rise, didn't smile. "I'm Striker."

"Oh . . . well, I'm a little early." Flashing a tentative smile, she crossed to his desk and extended her hand. "Lindsey Johnson. Thank you for seeing me on such short notice."

Her voice was low and husky and seemed incongruent with the rest of her. He accepted her hand, noting her firm grip, and felt another inappropriate tug.

"Nasty day," he said.

"It's cold."

There was something familiar about her, but he felt certain he'd never met her before. He would have remembered those eyes. He sure as hell would have remembered her body. Realizing he was still gripping her hand, he released her. "Have a seat."

She took the chair opposite his desk and crossed her legs. Striker watched her, trying to peg her the way he'd pegged people back when he'd been a cop. Eye contact. Mannerisms. Gestures. Speech. But he knew almost immediately that Lindsey Johnson didn't fall into a neat category. She was too aware of herself, and there were simply too many contrasts that didn't quite meld.

He saw some street smarts in her eyes, but she fell just shy of tough. She was attractive, but not classically beautiful. She wasn't quite rough around the edges, but she wasn't polished, either. The contrasts made for an interesting package and intrigued him more than he wanted to admit.

"What can I do for you?" he asked.

"I think I need to hire a private detective."

"Why do you think you need a PI?"

"My sister is missing."

He tried not to notice when she licked her lips. That her lower lip was fuller than the upper and slicked with moisture. "How long has she been missing?"

"Four days. Maybe longer."

"Is she an adult? Over seventeen?"

"She's twenty-four."

"Have you filed a missing person report?"

"Yes, but . . . I want to do more. I mean . . ." When she looked at him, he saw nerves in her eyes. "You do missing person cases, don't you?"

"Most of what I do entails finding people."

She looked relieved. "In that case, do you mind if I ask you a few questions? I mean, before we start?"

Striker tried not to be amused. The extent of most people's knowledge of PIs came from what they saw on television. Most wandered in expecting Mickey Spillane or Tom Selleck. Reality couldn't be further removed from those Hollywood images. Real-life PI work consisted of surveillance for insurance companies looking to catch some poor slob in a back brace washing his car, cheating spouses going at it like rabbits in the backseat of hubby's car, running down wayward teenagers whacked out on ecstasy and hormones and a severe shortage of brain cells.

"Ask away," he said.

"I guess the most important thing I need to know about you is if you have references."

Plucking one of his business cards from his pencil drawer, he turned it over and wrote three names and phone numbers on the back of the card, then slid it across the desk. "You might check with the detective first," he said.

She picked up the card, glanced down at it, and dropped it in her purse. "How long have you been a private detective?"

"About three months."

"You were a police detective before that?"

He resisted the urge to roll his eyes and wondered how someone could be so out of touch. His upcoming trial was a favorite topic among Seattle's media elite. "I was a cop for eighteen years." Growing impatient with her questions, he tapped his pen against his desktop and reminded himself that she was a prospective client, that he should be nice to her.

"Why don't you tell me about your sister?" he said.

"It's a little . . . complicated."

He waited, knowing there was more. There was always more.

"She's got a warrant."

Inwardly, Striker groaned. "She skipped bail?"

"No. I mean . . . maybe." She took a deep breath. "I don't think so."

He contemplated her, unable to shake the feeling that there was more to the story than she was letting on. She seemed nervous, but he didn't think it had anything to do with him personally. More like she was fishing for information. Holding that thought, he reached into the file drawer in his desk and pulled out a copy of his client contract. "I work off a contract."

"How much do you charge?" she asked.

"Seventy-five dollars an hour plus expenses."

She seemed to mull that over for a moment. "That's six hundred dollars a day, if you put in a full day."

"That's the going rate."

"That's a little steep for me. I don't have a lot of money."

He rolled his shoulder, waited, telling himself there was no way he was going to do something stupid, like offer her a discount just because she had amazing eyes. Or because she filled out those jeans the way he thought jeans ought to be filled out. He might be down on his luck, but he wasn't a sucker.

"Do you usually find the people you're looking for?" she asked.

"It depends on how complicated the case is. Most of my missing persons cases are for runaway teens. A couple of days of legwork, a few phone calls, and I can usually run them down. Most times it's a matter of finding out who they're with."

"I see."

He shoved the contract at her. "Why don't you take the contract home and read through it and give me a call if you're interested?"

She didn't budge. She licked her lips again, and he suddenly got the feeling she wasn't some prospective client who'd found his name in the book and called him up blind, hoping to find some long-lost relative. There was more coming. He could see it in her eyes. He looked at her closely, trying to recall if he'd met her before. She was so damn familiar . . .

"Can you give me the names of your last five clients?" she asked.

"My client list is confidential."

"I mean, for references."

"I just gave you references."

"I just . . . like to know who I'm dealing with."

"What you see is what you get, sweetheart. Take it or leave it."

She looked down at her hands, then met his gaze. "Do you know Traci Metcalf?"

The name zinged through his mind like a ricochet. For the first time, suspicion reared its head. An alarm began to wail inside his brain. He cut her a hard look, realizing he'd read her wrong. That she was something he hadn't anticipated. Something he detested. A vulture looking for carrion on a carcass that had already been picked clean.

"You've got two seconds to tell me what this is about," he said.

Her eyes went wide. "I just . . . want to know—"

"Bullshit. Who are you working for?"

"Nobody. I own . . . a catering—"

"Who the hell are you? Some kind of reporter? Tabloid?" The thought made him furious. "Don't you people ever get enough?"

"Reporter? No, I'm Lindsey . . ."

Her voice trailed when he rose. Leaning over the desk, Striker glared at her, aware that his temper was lit. This wasn't the first time some second-rate newspaper or magazine or tabloid had sent some scumbag reporter to his office fishing for a scoop.

He knew it was stupid to let it get to him. But in the last

four months, his fuse had been worn down to a nub. A strike of the match, and he went off like a bomb. The media knew that and loved to stick a camera in his face. Invariably, he gave them the fireworks they were hoping for. Since that fateful day in the police interview room, he was the hottest thing to hit the Seattle airwaves since Kurt Cobain had blown his head off with a shotgun.

"Who do you think you're fucking with?" he snarled.

Her eyes widened. "I—I'm not—"

"You're not here looking to hire me." He shoved his chair back and rounded the desk. "You're yanking my chain. Looking for some juicy tidbit to print in whatever rag you're working for."

"Look, Mr. Striker, I didn't mean to upset you."

"I'm not upset, lady. I'm pissed off. Believe me, there's a big difference."

She glanced over her shoulder toward the door, then started to rise. "I think I'd better leave—"

He rounded the desk and reached her just in time to keep her from getting up, then locked her into the chair with his arms. "Who the fuck are you?"

"I'm Lindsey . . . Metcalf," she said breathlessly.

Striker ground his teeth, aware that his temper had broken free, that it was like a raging beast that had burst from its cage, and there was no way in hell he was going to rein it in now that the monster was out. "Why did you give me a phony name?"

"I didn't want . . . you to—"

"Do you know what happened to the last reporter who came in here looking for a juice story?" he asked nastily.

Her eyes went wider. "No, I mean . . . I'm not . . ."

He had to hand it to her; she was good. She actually looked frightened. A little indignant. But he'd been around the block too many times to believe she was here for any other reason than to dig up some dirt so she could write a sensational story about how she'd gone deep under cover and infiltrated the lair of the infamous Michael Striker. Bloodsucking parasites.

"M—my sister is missing," she said.

"Wrong answer, sweetheart. Try again."

"You don't understand. Traci Metcalf is my sister."

The words penetrated the fog of anger like a hail of bullets. And suddenly he realized why this woman was familiar. He stared at her, shocked and unsettled and not quite sure how to respond.

Digging into her bag, she pulled a photo from her wallet. Her hand trembled when she handed it to him. "I haven't been able to reach her. I think she's in trouble."

Striker looked at the photo. A young woman with wavy blond hair, a lovely face, and engaging, mischievous smile. A face that was a hell of a lot more familiar than he wanted it to be. A face that would make it very difficult to turn this woman away no matter how badly he wanted to.

"I'm worried about her," she said. "I'm just trying to find out . . . how you know her. How you fit into this."

He glanced down at her, not sure how to reply without opening a can of worms he had absolutely no desire to deal with. "What makes you think I know her?"

"There was a message from you on her answering machine," she said. "I found your card on her desk. I thought maybe she'd called you about . . . a problem."

Striker felt a sinking sensation in his gut when he realized why she hadn't been straightforward with him from the get-go. "Or maybe you thought I was responsible for her going missing."

"No, I just—"

"But you came here to talk to me anyway." He laughed, but it was an ugly sound. "Christ, lady, I'm the last man a woman like you ought to come to for help."

"Why did you call her?"

"I was returning her call." He lifted a shoulder, let it drop. "She didn't call me back."

"How do you know her?"

"I met her at Club Tribeca."

"Oh." She stared at him with those amazing eyes.

He stared back, aware that they were having an effect. "Look, I appreciate your being worried about your sister, but I think maybe you ought to find someone else to help you."

"I don't want anyone else."

He laughed again. "Why the hell not?"

"Because she called you. Evidently, she thought you could help her. You know her."

"I don't know her. She's an acquaintance." He shook his head, incredulous. "Don't you know who I am?"

"So far you're my best hope of finding her."

chapter
4

It had been a long time since Striker had been anyone's best hope. Frankly, he wasn't sure he was up to the task. Expectations could be such a pain in the ass. Especially when the person doing the expecting was a woman with a body designed by the devil himself.

He thought about Traci Metcalf, and uneasiness niggled at the back of his brain. Beautiful, wild, fun-loving Traci. She was high heels and slinky dresses and the kind of sex appeal guaranteed to put a man on his knees. She was a free spirit and didn't mind the occasional walk on the wild side. She was reckless and troubled and lethal as hell. A danger to herself and anyone who cared because she got off on risk and the sky was the limit.

In the back of his mind he wondered if her card had finally come up.

He contemplated the woman before him, judging the similarities, the stark differences. He hadn't known Traci had a sister. He hadn't known much about her at all. But then, he hadn't asked.

Realizing he was still leaning over her, he straightened, then stepped back. "You're not from around here, are you?"

"I'm from Ohio. Columbus."

Midwest. He should have had that one pegged. She had that wholesome look about her. Not that she'd just fallen off the turnip truck. No, this woman had a few rough edges. But there was an innate kindness about her, too. A fragility her sister didn't possess. A softness life hadn't been able to harden.

Striker rounded the desk and sat down, trying to figure out how to handle this. "What makes you think Traci is in trouble?"

He listened intently as she explained the chain of events that had brought her to Seattle, starting with Traci's cryptic message and ending with her filing the missing persons report with the Seattle PD. "She wouldn't leave a message like that and then disappear without a trace."

"Unless maybe she doesn't want to be found."

"She knows she can trust me. No matter what kind of trouble she's in."

When Striker only frowned, she turned those eyes on him, and he found himself thinking about Caribbean rum. "She was scared when she left those messages," she said. "Traci isn't the kind of woman to scare easily."

No, he thought, Traci didn't have the good sense to know when to be afraid. "Have you called Club Tribeca?" he asked. "Any of her friends? Boyfriend? Neighbors?"

"I called Club Tribeca and was told she hasn't shown up for work for the last two days."

Striker rolled his shoulder. "Good attendance probably isn't real high on the job-skill requirement there."

When she only continued to look at him, he wondered if she knew what her sister did for a living. "You know your sister is a topless dancer, right?"

Flushing, she looked down at her hands. "Yes."

He gave her a moment, then asked the next obvious question. "What's the warrant for?"

Her eyes met his. "It's a felony drug warrant. The detective I spoke with said she was arrested during a traffic stop and the police found two grams of heroin. She also failed to appear for her court date."

He scrubbed a hand over his jaw. "If she skipped—"

"She didn't skip." Her eyes turned fierce. "I know my sister. She would have called me."

"Look," he said, "one of the things I've learned over the years is to look at the motivation behind people's actions. Motivation usually explains behavior. In this case, her leaving town without notice makes sense if she was trying to stay out of jail."

"She didn't skip town, damn it."

"If your sister is into drugs, she's probably running with a bad crowd. Partying. Getting bad advice. Using bad judgment. It all goes hand in hand."

"You're making blanket assumptions."

"I'm drawing upon my experience as a cop."

"My sister isn't 'into' drugs. Traci isn't like that. I mean, she may be fun-loving, but she's got a good head on her shoulders—"

"Look, Ms. Metcalf, let's get real. People who use good judgment don't get busted with two grams of heroin." Not that he was an expert on good judgment these days, but at least he could still tell the difference.

Indignation heated her gaze. "She's missing. She could be in trouble. Does it really matter if she has a warrant?"

"It matters because my experience tells me she skipped. My advice to you is not to waste my time or your money trying to find her. Call her friends; that's where she'll be."

She sat very still and stared at him for several long seconds. "I guess I was wrong about you."

"Look, I'm sorry if that's not warm and fuzzy enough for you, but that's what I think."

"Or maybe you think she doesn't matter because she's made some mistakes in her life. Maybe you think she's not worth your time because she doesn't rate high enough on your scale of decent. Maybe you think she doesn't count because of the way she lives her life."

The quick rise of indignation cut him cleanly. "Nobody said she doesn't matter," he growled.

"You just did." She rose abruptly. "And I got your message loud and clear."

Because she'd managed to ruffle him, he stood, too, and glared at her across the desk. "I know what I'm talking about."

"And I'm pretty sick of you self-righteous types judging a missing woman based on your perception of her lifestyle."

His temper strained against its leash, but he reined it in, held it back. "Getting yourself all worked up over what's probably nothing isn't going to help you find her."

"I'll see myself out." Before he could respond, she was striding toward the door. "You are *such* a loser."

Loser.

The word stung with surprising ferocity. Of all the things she could have called him, why did she choose that one? Why not cold-hearted bastard? Or apathetic son of a bitch? Striker figured he had those coming. But loser?

"Wait a minute . . ."

Without pausing or looking at him, she raised her hand as if to silence him. "Don't bother."

Striker watched her walk through the reception area, hating it that he was angry. Hating it even more because deep down inside he knew he'd just done to her the same thing the fine citizens of Seattle had done to him. Made assumptions and judgments based on flimsy impressions and preconceived notions, then let him twist in the wind.

Damn it, he didn't need this shit.

At the door, she turned, struck him with angry, dark eyes.

"When I find her, I'll be sure to let her know how concerned you were."

Striker stood at his desk and watched her jerk open the door and then slam it behind her, telling himself the nagging little voice in the back of his head wasn't his conscience. He didn't have anything to feel guilty about. Damn it, he didn't.

But no matter how vehemently he denied it, some of the things she'd said had gotten under his skin. He told himself it didn't matter. He'd done the right thing by sending her away. Finding a missing person was one thing. Trying to find a junkie who didn't want to be found was something else entirely.

Maybe you think she's not worth your time because she doesn't rate high enough on your scale of decent.

The words rankled. Maybe because she was right. Or maybe he hadn't given a damn for so long, he hadn't even realized it when doing the right thing no longer counted for shit.

And as he stood in his dank office and listened to the rain slap the windows, he felt like hell. For letting her walk out when he shouldn't have. For refusing to help her when he could have done plenty to make things right.

For not telling her the truth about her sister when she had every right to know.

Lindsey was still shaking when she left the business district and headed north on Westlake toward Belltown. She'd been hopeful that Michael Striker would offer to help her find Traci, or at the very least point her in the right direction. That he'd refused to do either of those things stung— and made her angry as hell.

"Loser," she muttered and rapped her palm against the steering wheel.

She didn't understand the connection between Striker

and Traci. He said he'd met her at Club Tribeca, that she
was an acquaintance. Did that mean he was a regular at the
club? Had Traci gotten to know him there and called him
because she was in trouble? Did that trouble have something to do with the warrant? Had she needed a private detective? Or had she called on him for a more personal
reason? The questions pounded at her with the same force
as the rain pounding the windshield, but there were no answers to be found.

Club Tribeca was located in a warehouse district comprised of tired brick buildings set against the backdrop of a
moody Lake Union. While many of the surrounding warehouses were ramshackle and vacant, Club Tribeca shone like
a big, gaudy ruby nestled amongst rough cut stone. The
location should have detracted from the appeal—the neighborhood wasn't exactly upscale—but the contrast between
derelict and chic added an interesting element that intrigued.

Lindsey drove by slowly. The two-story building had
been artfully renovated, with obvious care taken with regard to preservation. Pane windows had been replaced with
elegant glass block. The original steel grate fire escapes
had been painted and ran like black lace from the second
level to the alley on the north side of the building. Red
neon slashed across the building's façade touting the name.
A red and white canopy hovered over a stone walkway,
protecting waiting clientele from the rain. To the left of the
beveled-glass doors, a small army of uniformed valets
manned a mahogany dais.

Even at noon, the place was packed. Lindsey studied the
people lined up beneath the canopy. Young upwardly mobile professionals. Couples. Stockbrokers, bankers, and
corporate executives out for a liquid lunch and a peek at
some female flesh to get them through their afternoon
meetings. She was surprised by the number of female patrons and wondered how much the club scene had changed
since her college days.

She parked halfway down the block and sat in her car for several minutes, trying to muster the courage to go inside. This wasn't the first time she'd walked into a club alone, but the clubs she'd frequented during college hadn't been topless and were a far cry from the cold glitter of Club Tribeca.

Rain fell in sheets as she got out of the car and started for the canopy at a brisk clip. She was severely underdressed in her faded jeans, turtleneck, and black leather jacket, but there was no way she was going to drive back to the bungalow to change clothes.

The line moved quickly, and within a few minutes she was through the front doors. Inside, the techno-rock blared so loudly she could feel the vibration all the way to her stomach. Dead ahead and behind a granite-topped counter, an anorexic-looking man clad in a black leather vest collected the hefty cover charge. When Lindsey reached the counter, she pulled Traci's photo from her purse and slid it across the counter. "Have you seen her?"

He glanced down at the photo. "Sure, she dances. She's good."

"When's the last time you saw her?"

"Three or four days ago." He looked more closely at her. "Hey, are you a cop? Is she in some kind of trouble?"

Aware that the customers were piling up behind her, she took a twenty out of her purse and laid it on the counter. "She's my sister. Is there someone I can talk to about her?"

"Mason Treece runs the place. He came in about half an hour ago."

Spotting a vase of matches on the counter, she picked one out and jotted her name and cell phone number on the inside cover. "Her name is Traci Metcalf. If you see her or hear anything about her, would you give me a call? It's important."

He looked down at the pack of matches and smiled. "Sure thing."

Lindsey thanked him and followed the roped-off walk-way toward the main part of the club. At the door, a muscle-bound man in a silk suit and a bald head smiled at her and opened the door. "Enjoy," he said.

Taking a deep breath, she walked into the club. The warehouse was immense and jam-packed with people. From monstrous speakers mounted high on the walls, the rock group Pearl Jam screamed about Jeremy. The air smelled of cigarette smoke and eucalyptus and a collage of expensive colognes. Retro stainless and glass pendant lights hung down from high steel beams and cast muted light onto three massive bars teeming with noontime revelers.

Lindsey had never liked crowds and for several heart-beats she stood just inside the door, trying to take it all in. On the stage, a stunning blond woman wearing only a se-quined thong and acrylic platform shoes wrapped her legs around a chrome fireman's pole and slid into an open-kneed squat. Her body was dusted with glitter, and her flesh sparkled beneath a thousand pin lights. Head thrown back, she rose slowly, then kicked her leg high above her head. Her lips pulled into a seductive smile when she looked out over the audience. Then, hooking her thumbs over the waistband of the thong, she gyrated her hips and slowly eased it over her hips and down her long legs.

Turning away from the stage, Lindsey looked around for a waitress. Surely one of them knew Traci. If not, per-haps they could point her in the direction of Mason Treece.

"Hey, you in the leather jacket. You lookin' for work, or did you just wander into the wrong club?"

Lindsey turned at the sound of the rich female voice, found herself looking at a lovely young woman with blond spiral curls that reached halfway down her back, feline green eyes, and lips slicked with something red and glossy. She wore a tiny black thong with a matching bow tie at her throat and was carting a tray laden with cobalt martini glasses.

"I'm looking for Traci Metcalf." Lindsey kept her eyes squarely on the woman's face.

"Haven't seen her for a couple of days. Who's asking?"

"I'm her sister. Lindsey."

The woman arched a thinly plucked brow. "I thought you looked kind of familiar. I'm Jamie."

Lindsey would have extended her hand, but the waitress still had the tray hefted over her shoulder, so she offered a smile instead. "I haven't been able to reach Traci, and I'm very concerned. Can you tell me when she last worked? When you last saw her?"

"She worked her regular shift last week. Then she must have cut out, because she hasn't been here for a few days. Didn't even call, but then that's Traci for you."

Lindsey wanted to ask her to clarify, but the other woman seemed to be in a hurry. "Does she have a friend by the name of Brandon? A boyfriend, maybe?"

"Brandon Rakestraw. I see him around sometimes."

"Do you know how I can contact him?

"*Jamie?* Is there a problem?"

Lindsey turned at the sound of the deep male voice to see a well-dressed man with vivid blue eyes approach, his gaze moving from the dancer to her. "May I help you?"

He spoke with a hint of an accent Lindsey couldn't quite place and looked as if he'd just walked off of a Paris runway. He wore an exquisitely cut brown silk suit, linen shirt, and a contrasting gold tie. His hair was as shiny as Oriental silk and pulled into a neat ponytail at his nape. Everything about him was slick, she thought. His clothes. His hair. His smile. Even his eyes seemed slick. She guessed him to be in his mid-thirties. Successful. She wondered if he was the manager.

"I think she's looking for work." Casting an amused smile in Lindsey's direction, the blond hefted her tray of martinis and walked away.

The man turned his attention to Lindsey, and she had to suppress a shiver when his eyes slid over her.

"I'm Lindsey Metcalf," she said quickly. "I'm not looking for work."

His gaze sharpened. "Ah, we spoke yesterday on the phone. You're Traci's sister?"

She nodded. "I still haven't heard from her. I was hoping you could spare a few minutes."

"Of course." He extended his hand. "I'm Mason Treece." He grimaced, looking appropriately concerned. "There was a police detective here earlier, asking questions about her."

Relief flitted through her that the police were doing their job. "I filed a missing persons report."

"Good, good." He touched his chin thoughtfully. "We can talk in my office. It's quieter. A bit more private." He motioned toward an illuminated EXIT sign at the back of the room. "Right this way."

Treece led her through the throng of people, pausing to speak to several patrons along the way, laughing with them, touching their shoulders. A manager who knew his clientele well, she thought. The curious glances cast her way didn't elude her, but no one spoke to her. She followed Treece through the EXIT door and into a dark, narrow hall. To her right was a dressing room with private stalls and several lighted makeup mirrors. The next room was a small break room with a table and chairs and soda machine. At the end of the hall, Treece stopped at a door and punched numbers into a security keypad.

The door opened to steel grate stairs that took them to the second level and another hall. Recessed lighting reflected off walls chock full of black and white photographs in trendy stainless steel frames. Lindsey recognized several of the faces and names. Kurt Cobain. Courtney Love. An obscure Hollywood actor whose name she couldn't remember. A quarterback with the Seattle Seahawks. Each of the photos had been autographed.

"Here we are." Treece stopped outside a paneled wood door, produced a key, and unlocked it. Stepping inside, he flipped on the light. "Please forgive the mess."

Lindsey didn't see a mess. In fact, she didn't see anything out of place, unless you took into account the dozen or so folders on his desk.

"Please. Sit down. Make yourself at home." He motioned toward one of two chairs opposite his desk. "Would you like a cappuccino? Brandy?"

Caffeine was the last thing she needed, but because she was chilled and wanted as much of his time as he would give her, she asked for cappuccino.

She took one of the chairs and looked around his office, while he scooped and measured and poured. It was small but classy and smelled vaguely of sandalwood. Retro sixties furniture was arranged tastefully on a glossy hardwood floor. A barrister bookcase. A drop leaf desk with a sleek table lamp and a laptop computer. Slick, Lindsey thought, just like him.

"I'm sure you've surmised by now that I manage Club Tribeca."

She nodded, wondering if he had any idea how much that disgusted her. "I still haven't heard from Traci. I'm very concerned. I'm wondering if you've seen her. If she's called in. If you know of anyone I could contact. Friends, maybe."

"I wish I had better news, Ms. Metcalf, but I'm afraid I must tell you the same thing I told the detective this morning. Traci didn't show up for her shift again this afternoon."

"Did she call? Has anyone heard from her?"

"I haven't heard from her. Of course, I haven't checked with all the other dancers yet, but I've called another meeting after closing to see if any of them have heard from her."

"Traci is a dancer?" she asked.

A glimmer of something that was more shrewd than

slick flickered in his eyes, and she suddenly knew that beneath the expensive clothes and good manners the man was a shark. "She's a dancer, of course. One of our best talents, actually. Creative. Athletic. Uninhibited."

Lindsey hadn't wanted to hear any of those things, but couldn't deny them, so she simply absorbed the information and tried not to let it disturb her. "How long has she worked here?"

"About six months. I hired her myself." He smiled as if that was something to be proud of. "Is there anything in particular that has caused you to be so concerned about her?"

Lindsey told him about Traci's message and that she hadn't returned any of her calls.

"I certainly understand your concern." He leaned forward as if he were about to share a secret. "But Ms. Metcalf, I'm afraid I must ask: How well do you know your sister?"

"Well enough to know she wouldn't call me to tell me she's in trouble and then not return my calls."

"Your relationship with your sister is none of my concern. I've only known her for about six months, after all. But I can tell you, this isn't the first time she's taken an unscheduled holiday."

"This has happened before?" But she already knew what he was going to say and braced.

"Actually, there have been several occasions in the last six months when Traci has gone missing."

"How long has she stayed away in the past?"

"It varies. A few days. The other dancers cover for her." He shrugged. "We always welcome her back. Our clients love her. They come to see her dance. If it's any consolation, I can tell you that Traci will be back."

Lindsey struggled to understand how someone could live their life that way. With Spice of Life to run, she couldn't imagine dropping out of sight without telling anyone. But then she'd always been the responsible one. Traci had always been . . . Traci. "But why does she disappear? Where does she go?"

He looked at her as if she were a dense child. "She is a lovely young woman. Spirited. Talented. But she's also adventurous and, some would say, irresponsible."

She heard something in his tone and asked, "What do you mean by irresponsible?"

"I really don't want to speculate—"

"What have you heard?" she pressed.

He shrugged. "Traci's a party girl. She likes to get high. Have a few drinks. Have a good time. You understand."

Lindsey didn't understand. But a picture was beginning to emerge. A very dark picture that disturbed her deeply. "Drugs?"

He nodded. "Recreational, if there is such a thing."

She knew there was no such thing as recreational drug use. Sooner or later, the lifestyle caught up with the user and they ended up paying a price. "Does she have any friends here that I could speak with? One of the other dancers, maybe? Someone she might have confided in?"

"Certainly. Some of the dancers are very close. They form bonds. We're sort of a family here at Club Tribeca."

A dysfunctional one, Lindsey thought. "Who can I talk to?"

"Traci and Jamie Mills are friendly. Tana."

"I'd like to talk with Tana."

He looked at his watch. "I'm afraid she just went on stage a few minutes ago."

"I don't mind waiting." She considered him a moment. "Do you know someone by the name of Brandon Rakestraw?"

His expression didn't change. "He's one of our regulars. Why do you ask?"

"Traci mentioned him. I think she was involved with him. Do you know anything about that?"

He raised his hands disarmingly. "I'm afraid I do not

keep up with the love lives of the dancers. I suspect that would be a full-time job. If Traci and Brandon are involved, I'm not aware."

"Do you know how I can contact him?"

"No."

There was a finality in the word that made her wonder if he was going to remain as helpful as he wanted her to believe. "When does he usually come in?"

Leaning back in his chair, Treece folded his arms over his chest and frowned. "Look, Ms. Metcalf, I appreciate your concern about your sister. I really do. It's a big and sometimes scary world out there. But as much as I'd like to help, I'm afraid I must ask that you not harass my customers."

"I just want to ask Brandon a few questions."

"People come into Club Tribeca to forget about their worries for a little while. They come here to have a good time. To escape their everyday worlds. They want anonymity. Fantasy. Atmosphere. Interaction with beautiful dancers who know how to please. I am dedicated to giving my clients what they pay for. With all due respect, they do not want to answer questions about someone's missing sister. I'm afraid that while I sympathize with your situation, I must ask that you not harass my clients with unpleasant questions. I'm sure you understand."

Of all the things he'd said, the word *unpleasant* was the one that struck a nerve. As if the disappearance of a young woman was nothing more than an annoyance that needed to be dealt with.

"What I understand, Mr. Treece, is that you don't give a damn about my sister, but you'll keep up the pretense that you do as long as it doesn't inconvenience those perverts you call clients."

"Your words, not mine."

"Maybe you'd rather the police haul them downtown." Lindsey didn't think the police would actually do that since they'd already been to the club asking questions, but she wanted to at least plant the thought.

His eyes hardened. "I suggest you refrain from idle threats if you want my cooperation."

"While we're on the subject of cooperation, why didn't you tell me you bailed her out of jail?"

Something dark flickered in the depths of his eyes. Annoyance. Anger, maybe. Not because she'd found out something he didn't want her to know, but because he'd been caught in a lie, if only by omission.

He shrugged disarmingly. "Traci made a bad decision and got into trouble. She asked me for help. I provided help. I don't make it a habit of broadcasting that kind of information."

"I'm her sister."

"If she wants you to know about that particular . . . transgression, I'm sure she'll tell you."

"Look, Mr. Treece, all I care about is finding her. Whatever else she's done . . . it doesn't matter. But I need your cooperation. Please, I'd like to speak with Tana and Brandon Rakestraw."

Mason Treece stood. "I'm afraid you'll have to do that another time. Now, I must get back to work." He reached for a notepad and pen and rounded his desk to hand them to her. "If you'll leave your name and number, I'll see to it that you're contacted immediately when we hear from Traci."

Trying not to acknowledge the fact that he was now standing too close, that his hips were almost at eye level, she reached for the pad and scribbled her name and cell phone number.

He leaned forward and would have locked her into the chair with his arms, but she rose quickly. "What do you think you're doing?"

"Just getting a better look at you."

Uneasiness slithered through her when he took a step

toward her. She didn't even realize she was backing up until her rear bumped the desk. He continued his forward progression until he was standing less than a foot away, blocking her path to the door.

She met his gaze levelly, but her heart had begun to hammer. "I have to go."

"The likeness between you and Traci is remarkable," he said softly.

His face was only a few inches from hers, so close she could feel the warm puff of his breath against her cheek. She heard the whistle of air in his nostrils, knew he was taking in her scent, and the thought made her shudder inwardly.

"Have you ever done any dancing?" His gaze flicked over her, lingering on her breasts. "The pay would be exceptional for a woman with your . . . talents."

It took several seconds for her brain to comprehend the connotation. The slow burn of anger made her grind her teeth. She wanted to say something nasty. Something to let him know she wasn't intimidated, that she wasn't impressed by all the glitter, that it took more than expensive aftershave to disguise the reek of garbage. Then she reminded herself why she was here, and decided he would be a lot more helpful if she stayed calm and kept this civil.

"I'll never be that desperate."

His mouth curved as if she'd just told an amusing anecdote, but his eyes never left hers. "It's all in the eyes," he whispered. "Something special that puts men under a spell, makes them do stupid things. Traci has it, too. I noticed it the moment I met her."

He raised his hand as if to touch her face, but instinct kicked in and she slapped it away. "If you touch me, I swear I'll call the cops and press charges."

He held on to his smile as he stepped back, but Lindsey saw the meanness in his eyes and knew she would have to be very cautious when dealing with Mason Treece.

Giving him the best go-to-hell look she could manage,

she pushed past him. "If I don't hear from you by tomorrow morning, I'll be back with the police." She said the words with firm resolve, but her legs were shaking when she crossed to the door.

"Let me know if you change your mind about dancing," he said.

"Don't hold your breath." Lindsey yanked open the door. Once safely in the hall, she risked looking at Treece. He stood behind his desk, watching her, looking slick and elegant and European in his silk suit and hundred-dollar tie.

He had the gall to smile. A smooth mocking smile that set her teeth on edge. *Bastard,* she thought, and slammed the door.

For a moment she stood in the dimly lit hall, ordering herself to calm down. She hated it that she'd let him rattle her. But Lindsey hated his kind. She hated the way he looked at her. Hated the way he made her feel, like she was fourteen years old again and didn't have any control over what happened to her. She'd wanted to believe she was tougher than that. Wanted to believe she could handle this. That she could handle Treece.

But her heart was still pounding when she reached the stairs. Her boots clicked loudly against the steel grating as she took the steps two at a time to the lower level. She glanced behind her when she reached the ground level and spotted Treece at the top of the stairs, watching her. She wanted to believe it was anger churning inside her. She'd faced down monsters far more dangerous than Mason Treece. But that didn't explain her sudden need to get out of there.

She hit the door to the main section of the bar with both hands, and it swung wide. Music and voices and cigarette smoke filled her senses. Out of the corner of her eye, she saw the throng of people at the bar. The sparkle of glittered flesh. The lights glinting off sequins. The promise of sex.

Sweat broke out on the back of her neck as she strode past the main bar. A dozen faceless, nameless bodies jostled her as she made her way toward the entrance.

"Hey, farm girl."

She turned, found herself face-to-face with Jamie Mills. The other woman looked dramatically different in a long denim coat and acid washed hip hugger jeans. She held a martini glass in one hand, a cigarette in the other. Not friendly, but approachable. For several heartbeats Lindsey waited, not sure what to expect.

"Brandon Rakestraw's here," Jamie said. "I saw him a couple of minutes ago. At the bar."

Lindsey glanced over her shoulder toward the bar where dozens of patrons crowded elbow to elbow. "Can you point him out to me?"

She followed Jamie's gaze to the end of the bar. "He's the one in the snazzy suit," she said. "Lavender shirt. Smells like cloves."

"Cloves?"

"Cigarettes."

Lindsey spotted him then. She turned to thank Jamie, but the other woman had already walked away.

"Thanks," she muttered and, keeping her eyes on the man in the lavender shirt, started for the bar.

He was embroiled in a lively conversation with another man. Both were in their late twenties. Well dressed. Attractive. *Club scene regulars,* she thought.

She reached him a moment later and stopped just behind him. "Brandon Rakestraw?"

He turned on the stool and slowly appraised her with unconcealed male appreciation. "Do I know you?"

He had the bluest eyes she'd ever seen. A patrician nose topped a mouth that was a tad too thin, but smiled readily. A tiny gold hoop glinted at his left earlobe. His dark hair was cut short and bleached blond on the ends. He looked classy, hip, and oozed confidence.

"I'm Lindsey Metcalf. Traci's sister."

He gave her a friendly, genuine smile that warmed her, despite the fact that she didn't know him from Adam, and didn't trust him as far as she could throw him. "Ah, the caterer from Ohio. Traci's talked about you." He leaned back on the stool, and his eyes did another slow perusal. "You look like her. Same mouth. You're hair's darker. A little more reserved, but every bit as pretty. What brings you to the Emerald City?"

Lindsey knew better than to let herself be charmed, but he was doing a stellar job of it. "I'd like to talk to you about Traci."

His eyes went a little wary, and he raised his hands. "Look, if this is about what happened last weekend, I already told her I'd pay for the damage."

"Damage?"

"The lamp."

"You broke one of her lamps?"

"It wasn't my fault, but, yeah, I broke it. Last weekend. At the party. Boy, was she pissed. It was some antique Oriental thing, and she wants my next six paychecks."

"Look, Brandon, I'm not here about the lamp. I just want to know when you saw her last. If you've spoken to her. Or if you know where she is."

He lost the grin, and his expression sobered. "What's up? Is she in some sort of trouble?"

"I've been trying to reach her for several days. She hasn't returned any of my calls, and I'm beginning to worry."

"You're kidding?"

"I'm afraid not. I was hoping you might know where she is."

Studying her, he brought a thin brown cigarette to his lips and drew deeply on it. Burning cloves mingled with the scent of expensive aftershave. "I haven't talked to her in a while, but I'm not exactly her favorite person these days."

"But I thought . . ." Lindsey paused, not quite sure how

to phrase the question. "Aren't you two seeing each other?"

His smiled was wistful. "We were an item for a few months. It was primo for a while. But we broke up a couple of weeks ago."

"Do you mind if I ask who broke up with whom?"

Another smile emerged, but this one was self-deprecating. "A beautiful woman like Traci? What do you think?"

She smiled back, but she wasn't buying the I'm-a-charming-guy act. He was just a little too smooth. "Was it amicable?"

"For one of us." When she only continued to stare at him, he rolled his eyes. "A guy has a tendency to get his heart broken when a beautiful woman dumps him."

"Any idea where she might be?"

He shook his head. "I don't know. I mean, she's got some favorite hangouts and lots of friends. But you know how she is when she gets pissed."

"No, I don't."

He looked at her as if she were the only person on earth who didn't know, and Lindsey felt a slice of guilt that maybe she should have tried a little harder to stay close to her sister.

"She's like independent, you know?" He paused for another drag on his cigarette. "I mean, she blows Dodge and doesn't tell a soul. I swear she gets off on people worrying about her." He turned thoughtful. "Have you talked to Jamie or Tana?"

Lindsey looked over at the stage where Tana was prowling like a big, sleek cat. "I spoke with Jamie and Mason Treece, but they weren't very much help."

"Yeah, Treece isn't known for his kindness and compassion."

"Do you know him well?"

"Well enough to know he's a dickhead."

"What makes you say that?"

"Anyone who spends five minutes with the guy pretty much draws the same conclusion."

"So when did you last see Traci?"

"Last week. Thursday, I think. I was here, having a drink. She was dancing." He shrugged. "Ignoring me."

Then his expression sharpened. "Hey, wait a minute. You don't think her going missing has something to do with me, do you?"

"I don't know what to think."

He lost some of his charm. "If you're that worried about her, maybe you ought to call the cops."

"I did." Lindsey watched him closely, but he didn't look perturbed by the news.

"So this is some serious shit then, huh?" he asked. "I mean, she could be in trouble?"

"I don't know," she said honestly. "I hope not."

Realizing she wasn't going to accomplish anything more here tonight, Lindsey dug into her purse for one of her cards and handed it to him. "My cell phone number is on the back. Will you call me if you hear something?"

He took the card, then smiled up at her. "Sure."

Disappointment pressed into her as she started toward the door. She'd been hoping for answers, but all she'd gotten were more questions—and a very bad feeling about Club Tribeca.

chapter
5

IT WAS DARK BY THE TIME LINDSEY ARRIVED BACK at the bungalow. After leaving Club Tribeca, she'd stopped by the police department to let Detective Renner know about her conversations with Mason Treece and Brandon Rakestraw. To her dismay Renner hadn't been in, so she'd left a message with one of the other detectives. Hungry and discouraged, she'd stopped at the grocery store, picked up enough food to get her through the rest of the week, and headed back to Traci's.

At least the rain had stopped, she thought as she gathered the bags and started for the door. She let herself in and carried the groceries to the kitchen. Methodically, she put them away, then set to work pouring soup into a saucepan. While it heated, she walked through the house, turning on lights as she went.

In the study, a photograph on the bookshelf caught her eye. Lindsey crossed to it, picked it up, found herself looking at Traci's smiling face. She saw vivid blue eyes. A wide smile filled with mischief. Long blond hair tousled by the wind. She was standing on a fishing pier with her arm around an attractive man whose smile was every bit as engaging. She wondered who the man was.

"Where are you, kiddo?" she whispered.

A pang of melancholy assailed her. Traci should be here, she thought. They should be exploring new restaurants and going to movies and arguing about the things sisters argued about. Lindsey missed her, she realized, and the worry she'd been feeling all week now had a very sharp edge.

She set the photo on the shelf and looked around. She didn't want to go through any more of her sister's things; even the cursory search she'd done the night before had felt wrong. But the situation had moved beyond propriety, and Lindsey knew she no longer had a choice.

Crossing to the desk she pulled open one of two file drawers. Hanging folders were stowed neatly inside. Utility bills. Two credit card accounts. Bank statements. On impulse, she pulled out a couple of the bank statements, shaking her head when she found that they hadn't even been opened yet. How very like Traci to leave her account unreconciled.

Lindsey opened one of the envelopes and began to skim. The checking account had a healthy balance of six thousand and change. Canceled checks made out to a local department store. Pandora's Box Hair Design. Boston Tea Party Health Food Store. A local drug store. She paged through each item, not sure what she was looking for. Finding nothing of interest, she stuffed the statement and checks back into the envelope and put it in the folder. She opened the next statement, realized it was for a savings account under the name of T. I. Metcalf. *Traci Irene*. Lindsey absently paged to the balance—and felt a jolt of surprise.

One hundred and forty-seven thousand dollars.

While the amount wasn't huge, it wasn't the kind of money a single, twenty-four-year-old dancer would have in her savings account. How had Traci come across that kind of money?

Methodically, Lindsey went through the rest of the statements. The checking statement balance had remained generally even. But the savings account balance had grown in huge increments over a very short period of time. Traci had opened the account a little over four months earlier with a fifty-thousand-dollar deposit. One month later, she'd added another thirty-two thousand. A few weeks after that she'd made a third deposit in the amount of sixty-five thousand dollars.

Puzzled, Lindsey pulled out the desk chair and sat down. The first explanation that came to mind was drugs. Traci had been busted with two grams of heroin. Was she selling drugs?

For the first time, Lindsey seriously considered the possibility that Traci had, indeed, skipped town to avoid arrest. That she led a double life. That maybe she didn't know her sister as well as she'd once believed.

It hurt to think that her sister had taken the wrong path. But the pain was infinitely worse when she considered the possibility that she herself had played a part in the course her sister had ultimately chosen. After all, Lindsey hadn't been there when Traci had needed her the most. And like a thousand other times in the last eleven years, she could feel the weight of that responsibility pressing down on her.

Lindsey and Traci had gone through hell together as children. They'd faced a common monster as a single, combined force. They spent their formative years terrified and violated and sometimes hopeless. Older by four years, Lindsey had promised to protect her younger sister. But it was a promise she hadn't been able to keep. . . .

Leaning forward, she lowered her face into her hands. Guilt churned like acid in her stomach. Even when she'd been seventeen, she'd known in her heart what would happen when she left for college. She'd known Traci was vulnerable. She'd known even then that she should have done something about it. That Jerry Thorpe was a cop shouldn't have mattered. Instead, she'd left her little sister in the hands of a monster. . . .

Shoving the memories to a place where she kept them locked away, Lindsey turned on the computer and pulled up her sister's E-mail software. Sure enough, Traci had an active electronic social life. Lindsey skimmed some of the E-mails, several of the names catching her attention. She'd written to Jamie about Brandon Rakestraw.

. . . the little son of a bitch actually thinks he can tell me what do to. I can't believe I got tangled up with him . . .

An E-mail from Brandon.

I thought you were different, Traci. But you're just like the rest of them. The only person you care about is yourself. I don't think I'm being unreasonable when I ask you to stop fucking every guy you meet. Treece was the last straw. He's got an entire stable of whores to choose from. I can't believe you want to be included among them.

Traci and Mason Treece? The thought made her shiver. But she knew Treece was the kind of man who would appeal to her sister. Traci had always been attracted to pretty packaging, even if it was thin and frayed. She wondered why Treece hadn't seen fit to mention it.

She printed the E-mails, then logged on to the Internet and signed onto her own E-mail account. She drafted an E-mail asking about Traci's whereabouts in very general terms and sent it to all thirty-five E-mail addresses from Traci's address book, including Jamie's and Tana's. Hopefully, one of them would contact her with information.

Feeling exhausted and frustrated, Lindsey left the study and headed upstairs for a shower. As she stripped and stepped beneath the hot spray, she tried to reassure herself that Traci was with a friend. That she'd dropped out of sight because of the warrant. That she would show up in the next day or so to get things straightened out.

But Lindsey knew in her heart that if Traci were able, she would have called by now.

* * *

She knew he would come to her tonight. He always did on the nights her mother worked. She closed her eyes tightly, put her hand over her mouth to smother the whimper that escaped her. The waiting was almost worst than what he did to her. Almost. She hated him. Hated the way he looked at her. Hated the way he looked at Traci. She wished he was dead.

It was summer and the night was sweltering. Sweat slicked her body, but she didn't dare uncover. Even though she knew the blankets offered no protection.

Her heart crashed against her ribs when her bedroom door creaked. Oh, God. Oh, God. He was coming. Please, God, don't let him hurt me. Lindsey squeezed her eyes closed, trying to regulate her breathing, hoping against hope that he would think she was sleeping and go away. But she could hear the ragged tear of her breaths. She could feel the scald of tears on her cheeks. She could feel the scream building in her chest.

"Sweetheart?"

She didn't answer. Didn't dare. If he thought she was asleep, maybe he would go away. Mama, please make him go away.

But he didn't leave, and her pulse skittered madly when she heard the door close. Her breathing quickened when she heard his footfalls against the carpet. The scream echoed inside her head when she heard him cross to the window, close it, lock it.

And she was trapped and alone with a monster.

She jolted when he sat down on the bed and put his hand on her hip. "Lindsey, honey. You awake? I came in to kiss you goodnight."

Go away!

She tried to say the words, but her throat locked up tight. It always happened that way. And it always made her feel helpless and stupid and indescribably dirty.

She lay beneath the covers, unable to breathe, her heart

pounding so hard she thought it would explode. She wished it would. She would rather die than have him touch her. Hatred welled inside her. Oh, God, she hated him so much. . . .

A sob escaped her when he peeled away the blankets. Her teeth began to chatter. She opened her eyes and saw his silhouette against the slash of light coming in beneath the door. She smelled his smell. Beer and cigarette smoke he tried to mask with spearmint gum. The combination made her want to vomit.

"Lindsey . . ."

"No."

"Don't tell me no, honey. I'm your daddy now."

You're not my daddy. Go away.

She heard the words inside her head, but wasn't sure if she'd actually spoken them. The blood rushing through her veins was too loud for her to hear anything but its steady roar. She wanted to lash out at him. Hurt him. Hurt him so badly he'd never come back. Not to her room. Not to Traci's. Or her mother's. Not ever.

A sound escaped her when he put his hand on her leg. She shuddered as that hand crept up her thigh like a poisonous spider. All she could think was that he shouldn't be doing this. That it was dirty, that she was dirty, and it was somehow her fault. She should have told Mama. Mama wouldn't blame her, wouldn't blame Traci. He might be a policeman, but mama would believe her. Mama loved her; she loved Traci.

"Don't," she whimpered.

"This is our special secret, Lindsey. Remember?"

"I'm going to tell."

"You know what will happen if you open your filthy little mouth, don't you?" He was breathing hard. His hands were on her, inside her, touching her in places he shouldn't touch. Oh, God, please let me die. . . .

"Mama. . . ."

"She can't hear you, Little Lindsey. She doesn't care

*about you. You're nothing," he panted. "You're nothing but
a little whore, and nobody will ever believe you, especially
your mama. She loves me more than she loves you. And if
she ever finds out you let me do this to you, she'll send you
away for good. Traci, too. You know she'll choose me over
you. Look at what you let me do to you. . . ."*

*Shame burned her, a red-hot brand held against her heart.
Mama please come home, she silently begged. Mama . . .*

Lindsey woke abruptly, a scream buried in her throat,
outrage exploding inside her. Shaken and disoriented, she
sat up, aware of her labored breathing, nausea seesawing in
her gut, sweat slicking her body. She fought to rid herself of
the nightmare, but it clung to her, sticky and putrid and dark.

"Jesus."

Slowly, the world around her came into focus. She was
in Traci's house. The guest room. Alone. Safe. It was dark,
but light from the streetlamp slanted in through the window
facing the street. Slowly the old fears retreated, like an oil
slick receding into the depths of the sea.

At the foot of the bed, the cat looked at her with owlish
feline eyes. Lindsey choked out a sound that was half
laugh, half sob, inordinately comforted by the animal's
presence. "We're sleeping together, and I don't even know
your name," she whispered.

She reached for the animal, but it had evidently decided
it had had enough human contact and jumped off the bed
and darted into the hall.

Feeling steadier, she threw her legs over the side of the
bed, put her face in her hands and took a deep, steadying
breath. It had been a long time since she'd had that particular nightmare. Why it would return now she had no idea.
Stress, maybe. Worry over Traci. The last couple of days
had been nerve-racking to say the least.

Knowing sleep wouldn't come again, she got out of bed
and crossed to the door. She'd just stepped into the hall
when a noise from downstairs stopped her. It wasn't a loud

noise. Just the quiet clatter of dishes. The kind of sound a cat might make if it were in the kitchen sink and drinking from a dripping tap.

But while Lindsey wasn't unduly alarmed, her senses went on alert. Silently, she walked to the rail overlooking the stairwell and gazed into the shadows below, listening. She could hear the ticking of the grandfather clock. Water dripping in the bathroom down the hall. The furnace had kicked on, and she could hear the hiss of warm air coming through the vents.

She reminded herself that she'd had the locks changed. Nobody had a key except for her—not even Traci. If someone were in the house, they would have had to break a window or kick in a door. Lindsey was a light sleeper. She would have heard it.

But fate had taught her to never take anything at face value. She'd learned at a formative age that monsters really did exist, even when the adults in her life had assured her they did not. She'd learned that the world wasn't necessarily a safe place. And she'd learned the hard way that fate didn't always play by the rules.

Staring into the darkness, she found herself thinking of the gun in Traci's room and wishing she'd taken the time to see if it was loaded. Not that she knew anything about guns. But it would be a comfort knowing she had a way to protect herself if something happened. If Traci was hanging around with people who were involved with drugs, it was possible those people knew she was out of town and figured her house would be easy pickings for a burglary.

Then again maybe the dream had spooked her.

"Get a grip, Linds," she told herself, annoyed that she'd let her imagination run amok. Chances were she was standing in the hall freezing her tail off because Traci's psycho cat was thirsty. Even so, Lindsey knew she would feel better if she took a quick look around, if only to pacify her overactive imagination.

Downstairs, the living room stood in shadows. The only light slanted in between the mini-blind slats. Her eyes had adjusted to the darkness, and she could make out the large screen television to her right. The sofa stood in silhouette against the French doors. She looked through the doors, saw the outline of the Adirondack furniture beyond. The glitter of rain on the glass.

Sighing, she crossed to the kitchen. The light above the stove was on, giving the kitchen a warm glow that comforted. Her eyes scanned the counter for the cat, but he was nowhere in sight. She crossed to the window above the sink and checked the lock, found it secure.

Confident that the house was locked down tight, Lindsey opened the refrigerator and reached for the carton of milk. She pulled a mug from the cabinet, poured milk, then put it in the microwave to heat. The chocolate chip cookies she'd bought at the grocery were on the shelf in the pantry. She opened the bag, pulled one out, and ate it while she waited for the milk to warm.

The microwave beeped. She retrieved the mug, then headed toward the study to find something to read. She was halfway through the living room when a cold draft against her bare legs gave her pause. Puzzled, she stopped outside the half bath and slowly turned her head. Every cell in her body froze when she spotted the broken window above the toilet.

Fear slashed like a knife, a brutal cut that opened her from end to end. Adrenaline jolted and burned in her belly. Spinning, she darted toward the phone in the kitchen. She was halfway there when she saw the silhouette of a man in the doorway. He lunged at her. Screaming, she threw the mug of hot milk at him and ran.

"Bitch!"

She was halfway across the living room when she heard him coming after her. She streaked to the stairs, used the banister to whip her body around, then took the steps two at a time. In her peripheral vision she saw him behind her, closing in at an astounding speed, and her fear notched up into terror.

She hit the landing running. She could hear him pounding up the steps. Cursing. Heavy on his feet. Breathing hard. She was going to make it to the bedroom. She was fast. In good shape . . .

Claw-like fingers closed around her ankle, jerked her leg out from under her. Lindsey screamed, fell hard on her stomach. "Get away from me!" She twisted onto her back, lashed out with both feet, but he was faster and grabbed both ankles.

"Shut your fuckin' mouth!"

He dragged her down several steps. The sharp edges of the wood thumped against her head and back, stunning her. Then the blow came out of nowhere. Her cheekbone felt as if it exploded on contact. Her head slammed against the step. She saw stars. Great explosions of white light that dazed her. She opened her eyes to see a man looming over her. She blinked, shook the dizziness from her head, realized he was wearing a ski mask. Then she saw him draw back to hit her again. *He's not going to do that to me,* she thought, and rolled. Wood splintered when his fist slammed against the step. A strangled sound rumbled out of him. Pain, she realized, and seeing an opening, lashed out with both feet.

Her left foot caught his hip and sent him backward. His arms flailed, then he tumbled down the steps. Using her hands and feet, Lindsey scrambled up the remaining stairs. She didn't look, but she could hear him cursing, coming after her. Gaining ground. Getting closer . . .

Oh, God!

At the top of the stairs she stumbled to the console table and heaved it down the steps. Glass shattered and flew like bullets. The sound of iron tearing into wood echoed as the table tumbled down. A bellowed curse burned through the air.

Remembering the gun in Traci's room, she darted past the guest room and sprinted to the door. Once inside, she slammed the door, prayed there was a lock. A sob escaped her when she twisted the knob, felt it click.

"Ohmigod. *Ohmigod!*" Lindsey lunged across the bed, expecting the door to splinter behind her at any second. She snatched up the phone, punched 911 with violently trembling fingers.

"911 what's your emergency?"

"Someone's in the house!" Taking the phone with her, she backed into a corner and crouched, terrified to take her eyes off the door. "Please! Send the police! *Hurry!*"

"Are you at 3553 Calimesa?"

"Yes! Please, send someone! Jesus!" She heard panic in her voice. Ragged breaths tearing from her throat. Her heart crashing against her ribs like a violent sea against a rocky shore.

"Is the intruder armed?"

"I don't know!"

"Male or female?"

"Male! Hurry, *please!*"

Computer keys clicked on the other end of the line. She didn't know why, but the sound took her panic down a notch. Vaguely, she was aware that the house had gone ominously quiet.

"Ma'am, there's a unit en route, okay?" More keys clicking. "Are you in imminent danger?"

"Yes! I'm locked in the bedroom." She dropped her voice. "For God's sake, it's a flimsy lock. Get someone out here *now!*"

Holding the phone at the crook of her neck, she scrambled across the bed to the night table, yanked open the drawer, fumbled around until her fingers closed around the butt of the gun.

"Is the intruder still in the house, ma'am?"

"I don't know." Lindsey pointed the gun in the general

direction of the door, curled her finger around the trigger. She didn't know if it was loaded. Had no idea if it needed to be cocked. It was dark. She couldn't see. Her hands wouldn't stop shaking. . . .

She strained to listen, but couldn't hear anything over the wild drum of her pulse.

"The unit should be there in just a few minutes, okay? Don't hang up. I'll stay with you until an officer arrives."

"Okay. Okay." She wondered if she should mention the gun, but decided against it. She wasn't sure if it was a legal weapon. She didn't want to get Traci into any more trouble than she already was.

But Lindsey knew she would use it if she had to. She'd promised herself a long time ago no one was ever going to hurt her again. She would kill him before she let him touch her. All she had to do was hang on until the police arrived.

chapter
6

STRIKER LANDED A PUNISHING BLOW TO THE PUNCH-
ing bag, felt the shock of pain all the way to his spine. He
hadn't bothered with gloves this morning, but he didn't
give a shit about his knuckles. He didn't give a shit about
the bones in his hands and wrists. All he knew was that if
he didn't work off some of this rage, he was going to hurt
somebody.

He leaned into the bag, pounding it with quick, even
blows, ignoring the pain zinging up his arms. When the bag
rocked back, he spun, landed a kick that sent a satisfying
shock of pain up his calf. Sweat poured down his back and
chest. His T-shirt had long since been soaked, but he barely
noticed and he didn't stop.

Thwack! Thwack! Thwack!

He'd gotten an urgent call from his lawyer less than an
hour earlier. Two minutes into the call, and Striker had
known he was in trouble. As far as lawyers went, Prentice
Blumenthal was good. One of Seattle's best, in fact. Striker
had seen his legal mind in action plenty of times over the

years, and, as a cop, he'd despised him. Blumenthal thrived on high profile cases. He knew how to manipulate the media. He was slick and ruthless and utterly brilliant when it came to keeping scumbags out of jail.

The irony that it was Striker who was now relying on his brilliance burned like acid.

According to Blumenthal, the King County prosecuting attorney had decided to make an example of him. With an election looming, it was the perfect time to hang an out-of-control cop up by his balls. There would be no deal making. No legal wrangling. The senior deputy prosecutor was going for the gold. First degree felony assault. Resisting arrest. The whole nine yards.

Thwack! Thwack! Thwack!

It took Striker several moments to realize the ringing wasn't inside his head, but the phone. Trembling from exertion, breathing hard, he stilled the bag and glared at the phone, wondering if he really wanted to answer. He'd had just about all the bad news he could take for one day, and it wasn't even eight o'clock yet.

The answering machine clicked on. He heard his own voice growl, "Leave a message." Then his ex-partner's voice blared like a foghorn. "I know you're there, Striker. Pick up the damn phone."

Striker snatched it up with a rough, "Yeah."

"Trying to avoid someone?"

"What do you think?"

"I think your ass is in a sling, my man."

"Tell me about it."

"Ignoring your phone isn't going to do a damn thing for your business."

Striker made a rude noise. "You and I both know that after my trial I'm going to be shutting down shop for about ten years, anyway. What the hell does it matter?"

Shepherd "Shep" Murray waited a beat. "How did it go with Blumenthal?"

"They're going to fry me."

"Felony assault?"

"First degree."

Shep whistled. "Shit. That's a tough break."

"Yeah, instead of retirement I get ten years in Walla Walla. How's that for irony?" The bitterness in his laugh rang loudly. The betrayal sliced to the bone. Striker had never felt sorry for himself in his life. That he did now infuriated him. He may have screwed up royally, but he didn't deserve to get railroaded. He didn't deserve to have his life destroyed because some politician wanted to look good at election time.

"Shroeder lawyered up with Johnny Glenn," Striker said, referring to a nationally known, high-powered criminal attorney.

"How the hell's he going to pay for Glenn? He doesn't have that kind of money."

"Shroeder's suing the department and the city for eleven million. You can bet Glenn's going to get most of it."

"If he wins."

"Even if he settles out of court, he'll get a lot of money."

"So is this official or what?"

"Glenn's camp sent out a press release this morning. It'll be on the noon news. Glenn's going to hold a press conference later."

"Bloodsucking shark."

Striker didn't mention he could use a bloodsucking shark like Glenn at the moment. "Yeah."

An uncomfortable silence ensued. Striker knew the other man was still absorbing what he'd been told. Weighing just how bad it looked for Striker. He figured they both knew it couldn't get much worse.

"They set a date for your trial?" Shep asked.

"January twenty-fifth." Two and a half weeks away, and Striker could already feel the noose tightening around his throat.

"Jury trial?"

"Probably. Any way you cut it, I'm fucked."

"Come on, Striker. There were extenuating circumstances. For God's sake . . . what that son of a bitch did to Trisha. That's enough to send anyone off the deep end. . . ."

Striker figured he had, indeed, gone off the deep end. He'd gone so deep that four months later he still wasn't absolutely certain he'd surfaced.

"She didn't deserve to die," Shep continued. Not like that. As far as I'm concerned Shroeder got what he had coming."

Striker closed his eyes, trying not to remember how his partner had died. But the memory came anyway, and he felt the sweat on his body go cold.

As if realizing he'd entered territory that was best left alone, Shep muttered a curse. "The department might have left you swinging in the wind, but you know the cops are with you. If you need anything . . ."

But both men knew there was nothing Shep could do.

Because neither man wanted to take the conversation any further, Striker moved to let him go. "I gotta run."

"Oh, I almost forgot. The reason I called . . . you know that topless dancer you were asking about the other day?"

After his meeting with Lindsey Metcalf, Striker had called Shep to have her run through the computer. "What about her?"

"911 dispatch took a call from 3553 Calimesa a little after three this morning. One Lindsey Metcalf reported an intruder. Uniform took the report."

"An intruder, huh? Anyone hurt?"

"Simple assault. She refused treatment, so it must not have been too serious. I thought you might want to know."

"Thanks for the heads up."

"Hang tight, my man."

Striker disconnected, then stood staring at the phone, trying hard not to think about the state of his life, or the fact that he didn't have anyone to blame but himself.

He'd rather cut out his tongue than admit it, but he missed being a cop. He missed the boredom of the slow days. The high-octane excitement when something was going down. He missed his cluttered desk. The bad pay and long hours. The fucked-up city politics. Most of all, he missed doing what he loved. What he'd loved for eighteen years of his life. What he'd once been good at.

He couldn't believe he'd thrown it all away. Couldn't believe an instant of bad judgment had cost him everything he'd ever worked for.

But Striker knew what he'd done to Norman Shroeder in that interview room was a hell of a lot worse than an instant of bad judgment. Striker had lost control that day. As Shep had so aptly pointed out, he'd gone off the deep end. He'd nearly killed Schroeder with his bare hands, while four cops and a lawyer tried to pull him off.

From the looks of things, the State of Washington was going to make damn sure he paid for it.

Raking his hands through his hair, he looked down at his bloodied knuckles and shook his head in disgust. He was going to have to get through this. Sure, he'd been put through the ringer. Some would say by his own hand. In the last four months he'd faced some of the toughest things a man could face. The death of a friend. The ruination of his career. The loss of his home. The media using ugly words like *unstable* and *bad cop. Personal dishonor.*

But Striker knew the worst was yet to come. A trial. The very real possibility of hard time. Of all the things he faced, the thought of going to prison disturbed him the most. Scared the hell out of him, in fact. Striker didn't scare easily, but the fear of having his dignity and freedom stripped away kept him up nights. He could get ten years for what he'd done. And while prison was a hellish place even for the most hardened of criminals, it would be infinitely worse for an ex-cop. . . .

Cursing, he yanked his towel off the barbell rest and

looped it over his shoulders. He wasn't doing himself any favors by dwelling on it. There wasn't a damn thing he could do about anything that was going on in his life. He could either keep himself busy by working, or he could spend the next two and a half weeks going nuts or maybe drinking himself into oblivion. Knowing he would be better off going to the office, keeping to some kind of routine, he used the towel to wipe the sweat from his face and started for the shower room at the rear of the loft.

Loft was a term his landlord used liberally for the warehouse apartment he rented by the month. The place had been a fire station back in the 1930s. After that, a furniture manufacturing plant. Striker called the 2,200-square-foot warehouse a drafty, musty disaster zone that needed a wrecking ball a hell of a lot more than it needed renovation. But for now, it was home.

Four months ago he'd owned a nice house in Magnolia Bluff. But after the fiasco with Shroeder, his legal bills had soared and he'd been forced to sell. He'd rented the loft because he hadn't had to sign a lease, because it was close to his office, his attorney's business district office, and, of course, the King County courthouse.

The landlord gave him a break on the rent and left him the hell alone for the most part—which suited Striker to a T. He'd set up his weights and punching bag in the far corner against the scarred brick wall. He'd bought a used sofa and television and set them up nearest the old steam register, where he was slightly less likely to catch hypothermia. He'd put his bed beneath the massive skylight because he liked looking up and seeing the rain run in silver rivulets across the glass. His kitchen consisted of a microwave, a hot plate, and a coffeemaker set up on an old wooden table, and a freestanding sink that leaked like a sieve. He showered in the "shower room" at the rear, an enclosed area with three tiled stalls that had once been used by the firefighters back in the 1930s.

When he'd first moved in, Striker had agreed to help the landlord with some of the renovation for a break on the rent, but he never seemed to get around to it. Motivation was hard to come by when he knew in a little over two weeks he wouldn't be around to enjoy the fruits of his labor.

Shoving thoughts of his precarious future aside, he set his mind instead to what Shep had told him about the 911 call. He wondered if the break-in had anything to do with Traci Metcalf or the shady people she hung out with. He thought about Lindsey Metcalf and felt a tinge of conscience for having blown her off. At the very least he should have told her to forget about Traci and go back to her life in Ohio. Judging from what he knew about Traci, big sister was out of her league.

Glancing at the alarm clock next to his bed, he figured he had time to swing by Traci's bungalow before going to the office. Just to make sure her sister was all right, he told himself. Maybe find out what that 911 call had been about. It didn't have a damn thing to do with his conscience, he assured himself.

Holding that thought, Striker stripped off his sweatpants and started toward the shower room.

Lindsey jolted awake to the peal of the doorbell. She bolted upright, disoriented and startled, the blur of everything that had happened the night before rushing back like the vague memory of a bad movie. The broken bathroom window. The masked man chasing her. The shock of violence when he'd struck her . . .

She sat up and looked around. Gray light slanted in through the French doors, and she realized with some surprise that it was morning. The last thing she remembered was lying down on the sofa because she'd been too afraid to go back upstairs. If someone was going to break in to do her harm, she wanted to see them coming. But somehow, she must have nodded off.

The doorbell rang again.

Feeling vulnerable and uneasy, she rose and padded barefoot to the door and checked the peephole. Surprise rippled through her when she saw Michael Striker standing on the porch. He was the last person she'd expected to find at her door. She wondered why he would show up now when he'd been so opposed to helping her the day before.

For an instant she considered not letting him in, then realized he could have news about Traci.

Taking a deep breath, Lindsey opened the door. His eyes swept the length of her, then settled on her face and narrowed. "I heard you had some trouble last night," he said.

The urge to slink back inside and lock the door was strong, but she resisted. This man might have been a detective once, but he had danger written all over him in big bold letters. He was six feet two inches of bad disposition and world-weary cynicism rolled into one very unsettling package. His eyes were the color of polished mahogany and as cutting as black diamonds. His raven hair was cropped short and shot generously with gray at his temples. A scar in the shape of a crescent moon marred his left cheek. The lines of his face spoke of hard knocks delivered on a regular basis—and he'd never quite gotten the hang of rolling with the punches.

"What are you doing here?" she asked.

"Just trying to do the right thing." He shifted his weight from one foot to the other. "Are you going to tell me what happened?"

"How did you find out about it?"

"A little bird at the precinct keeps me informed."

She lifted her shoulder, let it fall. "Someone broke in last night."

"How did your face get bruised?"

She hadn't yet checked the damage, but was well aware of the throb. "He punched me."

Something dark and dangerous flashed in his eyes. "Are you okay? How badly did he hurt you?"

"No, I'm just . . ." She touched her bruised cheekbone and tried not to wince. "A little shaken up."

"Yeah, well, he gave you one hell of a bruise."

"You should see the other guy." She wanted to laugh—just to prove to him she wasn't some piece of fluff. But getting slugged by a masked intruder in the middle of the night had peeled away the last of her humor.

"One guy?" he asked.

She nodded.

"How'd he get in?"

"Broke a window in the bathroom."

"Mind if I take a look?"

She hesitated, a dozen reasons why she shouldn't let him in spinning through her mind. She didn't like him, didn't like his attitude or the way he'd treated her the day before. Wearing a midriff T-shirt and drawstring pants, she certainly wasn't dressed for company.

He glanced over his shoulder toward the street, then back at her. It was raining. He hadn't bothered with an umbrella and was slowly getting wet. "Are you going to let me in, or are you going to let me stand here all morning and get soaked?"

"If you're offering to help me find my sister, I need to tell you right off the bat that I don't have the money to pay your fee," she said.

"No one said anything about money."

"You did," she pointed out. "Yesterday."

"Look, I was . . . preoccupied with some other things when you came by."

"If that's the way you treat your clients when you're pre-occupied, I'd really hate to see what you do to them when you're having a bad day."

The crescent shaped scar on his cheek deepened when he frowned. "Look, I just came by to make sure you're okay."

"Like you care."

"I wouldn't be here if I wasn't concerned."

She hesitated an instant longer, mostly because she didn't want him to think she was a pushover, then opened the door and moved back. He stepped into the foyer. Lindsey watched as his cop's eyes skimmed the room, the stairs, assessing the damage, weighing the situation. When his dark eyes swept to her she felt a chill and suddenly wished her robe wasn't upstairs in the bedroom.

"You shouldn't be running around barefoot," he said.

Lindsey looked down at her feet, wriggled her toes.

"Glass," he said, motioning with his eyes toward the stairs where shards from the console table glittered like crystal.

"Oh." Folding her arms over her chest, Lindsey walked over to the sofa and slid her feet into a pair of fuzzy slippers.

"Any idea why this guy broke in?" he asked, leaving the foyer and entering the living room.

She shook her head. "The police think it was an attempted burglary. They think he might know Traci, knew she was out of town and came in to rip her off. I surprised him. He panicked."

"Did he take anything?"

"I don't think there's anything missing, but I'm not familiar with her things."

"Did he say anything to you?"

"Just a few curse words." She thought about it for a moment, asked the question that had been burning. "Do you think this could have something to do with Traci's disappearance?"

He grimaced.

"Oh, I forgot," she said. "You're still assuming she skipped town to avoid getting arrested."

"Traci has been known to hang around with some unsavory characters," he said. "Unsavory characters do unsavory things."

"Like break into their friend's house?"

"*Friend* being a relative term in the world of the unsavory."

"How do you know so much about unsavory characters?"

His gaze locked with hers. "Let's just suffice it to say I've seen my share and leave it at that, okay?"

Unsettled by the intensity of his gaze, she picked up the chenille throw, draped it over her shoulders, and curled up on the sofa. To face Michael Striker while fully dressed was difficult enough, but to face him wearing her pajamas made her feel uncomfortably vulnerable.

Striker took the loveseat opposite her, his eyes settling on the gun lying on the coffee table between them. "That yours?"

"I'm assuming it's Traci's. I found it in the night stand next to her bed."

Leaning forward, he picked it up then quickly and adeptly ejected the clip. "Full clip with a bullet in the chamber. You were ready to plug him, huh?"

"If I had to choose between me and him, I would have chosen me."

He set the pistol and clip on the table. "That's a Colt Mustang .380. Nice gun. Expensive. A woman's gun."

"I don' t know anything about guns.

"It looks like maybe your sister does."

She shrugged. "Lots of people have guns."

"For lots of different reasons." He leaned against the back of the loveseat and contemplated her as if she were a puzzle he couldn't quite figure out. "Why don't you start at the top and tell me everything that happened?"

She didn't want to relive it yet again. The memory was still too vivid, the fear too fresh. But logic told her if she wanted this man's help, she was going to have to go through it at least one more time.

Reaching for the throw pillow, Lindsey hugged it against her and told him everything, starting with her being wakened and ending with her statement to the police. Residual fear gripped her when the dark silhouette of the intruder flashed in her mind's eye. She shuddered when she recounted the struggle on the stairs. The utter helplessness she'd felt when he'd been on top of her. The shock of violence when he'd struck her.

When she finished, Striker rose. "I'll get you some ice for that bruise."

"I iced it last night."

"Not enough, evidently."

She watched him walk into the kitchen, surprised by his concern, trying not to notice that for a man with gray in his hair he was in damn good shape. He wore a leather bomber jacket over faded jeans that delineated muscular legs and a very nice butt.

"You should have gotten yourself checked out at the hospital," he said from the kitchen.

"I didn't need some doctor to tell me I have a bruise."

He returned with a damp kitchen towel and a bag of frozen vegetables. "Were you unconscious at all?"

"No. And I don't have a concussion." She looked at the bag in his hand. "Frozen corn?"

"Better than an ice pack. Conforms to the face."

"You sound like you know that from experience."

"I get punched a lot."

Despite the situation, she laughed. "I bet."

He sat down next to her. "Lean back. Tilt your head a little."

She sank back into the sofa cushions and watched him wrap a kitchen towel around the bag. Leaning close, he set it against her cheekbone.

"Hurt?" he asked.

"Only when I laugh."

An uncomfortable moment ensued when their eyes met. His stare was penetrating. Within its depths she saw razor sharp intelligence, a keen perceptivity, and an intensity that unnerved her so completely that for several seconds she couldn't look away.

She jolted when he took her hand and pressed it to the makeshift icepack. "Ice for the first twenty-four hours, then heat."

The tension inside her eased when he rose and walked over to the stairway and looked down at the broken glass and what was left of the console table. "You're not planning on staying here, are you?" he asked.

"I was thinking about checking into a hotel for a couple of days."

"Probably a good idea."

Sighing because she hadn't wanted to do that, Lindsey glanced toward the stairwell where glass sparkled like bits of ice. "Traci loved that table. She's going to kill me when she finds out I threw it down the stairs."

"You tossed the table at our perp, huh?"

She nodded.

"Nice move."

"He didn't seem to think so."

One side of his mouth curved. "I don't imagine he did."

It was the first time she'd seen him smile, and it changed his face dramatically. Made him look a little more human. A little less intimidating. Rising, she walked over to the stairwell, looked at the glass, the chunks taken out of the wood steps, and sighed. "It was an antique. We bought it at the Pike Street Market the last time I was here."

"Tables can be replaced." He looked over at her and frowned. "Sisters can't. Things could have turned out a hell of a lot worse."

The thought of just how bad things could have been made her shiver.

His shoes crunched glass as he stood the table up. "A cleaning service would make short work of this. I can call the guy who cleans my office, have him send a crew."

"I'll take care of it." She didn't want to pay for a cleaning crew when she was more than capable of doing it herself. "To be perfectly honest, Mr. Striker, I'm still trying to figure out why you're here."

He should have been asking himself the very same question. He was in no position to be taking on a client. Especially a client with pretty brown eyes and a body designed by the devil himself. But he knew what it was like to need help and know you didn't have a snowball's chance in hell of getting it.

"Look, I know Traci," he heard himself say. "Maybe I can look in to some things for you. As a friend to her."

She seemed to mull that over for a moment. "Are you and Traci . . ."

"Just so we're clear," he began, "I met Traci at Club Tribeca when I was working there." When she only continued to stare at him, he added, "Security."

"Oh." She looked relieved. "Do you still work there?"

"No." Because his departure from Club Tribeca hadn't been amicable, he didn't elaborate.

"So how much are you going to charge me?"

"A couple of hundred to cover expenses."

"I think I can live with that. Can I write you a check?"

"A check's fine."

Turning away from him, she started toward the kitchen. "I was going to make coffee," she said over her shoulder. "Would you like some?"

Striker's eyes did a slow, dangerous sweep of her. The pajamas didn't do much for her figure, but he could plainly see she had some nice curves beneath all that cotton. She had a narrow waist, a nicely rounded ass and mile-long legs. Judging from the way her breasts were jiggling, she wasn't wearing a bra. The T-shirt was cropped and twice he'd gotten a glimpse of her navel. Twice he'd felt a stir of lust low in his belly.

"Coffee would be great," he said and wandered toward the

small bathroom, where the perpetrator had entered the house.

Sure enough the window above the commode had been broken. There was duct tape on the glass. Striker wondered if the perp had known there was someone in the house or if Lindsey's presence had caught him by surprise. He wondered if she had been his target, if maybe some scumbag had spotted her and decided he wanted a piece.

He left the bathroom and headed toward the kitchen, wondering if she could give him a description of the guy. Sometimes people remembered details once they'd had a chance to calm down.

He was entering the kitchen just as she came out, and they collided hard enough to make him grunt. He caught a whiff of something sweet an instant before his sense of smell conceded to his sense of touch. Then he wasn't aware of anything except for soft curves and warm flesh. Pleasure jolted him when her breast brushed against the top of his hand. He grasped her biceps to steady her, only to have a lock of reddish brown hair sweep over his fingers.

She scrambled back, then looked at him with wide eyes. She had incredible skin. Pale and flawless, like a baby's. He knew it was crazy, but for a moment he wanted to reach out and touch her, just to see if she was really as soft as she looked.

Something he didn't want to acknowledge stirred inside him. Something elusive and powerful that he hadn't felt for a very long time. Something that made him feel damningly human and a lot more vulnerable than he wanted to admit.

"I was just checking the broken window," he said and stepped back.

She let out a breath, her gaze darting toward the half bath behind him. "I need to put something over it to keep out the rain."

"I can pick up a pane for you. Some glazing compound. Shouldn't take much."

"Okay. Just . . . let me know how much I owe you."

"I can take it out of the two hundred." He studied the bruise on her cheek, felt a surge of male outrage that some goon had seen fit to mess up her face.

"Coffee's on," she said and took another step back. "I need to get dressed."

"Did you get a look at the guy?" he asked. "Get an impression of him? Height. Weight. Anything like that?"

She crossed her arms over her chest in a protective gesture. He tried not to notice the way it plumped her breasts, but he ended up looking away. "It happened too fast," she said. "It was dark. I was scared. He had a really hard fist."

"Do you think you surprised him? Or do you think maybe he broke in because he knew you were here?"

Her gaze met his, then skittered away. "I don't think he knew I was here."

"Did he touch you inappropriately? Say anything of a sexual nature? Foul language? Anything like that?"

She shook her head, but he didn't miss the shiver that ran the length of her. "No."

"If he broke in to steal, it doesn't make sense that he went after you the way he did. I mean, why didn't he just take what he wanted and leave? If you surprised him, why didn't he just run?"

"I walked right up on him. Maybe he panicked." Her gaze met his. "You're the cop. You tell me."

Striker didn't like the idea of one of Traci's druggie friends breaking in and roughing up her sister. But he knew the kind of people Traci ran with. The party crowd out for a good time at just about any cost. Heroine. Cocaine. Crystal meth. Trouble waiting to happen.

"So you're going to help me find her?" she asked.

He looked at her, felt the inevitability of the mistake he was about to make, knew he had been destined to make it since the moment she'd walked into his office the day before.

"I'll see what I can do," he heard himself say. "Get dressed, and we'll see if we can come up with a plan."

chapter
7

STRIKER WAS STANDING IN THE LIVING ROOM, drinking his second cup of coffee when Lindsey came down the stairs. She'd pulled her hair into a ponytail that revealed high cheekbones and large, fragile eyes. She'd tried to cover the bruise with makeup, but it was dark and swollen and hadn't covered well. She was wearing low-rise bell-bottom jeans and an off-white turtleneck. He watched her walk into the kitchen and tried very hard not to acknowledge the fact that she had one of the nicest asses he'd ever laid eyes on.

She returned a moment later carrying a cup of coffee and settled onto the sofa. Without looking at him, she pulled her checkbook from her bag and proceeded to write a check. "Two hundred? Make it out to you?"

"Yeah." He watched her, refusing to feel like a two-bit crook for taking her money. "I measured the broken pane while you were upstairs. I can swing by the hardware store and pick up a new one."

"Thanks." She signed the check and slid it across the

table. "I probably would have slapped some cardboard and tape over it."

He considered the check for a moment and wondered how much she knew about his own situation. About the fiasco his life had become. Even though she was from out of state, he laid odds that she'd heard something about it because the media had been relentless in their coverage. "I guess now would be a good time to tell you I'm involved in a high-profile legal case. You've probably heard. If you haven't, you will." He studied her face, waited for the moment when her brain made the connection and was surprised when it didn't come. "If that bothers you, I can tear up this check and walk out the door right now. No hard feelings." When she didn't say anything, he added, "The national media has been carrying the story."

"I work a lot." She eyed him over the rim of her coffee mug. "I mean, I try to keep myself informed, but for the last couple of months I just haven't had time to follow all the news. Maybe you ought to fill me in."

She was the first person he'd met who hadn't heard about what he'd done. Probably the only person in Seattle who hadn't formed an opinion, either condemning him for police brutality or wanting to give him a medal for socking it to one of the bad guys.

Striker didn't know where the hell to begin, so he opted for a vague explanation and the hope that she would let it drop. "The reason I'm working as a private detective is because I was fired from the police department. I'm involved in a police brutality case. I've got charges pending. Serious charges."

God, he hated the way that sounded. Like he was some rogue yahoo . . . or maybe the kind of cop he'd always despised.

She stared at him. Striker stared back, trying to read her reaction, waiting for the disgust, the revulsion to register in her expression. God knew he deserved it.

"You struck a suspect?" she asked.

"I did a hell of a lot more than hit him."

"How badly did you hurt him?"

"I put him in the hospital." For the life of him he couldn't bring himself to tell her the rest.

She blinked, clearly shocked. "My God."

"Yeah, well, even cops have their limits." Rising, he reached into his pocket for the check, thrust it at her. "Take it, and I'm gone. No hard feelings."

She got to her feet. Her gaze flicked from the check to his face, but she made no move to take it. "Why did you do it?"

He stared hard at her for a long moment, trying to gauge her sincerity, his own frame of mind, how one might affect the other. "Because he had it coming."

He set the check on the table between them, snagged his jacket off the sofa arm and started for the door.

"What are you doing?" she asked.

"Saving you the hassle of firing me."

"I'm not going to fire you."

Gripping the jacket in his fist, he swung around to face her. "If you're looking for an explanation that will make what I did all right, you're not going to get it."

"I don't condone what you did." She crossed to him, her gaze searching his. "But I still need your help."

Striker figured he wasn't in the best position to help her, but the part of him that was still human enough, still man enough, to know when a woman was into something that was miles over her head wouldn't let him walk out the door.

For an interminable moment he stood there, looking at her, not quite sure what to do. "I'm probably not what you think I am," he said after a moment.

"Right now I think you're the only person in this city who might be able to help me find my sister."

Striker stared hard at her, wondering if she understood what he'd just confessed. "Didn't you hear what I just told you?"

"This doesn't have to be about you. All I want is to find my sister. If you can help me, then the rest of it doesn't matter."

"I've only got a couple of weeks before my trial," he said. "I can only give you a few days."

"I'll take what I can get."

He stood unmoving by the door and watched her walk back to the living room. She sat on the sofa, then looked at him over her shoulder expectantly. "If you've only got a few days, I think we should get started."

Not sure if he was impressed by her no-nonsense approach or annoyed because he'd gotten himself into this for all the wrong reasons, Striker left the foyer and sat down on the loveseat.

"What have you done so far?" he asked.

"I went to Club Tribeca yesterday. I met with Mason Treece. He told me no one has seen Traci since her shift several days ago."

"Was Treece cooperative?"

"I think he wanted me to believe he was cooperating. But there were a couple of things he didn't mention that he should have."

"Such as?"

"For starters, I found out later that he and Traci were involved."

"How do you know that?"

"I saw an E-mail on her computer."

Striker was impressed. "What else?"

"Treece posted bond after Traci was arrested. He didn't even bother to tell me she'd even been arrested."

"Yeah, he's a real stand-up guy," he said dryly.

"He told me two of the dancers are friendly with Traci. Jamie and Tana. I spoke briefly with Jamie, but she was busy. Do you know them?"

"I know them. Tana is smart and relatively straight. Jamie Mills is a piece of work. She's probably into some shit."

"You mean drugs?"

He nodded. "Ecstasy. Coke. Heroin, maybe. Not selling, but using. She's a pain in the ass. I'll make it a point to talk to them."

"I also spoke with Brandon Rakestraw. He and Traci were involved for a while, but he told me she broke up with him."

Striker turned the name over in his mind. It was familiar, but he couldn't conjure a face to go with it. "I'll find him, talk to him."

"Treece let me know in no uncertain terms that I wasn't to harass his clientele."

"I can work around Treece." He thought about that for a moment. "Did you find anything else on her PC?"

"Nothing to indicate where she is or who she might be with." She paused, her brows knitting. "I was going through some of her things and found some bank statements. There were some large deposits into a savings account."

"Topless dancers make pretty good money."

"A-hundred-and-forty-seven-thousand-dollars-in-four-months good?"

He frowned. "Mind if I take a look?"

She led him into the study and handed him the statements. Striker scanned the deposits, the running balances, the dates. "Four deposits in a four-month period equaling a cool one hundred and forty-seven thousand dollars."

"I don't see how she could be making that kind of money. And so sporadically."

"Any number of ways."

She shot him a questioning look. "Such as?"

"If she got busted with two grams of heroin, then it's possible she's dealing."

"I can't believe Traci would sell drugs."

"Come on, Lindsey, I'm sure you didn't think she would become a topless dancer either, did you? Shit happens. People change. They . . . make mistakes."

She stared at him for a moment before turning on her heel and walking from the room. Striker didn't follow. Instead, he looked down at the statement in his hand and wondered what the hell he was doing here when he could be down at the Red-Eye Saloon getting drunk. Picking up a bottle of scotch sure took a hell of a lot less effort.

But he knew why he hadn't walked away. While the cynical side of him still believed Traci Metcalf had hightailed it to avoid arrest, the side of him that had known her on a more personal level wanted to make sure she was all right. It didn't hurt that Lindsey Metcalf looked so damn good in those jeans. . . .

He found her in the living room, lugging a vacuum cleaner from the hall closet. "She could be blackmailing someone," he said.

She closed her eyes briefly, then sighed. "What information could she possibly have on someone who would have that kind of money?"

He shrugged. "Hard telling. But that would explain the large, sporadic deposits. The high rent. It might also explain why someone broke in here last night."

Her gaze snapped to his. "They were here looking for something."

He nodded, not liking the direction his mind had taken.

"So what do we do next?" she asked.

"I say we take a look around and see what we can come up with."

"What are we looking for?"

"Correspondence. Evidence of large expenditures. Cash. Photographs. Film. Negatives. Disks." He thought about it for a moment. "You know there's a possibility that she's gone away for a few days with her boyfriend and she's going to be pissed as hell when she gets back and finds out we've gone through her things."

"I'll take responsibility. I'm sure once she realizes how worried I was, she'll understand."

Striker didn't tell her that he considered the possibility of Traci's having left town a best-case scenario.

Two hours later Lindsey sat at the desk in her sister's study, trying hard not to be disheartened. So far, she'd searched every drawer and cabinet in the kitchen—including the small built-in desk—then moved on to the coat closet in the hall off the living room. Her efforts had produced enough merchandise to stock a department store—but not a single clue that would explain the bank deposits or reveal where Traci might have gone. She hoped a thorough search of the study would produce something useful.

She crossed to the cherry wood file cabinet and tugged at the top drawer, only to find it locked. "Of course," she muttered and went to the desk in search of a key.

From the other room, she could hear Striker scraping the old caulking from the bathroom window where the glass had been broken. He'd left briefly to buy a new pane at the hardware store and talk with the neighbors. None of them had seen or heard from Traci in several days.

Lindsey began rifling through the desk, finding pencils, pens, a scratch pad and a letter opener, but no key. She closed the drawer and opened another, shoving aside a legal pad and a leather address book. She lifted a paper clip holder, heard the rattle inside, and popped off the lid. Two shiny brass keys winked at her.

"Bingo."

Snatching up the keys, she moved to the file cabinet and unlocked it. The top drawer contained dozens of labeled manila folders containing payroll stubs from Club Tribeca, a health insurance plan through a major carrier, income taxes for the last two years, an auto insurance policy.

She skimmed through the files, closed the drawer, and tugged open the next. Several expensive-looking gold embossed leather portfolios stared up at her. Curious, she pulled out the first one, set it on top of the cabinet, and opened it.

A glossy black and white photograph of Traci smiled up at her. It was a modeling portfolio. Professionally done judging from the quality of the photos. The rest of the pages contained a dozen different headshots of Traci with different hairstyles and shades of makeup. Some of the photos were black and white, others were in color.

Lindsey hadn't realized Traci was interested in modeling. That she knew so little about the sister she'd once been so close to made her sad, and she vowed that once Traci was home, she was going to spend some time getting reacquainted with her.

She lingered over the portfolios, a sense of pride swelling in her chest. Traci was exceptionally photogenic with high cheekbones, flawless skin, and electric blue eyes. Lindsey wondered if she'd done any modeling. Hope jumped through her when she realized it could explain the large deposits. Maybe Traci hadn't been involved with drugs or blackmail or anything illicit. Maybe she'd found her calling in modeling. She was certainly beautiful enough. She had the height for it, the body, the poise. It was a tough business to break in to, but if anyone could do it, Traci could.

Feeling giddy with newfound hope, Lindsey dropped the portfolio back into the drawer and tugged out the next. The photos were in stark black and white. Traci on the beach in a long, gauzy gown, holding the dress up to keep the hem from getting wet. Her head thrown back in laughter. Her legs were long and slender and wet all the way to her thighs.

Lindsey looked through the dozens of shots, then put the portfolio away. She opened the next drawer, found a small lockbox and pulled it out. It was locked, but she found the key taped to the bottom and opened it. A brown envelope was tucked inside. She pulled it out, opened it, emptied the contents onto the blotter.

Her blood ran cold at the sight of naked flesh. Traci standing in a hot tub, nude, a stemmed champagne flute in her hand. Lindsey stared, shock and disappointment jolting her with equal force. Denial reared, but the image remained in vivid, damning color.

"Oh, Traci," she whispered, a terrible new sadness rising inside her.

Lindsey didn't want to see more, but knew she didn't have a choice. Her hand flipped over the first photo, her eyes going to the next. Traci standing in the same hot tub, nude, her hands stretched over her head. It was snowing. She was laughing, her eyes reckless and alive. She held the fluted glass in her hand and was pouring the contents of the glass over her breasts.

Lindsey banked the slash of pain, told herself this didn't mean anything. So her sister had a few nude photographs tucked away in a lockbox. A lover could have taken them. . . .

But each picture became progressively more risqué and added a dark and troubling facet to the situation. Traci standing in the hot tub, bent at the hip, brutally exposed and smiling seductively at the camera. Traci in the shower, water cascading over her. Traci lying within a frame of silk sheets, her blond hair spread out like gold, her hands on her breasts. Traci lying in bed looking rumpled and sated, her most intimate places exposed.

Lindsey closed her eyes against the burn of tears, but she couldn't cry. There were too many emotions barreling through her. Anger. Outrage. Shame for her sister. But most of all, she felt guilt. Guilt because her troubled, beautiful sister had let herself be exploited in a way that was as insidious as cancer. The sister she'd promised to protect all those years ago. A promise Lindsey hadn't kept.

The pain was so sharp, she couldn't catch her breath for a moment. She felt sick inside and completely unable to comprehend why an intelligent young woman with her entire life ahead of her would let herself be used in such a terrible way. Sinking into the chair, Lindsey put her face in her hands. She wanted to slam her fist against the desk, tear the photographs into small pieces, deny they existed. She wanted to rage at the unfairness of life. At the road her sister had chosen.

For a crazy instant, she considered shoving the photographs back into the box, locking it, forgetting about them. But she knew she couldn't do that because deep down inside she knew the photographs could be relevant to Traci's disappearance.

Struggling to pull herself together, she took a deep breath, tried to put things into perspective. Maybe Traci had encountered some serious financial problems. Maybe some sleazy bastard had gotten her hooked on drugs so he could take pornographic pictures of her. Maybe the photos hadn't been published. . . .

"Lindsey."

Striker's voice jolted her. She glanced up, saw him standing at the door, watching her. Dumbly, she spread both hands over the photographs in front of her, like a school kid trying to keep another from copying her work.

His eyes flicked to the photos, then back at her.

She didn't want to show them to him. Damn it, she wouldn't do that to her sister. She wouldn't degrade or humiliate or embarrass. But Lindsey knew Traci had already done all of those things to herself.

"What are those?" he asked after a lengthy silence.

"Nothing." Without looking at him, Lindsey swept the photos into a pile and with shaking hands shoved them back into the lockbox.

"Nothing seems to have you pretty shaken up."

"I'm just . . ." Her chest was so tight she could barely draw a breath. "I'm just . . ." At the moment, she didn't know what she was. Angry. Outraged. Incredibly sad.

Striker watched her close the box. When he said nothing, she finally met his gaze. She saw suspicion in its depths, as hard and uncompromising as black granite.

"What's in the box?" he asked.

"Photographs."

"What kind of photographs?"

A hundred answers scrolled through her brain, but Lindsey couldn't bring herself to say any of them. Instead, she leaned forward and put her face in her hands. She heard Striker cross to the desk, unlock the box, open it. The part of her that was Traci's protective older sister cringed at the thought of anyone seeing those pictures. But the part of her that cared only about finding her—whatever the cost—let him look so they could get on with what they needed to do next.

He made a low sound in his throat, then cursed quietly. Lindsey raised her head, watched him as he looked at several of the photos. He wasn't an easy man to read, but she recognized disappointment when she saw it.

"Aw, man." Tossing the photos onto the desktop, he raked a hand through his hair. "Damn it."

"I can't believe she would do that."

"I thought she had a better head on her shoulders."

"What do you make of them?" she asked.

"I don't know. It's been a long time since I worked vice. They look professionally done. The quality. The lighting." He sighed and shook his head. "Could be they're not published. Could be she hooked up with someone who runs an Internet porn site." He sighed. "That might explain the deposits."

Lindsey thought about that, but couldn't keep her mind from racing for explanations that would exonerate her sister from what they were both thinking. "Maybe her boyfriend took them. I mean, it's possible, isn't it? Maybe she met someone who's into photography. Maybe he's a student, has his own dark room."

"It's possible, but whatever the scenario, she's definitely headed down the wrong road." Scowling, he looked around the room. "Did you finish going through everything?"

"There are two more drawers left in that file cabinet." But she would rather cut off her own hand than go through them.

"I can do it if you want," he said.

She shook her head. *No,* she thought. *It's my responsibility. My fault. . . .*

He glanced at his watch. "I'd like to talk to a few people at Club Tribeca yet tonight."

"I'm going with you."

He gave her a pained look. "Lindsey, you don't want to go there."

A quiver of anger went through her. "I need to talk to those people, too, Striker. I'm involved in this."

"Don't expect me to keep the bloodsuckers off you."

She doubted he had any idea just how much experience she had at handling bloodsuckers. "I know how to handle myself."

For a moment, the only sound came from the rain pounding on the window, then he said, "If we're going to finish searching that cabinet before we leave, we'd better get started." The lines at the corners of his mouth deepened when he scowled. "We still need to get you a hotel reservation."

She locked the box, then walked over to the file cabinet and set it inside. She tugged open the fourth drawer. A quiver of unease went through her when she saw the compact disk file. It was locked, but the cover was transparent and she could see that there were dozens of tiny iridescent disks inside. Striker came up beside her. He lifted the disk file and set it on the desk.

"She's pretty careful about security," he said.

"I'm sure she doesn't want anyone getting their hands on those photographs."

"Can't blame her." He hit the power button on the computer, then lifted the file, ran his hand underneath it and located the key taped to the underside.

Lindsey watched him remove one of the disks and slide it into the drive. Taking the chair, he clicked the mouse a few times. The CD whirred softly. A moment later, the screen blinked to life. A lovely villa with stucco walls and a red tile roof nestled on a hillside materialized on the screen. The house was elegant and stylish and very European. The kind of place anyone would want to live.

The camera cut to a spacious living room. A leather sectional sofa was piled with velvet pillows. A dozen pillar candles flickered atop an ornate glass and steel coffee table. Abstract art set into velvet and gold leaf brooded on stuccoed walls. A wet bar stocked with gleaming stemware, crystal decanters, and a multitude of top-shelf liquors beckoned one to pour a drink. Beyond, a wall of French doors opened to a large patio replete with tropical plants, rattan furniture, and a picturesque view of a turquoise sea.

Lindsey took in the scene, dread building inside her like a storm. Her chest tightened uncomfortably when she saw Traci enter the room. Her sister looked stunning in a snug bolero jacket and a matching short skirt. Her blond hair was tossed carelessly over her shoulder. Her smile was reckless, her mouth full and red and far too sensual. There was a bounce in her step as she crossed to the sofa.

Even when they were kids, Traci had always been the beautiful one. The funny one. The extrovert who'd liked having an audience. As a teen she'd been fun-loving and a magnet for trouble. But Lindsey had always seen right through the thousand-watt smiles and laughing eyes to the sad and frightened girl beneath.

The woman commanding the screen now was nothing like the girl Lindsey had once known. But she was everything Traci had always wanted to be. Sophisticated and confident and so lovely it hurt just to look at her.

As Lindsey watched the scene unfold, her only thought was that she did not want to know her sister's secrets. She knew those secrets were going to hurt her. She knew they were going to change her.

Deep inside, she knew her sister's secrets were going to change everything.

chapter
8

LINDSEY WATCHED HER SISTER SASHAY ACROSS THE
palazzo-tiled floor on spiked heels. Her tiny red skirt rode
dangerously high on her thighs when she seated herself on
the sofa and crossed her legs. But she seemed utterly at
ease with the situation and very pleased with herself. She
tilted her head when the doorbell rang. A smile curved her
mouth as she rose and crossed to the foyer. She opened the
door, and two men appeared. Both were dressed in exquisitely cut suits, silk shirts, and colorful ties. The man in the
foreground was tall and lean with sun-bleached hair pulled
into a chic ponytail. The other was short, darkly handsome,
and wore a day's growth of beard.

Traci walked with them back to the living room, gestur-
ing and making small talk. Three friends meeting for a
drink before an evening on the town. The short man took a
seat on the sofa. Traci crossed to the bar and poured three
drinks into crystal tumblers. She returned to the sofa and
handed the drinks to the men, then retrieved her own. The
short man drained his glass then leaned back and spread

his arms along the sofa back. The tall man remained standing. Traci turned, smiled at him from beneath her lashes, sipped her drink.

"The audio is poor," Striker said.

Vaguely, Lindsey was aware of him using the mouse in an effort to enhance it. But she couldn't take her eyes off the screen.

For several minutes, Traci and the two men made small talk and laughed. Then Traci set her drink on the coffee table and slowly removed her jacket. The blouse beneath was shockingly sheer, exposing taut flesh trapped within a lacy bra that was cut very low. With the grace of a dancer, she turned away from the tall man in the ponytail, went to her knees in front of the short man sitting on the sofa and put her hands on his thighs. Leaning forward, she reached for the zipper of his trousers and unzipped his fly.

Lindsey stared at the screen, her heart raging, her brain denying what she knew would happen next. The outrage of it choked her. The pain that followed was dark and bottomless and heartbreaking.

"Oh, Traci." Lindsey put her hand over her mouth.

Traci pulled the man's erect penis from his fly, leaned forward and put her mouth around him. The tall man moved in behind Traci. Using both hands, he lifted her skirt, exposing her bare buttocks and a tiny red thong.

Mortified and shocked to her core, Lindsey closed her eyes against the ugliness of what she knew would happen next. She couldn't bear to watch it. But she could hear Traci crying out in a grotesque imitation of passion. Her sweet little sister. The young girl she'd grown up with, gone through hell with, promised to protect. The sister she'd abandoned to save herself . . .

"Son of a bitch," Striker muttered.

Lindsey opened her eyes, but she couldn't look at him. Instead, she stared at the desktop and concentrated on getting oxygen into her lungs. Dimly, she was aware of him clicking the mouse, ending the video. She wanted to say something, but there were no words for the emotions exploding inside her. She wanted desperately to defend, but there was nothing she could say that would change what they had just witnessed.

She looked down at her hands, realized with some surprise that they were shaking violently. She was aware of Striker rising, looking at her as if he thought she might crumple. "Lindsey . . ."

She raised her hand as if to fend off an attack. "Don't say it," she said in a strangled voice. "Just . . . don't say anything."

Suddenly, she needed to get out of there. Out of the house. Away from Striker's knowing gaze. Away from her sister's mistakes and the terrible things she'd done with her life.

Her boots clicked smartly against the hardwood floor as she left the study and ran to the French doors. She fumbled with the lock, aware that she was breathing hard, that her hands were shaking so badly she could barely manage the lock, that there were tears on her cheeks.

The door swung open. Cold air rushed over her as she stumbled to the patio. She felt rain on her face, but she welcomed the wet and cold. Anything was better than the pain cutting her from the inside out.

For several seconds she stood in the rain, her breath puffing out in a thin white cloud. She closed her eyes and turned her face up to the sky, wished desperately that the cold drops could wash the images of her sister from her eyes.

She didn't know how long she stood there. It could have been minutes, or it could have been an hour. She jolted when Striker came up behind her and put his hands on her shoulders.

"You're getting wet," he said. "Come back inside."

She turned to him, sought his gaze. "Don't you dare judge her," she said fiercely.

"I'm not exactly in a position to judge anyone, Lindsey," he said. "Come inside."

She shook off his hands. "I mean it, damn it. You don't know her. You don't know what she's been through." A breath shuddered out of her. "I don't know what's going on, but that woman . . . that wasn't Traci. I know my sister. She wouldn't . . ."

But they both knew she had.

When she made no effort to go inside, Striker took her arm and guided her through the French door. "We can talk about this inside."

"I don't want to talk about it."

"Neither do I, but if you want to find your sister we probably don't have a choice."

Then she was in the living room, dripping water on the floor. Striker walked to the bathroom and returned with a towel, handed it to her, then crossed to the French door and looked out at the early evening shadows beyond.

Lindsey looked down at the towel in her hand. She was cold, both inside and out. She wanted to cry, but she felt empty, hollowed out. She wanted to rant and scream and deny what she'd seen on that disk, but all of her energy seemed to have been sucked out of her. For the first time anger burgeoned and she realized she was angry with Traci. With the person who'd demoralized her. With herself because in some far corner of her mind, she thought maybe this was her fault.

"If Traci's involved in the pornography industry, that would explain how she affords this house," Striker said. "It would explain the deposits. The new car. The clothes and shoes and expensive furniture."

Pornography.

The word made her cringe. It sounded so filthy. A dirty word that conjured up images of perverts and drug-addicted

prostitutes. Never in a thousand years would she have sus-
pected Traci.

"I can't believe she would do that," she said. "I just can't
get my brain around it."

Striker turned to her, and for the first time she saw compassion in his dark eyes. It was the first emotion she'd been
able to read, and she wondered if he had any idea how much
it meant to her at that moment. "People make mistakes," he
said. "They use bad judgment. They screw up. It's part of
being human."

"But for her to get involved in . . ." She couldn't say the
word. "She wouldn't do that."

"You saw the disk. There was no evil villain holding a
gun to her head."

"Not a gun. But you know as well as I do that there are
other ways to coerce a person. Maybe somebody drugged
her or threatened her in some way. Maybe they were blackmailing her, and she didn't have a choice." But even to her
the words sounded like a desperate attempt to deny the
undeniable.

The truth of the matter was that Traci led a secret life.
She sold her soul for money. Traded her self-respect and
pride for fifteen minutes of fame and fortune.

"Isn't that kind of hard-core pornography illegal?" she
asked.

He shrugged. "Some is. Most isn't. Some states have
sodomy laws, which would prevent certain kinds of movies
from going to production. At least legally, anyway. There's a
pretty healthy black market."

Lindsey looked down at the towel in her hands, felt the
heat of a blush on her face. Sodomy laws. Oh, dear God,
she didn't want to think about that.

"When I get my hands on her . . ." Sudden fury made
her clench her hands into fists. "I'm not going to let her do
this to herself. Even if I have to drag her back to Ohio with
me. I'm not going to let her ruin her life."

The next thought that struck her chilled her. "Do you think Traci's being involved in the porn industry could have something to do with her disappearance?"

"She's running with a bad crowd. She's making some bad choices. That probably puts her in a higher risk bracket."

"Higher risk for what?"

"Take your pick. The porn industry is chock-full of drugs and sharks."

Lindsey felt a little sick. "Traci may have made some bad decisions, but she's got good instincts. Striker, she's a survivor."

He looked away and for a moment the only sound came from the tinkle of rain against the windows. "Did you notice the tattoo on her shoulder?" he asked after a moment.

She'd been too shocked to notice much of anything, but shook her head. "Traci doesn't have any tattoos."

"She does now." He sighed. "It looked like letters or initials. I need to take another look and see if I can magnify it."

"You think it could be important?"

"I think most people don't have initials tattooed on their bodies unless those initials mean something." He paused. "I can have a look at it while you get into some dry clothes."

He was giving her an out. Lindsey knew she should take it. The last thing she wanted to do was see that disk again. But she knew that sticking her head in the sand wasn't going to make it go away.

"No," she said. "I need to see it."

"You don't have to put yourself through this."

She didn't answer.

Back in the study, Striker went directly to the computer. Lindsey hung back and watched from the doorway. He turned off the sound, which helped, but seeing her sister writhing on the screen with two men was like getting punched in the gut.

"The camera work isn't the best," Striker said. "Resolution sucks." He used the mouse to isolate and select a relatively clear shot of the tattoo, then saved the image to the hard drive, using the graphics software.

Lindsey watched, dread roiling inside her as he used the software to enlarge the still, then began enhancing the resolution. A few minutes later, the letters J. B. stood out in stark blue against milky white flesh.

"Bingo." Striker leaned back in the chair, then turned to Lindsey. "Did Traci ever mention anyone with the initials J. B.?"

"The only guy she mentioned was Brandon."

He turned back to the computer, reopened the disk, and skipped forward to the credits before normalizing the speed.

"What are you doing?" she asked.

"We might get lucky and find a J. B. in the credits. Most people in this business don't use their real names, but occasionally you get some *artiste* with an ego who can't bear the thought of giving the credit to some pseudonym."

Lindsey watched the credits roll. If she hadn't been tied up in knots on the inside, she might have laughed at some of the aliases used by the actors and actress and crew. Honey Suckle. Rod Strong. Peter Thrust.

"We've got a match." He clicked the mouse, and the credits froze. Leaning close to the monitor, he squinted. "Did Traci ever mention anyone by the name of Jason Blow?"

"No." Lindsey looked closely at the name, realized Jason Blow was one of two cameramen.

"Sounds like an alias."

"The initials being the same as the tattoo could be a coincidence, couldn't it?"

"Maybe. I can do a search, then run a couple of checks and cross checks on the name and see what we get."

"How long will that take?"

"A day. Maybe two."

"Then what do we do?"

"If I can come up with an address, we pay the little

pervert a visit and rattle his cage." Striker turned to her. "In case you hadn't noticed, that's my specialty."

"I've noticed."

His gaze lingered on hers for a moment, then he popped the disk out of the drive and set it back in its case. "If it's all right with you, I'd like to make a copy of this and have it analyzed."

"By whom?"

"I have a friend in vice. He can send it to the lab for me, courtesy of the city. They might be able to lift some latent prints. Find something we missed."

"And in the interim?"

"We go to Club Tribeca and talk to Jamie and Tana. We see if we can find Brandon Rakestraw again."

She didn't like the idea of going back to the club, but the prospect of getting solid information about Traci wouldn't let her walk away from the opportunity. "I just need to change clothes."

"I'll see what I can dig up on Jason Blow." Striker was already logging in to a Web site that ran background checks for $24.95. "If we're lucky maybe we can kill two birds in one night."

The drive to Club Tribeca was silent. Striker wove the jeep through heavy rush-hour traffic made worse by the rain. Usually he despised Seattle traffic. Tonight, he was glad he had something to concentrate on besides the woman sitting next to him and a case that was becoming more troubling by the minute.

Of all the things Traci could have been into, porn was one of the worst. He ranked it at the top of the trouble scale—right next to drugs. The adult film industry was full of predators, easy money, and the exploitation of the innocent. Not that the stars and starlets were all that innocent. But most were too young or dazzled to even realize they were being used. By the time they did, they were already hooked on drugs or the money or both.

He'd worked vice for two years. He knew the havoc the industry could wreak on people's lives. He didn't want that to happen to Traci Metcalf. He didn't want Lindsey to have to deal with the aftermath.

Even though it was a weeknight, Club Tribeca was packed to the hilt. Striker parked the jeep in a quiet lot a block away and waited for Lindsey to get out, then approached her. "You sure you want to do this?" he asked.

She glanced toward the crowd milling about outside the front doors of the club and nodded. "We'll be able to cover twice as much ground."

It sounded good in theory, but he had a bad feeling about bringing her along. He could see that she was wound tight after seeing that disk. Club Tribeca wasn't the kind of place you wanted to go when you were wound tight. It might be upscale, but the place was teeming with sharks. Big ones that were very high on the food chain. He didn't want any of those sharks taking a bite out of her.

He watched her out of the corner of his eye while he locked up the jeep. She'd changed into snug black jeans and paired them with a black velvet pullover, clunky boots, and a pair of dangly earrings. She'd piled her hair on top of her head, leaving tendrils to frame her face and curl at the back of her neck. Not dressy in terms of how most of Club Tribeca's female patrons dressed, but she looked good. Too good if he wanted to be honest about it. And he was a damn fool for noticing.

"I keep trying to put myself inside her head," she said as they started toward the club. "As close as we once were, I just can't do it."

He fell into step beside her. "People grow and change over time," he said. "You and Traci chose different paths, different lives."

"How did she feel about working here?" she asked after a moment.

He glanced over at her, wondered what she was really asking, if she really wanted an answer. "I don't think she hated it. I don't think anyone was forcing her, if that's what you're asking."

"I'm just trying to understand her."

"Money was probably a factor. She's a pretty girl. She liked people, liked to dance. She used those things to her advantage, and she got paid for it." He shrugged. "She made friends here. Had a social life. Maybe those friends influenced her. It's hard to say what she was thinking. What factors were involved."

She seemed to mull that over for a moment, then asked, "How long did you work security here?"

"About a month. After I got canned from the department. I needed the cash. Worked here to pass the time while my PI license was being approved."

"What did you do?"

"Plainclothes. Blended with the crowd. Made sure all the boys and girls behaved themselves and followed the rules."

She nodded. "A month isn't very long. What happened?"

That was the question Striker hadn't wanted to answer. But he figured she deserved the answer. "I pissed off the boss."

"Treece?"

He nodded.

"You're good at that, no?"

"A little too good, I guess."

"So what did you do?"

Striker sighed. "There's an alley at the rear of the club. The employees go out there to smoke. Hang out during breaks. One night I was out there, getting some air, and out comes your sister."

She looked at him sharply.

"We talked for a while," he said. "She'd just finished her

shift. She'd been doing shots. She was disgruntled about something insignificant and wanted to bitch. Or so she led me to believe." Not sure how she was going to take it, he grimaced. "You sure you want to hear this?"

"No. But judging from the way you're stalling, I think I need to."

He frowned. "So we're talking. She's bitching. I'm listening. Then the next thing I know she's all over me. Before I could figure out what the hell was going on, Treece flies out the door, looking for her, pissed as hell."

Lindsey stopped walking, gave him her full attention. "Were you involved with her?"

Striker shook his head. "Never. She liked to flirt. We cut up a couple of times. But that night it was all about Treece. She wanted him jealous, and I just happened to be convenient."

"That's terrible."

"She was into playing games like that."

"So she and Treece *were* involved?"

"Or maybe they were just having sex on a regular basis." He shrugged. "Whatever the case, he got pissed. Fired me on the spot, tried to sic a couple of his bouncers on me."

"Why didn't you mention this sooner?"

"I figured that was something you wouldn't want to hear about your sister. If it had been relevant to the case, I would have told you, but it wasn't, so I didn't."

They resumed walking, and she shook her head. "God, Striker, the more I learn about her, the less I feel I know her."

They reached the sidewalk in front of the club. A throng of Seattle's upwardly mobile lined up beneath the red and white canopy outside the beveled glass doors. There were a few couples and a surprising number of women, but most were single men in custom suits and hundred-dollar haircuts. They drank from silver flasks, smoked thin brown cigarettes, and talked about the stock market and the price of real estate.

Striker found a place in line, took Lindsey's arm, and put her in front of him. Ahead, the double doors stood open. He could see the cashier's cage beyond. Techno-rock blasted from tiny Bose speakers mounted above the doorway. He watched the valets hustle and park hundred-thousand-dollar cars. On another level, he was aware of the male eyes seeking out the woman he was with, and he found himself feeling uncharacteristically territorial.

When the line began to move, he ushered her toward the doors. "I'm going to try to corner Jamie first," he said. "She and Traci are pretty good friends. She might know something. But I need to warn you, she can be difficult."

"What do you mean?"

"For lack of a better term, she's a damn flake. Don't let your guard down around her. And don't trust her."

She nodded. "I'll watch for Brandon Rakestraw."

Striker paid their cover, and they walked into the club. It had been almost three months since he'd set foot inside, but nothing had changed. Same modish crowd. Same loud music. Same smell of recirculated air, cigarette smoke, and designer cologne. He spotted a dancer he knew and raised his hand to catch her attention. "Showtime," he said.

Wearing the customary red sequined thong and bow tie, she approached them with a tray hefted on her shoulder. She was nearly as tall as he was, rawboned and with flawless skin the color of dark roast coffee. She shoved her mane of black curls over her shoulder and grinned. "Ah, my favorite detective. Good to see you, Striker. You working tonight, or are you here on pleasure?"

"I'm working, but it's good to see you, too, Tana."

Her gaze flitted to Lindsey, then back to him. "I've missed seeing you around. New security guy's a jerk."

"All cops are jerks."

She tossed her head back and laughed. "I miss your sense of humor."

Striker had long since grown used to working around the dancers. Most were friendly and outgoing and he'd gotten along with them well. But he'd worked vice for too many years to be taken in by their female charms. Tana was one of the smart ones. She attended college during the day. Once, he'd asked her why she took off her clothes for money, and she'd told him she was putting herself through law school and raising two little girls on her own. Despite the way she made her living, that had impressed him.

"Have you seen Traci around?" he asked.

"Not for a few days. Vicki covered for her a couple of times, I think. But Treece is pissed. He's been ranting about firing her this time."

"Do you have any idea where she might be?"

She shook her head. "I haven't talked to her much lately. We've been shorthanded, and it's been busy as hell."

"Do you know anyone by the name of Jason Blow?"

Tana chuckled. "You're kidding me, right?"

Striker sighed. "Never mind." He kept his expression bland, but friendly. "Is Jamie working tonight?"

"She's around here somewhere." Tana glanced over her shoulder toward one of the stages. "You want me to send her your way if I see her?"

"Yeah, I need to talk to her."

"Is Brandon Rakestraw around?" Lindsey put in.

The dancer shot her a measuring look. "Haven't seen him yet. You look familiar."

"I'm Traci's sister, Lindsey."

Tana shot her a dazzling smile. "Nice to meet you." Her gaze swept back to Striker. "I've got to get going. What can I get you?"

"Heineken."

"Club soda," Lindsey said.

He dug a twenty dollar bill from his wallet and put it in her palm. "Keep it."

Smiling, Tana tucked the bill into the front of her thong. "It's about time you caught a nice one," she said and hustled away.

By the time Lindsey realized Tana had gotten the wrong impression about her and Striker, the dancer was already moving away. She started to say something to him, but he took her arm and was already steering her through the crowd.

"Let's see if we can spot Jamie," he said over the blare of music.

She fell into step beside him, trying to avoid being jostled by the crowd, watching for Jamie, a small corner of her mind keeping an eye out for Traci. On the stage to her left, a petite dancer in a scanty cat costume performed an anatomically difficult exercise with the vertical brass pole that ran from the dance floor to the ceiling. Brown glitter covered her bare breasts and sparked like gold and copper beneath yellow lights. She wore a tiny thong with a faux fur thatch at the front and a long tail at the small of her back. Matching cat ears attached to a headband crowned her head. She undulated to the Red Hot Chili Peppers' "Californication" and demonstrated exactly what a woman could do with double jointed hips.

Lindsey tried not to feel claustrophobic as they pushed through the mass of people, but she'd never liked large, tight crowds. As they neared the bar, the air grew heavy with the heat of a hundred bodies packed into a too small area.

Next to her, Striker watched the crowd with those shrewd cop eyes of his, and she found herself pleased that he hadn't succumbed to the show on the stage. She surveyed his profile unnoticed, the straight slash of his nose, the crescent scar on his cheek, the too strong jaw, eyes that didn't miss a beat. He might have had the title of detective stripped away, she thought, but he was still a cop.

"There's Jamie."

She followed his gaze across the bar to see the attractive

blond heading toward a table at the back of the room, a tray propped on her shoulder. She was wearing the same getup as she had been the day before—sequined thong and matching bow tie.

Hope jumped through Lindsey at the prospect of getting some solid information about Traci. Before even realizing she was going to move, she found herself pushing through the crowd, determined not to lose sight of Jamie.

She was aware of Striker behind her. The ebb and flow of people all around. The music pulsing in her brain, vibrating her bones. Red lights slashing down. She watched Jamie stop at a small table in a relatively quiet corner, set down her tray. She turned, spotted Lindsey just as she broke from the crowd. "Listen, babe, if you want a lap dance, it's not my night for girls."

Lindsey hesitated, but she didn't stop until she was standing just a few feet away from her. "I'm Traci's sister. You and I spoke briefly yesterday. I just want to ask you some questions."

Ignoring her, the woman's amused eyes flicked to Striker as he crossed toward them, and her mouth pulled into a slow, seductive smile. "Well, well, well, if it isn't my favorite cop come to rough me up with those bad boy hands of his. Tana said you were around here somewhere." Snagging a Heineken and a tall glass from the tray, she strode to Striker, handed the beer to him.

"How's tricks, Striker?"

chapter
9

STRIKER ACCEPTED THE BEER, BUT HE DIDN'T
return the smile. He knew better than to indulge a head case
like Jamie Mills. She might be beautiful, but she was as
dangerous as a black widow, just as unpredictable, and ten
times as deadly.

"I thought you'd be out of this dump by now," he said.
"You had big plans for yourself."

She gestured toward the stage, her breasts swaying
slightly with the movement. "And miss out on all the fun?
Come on, Striker, I love this shit."

"Still making all the right connections, huh?"

She laughed. "God, I've missed your smart mouth."

He felt himself tense when she leaned close and pressed
a kiss to his cheek. "All the chicks miss you. We're all root-
ing for you, you know. Big, bad Michael Striker against a
world that doesn't give a shit about justice."

"I appreciate that, Jamie." Aware that Lindsey was
watching him, that he'd broken a sweat beneath his jacket,

he uncapped the beer, took a swig, and he was very glad it was cold. "Have you seen Traci?"

She flashed shockingly white teeth, first at Lindsey, then back at him. "Ah, a Striker interrogation. I hope you brought your cuffs and baton. You know that cop shit turns me on."

Turning away from him, she handed Lindsey the tall glass with a thin straw. "Club soda with a twist?"

Lindsey reached for the drink. "Thanks."

The dancer's eyes narrowed. "Now I remember you. You've got one of those unforgettable faces, you know? Something in the eyes. Traci has it, too."

"Have you seen her?"

"Not in a while." Jamie turned an amused look to Striker. "You still got it bad for Traci, huh? I gotta tell you, she talks about you all the time. Treece is still hot about that."

He felt Lindsey's eyes on him, but he didn't look at her. "Cut it out, Jamie."

"It's driving Treece nuts," she said. "He thinks you're fucking her, and we're all laughing behind his back."

"When's the last time you saw her?" he asked.

"I don't know." She shrugged. "A few days."

"Can you be more specific?"

"You going to cuff me and haul me in?"

He sighed. "A straight answer would be a big help right now."

She threw her head back and laughed. "God, I love it when you get pissed, Striker. That just *does* it for me. Bad boy pretending to be good. We all know you're not, though, don't we?"

"You're making a fool of yourself," he said.

"Or maybe I'm telling all of your secrets, and you don't like it."

Lindsey said, "Jamie, please, we just want to know about Traci."

The dancer shot her a dazzling smile. "Don't worry,

honey, he doesn't play with us bad girls. He grew up with all that apple pie bullshit." Her eyes flicked to Striker. "Didn't you?"

"Traci's missing," he said. "We think something might have happened to her."

"What makes you think that?" Putting both hands at the small of her back, Jamie arched, stretched like a cat.

Striker looked away, waited.

Jamie laughed outright. "You're a hard case, Striker."

"You're not being very cooperative."

"Maybe I want you to earn my cooperation. I mean, fuck, I could be out there earning tips, and here I am talking bullshit with you, and you're not paying me shit."

"You talk like a truck driver, Jamie. It's not very becoming."

Her smile turned nasty. "You want to see something becoming?"

"Not particular—"

He broke off when her hand snaked out, went in low. He felt her fingers brush his fly. He twisted away just in time to keep her from grabbing a part of his anatomy he didn't want her getting anywhere near. "Knock it off," he snapped.

"Come on, Striker. I answer questions a lot better when I'm having a good time."

She reached for him again, and his temper kicked. He grabbed her wrist, twisted just hard enough to get her attention. "You know the rules about touching in this joint, don't you, Jamie?"

"That only goes for the dancers, asshole. Let go of me, or Treece is going to do what he's been wanting to do since the day he caught you and Traci going at it out in the alley."

Remembering there was a break room through the door at the rear of the club, he tightened his grip on her wrist. "Let's go for a walk," he said and hauled her toward the door.

"Let go of me, you bastard!" she tried to twist away, but he held her firm, shoved open the door.

Vaguely, he was aware of Lindsey saying his name, but he didn't stop. He knew this was probably going to cause him more problems than it was worth, but he had a feeling Jamie knew something about Traci. What he couldn't figure out was why she didn't want to talk about it.

"What's your problem?" He hauled her into a dimly lit hall. "Are you high on something tonight?"

"I'm high on life, Striker. You ought to try it sometime."

"I think you know something about Traci."

"I think you're full of shit."

He opened the break room door and muscled her inside. A table and several chairs were arranged in the center of the room. A red Formica counter ran along the wall and held a microwave and mini fridge. Opposite, a red exit sign flickered over a security door with a push bar that led to the alley beyond where the employees congregated to smoke.

He dragged her across the room and shoved her into a plastic chair. "Sit down and act like you've got some self-respect," he growled.

"You *prick*! Don't lecture me about self-respect!"

She tried to rise, but he put his hand on her shoulder and pressed her back into the chair. "Pull yourself together." He crossed to the roll-away closet, jerked a bright pink blouse from a hanger, flung it at her. "For chrissake, put that on and cover yourself."

Face red with fury, Jamie stuck her arms into the sleeves and yanked the shirt over her breasts. "The bouncers aren't going to let you treat me like this. You don't work here anymore, Striker. You're not even a fuckin' cop anymore. Just another piece of shit off the street, coming in here to hassle the dancers."

Too angry to speak, he crossed to the soft drink machine against the wall, pulled two quarters out of his pocket and pressed the button for a Coke. He held out the can to Jamie. "Take this and sober the hell up. I'm tired of playing games with you."

She slapped his hand hard, sent the can of soda to the floor. "Maybe I don't want to sober up."

It didn't hurt, but it made him angrier. "If you know something about Traci, you'd better start talking, or I swear to Christ I'll haul you down to detox and let the doctors have you for the next couple of days."

"I don't know shit about Traci."

He glanced up to see Lindsey standing in the break room doorway, her face ashen, and he scrubbed a hand over his face. Damn it, he hadn't intended for this to happen. He hadn't intended to lose his temper, make a scene. But he'd never had much patience for some smart mouth jerk stonewalling him.

Grimacing, he looked down at Jamie, decided now might be a good time to change tactics. "I need your help," he said quietly.

"Since when has anybody ever helped *me*? Where's *my* cavalry, Striker? Huh? Where's my knight in shining armor, for God's sake?"

"If you care about Traci, you'll tell me what you know. She'd do it for you." When she didn't say anything, he added, "All I'm asking for is a little cooperation."

Jamie glanced toward the door, and some of the belligerence leached out of her. "Maybe I'm not supposed to cooperate with you."

The hairs at the back of his neck prickled, and he felt his cop's suspicions kick into gear. For the first time since Lindsey Metcalf had walked into his office, he got the feeling there was more going on than either of them had considered.

He leaned close to Jamie. "Are you afraid of someone? Is that what you're telling me?"

"What the hell's going on here?"

Jamie visibly jolted at the sound of Mason Treece's voice. Striker rose to his full height to see Treece stride through the door as if he were a lead actor walking onto a movie set. His hair was slicked back in a neat ponytail. His impeccably cut jacket flying open to reveal a white silk shirt. Two thugs sporting crew cuts and suit jackets stretched taut over steroid-enhanced muscles flanked him.

Lindsey had sidled toward the counter. Striker saw the uneasiness in her eyes, nodded his head at her. "It's okay," he said.

Treece's eyes swept from Striker to Jamie. "Are you all right?" he asked her.

Jamie sprang out of the chair, her eyes darting wildly. "That son of a bitch manhandled me, bruised my wrist."

Striker could see her trembling as she fumbled with the sleeves of her shirt, shoved the cuff up to her elbow to reveal the red mark he'd put on her wrist. It wasn't a bruise by any stretch of the imagination, but he knew it was enough for Treece to sic his pit bull bouncers on him. In the back of his mind, he wondered what had tough-talking Jamie so spooked that she was willing to turn to Treece to get out of talking to him.

Striker felt his muscles tense when Lindsey shoved away from the counter. He shot her a warning look, hoping she would keep her mouth shut and sit this out, but either she didn't see his signal or chose to ignore it.

"I wanted to talk to her about Traci," she said to Treece.

The club manager looked her over, smiled. "I can only assume our chat yesterday didn't satisfy you."

"I just had a few more questions for her," she said. "The music was too loud in the bar. We couldn't hear, so we came back here."

"Ah, and you brought the cavalry." He sighed in overstated exasperation, then glared at Striker. "I'm sure you have a multitude of reasons for being here, but I'm afraid you are no longer welcome in my club."

"In case it's slipped your mind, one of your employees is missing. I've been hired to find her."

Treece looked around the room, made a sweeping gesture with his hands. "She's not here."

Striker ground his teeth. "This is the last place she was seen. Either you can talk to me or I can have the cops breathe down your neck for a while."

Looking confident and amused, Treece walked over to Jamie, took her hand, caressed the fading red mark on her wrist. "Did he hurt you?" he asked quietly.

She lowered her eyes, nodded.

"Do you know where Traci Metcalf is?"

"No."

Striker watched the exchange, felt something deeper than temper stir inside him. He'd known too many men like Mason Treece in his lifetime. Corrupt. Immoral. With a glossy sheen that covered all the dirt. He hated his kind. Hated what he stood for. Hated what he did to those who were weaker.

Treece patted Jamie's hand. "I can see you're upset. Why don't you take the rest of the evening off? I'll see to it that you're paid, including the tips you would have earned."

Jamie glanced at Striker. He stared back, noticing she was now clutching the shirt around her.

She looked away. "Sure. Why not?"

The room fell silent as she walked out the door and closed it behind her. Then Treece turned to Striker, contemplated him as if he were a problem he didn't quite know how to solve. "Tell me, Mr. Striker, am I going to have to get a restraining order to keep you out of my club?"

"We were just leaving," he said.

"I'm sure it would cause you a host of problems if Jamie chose to press assault charges against you. I'll see what I can do to keep that from happening." Treece's mouth curved as if the thought pleased him. "But I can't make any promises. I think we both know what an additional assault charge on top of your current record would do for your upcoming trial. People, jurors might assume you're a loose cannon."

"Everyone in this room knows I didn't assault her," he said evenly.

"Ah, but you put your hands on one of my dancers. She has the marks to prove it."

"Jamie's the one who has a problem with her hands," Lindsey put in.

Out of the corner of his eye, Striker saw one of Treece's goons sidle closer, and he knew this wasn't going to end nicely. He started toward Lindsey. "Let's go." He didn't think Treece would hurt her, but he didn't trust him.

Treece looked at Lindsey. "I'd like to have a private word with Mr. Striker, if you don't mind. Why don't you go to the bar and get yourself something to drink?"

Her gaze went from Treece to Striker, then back to Treece.

"Whatever you have to say to him you can say to me."

Striker didn't miss the nod Treece sent the goon nearest her. "Aaron, why don't you escort her to the coatroom? Make sure their cover charges are fully refunded."

She stepped back when the big man moved toward her. "I'm not leaving without—"

"Go ahead." Striker cut her off. He had a pretty good idea what Treece had planned for him, and he didn't want her involved. "I'll meet you out front in a few minutes."

She resisted, her eyes sweeping from Striker, to Treece and back to Striker.

"Two minutes," he said. "It's okay."

The goon tried to take her arm to escort her from the room, but Lindsey shook him off roughly. "Get your hands off me."

Treece waited until she left, then crossed to the door and locked it. His eyes were flat when he turned to Striker. "You know the rules about touching my dancers."

"I know a lot of things about you, Treece. I know you're a piece of scum. And I know your number is going to come up one of these days."

"I hear the inmates at Walla Walla already know you're going to be joining them. I hear they're looking forward to having a cop in their ranks. I think they'll have you cut down to size in no time, don't you think?"

Striker glared at him, his heart pounding, and found himself wishing for his sidearm. "Fuck you."

Treece smiled. "Ah, Mr. Striker, I'm going to enjoy making you bleed." He looked at the two men at his side. "I believe he needs a lesson in club etiquette."

In his peripheral vision Striker saw both men move toward him. Dread curdled in his gut when they slid expandable police batons from beneath their jackets. He'd hoped to avoid a physical confrontation, but it didn't look like he was going to get his wish.

Striker wasn't afraid of taking a beating. It wouldn't be the first, and it probably wouldn't be the last. But he sure as hell wasn't going to go down without a fight.

Treece motioned toward the alley door. "Shall we step into the alley, gentlemen?"

Knowing he only had a few seconds before they incapacitated him, Striker said, "you first," and charged Treece.

He caught a glimpse of Treece's shocked expression an instant before he landed an uppercut to the other man's chin. Pain radiated up his knuckles all the way to his elbow on contact. Satisfaction flashed when he heard Treece's teeth snap together. Vaguely he was aware of the shuffle of shoes against tile, the other two men closing in from behind.

As Treece reeled backward, Striker spun, landed a kick in one of the men's abdomen. He heard a grunt. From his other side a baton flashed, came down with bone-crunching force on his thigh. He cursed as brilliant pain streaked up his leg, but he didn't go down. He spun, threw a punch, but it went wide, grazed the man's cheek. The second baton came out of nowhere and slammed into his ribs like a concrete block shot out of a cannon. Striker heard bone crack, felt all the oxygen leave his lungs. He tried to suck in a breath, ended up making an undignified sound. Another blow landed between his shoulder blades. Pain zinged down his spine, and his head began to reel.

Vaguely, he was aware of Treece cursing. One of the other men moving quickly around the room. He tried to focus, but his vision blurred. He sucked in a breath, and his ribs screamed in pain.

He looked up to see one of the goons circling him, grinning like an idiot, holding the baton ready. "You want some more of this?"

Striker knew they weren't going to stop. He knew he was going to have to rely on himself if he wanted to get out of this without serious bodily injury. Grinding his teeth in anger and pain, he kicked the baton from the man's hand. It clattered away, slid beneath the table.

"Watch his feet," the man said.

Striker dove for the fallen weapon. He heard a *whoosh*! an instant before the baton impacted solidly against his spine. A baseball bat slamming in a home run. The concussion jarred his kidneys. Vivid pain streaked down his body all the way to his toes. Surprise rippled through him when his knees hit the floor. He heard himself gasp for breath, and knew it was over. All he could do from here on out was try to protect himself and hope they didn't hit anything vital.

Striker didn't see the next blow coming. The end of the baton slammed against his right temple. He raised his arms in an attempt to grab it but wasn't fast enough. A steel-toed boot rammed into his stomach just below his ribs. Nausea climbed up his throat. He heard himself retch. He reached out to break his fall just as the cold tile floor rushed up to greet him. He tried to roll, but another boot crashed into his chest. Again in his side. Pain exploded across his rib cage. He tried to roll away, but another kick caught him in the back of the head. Darkness crowded his vision.

Vaguely, he was aware of cool tile beneath his cheek. The door to the alley opening. He tried to get his arms under him, but rough hands were already dragging him across the floor. Pain ground through his body as they hauled him over the threshold and into the alley.

Then he was lying on his back. He heard the door close, the lock being turned. He felt rain on his face. Water seeping through his slacks. He opened his eyes, saw a fire escape against a night sky. He smelled garbage and motor oil and wet asphalt. He rolled onto his side, tried to sit up, and a tidal wave of pain swamped him. Took his breath. Dimmed the lights.

He thought about Lindsey in the club all alone and hoped she was smart enough to stay out of trouble. He didn't think she'd had much experience with sharks. Then again, he'd had plenty, and look what happened.

chapter
10

LINDSEY'S HEART WAS STILL POUNDING WHEN SHE left the break area and entered the main part of the club. She told herself she wasn't worried about Striker. He was an ex-cop and more than capable of taking care of himself.

But she didn't like what had gone down in that break room. She didn't like Mason Treece. Didn't like the business he ran or the company he kept. She certainly hadn't liked the looks of the two thugs who'd been with him.

Uneasiness followed her as she made her way toward the bar. Beyond she could see one of the dancers squatting on the stage, the brass pole sliding between her thighs. Revelers crowded around the stage, offering hundred-dollar bills, lewd comments, and hungry leers.

As she elbowed through the crowd, she realized that her head was feeling fuzzy. She wanted to blame it on the loud music and cigarette smoke, or maybe residual adrenaline from the confrontation with Treece. But she was having a difficult time concentrating. Her thoughts were disjointed. Her mind seemed to be moving in slow motion.

By the time she reached the bar, Lindsey felt light-headed and out of sync with her surroundings. When her vision blurred, worry niggled at the back of her brain. She tried to recall if she'd eaten, but couldn't. She caught the bartender's attention and asked for a Red Bull energy drink on ice. He grinned, picked up a tall, narrow glass, spun it in the air like a baton, then filled it with ice and the amber liquid. Lindsey set four dollars on the bar and drank, hoping the caffeine would clear her head.

But when she glanced toward the exit sign that led to the break room where she'd left Striker, the room began to swim. Alarmed, she blinked and rubbed at her eyes, but it didn't help. At some point her mouth had gone dry. She could feel the blood pounding through her veins. The music pulsing inside her body.

What in the name of God was happening to her?

Frightened now, Lindsey started toward the ladies rest room. She needed a few minutes of quiet. Some cool water on her face. But after a few steps she realized she was no longer steady on her feet. It was as if she were walking through a tunnel that kept getting longer and longer. She could feel her legs moving, but she didn't seem to be getting any closer to her destination.

The music was vibrating inside her head, jarring her brain, making it difficult to think. The crowd seemed to ebb and flow around her, an ocean of laughter and conversation melding into deafening and meaningless babble.

She was halfway to the rest room when she bumped into someone hard enough to jar her teeth. She would have lost her balance if a set of strong hands hadn't reached out to steady her.

"Whatever you're on, honey, you took too much."

"I'm sorry," she muttered.

"Hey!" The hands tightened on her biceps. "You're Traci's sister. Lindsey, right?"

She looked up to see Brandon Rakestraw smiling down

at her, his expression surprised and a little amused. He was wearing a charcoal suit with a shirt the color of orange sherbet. He smelled like cloves.

"Hey, are you okay?" he asked.

"I don't know what's happening to me." To her horror, her words slurred. "I think I need to sit down."

"Let's just take a walk over to the bar, okay? I'll find you a place to sit."

Vaguely, she was aware of him guiding her through the crowd. Bodies jostled her from all sides. She tried to sip her drink, but was suddenly afraid she would drop the glass, so she held it in front of her, gripping it tightly.

"Here we go."

They'd reached the bar. Lindsey tried to set down her drink, but she knocked over the glass, spilling Red Bull and ice. "I'm sorry," she muttered.

"Hey, no problem." Smiling, Brandon picked up several napkins, dropped them over the spill. "You having a good time?"

"No. I just . . . I'm feeling really dizzy." The room dipped, and she had to grasp the bar to maintain her balance.

"Whoa." He patted the barstool next to her. "Why don't you have a seat? Let me order you an espresso, get a little caffeine in your system. If you don't mind my saying so, you look like you could use it."

When she tried to scoot onto the stool, her hand slipped. She would have fallen if he hadn't reached for her, gotten his hands beneath her armpits.

"I've got you." He guided her onto the stool, then wrapped an arm around her waist to support her. "Damn bartenders are lethal, aren't they?"

The man sitting next to her leaned forward to get a look at her. He was young and slightly built with a dark goatee and a pierced eyebrow. He laughed when she made eye contact with him. Vaguely, she was aware of the bartender watching her, looking perturbed as he cleaned up the drink she spilled. And she realized all of them thought she was drunk.

"I haven't had anything to drink," she slurred. "I don't know why this is happening to me."

Rakestraw snagged the bartender's attention. "Why don't you get me a double espresso for her?"

Lindsey prayed the caffeine would help her regain her equilibrium. She didn't know what was wrong with her. She didn't think she was ill. She felt as if she'd had too much to drink, but the only drink she'd had was the club soda Jamie had given her earlier. . . .

Her next thought sent a wave of fear slicing through her. What if someone had drugged her? She tried to remember who'd had access to her drink.

"So have you had any luck locating Traci?" Brandon asked.

Lindsey had forgotten he was standing beside her. She tried to focus on his face, concentrate on what he'd said. But the room spun and bucked in her peripheral vision. She could feel his arm around her, supporting her. His hand was brushing her left breast. She wanted to push him away, but knew if she did she would slide to the floor in a heap.

"Can't find her," she slurred.

"So how long will you be in town?"

When she didn't answer, he leaned forward and looked closely at her. "Hey, are you okay?"

"You don't understand . . . "

The bartender set the espresso in front of her. She wanted to drink it down in the hope that the caffeine would clear her head. But she didn't trust her hands to pick up the demitasse cup without spilling it, so she left it.

"Whatever the case, I don't think you're in any condition to be wandering around Club Tribeca looking for your sister."

"Do you . . . know . . . where . . ." Unable to remember how she'd intended to finish the sentence, Lindsey pressed her fingertips against her temples and massaged, but the dizziness and lethargy were getting worse.

"I need to . . . go home," she slurred.

"Do you have a ride?" he asked. "I mean, there's no way in hell you can drive. If you don't wrap your car around a telephone pole, the cops will get you. They can be real bastards when it comes to DUI."

Lindsey looked down at her hands, and was shocked to see them pulsing like balloons. She touched her face. A layer of fear settled over her when she realized her cheeks were numb. Worse, she could feel herself sagging on the barstool, pitching forward. Her spine felt like rubber, her head as if it weighed a hundred pounds.

Rakestraw was holding her more tightly now, talking quietly to her, trying to keep her upright. She could no longer tell how close his hand was to her breast. She didn't trust him, didn't want him to touch her. All she wanted was to find Striker and go home.

"Let go of me," she said.

He said something, but for the life of her she couldn't understand what. "I have to go."

"Why don't you let me call you a cab?"

"Find . . . Striker."

"Is that a person, place, or thing?"

She could feel his arms around her, like steel bands, holding her upright, touching her. "Get your . . . hands off me."

Shaking off Rakestraw's arms, she slid from the stool. Shock punched her when her knees buckled. She fell forward. Her knees hit the floor. She tried to break her fall with her hands, but her elbows gave way. She landed belly down on the cold tile.

"Whoa!"

Rakestraw's voice. Above her. Lindsey tried to push herself up, but couldn't and floundered like a fish out of water. She lifted her head and looked around, but her hair was in her eyes. All she could see were dozens of legs, shoes, spiked heels.

People were looking at her. Laughing and pointing. They

thought she was drunk. Lindsey never drank. The smell of it nauseated her. Jerry Thorpe had been a drunk. His breath had reeked of it when he came to her bed at night . . .

Humiliation and embarrassment washed over her, but those two emotions were dwarfed by the knowledge that she was in trouble. That she was vulnerable and unable to protect herself.

A strong hand closed around her bicep. "Upsy daisy, honey. Let's go, sister. Come on, hon, you can do it."

Rakestraw's voice reached her as if through a veil of fog. She struggled to get her legs under her and somehow made it to her feet.

"I think it's time I either put you in a cab or took you home myself."

"Don't want to go . . . with you."

She caught a glimpse of his blue eyes an instant before her head lolled back. "I want Striker," she whispered. Then the world around her turned monochrome.

Striker had been in enough brawls to know when he was on the losing end of one. Not that this one had entailed much in the way of brawling. It had been more of a straightforward, no-questions-asked ass kicking.

His forty-two-year-old body was feeling every second of that beating now. His ribs hurt. His brain felt as if it had been run through a meat grinder. But of all the places he'd been hit—and he'd lost track after about the third blow—his thigh hurt the most. The baton had come down hard on his right quadriceps, and it had felt as if his leg had shattered.

Goddamn Mason Treece.

Leaning against the wet brick, Striker spat blood and looked at his watch. Surprise kicked through him when he realized he'd been lying in the cold drizzle for half an hour. He'd told Lindsey he would meet her in just a few minutes. He wondered if she was waiting. If she was looking for him. If she'd gone back into that break room . . .

He struggled to his feet and limped toward the mouth of the alley. He wasn't sure what he was going to do about Treece. A smarter man might have called the cops and filed assault charges. But Striker had a newfound reputation for having a fire keg temper and a propensity for beating the shit out of people. It wouldn't take much for Treece to convince the cops Striker had instigated the fight.

No, he thought bitterly. It might be best just to let this one slide. Chalk it up to experience. Or maybe he'd just wait for a better time to make things right.

On the sidewalk beneath a streetlamp, Striker got a good look at the condition of his clothes. His jeans were torn at one knee. His jacket was wet and smelled like dirty asphalt. He was pretty sure the dark stain on his shirt was blood. He took a moment to tuck in his shirt, straighten his jacket, and wipe the grime from his hands onto his pants. Once his clothes were tidied, he started toward the entrance of Club Tribeca.

The late-night crowd was lined up at the front door like a herd of high-dollar show cattle. Two bouncers stood sentry on either side of the doors. Striker scanned the crowd, looking for a slender woman with reddish brown hair and a pretty smile. That was when he noticed the small group that had gathered on the sidewalk near the taxi lane, and he got a bad feeling in the pit of his stomach.

Forgetting about the pain in his thigh, he started toward the group. Through the throng of bodies he could see someone staggering around. A woman who looked to be falling down drunk. Several people had come to her aid. Then he saw reddish brown hair and a pale face and something went cold inside him.

Striker broke into a run. "Lindsey!"

He reached the crowd, elbowed past several onlookers. Something protective and decidedly mean stirred inside him when he saw her go down on her knees. Some joker in a five-hundred-dollar suit was trying to lift her. Her shirt had ridden up, and he could see the bare flesh of her belly, the white flash of her bra, and Striker saw red.

"Get your hands off her now!" he snarled.

Before the man could answer, Striker brought his hands down hard on the man's shoulders, spun him around. "What the hell did you do to her?"

The man snarled, tried to jerk away. Then he must have seen something in Striker's eyes because his face blanched. "I didn't do anything. She's fuckin' wasted. I was just trying to help."

Shoving him aside, Striker crossed to Lindsey, bent to her, "Lindsey. Hey, it's me. What happened?"

She looked up at him with glazed eyes. "Striker . . ."

"She's drunk as a skunk," someone said.

"Better keep a closer eye on your woman, buddy."

Laughter sounded, and then the crowd began to disburse. Striker looked at Lindsey in disbelief. Of all the people he might have expected to get shit-faced, she was not one of them.

What the hell had she been thinking?

Relieved that she was unhurt, annoyed that she had been so irresponsible, he put his hands beneath her armpits, lifted her to her feet. "Come on, Lindsey. Party's over. I'm taking you home."

"Need to find . . . Traci."

"You should have thought of that before you tried to drown yourself in whatever the hell you've been drinking."

"I . . . haven't . . . been . . ."

"Yeah, and I'm a nice guy."

"No . . . Striker. Rakestraw . . . talking." She tried to dig in her heels, but her knees buckled.

He caught her before she fell, looped her arm around his neck, and held her upright. "You're in no condition to talk to anyone tonight. Let's go."

Only he wasn't quite sure where to take her. He didn't think it was safe to take her back to Traci's house. He considered checking her into a hotel, but that would leave her with a transportation problem come morning. The last thing he wanted to do was take her to his place.

She leaned heavily against him as he guided her down the sidewalk toward the jeep. He had one arm around her waist, the other held her left arm over his shoulder to keep her upright. Her body was pressed up against his, and for the first time he was aware of how soft she felt against him. How good she smelled. Damn it, he didn't need this.

"Striker." She slurred his name. "Wait . . ."

He glanced over at her, grimaced. He didn't like seeing her like this. He'd put her on some kind of a pedestal, he realized. The wholesome girl next door. A kid-sister smile that was pretty enough to turn a man inside out.

. He was annoyed with her for getting drunk. Annoyed with himself for noticing things about her he shouldn't be noticing.

". . . drugged me . . ."

The words drove into his brain like a dull knife. He stopped abruptly, a new and terrible suspicion hammering through him. He turned her to face him, looked hard at her. "What did you say?"

She looked at him from beneath heavy lidded eyes. She blinked furiously, trying to focus, but her head kept lolling back. ". . . drug . . . in my drink."

He put his hands on her shoulders, leaned close, and checked her breath for alcohol. All he smelled was the citrus scent of her shampoo. Sweet vanilla on her skin. Not a hint of alcohol. For God's sake, he should have realized.

Fury coursed through him at the thought of someone drugging her. As a cop he'd seen it before. A woman out on the town. Some scumbag drops a roofie into her drink, drags her out to the parking lot, and rapes her. With no memory of the event, no face to put with the crime, he gets away with it, and the female victim is left thinking it was her fault.

Scummy sons of bitches.

There were a plethora of date rape drugs readily available

on the black market. Rohypnol, the trade name for fluni-trazepam, otherwise known as "roofies," was the most popular. GHB or gamma-hydroxybutyrate was quickly growing in popularity. Both were powerful sedatives and could be dangerous as hell when used improperly. They were relatively common at some of the area clubs, the rave parties, and with sexual predators.

Striker wondered who'd seen fit to slip one into Lindsey's club soda. He wondered what their motivation had been and suddenly wished he'd gotten a better look at the man he'd found her with.

"Aw, man," he muttered.

She sagged against him. He caught her beneath her arms and tried not to think of how vulnerable she'd been in that club. He wondered why she'd been singled out, if it had been random. Or maybe it had something to do with Traci . . .

"Striker?"

He looked down at her. "Yeah?"

"I don't drink . . . can't stand the smell."

Beneath the light of the single streetlamp, she looked small and vulnerable, and he felt very badly that this had happened to her. "I know," he said.

At the jeep, he opened the passenger door and helped her inside. By the time he walked around to be driver's side, she was lying across the seat. He got in, propped her upright, and snapped her safety belt into place.

"I want to go home," she whispered.

"Change of plans, partner." He started the engine.

"Where? . . ."

"We're going to make a stop at the emergency room and get you checked out."

"Don't like . . . doctors."

"Neither do I, but I don't think we have a choice," he said and pulled onto the street.

chapter
11

LINDSEY WOKE TO A FIERCELY POUNDING HEAD AND a mouth that tasted like dirty socks. She was lying on a bed, on her side. The sheets smelled familiar and made her think of Striker. Somewhere in the distance she could hear water running. Or maybe it was raining again. She was beginning to hate Seattle weather.

Vaguely, she remembered there was something she needed to do. Something important that niggled at the back of her brain. Something having to do with Traci.

The thought of her sister opened her eyes. She rolled onto her back and found herself staring up at an ancient skylight where rain pounded down, turning mullioned glass into a hundred silver streamers. The sky beyond was the color of wet slate. She watched the water cascade and wondered who would put their bed right beneath a mammoth skylight.

Suddenly, it dawned on her that she didn't have the slightest idea where she was. The realization sent her bolt upright. Disoriented, she looked down at the navy comforter tangled around her and waited for the familiarity that didn't come. She was wearing her turtleneck, bra, and panties, but her jeans and boots had been removed.

"Oh, my God."

She remembered going to Club Tribeca with Striker. She remembered speaking to Jamie Mills. The scene in the break room with Treece and his goons. And then nothing.

Lindsey looked around, confusion and uneasiness stealing through her. She was sitting on a king-size brass bed in what was apparently some type of warehouse loft. The place was immense and uncomfortably cold. Judging from the polyurethane sheets hanging along the far wall, it was also undergoing renovation. The air smelled of recently cut lumber and fresh paint, with the underlying redolence of old building. To her left, a scarred brick wall ran the length of the room. To her right was a painted brick wall and a single, open doorway. Above her, steel rafters and a labyrinth of suspended steel pipe and ductwork comprised the ceiling. Immense arched windows locked out the pouring rain. A few feet away from the bed, water dripped from the ceiling into a rusty gallon bucket.

Where the hell was she?

She looked around for her jeans—trying desperately to quiet the voice in her head that wanted to know who had taken them off of her—and found them draped neatly across a chair next to the bed. Ignoring her aching head, she swung her legs over the side of the bed and reached for her pants. Her boots came next. She looked around, spotted her purse on the night table. Next to it, an alarm clock told her it was one o'clock. She gaped at the dial, shocked that she had slept so late.

How in the world had she gotten here? Why couldn't she remember last night?

A noise off to her right made her jump. She spun and realized the sound had come from an antique steam register that had begun to heat. Pressing her hand to her chest, she cautiously walked over to a sofa, television, chair, and coffee table that had been grouped together and comprised the living area. The television was turned on to an all news cable channel. Beyond, in a makeshift kitchen, a coffeemaker gurgled and spat into a carafe.

Her first instinct was to call out. But Lindsey had absolutely no idea to whom she would be calling, so she didn't. Ordering herself to stay calm, she started toward the rear of the warehouse where she heard the sound of running water. A wide doorway took her to a tiled room with low ceilings. It was warmer, and humidity hung in the air. Some of the tiles were broken in places; some were missing completely, and she had the feeling of walking into an ancient high school shower room.

She followed the sound of the water. A shower if she wasn't mistaken. The corridor took her to a smaller room filled with steam. Industrial gray tile comprised three open shower stalls. In the last stall, Michael Striker stood naked beneath the spray of a big round showerhead.

For the span of a heartbeat, Lindsey just stood there, shocked, unable to look away. He was built like a marathon runner. Lean without being thin. Long limbed with well-defined muscles that looked hard as rock. A thatch of black hair covered his chest and tapered to a flat belly. Her gaze went lower, and she felt the heat of a blush on her cheeks.

Her embarrassment transformed to shock when he turned and she spotted the bruise. It was the color of eggplant and stretched from his shoulder blade to the small of his back. Even from twenty feet away, she could see that the flesh was angry and swollen. A second bruise striped his thigh. It was lighter in color, but she could see that he was favoring his leg. What on earth had happened to him? Had he gotten into a fight? With Treece and his goons?

Vaguely, she heard the squeak of faucets. The water shutting off. Before she could duck back into the hall, he spotted her. But he looked more amused than embarrassed as he jerked a towel from the rack and wrapped it around his hips. "I'm not even going to ask you how long you've been standing there," he said.

Mortified, Lindsey lurched into the hall, her heart pounding wildly in her chest. She told herself she was shaking because she was startled, because she didn't know what the hell she was doing in Michael Striker's loft or how she'd gotten there. But none of those things explained the quick slice of heat low in her belly.

"You're probably wondering what you're doing here," he called out.

Closing her eyes, she pressed her back against the wall and willed herself to calm down. "I—I didn't know you were showering," she said. "I . . . heard the water running and . . . for God's sake, there are no doors in this place."

He entered the corridor a moment later, a second towel draped over his shoulders. "No harm done."

She had a difficult time holding his gaze. "Striker, my God, how did you get those bruises? What happened?"

"Forget about the bruises, Lindsey."

"They look serious."

"I'll live."

"But how did you get them?" Her gaze slid toward the bruises in question. She caught a glimpse of hard male skin, still damp from his shower, and jerked her eyes back to his, her cheeks heating. "D—did you get into a fight last night? With Treece?"

"I think the bigger question is what happened to you."

She pressed her hand to her stomach and looked away. "I don't even know where I am."

"This is my place." He contemplated her. "How are you feeling?"

"I have a headache."

"How much do you remember?"

"I remember being at Club Tribeca. After that . . . it's all a blank." A terrible, black void.

"I think some scumbag dropped a roofie into your club soda," he said.

The words struck her like a slap. "A roofie?" She had a pretty good idea what that was. "How did I . . . I mean, I wasn't . . . " Panic rose swiftly inside her at the thought of all the things that could have happened, what might have happened, that she wouldn't even remember.

Striker must have ascertained her thoughts. "Nothing happened," he said. "I took you to the emergency room at Harborview and had the doc check you out."

"I have no recollection of being in the emergency room." She lowered her head, put her fingers against her temple, and rubbed. "My God, I don't remember anything."

"Blackout," he said. "It's typical of date rape drugs."

She looked up at him, trying to get her brain around what he was telling her. To think that someone had incapacitated her, left her vulnerable and helpless was unthinkable.

"You brought me here?" And undressed her and tucked her into his bed.

"The doc said not to leave you alone. I didn't think it was a good idea to take you back to Traci's." He looked uncomfortable for a moment. "Your clothes were damp, so I hung them to dry for you. I hope that's all right."

She stared at him, feeling angry and incredibly violated. "I don't understand why someone would drug me."

"Look, I know this is upsetting. But you're okay. Everything turned out all right."

"Nothing is all right," she snapped. "I was drugged. That's . . . unspeakably malicious."

"It could have been a lot worse," he pointed out.

She knew he was right, but it didn't make it any easier to accept. "Can the police do something? Arrest someone? I mean, those kinds of drugs are illegal, aren't they?"

"Who would they arrest?"

"They could start with Mason Treece."

"Do you have the proof that he drugged you? Did you see him do it? Does he have drugs in his possession?"

She realized where he was going and felt even more outraged. "No, but . . . it's his club."

"Unfortunately that doesn't make him a criminal. It doesn't even make him a suspect."

"Well, since you're the cop, why don't you tell me what we can do about it."

He shrugged. "I called in a report last night, talked to one of the detectives. The doctor drew a blood sample while you were in the emergency room, so in a few days we'll have proof you were drugged. Once that happens, vice will send a detective to hassle Treece and ask a few questions. But without an eyewitness to the crime or the discovery of drugs in his possession, nothing's going to happen."

"I hate the idea of someone getting away with that."

"I don't like it either, but that's the way the system works."

She rubbed her temple where the headache was pounding like a drum. "Was the entire night a bust?"

"We spoke with Jamie Mills. She wasn't very cooperative, but I got the impression she knows more than she's letting on." He shrugged. "We can keep pushing her, maybe wear her down. But her refusing to talk to us could be something as innocuous as Traci swearing her to secrecy. I mean, as far as we know, Traci could be in rehab. She could be having some plastic surgery done. I don't know." He paused. "You mentioned Rakestraw last night. Did you talk to him?"

"I think so." Images flashed in her mind's eye. Rakestraw wearing a black suit with a shirt the color of orange sherbet. He'd thought she was drunk. The smell of clove cigarettes . . . "I don't remember much about the conversation."

"Think about it. It may come back to you." He lifted the towel from his shoulders and began drying his hair. "I've got a meeting with my lawyer in an hour. You're welcome to stay here if you want."

She opened her mouth to refuse when she caught a glimpse of his chest, and the words died on her tongue. He was still damp from the shower and little droplets of water clung to thick swirls of black hair. His pectoral muscles looked as if they'd been sculpted from steel and flexed as he toweled his hair.

Ridiculously embarrassed, she dropped her gaze. "Thank you, but I should go. I need to . . . follow up on a few things."

"Suit yourself." Draping the towel over his shoulders, he started down the corridor toward the main part of the loft. "I made some coffee. Don't take this the wrong way, but you look like you could use it."

Lindsey watched him walk away, telling herself it was the aftereffects of the drug she'd been given that had her thinking of him in terms of his chest instead of the man she'd hired to find her sister.

Because if she knew anything about herself, it was that she was immune to rough-around-the-edges males like Michael Striker. And she was far too smart to fall victim to something as banal as her own hormones.

Holding that thought, she started after him.

Striker had never been shy. As a kid, he'd always been the first one to strip off his jeans and jump into the quarry for an ice-cold skinny dip. When he'd seen Lindsey standing just outside the shower room, watching him, he hadn't reached for the towel out of modesty. He'd reached for the towel to cover his physical reaction to her because he'd suddenly found himself remembering what it had been like tucking her into his bed the night before.

After carrying her into the loft and laying her on his bed, he'd spent twenty minutes trying to decide if it was appropriate for him to remove her wet clothes. With her barely conscious, undressing her simply hadn't felt right.

But there was no way his conscience would let him leave her in wet clothes all night. So as quickly and impersonally as possible, he'd tugged off her boots and peeled off her damp jeans. And even though he'd gone to great lengths to avoid touching her, he'd looked.

Giving himself a hard mental shake, he crossed to the bedroom area and jerked a pair of Dockers off a hanger. He was aware of Lindsey behind him and glanced at her over his shoulder. "This might be a good time for you to turn around," he said. "There's not much privacy in this loft, and I need to get my clothes on."

"Oh." She spun away from him, then headed toward the living area without looking back.

Watching her retreat, he stepped into his boxers and slacks and draped the towel over the footboard of the bed. Grabbing a pullover from the rack, he started toward the kitchen area for coffee. Lindsey was standing in the living area, and he was suddenly, painfully aware that she was looking around, that the place was a mess. And for the first time since he'd moved in, he found himself wishing he'd spent a little more time making it habitable.

"Are you going to tell me how you got those bruises or not?"

He'd been hoping she would forget about the bruises, but it didn't look like he was going to get his wish. He might as well come clean and let her know just how dangerous Mason Treece was. "I had a little altercation with a couple of Treece's goons last night."

"Little altercation?" She walked over to him, her expression incredulous. "It looks like someone flogged you with a telephone pole!"

He stopped what he was doing and looked down at her. "It's not a big deal, Lindsey."

She searched his gaze. Her eyes widened, and he knew she'd spotted the darkening bruise at his hairline just behind his temple. Damn it.

"Those two gorillas beat you," she said. "That's a big deal."

"Like I told you, Treece thinks he has a score to settle with me." He set two mugs next to the coffeemaker. "Last night he figured he had an opportunity to make good on it."

"But, that's assault, isn't it? Why didn't you press charges?"

"I'm involved in a high-profile case right now, and I'm trying like hell to keep my nose clean."

"But it wasn't your fault."

"Unless Treece's lawyer convinces a jury I threw the first punch."

"You can't let him get away with assaulting you."

"I wasn't assaulted," he snapped. "I got into a fight. I got my ass kicked. End of story."

Striker watched her walk to the sofa and tried not to feel bad for having snapped at her when she'd only been trying to help. But he didn't need some female hovering over him. The way he saw it, the bruises he'd suffered last night were the least of his problems.

Wanting to make things right with her, but not quite sure how to do it, he poured coffee into the mugs and carried both into the living area. He handed her one of the mugs. "Here's a peace offering. It's hot."

"Thanks."

For a moment neither of them spoke, then she surprised him by asking, "Do you think my getting drugged could have something to do with my looking for Traci?"

Striker had spent half the night pondering the whos and whys of how Lindsey had ended up with a roofie in her drink. He didn't like any of the scenarios that had come back at him. "It's hard to say," he said. "It could have been random. Some sexual predator looking for a score. Guy sees you alone in the bar. He likes what he sees." He didn't miss the minute shiver that ran the length of her and in the back of his mind wondered about its source. "Did you set your drink down at any time?"

She shook her head adamantly. "That drug went into my drink before we went into the break room."

"Jamie could have done it," he said.

"But why would she drug me? What could she possibly have to gain? Especially if she and Traci are friends?"

He thought about it for a moment. "Maybe she's just doing what she's told."

"By whom? Treece?"

"He's enough of a scumbag to do something like that, though I can't figure his motivation."

"To get back at you?"

"Maybe, but the timing of this bothers me."

"That takes us back to Traci, doesn't it?"

He met her gaze. "It coincides with your asking questions about your sister."

"I have a news flash for Treece," she said, her expression turning fierce. "I'm not going to let him or Jamie Mills or any one else keep me from doing what I need to do."

Suddenly, Striker didn't like the stubborn determination he saw on her face. "Since you're paying me, why don't you leave Mason Treece and Jamie Mills to me?"

"Because I happen to think two heads are better than one."

"I think you need to take a big step back and remind yourself what kind of people we're dealing with. This isn't some neat script where everyone plays by the rules."

"Don't ask me to sit this out, Striker. It's not going to happen."

"All I'm asking you to do is to think before you act," he said. "Be smart about this. Treece is a shark. If he's running some sort of con at that club and you get in the way, he'll run right over you."

"Are you saying he's dangerous?"

"Dangerous to someone who isn't used to dealing with sharks."

She looked away, but not before he saw her pale. He didn't like frightening her, but he'd been around enough to know that there were times when good old-fashioned fear was a healthy thing.

He looked at his watch. "Why don't you let me drop you off at a hotel. You can get yourself checked in, and we can meet later."

Squaring her shoulders, she turned to face him. "I need to finish going through Traci's things at the house."

He admired her tenacity, but it annoyed him that she wasn't going to take his advice. "Lindsey, the house has already been broken into at least once—"

"I'll be careful," she said quickly. "Come on. It's broad daylight. I'll keep my cell phone handy. Keep the doors locked."

Bending his head, he pinched the bridge of his nose and muttered a curse. "Lindsey . . ."

"I mean it, Striker. I'm not going to sit this out. I need to do this. Not only for Traci, but for me."

"I hope she's worth it," he said and tried not to think about all the things that could happen.

chapter
12

LINDSEY STOOD AT THE FRONT DOOR OF TRACI'S bungalow and watched Striker drive away. He hadn't spoken to her during the drive from downtown to Bellevue. She didn't know if his cool silence had been because she'd bucked his advice about checking in to a hotel, or because he was on his way to see his lawyer. Whatever the case, he hadn't been very happy. But there was no way she was going to spend the day cowering in some hotel room just to appease him.

Locking the door behind her, she walked through the house, checking the windows and doors as she went, making sure her unwanted visitor hadn't returned during the night. After feeding the cat, she went directly to the study. The answering machine message light was blinking, so she grabbed a pad of paper and hit the PLAY button. Two hangups and a recording touting carpet cleaning for $69.00. Damn.

She checked her E-mail and found messages from several of Traci's friends, but none of them had heard from her. The E-mail she'd sent to Brandon Rakestraw had bounced. She E-mailed Carissa, letting her know she still hadn't located Traci and would be in Seattle at least a couple more days. Then she called a nearby hotel and made a reservation for the next two nights.

Settling behind the desk, she methodically went through the credenza and a small cabinet set in to the bookcase. She found a dozen more disks but couldn't bring herself to watch them, so she dropped them into her bag in the hope that Striker would do it for her.

Finding nothing more of interest in the study, she switched gears and went upstairs. She stood in the doorway of Traci's bedroom for a long time, trying to decide what to do next. Trying even harder to make sense of all the things she'd learned about her sister.

Lindsey didn't believe Traci had gone on the run. She didn't believe her sister would abandon her home, her job, her life. Traci was too much of a fighter. If anything, she would have hired some high-powered lawyer to get her off.

But Lindsey acknowledged the fact that at some point in the last few years, her sister had become a stranger. She thought about the pornographic movie and wondered how she could have gotten involved in something so reprehensible. Had she done it strictly for the money? Or had she been coerced? Had she been manipulated by love or drugs or both? Or did her sister's foray into the dark side of filmmaking have more to do with what had happened to them as children?

The latter explanation caused Lindsey the most pain. The most outrage. The most guilt. Intellectually, she knew she wasn't responsible for what had happened to them all those years ago. There was only one person responsible for the abuse they had endured, and that was Jerry Thorpe.

But on an emotional level, Lindsey bore the burden of blame right along with her stepfather. The truth of the matter was she hadn't told anyone what was happening. Not her mother. Not her teacher. Not the pastor at their church. There would always be a part of her that felt responsible. A part of her she couldn't forgive because she'd walked away and left her younger sister in the hands of a monster.

As an adult, Lindsey had worked hard to come to terms with what had happened to her. She'd spent years in therapy, educating herself, arming herself with knowledge. She knew all about the long-term effects of sexual abuse. She knew that adult survivors of childhood abuse spent years dealing with fear, anxiety, depression, and anger. She knew they were more apt to engage in inappropriate sexual behavior. That they had a tendency toward substance abuse and experienced difficulties with close relationships.

Traci fit the mold to a T.

While Lindsey had never abused drugs or had issues with anger or depression, she fell squarely into the "difficulties with close relationships" category. She'd dated during college, but could honestly say she'd never been in love. She was twenty-eight years old, but she'd only had one serious relationship in her life. A short and tumultuous association in which she'd engaged in sex twice. Both times the experience had been more of an I-need-to-do-this-so-I-can-be-normal undertaking than as an expression of love or passion.

As Lindsey stood in the dim light of the hall looking into Traci's bedroom, she wondered what demons tormented her sister when she was alone with her thoughts at night. She wondered if Traci ever blamed her for those demons. If they were the same demons that tormented her.

Lindsey spent the remainder of the afternoon going through every drawer, closet, and box in the house. Her efforts were in vain because at the end of the day she still had no clue as to where her sister might have gone or who she might be with. By dark she was exhausted and frustrated and just wanted to get checked in to the hotel so she could take a •

shower and collapse into bed. She had her purse and keys in hand when the phone jangled.

"Hello?"

"Lindsey Metcalf?"

A female voice. Familiar. Lots of attitude. Recognition dawned an instant later. "Jamie?"

The other woman didn't bother with small talk. "I need to see you."

Lindsey went with her instincts and said, "You have some nerve calling me after what you did last night."

Silence.

"I know you put something in my drink, Jamie."

The silence lasted longer this time. So long that for a moment, Lindsey thought she might hang up. "I could have gotten into serious trouble, Jamie. I could have been hurt or worse."

"I didn't call you to talk about last night."

Lindsey heard the other woman's quickened breathing on the other end of the line, and for the first time realized she was upset. Maybe even scared. Curiosity, irritation, and concern mingled into a strange mix. "What do you want?"

"I need to see you. I . . . found something. I don't know what to make of it, but it's freaking me out."

"What are you talking about?"

"A disk. I found a goddamn disk."

Lindsey thought about the disks in her sister's lockbox and closed her eyes briefly. "Look, I know Traci did some porn."

"This isn't fucking porn."

"What's on the disk?"

Silence.

The hairs at her nape prickled. "Jamie, do you know where she is?"

"No. I swear I don't know where she is. But . . . for God's sake . . . the shit on this disk. . . . If Traci's involved . . . My God . . ."

"Involved in what?"

"Something . . . horrible."

Lindsey didn't trust her. But there was a edge in the other woman's voice that pulled at her. "Jamie, all I care about is finding my sister. If she's in trouble, you have to tell me."

"I'm scared," she whispered. "I think something terrible is going on."

The words hung for an interminable moment, like the snap of violence after a gun blast. "Do you have information about Traci?"

"I think this disk could have something to do with her. I don't fucking know." A sigh hissed through the line. "You look at the damn thing and decide for yourself."

"Tell me what you know," Lindsey said.

"I can't!" she whispered furiously. "I'm scared, for chrissake!"

Somewhere in the back of Lindsey's mind an alarm began to wail. Her intellect told her to stay away from Jamie Mills. She wasn't the kind of person you wanted to meet alone after dark. But the part of Lindsey that was determined to find her sister told her this could be the break she'd been waiting for.

"Who are you afraid of?" she asked. "Treece?"

"If you want to know what I found, meet me. If not, I'm getting the hell out while I still can."

"Jamie, what do you mean?"

"Forget it. I gotta go."

"Wait." Indecision pounded at her for an interminable moment, then she sighed. "Where?"

"Terminal 46. Half an hour. I drive a black Jetta. I'll be by the big crane."

Lindsey remembered seeing Terminal 46 on the map. It was a shipyard not far from downtown. Not the kind of place she wanted to wander after dark. "I don't think the shipyard is a very good idea. We can meet at Club Tribeca—"

"No! Just . . . for God's sake, don't talk to anyone at the club or you'll fucking get me killed."

"Killed?" The word put gooseflesh on her arms. "Jamie—"

The line disconnected.

Lindsey gripped the phone for several seconds, telling herself she wasn't going to let Jamie Mills send her on some wild-goose chase. She wasn't stupid enough to meet her in a shipyard after dark. Not after the stunt she'd pulled last night. The woman had a drug habit and a host of unsavory friends. On the other hand, Traci may have some of the very same problems. . . .

I think something terrible is going on.

Lindsey looked at the clock on the mantel. Eight P.M. She knew going to Terminal 46 at this hour was a bad idea. She felt the wrongness of it all the way to her bones. But there was no way she could ignore the call and walk away. She'd walked away once before, and it had cost her a piece of herself she hadn't been able to get back.

"What the hell are you up to, Jamie?" she whispered.

Tugging her cell phone from her purse, she dialed Striker's number and started for the door.

Striker usually didn't get drunk so early in the evening. He normally liked to work up to it slowly. Drink a few beers. Cop a buzz. Play some pool. Then he would break the seal on something imported and eighty proof and lay into it like a man on a holy mission to save his soul by drowning it. Tonight, however, he had made an exception and gone directly to the eighty-proof shit.

The meeting with his lawyer hadn't gone well. In fact it had pretty much gone right into the toilet the moment he'd walked through the door and Blumenthal had told him the King County Prosecutor wasn't going to let him cop a plea. Striker had been holding out hope that the eighteen years he'd been with the Seattle PD would mean something to somebody. Besides himself, anyway. He hadn't counted on it being an election year, or that the prosecuting attorney was an ambitious son of a bitch.

Even though it was only a little after eight o'clock, the Red-Eye Saloon was hopping. Eric Clapton was belting out a tune about an illicit narcotic, while a couple of wannabe pool sharks tried a little too hard to impress the biker chicks racking up balls. Striker knew the regulars and the routine. He knew business picked up a little before midnight. He knew the first fight usually broke out around one A.M. He knew drugs changed hands in the men's rest room. And he knew the bartender kept a Louisville Slugger behind the bar and wouldn't hesitate to use it if some joker gave him any shit.

Striker knew how his own evening would go, too. He would drink until he couldn't see straight. Then at two A.M., he'd stagger to the front door, make a right on First Street, and walk to his loft. He would pass out on the sofa or in his bed only to wake a few hours later bathed in a cold sweat because he could still hear his partner screaming. . . .

"Hell of a nice cave you got here, Striker." Sergeant Detective Shep Murray sat across from him, nursing a Budweiser.

Striker finished his scotch whiskey and lifted the empty glass at the bartender. "Service could use some sprucing up."

Both men watched in silence as the bartender, a burly man with a full beard and a pronounced limp, walked over to their booth and poured Cutty Sark straight from the bottle. "It's on the house, Striker."

"What's the occasion?"

"Nobody likes it when the good guy gets the shaft. Legal system's gonna fuck you up bad." He leaned closer, lowered his voice. "I got some biker friends inside Walla Walla. Worse comes to worse an' I'll give 'em a call." He winked. "Believe me, nobody fucks with these guys."

"I appreciate that." Striker twisted his mouth, hoped it passed for a smile.

Shep watched the bartender limp away, then turned his attention back to Striker. "You think this is a good time for you to get shit-faced, buddy?"

"I think it's the perfect time for me to get shit-faced." Lately, every day seemed like a good time to get shit-faced.

"I take it your meeting with Blumenthal didn't go well."

"Fry isn't going to cut a deal. They're going all the way. First degree felony assault."

"Fry's a prick." Shep looked down at his beer. "Is Blumenthal going to let that stand? I mean, first degree . . . you didn't have a weapon."

"Prosecutor aims to prove my bare hands presented a substantial risk of death to Shroeder."

"Jesus, Striker." Shep looked away. "Isn't there some legal angle Blumenthal can pursue? Mitigating circumstances or something?"

"Half the cops in the precinct saw me go off on Shroeder. Add Schroeder's lawyer to that, and you have one hell of a case."

Shep looked uncomfortable, and Striker knew the other man was glad as hell he hadn't been there that day. A man didn't like having to choose between a friend and his job, especially when he was only five years away from retirement. "You looking at time?"

Striker leaned back in the booth, sipped the scotch whiskey, tried to look unaffected. "Probably."

The reality that in all likelihood he would be going to prison sent a quiver of fear through his gut. He hated being afraid; Striker had never been afraid of anything in his life. But this was like a monkey on his back, riding him hard.

Shep muttered a curse. "Even if you are convicted, there's no jury on earth that will give you ten years for what you did."

"That's what we're counting on. But we all know juries can be fickle as hell."

"After what that little prick did to Trisha . . ." Shep's hands flexed. "They ought to give you a medal instead of a damn trial."

"Blumenthal thinks I'll get a two or three years. With good behavior, I'll be out in eighteen months." Striker looked down at his glass, wished there were something stronger than whiskey inside. He didn't know what that might be, but he didn't want to think about this anymore. Not about prison. Not about *The Incident* and the havoc it had wreaked on his life. But as he sat in the booth and worked diligently on his second double, he knew it wasn't going to be enough to keep his brain from grinding it the rest of the night.

"I think there's some irony in there somewhere," he said after a moment.

"Good guy gets the shaft. Schroeder gets a book deal."

Striker looked over at the pool tables.

"Want to play some eight ball?" Shep asked.

"Not tonight."

Shep took a swig of beer, then looked over at him. "How are you dealing with the other thing?"

Striker wasn't sure if his recoil was physical or emotional, but he felt it deep inside. Like an insect curling up after being prodded with a needle. *The Other Thing* was the euphemism people used when they asked about his partner's rape and murder. The veteran detective Schroeder had tortured and then cut to pieces, while Striker listened to her screams on his cell phone . . .

Striker rolled his shoulder, tried hard not to look as strung out as he felt. "I'm getting by."

"Yeah, you look like you're getting by as you suck down that booze."

Striker felt Shep's eyes on him and wondered if the

other man thought maybe he was about to slide down some slippery slope. "Whatever works."

"So you lying to me, or what?" Shep pressed.

"I'm fine, damn it."

But even a passing thought of what had gone down that night was enough to make him break out in a cold sweat. Knowing Shep was watching him, Striker loosened his grip on the glass and watched the two wannabe pool sharks make fools of themselves. He listened to the music and forced the memory of that night back into its deep, dark hole.

His cell phone chirped. For an instant he considered not answering. Then he looked down at the display, saw Lindsey's number and an unusual ripple of anticipation went through him. He answered with a curt, "yeah."

"Jamie Mills called me," Lindsey said. "She claims to have information about Traci."

She was talking too fast, Striker thought. She was too excited. He heard background noise, realized she was in her vehicle. "Where are you?"

"I'm on my way to meet her."

He sat up straighter. "You don't want to meet her, Lindsey."

"Don't try to talk me out of this."

"Yeah that would be way too reasonable." He sighed. "What kind of information does she claim to have?"

"She wouldn't say."

"That's convenient as hell. She's yanking your chain."

"I know you're going to think I'm nuts, but she sounded scared."

"Lindsey . . ."

"Look, I'm just going to talk to her. I won't take any chances."

"That's like saying you're going skydiving only you promise not to jump out of a plane."

"This could be the break I've been waiting for," she said.

"I'm not going to ignore it because the source is a little shady."

"Jamie Mills is a hell of lot more than a little shady." He looked down at his glass and cursed. "Tell me where."

"Terminal 46."

He got a bad feeling in the pit of his stomach. "Lindsey, damn it. That's not the kind of place you want to go after dark."

"I'll take that under advisement. Hey, thanks for your help, Striker."

"Lindsey—"

The line disconnected.

"Damn it." He snapped the phone closed, looked over at Shep who was watching him with a little too much interest.

"That was a client," Striker clarified.

"Judging from the way you're grinding your teeth, I thought maybe it was a woman."

"That, too, but . . ." He sighed. "She's just a client."

"Whatever you say."

Frowning, Striker laid a ten-dollar bill on the table. "I've got to go."

"Problem?"

Striker slid from the booth. "Yeah, damn woman has a death wish."

chapter
13

LINDSEY EXITED THE ALASKA WAY VIADUCT AT Terminal 46 and parked the Taurus in a seedy lot next to an abandoned building. The smells of brackish water, dead fish, and oil-slicked asphalt met her as she got out of the car. A couple of sodium vapor streetlamps made a feeble attempt to light the area, but the winter fog rolling in from Elliott Bay cut visibility to only a few yards.

Trying hard to convince herself she wasn't an idiot for driving into a squalid section of town to meet a woman who probably didn't know squat about Traci, Lindsey looked around. On the other side of a tall chain-link fence, two huge petroleum tanks rose thirty feet out of the concrete and blocked her view of the bay. To her right, a long, low building ran alongside the waterfront, its loading bays watching her like a dozen vacant eyes. In a small building to her left, she saw the flickering blue light of a welder's arc. Dead ahead, the chain-link gate stood open, and in the distance she could see the skeletal outline of a massive crane that was used to load containers onto ships.

No sign of Jamie. No black Jetta anywhere in sight.

"Terrific," she muttered.

Reaching into her purse, she pulled out her canister of pepper spray, looped the cord around her neck, and hoped like hell she didn't have to use it.

The smells of seawater and shipyard oil became more pronounced as she ventured deeper into the terminal. She cut between two dilapidated buildings, and the black water of the bay loomed into view. At the edge of the pier, a massive container vessel sat in the water as silent and dark as a ghost ship. She should not be thinking about ghost ships on a night like this.

"Jamie?" she called out in her toughest voice. "You have two minutes to show yourself or—"

The hiss of tires on wet pavement spun her around. For an instant headlights blinded her. Raising her hand against the glare, she backed toward the relative protection of a steel parking post jutting from the asphalt. The vehicle stopped twenty feet away. The headlights went out. Lindsey identified the car as a black Jetta, and a measure of relief slid through her.

Jamie Mills emerged from the car. "I didn't think you'd show," she said.

"Yeah, well, my curiosity overrode my better judgment." Her hand on the pepper spray, Lindsey crossed to her, stopping a safe distance away. "This is a hell of a place to meet."

"I wanted someplace out of the way."

"This definitely qualifies. Why all the secrecy?"

Jamie looked over her shoulder. "I didn't want anyone to follow me."

Lindsey studied her, trying to ascertain her frame of mind and failing. "Why would anyone be following you?"

Jamie stepped closer, and for the first time, Lindsey noticed her appearance. Her hair was damp from the drizzle and fell in a tangled mass to her shoulders. She wore a ratty hooded sweatshirt, skin-tight jeans, and high-heeled boots.

A leather backpack was slung over her shoulder. Her face was devoid of stage makeup, revealing the haggard countenance and sleep-deprived eyes of a woman on the edge.

"Maybe I know something I shouldn't," she said.

"Like what?"

Sliding the backpack off her shoulder, Jamie reached inside and pulled out a disk. "I found this." She held it out to Lindsey. "I don't know what to make of it. I don't know if it means anything. I don't even know if it's real, but it's scaring the living shit out of me."

Lindsey looked down at the disk, saw that the other woman's hand was shaking. From drugs? she wondered. Or something else? She took the disk, turned it over. It was the same brand as the ones she'd found at Traci's. A sense of foreboding pressed down on her. "What's on it?"

"See for yourself." Jamie looked over her shoulder, her eyes scanning the fog-shrouded shipyard. "I gotta go."

"You said you had information about Traci."

"I just laid it in your hand, honey."

"Look, Jamie, I know Traci was involved in pornography," Lindsey said. "I want you to know . . . it doesn't matter to me. I don't care what she did. All I care about is finding her."

"For her sake, I hope you can."

Lindsey stared at her. "What is that supposed to mean?"

"Watch the disk. You'll get the picture." She turned and started for the car.

Lindsey didn't want her to leave. She couldn't shake the feeling that the other woman knew more than she was saying. If only she could get Jamie to trust her. "Wait."

Jamie paused, turned.

"You can't just throw me a tidbit and then leave. If you know something about Traci, tell me. Please. I want to help her."

When the other woman didn't say anything, Lindsey reached into her purse, fumbled around for one of her

Spice of Life business cards, and handed it to her. "My cell phone number's on the card. Call me. Please. Maybe I can help you, too."

"Yeah, and maybe I've been beyond help for a long time." But Jamie took the card, shoved it into the pocket of her sweatshirt without looking at it, and opened the car door.

The interior light came on, and Lindsey saw two suitcases and an overnight bag in the backseat. "Are you going on a trip?" she asked.

Jamie slid behind the wheel without answering.

Feeling a little desperate, Lindsey crossed to her, reached out and grasped her arm through the open window. "Please, if you know something about my sister, tell me."

Jamie yanked her arm from Lindsey's grasp. "Get off me," she snarled.

Lindsey stumbled back. The engine turned over and revved. An instant later the tires spun on wet asphalt, and she jumped away from the car just as it shot backward.

For several seconds she stood in the drizzle and swirling fog and watched the red taillights melt into the night. Only then did she realize she was shaking. That she was angry and frustrated and more worried about Traci now than she'd been when she'd driven to this godforsaken shipyard.

She looked down at the disk in her hand. She didn't want to see what was on it, but knew she didn't have a choice. "Damn it," she muttered and started toward the rental car.

Taking the same route as before, she cut between the two buildings and headed toward the yellow glow of the sodium vapor light in the lot where she'd parked. The fog had thickened in the few minutes she'd spoken to Jamie, and the shipyard appeared utterly deserted. Even the welder whose light she'd seen earlier had shut down shop and gone home.

Relief slipped through her when she reached the lot. She was halfway to her car when a sound behind her sent her heart slamming into her ribs. She glanced over her shoulder without slowing her pace, found herself staring into a swirling, white void. She quickened her stride, but the sound came again, to her left this time. The shuffle of shoes against concrete.

"I've already called the cops," she said in her toughest voice. "They're on the way, so whoever you are, I suggest you stay the hell away."

Clutching the canister of pepper spray, she broke into a run. Ten yards to go. She thought she heard something ahead of her, but she didn't stop. The car loomed into view an instant later. Lindsey already had her keys in hand when a man materialized from behind her car.

Fear stopped her dead in her tracks. "Don't come any closer," she said and raised the pepper spray.

He looked otherworldly silhouetted beneath the glow of the streetlamp. As he moved toward her, she got a vague impression of a long coat and a face obscured by a ski mask. In some small corner of her mind it registered that he was now blocking her path to the car. That her phone was lying on the front seat. That she was an idiot for getting herself into this situation.

A sound escaped her when his arm came up. She didn't need to see the gun to know he was pointing one at her. That he was going to use it if she didn't think of a way to stop him and quick. Without thinking, she raised the canister and sprayed.

"Bitch!"

Spinning, she flung herself into a dead run. Disbelief slammed through her when she heard what could have been a silenced gunshot. Too scared to look back, she opted to scream instead. "Help me! Help *me!*"

Lindsey was in good physical condition and ran at a dangerous speed. But she didn't know the layout of the shipyard. The fog disoriented her. Fear jumbled her thoughts. She couldn't remember if the water was left or right. If she ran into a dead end she would be trapped and unable to defend herself.

She looked around wildly as she ran, searching in vain for a passing motorist or lighted building or dockworker. She came to a corrugated steel building and skidded to a halt outside a door. She tugged hard on the knob, found it locked.

"Help me!" She pounded the door with her fist. "Help me! Please! Someone, *please!*"

The sound of shoes against asphalt spun her around. Through the fog, she saw the man running toward her. Just a few yards away. He was moving fast, his coat flapping behind him like an evil cape.

She left the building and sprinted toward the water. She ran blindly through the fog, searching for lights, an open door, any sign of help. But it was as if she were running through a blizzard in whiteout conditions.

At the end of a building, she cut hard to the right, then raced across a narrow lot toward the water. Halfway to the water's edge, she looked over her shoulder, saw the man come around the building. Oh, God. Oh, *God!* He'd gained an alarming amount of ground. Another five yards and he would be on top of her.

"Help *me!*"

She reached the water's edge, saw lights to her right and tried to veer toward them, but her boots slid out from under her. She went down fast and landed hard on her hands and knees. Pain flashed briefly as gravel bit into her palms and knees, then adrenaline took over and she scrambled to her feet, hurled herself into a run.

She ran as fast as she could, arms outstretched, animal sounds tearing from her throat. She didn't know where she was going. All she knew was that she couldn't let him catch her. That he wanted to hurt her. And she'd vowed a long time ago nobody would ever hurt her again.

She ran along the water's edge, past a container ship, toward the crane where she'd met Jamie earlier. She could no longer hear the man behind her, but her heart was pumping like a jackhammer. Every breath exploded from her lungs like fire. She was beginning to tire. Her legs felt as if her shoes had been set in concrete. If only she could find a way to double back and reach her car.

She glanced over her shoulder, but her pursuer was nowhere in sight. An instant later she heard a shout. She turned her head, but it was too late to stop. A scream tore from her throat as she plowed headlong into the looming shadow of a man.

chapter
14

THE IMPACT KNOCKED THE AIR FROM HIS LUNGS AND sent him reeling. Striker knew immediately the perpetrator was a female. He knew she was strong and scared and if he didn't get control of the situation quickly he was probably going to get his ass trounced.

Cursing, he reached out to subdue her only to find himself grappling with long hair and a soft sweater that made it hard as hell to get a decent grip.

"Get away from me!" she screamed.

Lindsey.

He got his fingers around her biceps and shook her. "Calm down, it's m—"

An instant later the heel of her hand slammed against his nose. Striker saw stars, felt his head snap back. Pain climbed up his sinuses and exploded like a firecracker in his brain.

At some point she'd gotten one arm free. He still had a hold on the other, so he jerked her toward him hard enough to knock her off balance. But he was too late because a second later he felt the unmistakable sensation of pepper spray against the side of his face and neck.

Son of a bitch!

The pain was instantaneous and fierce. Striker let go of her and stumbled back, put his hands to his face. His eyes felt as if someone had doused them with acid. Tears blinded him. When he took a breath, the oleoresin capsicum hit his bronchial tubes like a blast from a flamethrower.

"Lindsey . . . *damn* it!"

Bending at the waist, he coughed violently. The urge to rub his eyes was strong, but he knew from his police training that it would only aggravate the pain, so he didn't.

"Striker? *Striker?*" Her voice was shrill, and she was gasping for breath. "Oh my *God!*"

He looked up and tried to focus, but his eyes were filled with tears. "What the *hell* do you think you're doing?" he snarled between coughing spasms.

"I'm sorry. I—I thought you were—"

"Jack the Ripper?"

"N—no. There was a man. In the fog . . ." She was talking too fast, breathing hard, her voice shaking with every word. "He was . . . chasing me."

Striker didn't like the sound of that, but he was in no shape to do anything about it, and that only made him angrier. "Nice job with the pepper spray," he snapped. "I jump in to save your ass, and you mace me! *Jesus!*"

"Stop yelling at me."

"Honey, you'll know it when I start yelling."

"Striker, for God's sake, I think he had a gun. He could still be out there."

That got his attention, so he shut up for a moment and concentrated hard on clearing his vision. "Did you see a weapon?"

"No, but I think he shot at me. Only it sounded . . . I don't know, like he was using a silencer."

Something mean and protective stirred inside him at the thought of some goon taking a shot at her. Raising his head, he squinted into the blanket of white, listened for footsteps.

For the span of several heartbeats the only sound came from their labored breathing and the occasional *clink!* of the container ship tugging against its moorings. Striker leaned forward, put his hands on his knees and concentrated on getting air into his lungs. He coughed and let the tears run unchecked, hoping the natural lubrication would ease the burning and help clear his vision.

He didn't like being out in the open and unable to see. If some thug had been chasing her, there was a possibility he was still around and looking for trouble.

"Do you see anything?" he asked after a moment.

"No," she said, "the fog is too thick."

He spat, then rose to his full height, aware that his nose felt as if it had been jammed into his brain. "What the hell did you punch me with?"

"It's called *Shotei uchi.*"

"I'm not even going to ask what that is."

"Palm heel strike. I'm a . . . student of karate."

"For chrissake." But Striker laughed.

"I'm careful about my personal security." She stepped closer to him, looking appropriately guilty. "I'm really sorry. Are you okay?"

"No. That shit burns like a son of a bitch."

"Striker, I thought . . . I didn't know it was you."

"Stop apologizing, damn it." He was too annoyed to admit it, but it pleased him that she had the skills to defend herself. In the years he'd been a cop, he'd known too many people who hadn't. "You got a belt?" he asked.

"Green."

He was impressed. She probably didn't weigh much more than a hundred and ten pounds soaking wet, and yet she'd stopped him cold.

His vision was beginning to clear. They were standing

several feet apart, staring at each other. She raised her hand. "Your nose is bleeding."

He blotted his upper lip with his sleeve. "Imagine that," he said dryly, and for the first time he was glad for the fog. He felt like shit. His eyes burned. A headache was beginning to pound. Worse, he was feeling a little embarrassed because big, bad Michael Striker had just gotten his ass thoroughly kicked by a hundred-and-ten-pound female.

"What happened?" he asked irritably. "Last time we talked, you had some crazy idea about meeting Jamie Mills."

"Well, I did meet with her, actually."

Striker scanned the area. Since the city had put in the viaduct, the waterfront didn't get much foot traffic. It was the perfect place for an ambush.

"You didn't see a problem with that?" he asked.

"Of course, I did. But I was willing to put my reservations aside on the outside chance—"

"For someone who's earned a green belt in karate, you're pretty careless with your personal safety."

"I don't really want a lecture right now, Striker."

"Yeah? Well, it's free, sweetheart, so listen up." He crossed to her and poked her shoulder hard enough to send her back a step. "Common sense 101, Lindsey: Don't put yourself at risk. Ever. You're not going to do your sister any good if you're dead."

She swatted his hand away, but not before he noticed the shiver that ran the length of her.

"You should have called me right away," he said.

"I did."

"You called me *after* you had already decided to do something incredibly stupid," he said with some heat. "This could have turned out a lot worse than it did."

"Jamie wouldn't wait."

"She's not your only source of information."

"I've been here for three days and I have more questions about my sister now than I did before I left Ohio."

"Coming here by yourself was worse than foolhardy, Lindsey. Jamie hangs out with some bad people. Damn it, look what she did to you last night."

She squared her shoulders, met his gaze levelly. "Striker, Traci is the only family I have left. I love her. I would do anything for her. It hurts to think I'm the only person on this earth who gives a damn about her. So you can huff and puff until you turn blue, but there's no way I'm going to turn my back on a lead when it comes up."

"I might be working for you," he said, "but I'm not going to stand by while you take foolish risks like you did tonight. I'm not going to let you get hurt. Not on my watch. You got that?"

She folded her arms in front of her and looked toward the water. In the fog-shrouded light from the streetlamp, she looked stubborn and vulnerable and incredibly beautiful. Because he shouldn't be noticing any of those things, he took a mental step back and forced his attention back to the situation at hand. "So what did Jamie have to say?"

He listened intently as she described the meeting. "Did she tell you what's on the disk?"

"She wouldn't say. Just that I needed to watch it."

"I guess since that's all we got out of this close encounter we should at least have a look." He thought about the other disk they'd watched and wondered how this new one would fit into the mystery.

"Jamie had her suitcases with her," Lindsey said.

He thought about that for a moment, and something new began to niggle at the back of his brain. And he suddenly had a very strong suspicion that Jamie Mills wouldn't be coming back.

The shakes hit Lindsey on the drive to the loft. One moment she was following the taillights of his jeep, the next her entire body was trembling so violently she thought she was going to have to pull over. She knew it was a delayed reaction to adrenaline. But it had come on like a freight train and served to remind her that she'd been lucky to walk away unhurt.

By the time she parked at the curb outside the red brick warehouse, most of the shaking had subsided. Striker parked the jeep, then walked with her to the entrance. Without speaking, he shoved open the outer door, took her down a dark hall to a scarred wooden sliding door. He slid open the door, and they stepped into a small alcove where he unlocked the door to his loft.

The place smelled of coffee and old wood, with a faint hint of Striker's aftershave. Even though she'd been there just that morning, the hugeness of the loft surprised her all over again. She lifted her gaze to the high, arched windows, let it skim down the peeling brick to the antique steam register and found herself admiring the vastness and the historic feel of the building.

It wasn't a cozy place. It wasn't even comfortable if she wanted to be honest about it. But it had heart and a history and a hell of a lot of character. Kind of like the man who lived there.

She turned to see him standing just inside the door, watching her with those cop's eyes. It was the first time since the incident at the shipyard that she'd seen him in full light, and he was looking a little worse for wear. Several drops of blood stained his shirt just below the collar. His eyes were bloodshot and slightly swollen.

"You look like you had a close encounter with Mike Tyson," she said.

"That's just my bad cop look."

"I could have broken your nose."

One side of his mouth pulled into a smile. "Yeah, well, don't get any ideas about spreading that around. Bad for my reputation."

Even though she was still shaking inside, a smile emerged, and for an instant they grinned at each other.

Then his gaze shifted, skimmed down the front of her, and Lindsey felt it like the whisper touch of a feather brushing her skin.

"Looks like I'm not the only one who's bleeding." He pointed at her knees.

She looked down. "Oh." Sure enough her jeans were torn at both knees and stained with blood.

"Did he touch you? Push you down?" he asked.

"No, I slipped."

"I called this in to the cops on the drive over here," he said. "Even though this wasn't an assault, I told them you thought you'd seen a gun, so they dispatched a couple of officers to the terminal."

"I hope they get the guy."

His gaze flicked to her hands and he frowned. She lifted them and was surprised to see blood on her palms. "Crap."

A frisson of tension went through her when he crossed to her. A tiny electrical jolt followed when he took her hands in his. His hands were large and warm, and the sudden contact shocked her. But she didn't pull away. "It doesn't hurt," she said.

"Once the adrenaline wears off it will."

Her palms were deeply abraded and oozing blood. He made a sound low in his throat at the sight of the gravel imbedded in the flesh.

"You're still shaking," he said.

He was at least ten inches taller than she was, and she had to crane her head to make eye contact. For an interminable moment she looked into his dark, unsettling eyes. He stared back unflinchingly. She was aware of her hands shaking within his. A measure of surprise in his expression. And she wondered if his heart was beating as fast as hers.

"It's that dark-shipyard-foggy-night-guy-with-a-gun thing. Does me in every time."

His expression softened. "Traci's lucky to have you looking out for her."

"Hey, I'm her sister. That's my job." She'd meant for the words to come out lightly and was surprised when her voice quivered.

"Yeah, you're real tough, too, aren't you?"

Feeling the emotions creeping up on her, she eased her hands from his and turned to walk a short distance away. For a moment she thought he would follow, but he held his ground near the door.

Lindsey knew she should be thinking about what had happened at the shipyard and how it fit into the mystery surrounding her sister. But the residual adrenaline was messing with her emotions, her perceptions, making her feel things she shouldn't be feeling, things that probably weren't even there.

Determined not to let herself get distracted, she took a deep breath and turned to him. "Do you think Jamie Mills set me up?"

"Yeah." He cut her a hard look. "And in case you're not reading between the lines, that means you should stay the hell away from her."

"I got that about the time the guy showed up with the gun," she said dryly. But her mind was still on Jamie. On how she fit into the puzzle. What role she played.

As if reading her thoughts, Striker said, "I'll get an address on her. Pay her a visit away from the club. If she hasn't skipped town yet, maybe she'll open up to me."

Frustrated with their lack of progress, Lindsey sighed. "Have you found anything on Jason Blow?"

"I'm waiting for some background information to come back."

"I could help. I mean, tonight. We could—"

"I think you've had enough action for one day. Besides, we probably ought to have a look at the disk Jamie gave you." He looked down at the blood on his shirt and frowned. "Give me a few minutes to get this o.c. off me, then I'll see to your scrapes."

Lindsey felt a vast sense of relief when he started toward the shower room. She wanted to blame her jumpiness on the incident at the shipyard, but she was honest enough with herself to admit that some of the nerves zinging through her had more to do with Striker.

"That is *so* not you, Linds," she muttered.

While he showered, she amused herself by exploring the loft. The place needed renovation, but the potential for something magnificent was unmistakable. She saw it in the architecture. The color and texture of the brick. The antique steam registers. The high windows and even higher ceilings. She noticed things she hadn't before. The computer and printer set up on the dented metal desk near the living area. The tall, walnut bookcases beneath the windows. She strolled over to the wall of books and skimmed the titles, realizing immediately he was a reader. Mostly fiction. Police procedural. Thrillers. An array of true crime books. On the floor next to the bookcase, a cardboard box contained more volumes that hadn't yet been shelved. A nice collection, she thought. Michael Striker was full of surprises.

"I see you found the books."

She spun at the sound of his voice to find him walking toward her. He wore button down jeans and a faded City of Seattle Police Department sweatshirt. His dark hair was still wet from his shower and swept straight back to reveal a high forehead and thick, arched brows over piercing eyes the color of espresso. His cheekbones were wide and sharply angled, as if an artisan had chiseled away a little too much stone. It was a harsh face, she thought. Difficult to read. And, like the man it belonged to, hard and uncompromising.

Michael Striker was not a handsome man. The planes of his face were too severe. His hollowed cheeks were pocked in several places. The crescent scar on his cheek made a slight indentation. His mouth seemed to be curled into a perpetual snarl. His face was one of imperfections. Flaws that should have detracted from his appeal. But they didn't.

Lindsey stared at him, aware that her face was hot, her hands were trembling. She wanted to believe she was still shaken by what had happened in the shipyard. But she knew the quivery sensation in her belly didn't have a damn thing to do with fear—and had everything to do with the man standing so close she could smell his aftershave.

The realization stunned her. Lindsey had never been susceptible to her hormones. Even as a teenager she'd never been boy crazy. She'd learned very early in life that some things were simply not meant for her. She'd come to terms with that a long time ago. She was comfortable with that. She liked things just the way they were. Even keel. Predictable. Safe.

All of the things that Michael Striker was not.

"That was just a friendly statement," he said.

Realizing she was staring at him—and that he was staring back with a slightly perplexed expression—Lindsey looked down at the book in her hand, tried to remember why she'd picked it up. "You have a nice collection."

"Thanks." He cleared his throat. "I've been reading a little more since . . . leaving the department."

An awkward silence fell. Because she couldn't meet his gaze, she started to turn away, but he stopped her by reaching for the book. "I'll put it back for you." He motioned toward the sofa. "Have a seat, and I'll take a look at those knees."

For an instant, they were both holding the hardcover book, and she found herself staring down at his long, blunt-tipped fingers and neat, short nails. He had the most fascinating hands she'd ever seen. His knuckles were abraded and cut in places. She recalled seeing the punching bag dangling from a pipe in the far corner of the loft and wondered why he didn't wear gloves. She studied her own hands, so close to his, and realized how slender and white and undamaged they were.

She relinquished the book and stepped back. "Your eyes are still red."

"I flushed them with water, but it can take a few hours for the irritation to go away." He shelved the book.

"Striker, I am so sorry . . ."

"You mean about jamming my nose cartilage into my brain or blinding me with pepper spray?"

It took her a moment to realize he was teasing, and she choked out a laugh. "Both," she said.

"I didn't mention it back at the shipyard, but I was impressed as hell with the way you handled yourself."

She snorted, but felt a quick rise of pleasure at the compliment. "I could tell by the way you were cussing me out."

"I mean it. You've got some good moves."

"It's called running."

He laughed. Surprising herself, she joined him, and for a moment the sound of their laughter filled the loft. His was deep and natural. She liked the way his eyes turned up at the corners. The way his laugh lines cupped his mouth. She liked seeing his straight, white teeth.

She knew it was just the aftereffects of high adrenaline, but it felt good to laugh. "You should try that more often, Striker."

"Yeah?" Still chuckling, he wiped at his eyes. "Try what?"

"This is the first time I've seen you laugh. It looks really good on you."

He blinked at her as if she'd stunned him. For a split second his eyes weren't shuttered, and she caught a glimpse of an emotion that was uneasy and raw and uncomfortable. Slowly, his smile faded, and he looked at her as if seeing her for the first time, as if he were shocked by what he saw. His eyes flicked to her mouth, lingered an instant too long.

The air seemed to charge with electricity. Lindsey could almost feel the hairs on her arms stand up. And she thought that maybe if she reached out and touched him, she would see the spark of the current, feel the quick jump of heat as it arced.

She was standing so close she could see the black whiskers of his five o'clock shadow. She stared at his imperfect face, the harsh mouth, the hollowed cheeks and hard eyes, and realized abruptly that her pulse was racing. That her body was humming. That she didn't have the slightest idea what she would do if he leaned forward and pressed his mouth to hers.

Shocked by the direction of her thoughts, Lindsey stepped back. She wanted to say something cocky, something.to let him know the strange moment between them hadn't affected her. But she couldn't find her voice, couldn't find any words.

After a moment, Striker turned away and strode to the kitchen area where he opened a cabinet and withdrew a small first aid kit. Pressing her hand to her stomach, Lindsey walked over to the sofa and sank onto the cushions.

He met her there a moment later and knelt in front of her. She tried not to fidget as he removed sterile gauze, a roll of first aid tape and a tube of antibiotic cream from the kit and set them on the coffee table. He rolled the hem of her jeans to just above her knees, frowning when the abrasions came into view. "Looks like you've got some gravel imbedded in the skin."

She was surprised by the amount of blood. She watched him tear open the sterile gauze and saturate it with peroxide. Sitting back on his heels, he lifted her leg and set her bare foot on his thigh. "This is going to hurt," he said and began to gently scrub at the bits of gravel.

Lindsey barely noticed the sting. Her entire focus centered on the way his hand looked wrapped around her calf. His skin was darker than hers. His damaged knuckles contrasted sharply with the unblemished white of her skin. The gentleness of his touch seemed incongruous with the rest of him. And she wondered how such a hard man could have such a soft touch.

"So you think what happened tonight was random? Or do you think it's somehow tied to Traci?" she asked after a moment.

He raised his shoulder, let it fall. "I don't think it was random."

"How does Traci fit in to it?"

"We both know she's into some things she shouldn't be. She's got a boatload of shady friends. She's involved with drugs. Pornography. Any one of those things could add up to trouble for her or the people around her. Add one hundred and fifty thousand dollars to that and you have the potential for all sorts of nasty things."

"So do you think she earned the money by making adult movies?"

He glanced at her, then turned his attention back to her knee. "Probably." He used his fingertip to apply antibiotic cream. "The only other thing that comes to mind is blackmail."

"I hate to say it, but that's sounds like Traci."

"That could get her into some serious trouble."

A chill moved through her. "How serious?"

"Depends on who it is, what they did, and how far they're willing to go to keep it from coming to light. Ten bucks is killing money for some people."

Lindsey thought about that and shivered. She thought about the pornographic movie. Traci's lifestyle. The designer clothes. The expensive furniture. The felony warrant for drugs. The kind of people she ran with . . .

"Pornography and blackmail," she said. "I think there are plenty of people who would go to great lengths to keep their involvement in something so disreputable from coming to light."

"Blackmail would explain the break-in," he said. "If

someone thinks she's hidden something at the house, or has something in her possession, it only makes sense that they'd look for it." Striker's gaze met hers. "And then you come along and start asking questions. Maybe they think Traci told you something. Gave you something. Maybe they think you know something you shouldn't."

The possibilities raised gooseflesh on her arms. "What could Traci have on someone? Pictures? What?"

"Think about it, Lindsey. She gets around. Maybe she found out someone in high places is a pervert. Maybe she's someone's lady on the side, and she threatened to go to the wife if fat daddy didn't pay up. Maybe some high roller is a coke freak. The possibilities are endless."

"How does Jamie Mills fit into any of those scenarios?"

"The only tie between Jamie and Traci is Club Tribeca."

"Everything seems to go back to the club," Lindsey said, thinking out loud. "It scares me that she's missing, Striker. I mean, any one of those things you mentioned could give someone a reason to hurt her."

He grimaced. "The only thing we know for certain at this point, is that she's missing. The way things are shaping up, that's not necessarily a bad thing. You said yourself Traci is a survivor. If she thought she was in danger, she'd skip town, right?"

"She's a fighter, too. But I'm just not even sure I know her anymore." Frustrated, she started to rise, realized he hadn't yet cleaned her other knee and sank back onto the sofa. "There's something we're missing," she said. "There's something someone doesn't want us to find." She looked at Striker. "How do we figure out what that is?"

"If I can come up with an address for this Jason Blow character, we can go see him first thing in the morning," he said. "If he doesn't give us anything helpful, then we start from the top again. We look at all of our sources of information. People are generally going to be the most helpful, so we'll talk to the dancers. Her friends. Boyfriends. Everyone who knows her. See if we can start putting the pieces of the puzzle together."

"Her friends aren't very cooperative."

"Then we'll wear them down until one of them spills something we can use. We'll take another look at the house. Go through everything with a fine-tooth comb, see if there's something we missed."

Lindsey felt marginally better knowing that Striker was on her side, that they had some avenues to explore, that they hadn't reached a dead end. But the case seemed to be moving at a snail's pace.

"Maybe the disk Jamie gave you will tell us something we don't already know," Striker offered.

She knew it was counterproductive, but she'd been trying not to think about the disk. Her biggest fear was that it contained another pornographic movie. She honestly didn't think she could bear to see her sister like that again.

Striker must have read her thoughts because he said, "I can take a look at the disk if you're not up to it."

But Lindsey refused to bury her head in the sand. She'd done that once before, and both she and Traci had paid a very steep price.

"No," she said, reaching for the disk. "I need to see it."

chapter
15

STRIKER DROPPED THE DISK INTO THE DVD PLAYER and hit the PLAY button on the remote. "Here we go."

Lindsey watched as a small room materialized on the screen. It was about fifteen feet square with a concrete floor and some type of industrial fabric wall covering. The camera panned, and she could see that there were no windows, just a scarred wooden door. A single bare bulb dangled from the ceiling and cast harsh light onto an oblong platform about the size of a twin bed. The platform was constructed of plywood and raised about three feet off the floor. Clear polyurethane sheeting had been draped over it and secured with heavy duty staples.

It didn't seem like the kind of setting for a pornographic movie. The other one had been glamorized with expensive furnishings, an exotic-looking locale, and exquisitely dressed actors. This room was ugly and dreary and looked more like a prison cell in some third world country.

The door swung open and a man wearing black leather pants and an ornate mask entered the room. The sight of the mask shocked Lindsey. Even though it wasn't the same as the one in her dream, the similarities raised gooseflesh on her arms. The mask was made of black leather with silver accents and cutouts for the eyes, and covered the top of his head to just below his nose.

Lindsey got a bad feeling in the pit of her stomach as she watched the man begin to pace the room. His movements were jerky and agitated. His torso was bare, and she could see his muscles flexing as he moved. Unsure of the meaning of what she was seeing, she glanced at Striker. He stood a few feet away, watching the television intently, his legs wide, his arms folded, his face devoid of emotion.

"What is this?" she asked.

He glanced over at her and shook his head. "I'm not sure. Let's see what happens."

The actor paced, an animal that had been locked up in a too-small cage for a very long time. A predator that was restless and hungry and would be dangerous once it was free.

The door opened again. Lindsey jolted when another man in a less ornate mask entered the room with a young woman in tow. A chill passed through Lindsey when she noticed that the woman's hands were bound behind her back. Snarling something indecipherable, he shoved her hard. The woman stumbled and fell to her knees.

The camera zoomed in on the woman's face. She couldn't have been more than twenty-five years old. Tangled brown hair hung limply into a face that would have been pretty had it not been tear-streaked and filled with terror. She was wearing a short black dress with thin, rhinestone straps. Her legs were scratched and bleeding. Her feet were bare. When she raised her head to look at the man who had shoved her inside, Lindsey noticed the gag in her mouth, and a terrible fear began to build in her chest.

"What the hell is this?" she said to Striker, but her voice was little more than a whisper.

"Some sick bastard's idea of entertainment."

She didn't want to look at the screen. "I don't understand why Jamie would give this to me."

"Let's give it a couple of minutes to play out, see if we can figure it out." Then he looked at her, and his jaw flexed. "You don't have to subject yourself to this. Why don't you make some coffee, let me finish this, and I'll let you know if I think it's relevant to the case?"

It would have been easy to say yes. To walk away and let herself believe she was better off not seeing the disturbing images playing out on the screen. But something inside her wouldn't let her take the easy way out.

"No," she said and looked at the screen.

The two men were on either side of the woman, their hands on her arms, forcing her toward the platform. She fought them valiantly, lashing out with her feet and trying to twist away, but as hard as she fought, she was no match for the two men. Roughly they forced her onto the platform. Lindsey noticed the eye hooks jutting from each corner of the platform and a terrible realization dawned. For God's sake, they were going to tie her down.

One of the men pinned the woman by putting his knee in the center of her back while the other untied her wrists. Roughly, they flipped her onto her back and secured her wrists to the hooks with leather restraints. She kicked wildly, and her dress rode high on her hips, but she didn't stop fighting. Her knee caught the second man under the chin, sent him reeling. Snarling, he lunged, drew back, and viciously punched her in the face with his fist. The woman's head snapped back and hit the platform with a loud *thunk!* She didn't move while they fastened the leather restraints at her ankles.

A moment later, the woman lay spread eagle on the platform. When the woman raised her head, Lindsey saw blood tricking from her left nostril. She saw misery and terror and resignation in her eyes.

She tried telling herself it wasn't real. That the man

hadn't really struck the woman with his fist. That it was a trick of the camera or some kind of computer sleight of hand, or maybe just a good stunt. But deep inside, Lindsey knew it was real. Nobody could fake that kind of violence.

Sinking more deeply into the sofa, she pulled her legs up to her chest and watched the man in the leather mask walk over to a nondescript table in the corner of the room where he picked up a pair of shears. The woman had raised her head to watch him. Tears blackened with mascara streaked her face. When she spotted the shears in his hand, she began struggling against her binds, screaming against the gag.

Disgust and pity and a choking outrage rose inside Lindsey at the realization of what he would do next. She simply couldn't reconcile herself to someone wanting to create such a horrific scene on film. A few feet away, Striker stood stone faced, his eyes on the screen, his jaw taut with disgust.

The man cut away the dress and pulled it from beneath the woman. Then he put the shears to her panties and cut them away with a single snip until she lay naked and helpless on the platform. The man wearing the hood unzipped his fly and pulled out his erect penis.

Lindsey put her face in her hands and closed her eyes. *Oh, dear God . . .*

But while she could shut out the images, she couldn't block the sounds of the woman screaming into the gag. The audio was scratchy, but good enough for her to hear the scrape of shoes against plywood. The sound of his knees thumping against the plywood as he climbed on top of her. The guttural hiss of obscenities as he began to violate her.

"I can't watch this." Lindsey rose abruptly. She felt dizzy, her face hot. "For God's sake, I can't . . ."

Cursing beneath his breath, Striker raised the remote and began to skip through the DVD, the digital version of fast forwarding. "Go," he said. "I'll finish it."

But for whatever reason, Lindsey couldn't make herself walk away. Maybe because in some small corner of her mind she thought it was the cowardly thing to do. Maybe because she thought she owed it to the young woman on the screen to see this through. Because she owed it to Traci. Owed it to herself.

She stared at Striker for a full minute as he skipped through the DVD, but he didn't meet her gaze. After a while she turned her attention to the television. Revulsion rose inside her as the man in the mask rolled off the woman and zipped his fly. The second man stood at the table with his back to the camera. When he turned, the lens zoomed in on the knife in his hand.

Lindsey's blood ran cold. Her heart rolled over and began to beat out of control, pumping ice to every part of her body. Her vision tunneled on the knife. It was an expensive chef's knife, a brand name. The stainless steel blade glinted coldly in the harsh light coming off the bulb.

As if in slow motion, the man walked over to the platform and looked down at the woman. Lindsey knew what would happen next. Disbelief and revulsion churned inside her. Nausea seesawed in her gut.

The woman's eyes flicked from the knife to his face. Terror contorted her features. Tears streamed from her eyes. She jerked hard against her binds when he ran the pointed tip of the knife along her abdomen, over her breast, to her throat. The woman fisted her hands and threw her head back and tried to scream, but the gag muffled her cries. The man's mouth twisted into a cruel smile.

Then the camera zoomed in on the woman's face.

Lindsey told herself, it wasn't real. That the man really hadn't raped her. That it was a form of pornography, that the violence was a trick of the camera. She held on to that thought with silent desperation. She chanted the words inside her head, willing herself to believe them. But the panic and horror in the woman's expression, the revulsion she felt in her own heart, wouldn't let her believe them.

The man gripped the handle of the knife with two hands

and raised it over his head. The woman strained against her binds, her body bucking in a violent attempt to free herself.

"Oh my God. Oh, no." Lindsey's heart hammered like a piston against her ribs. "He's going to . . . Oh, God, Striker, he's going to . . ."

The knife came down in a perfect arc.

Lindsey reached out, but knew she couldn't stop what would happen next. Stainless steel glinted like blue ice. The blade plunged into the pasty white of the woman's abdomen, just above her navel. The woman made a horrible sound. Her body went rigid. Her eyes bulged and rolled back white. Her fingers and toes clenched as if she'd been hit with a thousand volts of electricity.

"Jesus Christ."

Vaguely Lindsey was aware that Striker had spoken. But she couldn't look away from the screen. Couldn't take her eyes off the woman. Her mouth opened and closed around the gag. She retched and then blood began to pour from her mouth. Her eyes blinked, then glazed. Her legs jerked. Slowly, her hands unclenched. And then she was still.

The man jerked the knife from her body. Blood spread in a brilliant red slick over the platform. Lindsey stared, horror welling inside her as the river of blood dripped to the floor and ran toward the drain. "Oh my God. Oh, no."

It isn't real. It isn't real. It isn't real!

But she felt the reality of it seeping into the deepest reaches of her mind. A young woman brutalized and killed. The savagery captured on film. Two men getting away with murder.

Lindsey turned away from the television, pressed her hand to her stomach. "Please tell me that wasn't real!"

Striker's face was pale when he looked at her. "Walk away," he snapped. *"Now!"*

When she didn't move fast enough, he crossed to her, turned her away from the television, and gave her a shove. "Go, damn it."

She didn't look at him as she crossed to the bed. She needed every bit of her concentration just to put one foot in front of the other. She needed air and space. Most of all, she needed distance from the horrors on that disk.

Even though the loft was spacious, she could feel the walls beginning to close in on her. Claustrophobia threatened. Cold sweat slicked the back of her neck. She could hear herself gasping for breath, but couldn't seem to get enough oxygen into her lungs.

She made it to the bed before her legs collapsed. She sat down hard, leaned forward, and put her face in her hands. A sob shuddered out of her. The horror of what she'd seen curdled like poison inside her body. She felt sick inside. Dirty. As if somehow the atrocity of what she'd witnessed had tainted her soul.

Lindsey had never had a weak stomach, but she tasted bile at the back of her throat. Knowing she was going to be ill, she left the bed and ran toward the shower area. She tried taking deep breaths, but at some point she had begun to cry and the sobs were choking her. She felt the wetness of tears on her cheeks. The sickness climbing up her throat, sour in her mouth. Her boots were loud against the old tiles as she entered the shower area. Her stomach heaved, and she made a retching sound as she crossed to the commode. Dropping to her knees in front of it, she lost the contents of her stomach.

For several long minutes she leaned over the toilet, breathing hard, spitting, waiting for the nausea to pass. Her hand shook when she reached up and pulled the cord to flush. She wanted to close her eyes, but every time she did she saw that girl lying on the platform. The blade of the knife glinting, arcing down. White flesh and the glossy black of blood . . .

Vaguely, she was aware of footsteps behind her. Of water running in the sink a few feet away. She jolted when Striker put his hand on her shoulder.

"Easy," he said softly. "Come on. I've got you."

Lindsey didn't move. She didn't trust her legs, didn't trust her stomach. She wanted to say something, but couldn't speak. There were no words to describe what she was feeling.

She didn't protest when he put his hands beneath her arms and lifted her, set her on her feet. She stood on her own power, but her legs felt like rubber.

"I'm sorry you had to see that," he said.

"Oh, God, Striker . . . that poor woman."

With a gentleness she hadn't realized he possessed, he turned her so that she was facing him and pressed a cool towel to her forehead, her cheeks, her temples. She felt his eyes on her, but she couldn't meet his gaze. She felt scraped raw, her every weakness exposed. She didn't want him to see her when she felt so fragile.

Gently, he blotted her mouth and chin, then left her to rinse the towel in the sink.

"They murdered that woman," she said, her voice shaking. "They raped her, and then they murdered her."

He twisted the water out of the towel, then turned to face her, his expression grim. Lindsey met his gaze, and wondered if he had any idea how desperately she needed him to tell her what they'd just seen on that disk wasn't real, if he had any idea how desperately she needed him to pull her back to a place where she felt safe and in control.

He didn't do either of those things.

"That was real, wasn't it?" she whispered.

He scraped a hand over his jaw. "I think it was."

chapter
16

STRIKER HAD SEEN A LOT OF THINGS IN THE EIGHT-
een years he'd been a cop. He'd seen rape and murder and
just about every crime in between. He'd seen men and
women and children gunned down in the street for a ten-
dollar piece of crack. He'd seen people cut to pieces because of the shoes they wore. He'd seen firsthand the dark
side of humanity. The kind of mindless brutality most people couldn't fathom. Things he didn't let himself think
about when he was alone in his bed at night.

But he'd never seen anything like what he'd just witnessed on that disk.

He could only imagine what those violent images had
done to Lindsey. She was decent and kind and still believed
people were good. She had no idea that evil was alive
and well and thriving in a society that wanted badly to believe it had risen above it. He didn't want to be the one to
break it to her that it hadn't.

She stared at him, her face the color of paste, her dark

eyes stricken with the horrors of what she'd seen. "What the hell was that, Striker?"

He raked his hand through his hair, surprised when his fingers trembled. "It's called snuff."

"Snuff? What does that mean?"

"It's a fringe genre of the film industry. The term came to being during the late 1960s and early 1970s when there were several low-budget films made depicting the murder of young women. Whether it was for promotional purposes or whatever, there were press releases put out hinting that the murders depicted in the films were real. Some people came to believe that the actors and actresses in these films were, indeed, murdered on tape. *Slaughter,* later retitled *Snuff* once the term caught on, began an urban legend of sorts.

"Over the years, several police agencies investigated the existence of these snuff films. At one point, even the FBI got involved. But I can tell you that literally every snuff film confiscated in the U.S. has been fake."

"But what we saw tonight . . . that poor woman . . . what they did to her. Striker, that was real."

He grimaced. "It looked real to me, but I'm no expert. With the advancements in software technology and computer animation, it's impossible to say without verification from a lab."

She lowered her head, pressed her fingers against her temples. "I'm having a real hard time making sense of this."

The need to go to her was surprisingly strong, but he resisted. "I'll give my ex-partner a call and see if I can get him to send it to the State Patrol Lab to have it authenticated and checked for prints."

"How long will that take?"

"I don't know. Depends on what kind of priority we can get. A couple of days. A week, maybe."

"That's too long. If there are people out there murdering women and putting it on disk . . ."

"We don't even know how old that disk is, Lindsey. Lab

boys might be able to tell us, but as far as you and I know it could be a year old."

She raised her head and looked at him. "I don't understand why Jamie gave the disk to me."

Striker had been wondering the same thing. And his cop's mind had already jumped ahead to all the ways Traci might be involved. The dots were tenuous, the possibilities worse than ugly, but he'd already made the connection. He knew it wouldn't be long before she did, too.

"You going to be okay?" he asked after a moment.

She raised her eyes to his. Her lashes were still wet from when she'd been crying. A little color had leached back into her cheeks, but she was still pale. "I'm okay." She looked down at her hands. "Thanks for the towel. It helped."

He took the towel from her and hung it over the edge of the sink. "I need to give my partner a call."

She looked incredibly fragile, standing there. Pale and trembling and small. But he could see that she was trying hard to appear brave. Striker had never been a comforting kind of guy, but there was a part of him that wanted to protect her from this. He wanted to put his arm around her. Draw her to him. Tell her everything was going to be all right.

He settled for touching her shoulder. "I think I've got some tea. In the kitchen . . ."

She shot him a grateful look. "Tea would be great."

"It's strawberry, or something."

"Striker, you keep surprising me."

"Don't read too much into it." He winked at her. "It was a Christmas gift from my niece."

In the kitchen, he filled a saucepan with water and set it on the hot plate. He found the teabags, dropped one into a mug, then picked up his cell phone and dialed Shep's home number.

His ex-partner answered on the seventh ring. "This had better be good."

"It's Striker. I need a favor."

The other man groaned. "Can't this wait until morning?"

"You know the missing persons case I've been working?"

"I can barely keep up with my own cases," he said crossly.

"Missing sister. Topless dancer. Club Tribeca. Last name Metcalf. Ring a bell?"

"Yeah. Yeah. What about it?"

Striker looked up to see Lindsey pick up the saucepan and pour the water over the teabag. She made eye contact with him, but he turned his attention to his phone call. "I want you to take a look at a disk. I want you to send it to the lab."

"What's on the disk?"

"A murder. Looks like a snuff film."

Shep didn't say anything.

"I want to have it analyzed," Striker said. "See if it's authentic."

"I don't have to tell you there's no such thing as a snuff film, do I? Or has all that free time and pressure you're under sent you off the deep end?"

Striker didn't want to think about the deep end with regard to his frame of mind. "I need to know if it's been touched up somehow to make it look real. I want latent prints. I'll run the names off the credits, but I'll need you to run them through the national database for me, see if you can get a hit."

"Well, for crying out loud, maybe you'd like me to buy you a new freaking car while I'm at it."

Striker didn't like the thin layer of sweat slicking the back of his neck. Shep was his best friend. His last friend, if he wanted to be honest about it. His only connection to the Seattle PD and his old life. If he turned him down . . .

"I'll see what I can do," Shep said after a moment. "I can meet you for lunch tomorrow. Bakeman's down on Cherry Street. Bring the disk. You're buying."

"I owe you," Striker said, but the other man had already disconnected.

Striker set down the phone and turned to see Lindsey on the sofa, holding her mug as if it were her lifeline to the rest of the world.

"Is he going to help us?" she asked.

"Yeah." He crossed to her, stopped before he got too close. "I'm going to meet with him tomorrow, but it could be a few days before we hear anything on the disk."

Setting her cup on the coffee table, she rose. "I've been working this over in my mind. I mean, about the disk and how Traci might be involved."

Because he knew where her mind would go next, he moved to stop her. "This isn't the time to let your imagination run amok. We need to concentrate on the facts."

"But what if Jamie is right? What if Traci *is* involved? What if? . . ." The color leached from her face, and for an instant she looked gut punched. "You don't think Traci got involved with those people and they . . . hurt her the way they hurt that girl, do you?"

Striker didn't want to tell her he'd already considered that scenario. "You're jumping to conclusions."

"I'm making logical assumptions."

"You're thinking with your emotions," he snapped. "Believe me, there's no quicker way to screw up an investigation."

For several long seconds she stood there, breathing hard, her nostrils flaring. Striker stared back, angry with her for pushing the issue when she shouldn't have. Angry with himself for letting that happen.

"What if I'm right?" she whispered.

"You've got a theory. It warrants looking into. But I don't think either of us are going to solve this thing tonight."

Turning away from him, she strode to the counter where she'd set her purse. He watched her fish out her keys, and for the first time, it struck him that it probably wasn't safe for her to leave. And that he was now in a position he didn't want to be in.

"Where are you going?" he asked.

"I have a hotel room for the next two nights."

He ordered himself to let her go. Damn it, he did not want her to stay. Her safety was not his responsibility. He had enough problems of his own without getting caught up in hers.

He stood his ground in the living area as she walked to the door. Sweat broke out on his back when she swung open the door.

"Wait a minute," he heard himself say.

She stopped and for several interminable seconds she stood with her back to him, facing the hall.

"Stay here." When she didn't move, he shifted his weight from one foot to the other, telling himself it didn't matter if she kept on walking. But he knew it did. "You can have the bed. I'll take the sofa."

Slowly, she turned to face him. He saw the questions in the whiskey depths of her eyes and knew she was wondering if he had an ulterior motive for asking her to stay.

"After what happened tonight, I'd feel a hell of a lot better if you didn't spend too much time alone," he said. "At least until we can figure out what's going on."

"I know how to take care of myself," she said. But there was no conviction in the words, and he could tell by the look in her eyes that, at the moment, she didn't believe them.

"Your staying here is just a precautionary measure," he said. "Probably not necessary, but it's better to be safe than sorry. Come back inside."

When she made no move to obey, he crossed to her, took her arm, and guided her back into the loft. "It's almost midnight," he said. "Let's get some rest, and we can start fresh in the morning."

"Do you think she's still alive?" she whispered.

"I don't know," he said. "That's as honest an answer as I can give you right now."

She nodded, but he could tell by the pain in her eyes that it wasn't the one she'd needed to hear.

chapter
17

LINDSEY RAN BLINDLY THROUGH THE DARKNESS
and fog. Breaths tore from her throat in ragged gasps. He
was so close she could hear his boots pounding behind her,
the rustle of his clothes, her name on his lips . . .

Lindsey . . .

She covered the ground at a dangerous speed, hurtling
obstacles and splashing through puddles with a recklessness borne of the primal will to survive. Fog curled around
the outbuildings of the shipyard like ghostly fingers. The
sodium vapor streetlamp glared down at her like a giant
yellow eye. In the distance she could hear the mournful cry
of a foghorn as a ship found its way to port.

She pushed her body to the limit, running as fast as her
legs would carry her. She ran until her lungs were on fire,
until she thought her heart would burst. She knew he would
kill her if he caught her. The horror of that pushed her forward when her body wanted to collapse.

Suddenly, the black water of the bay loomed like a bottomless, yawning mouth. She stopped inches from the edge

of the pier, just in time to keep herself from tumbling into the drink. For several seconds the only sound came from her labored breathing, the thundering of her pulse, the wild staccato of her heartbeat.

"Linny."

She spun at the familiar voice. Disbelief punched her at the sight of her sister standing a few feet away. "Traci?"

She knew it wasn't possible for Traci to be standing there smiling at her, much less be twelve years old again. But there she was. A pretty tomboy in blue jeans, a ratty T-shirt and her trademark expression that told the world she was going to make something of herself and anyone who doubted that could go straight to hell.

"Honey, is that you?" Lindsey asked.

"He's coming for you, Linny."

"Who?" she asked. But in her heart of hearts, she knew.

"Be careful."

Fear trembled through her at the sound of approaching footsteps. Only then did she realize she was trapped on the pier, with no way of escape, except for the water. She knew HE was coming for her, knew he wanted to hurt her. And even after all these years she was terrified.

She squinted into the swirling mist. She could hear his shoes against the concrete, but the fog was impenetrable, the night utterly dark. "What do you want?" she cried.

"Lindsey, it'll be our secret," came his whispered voice.

She spun back to Traci, ready to take her sister's hand and bolt. By God, she wasn't going to leave her behind this time. Not again.

But her sister was gone.

"Traci?"

Suddenly terrified for her, Lindsey reached out, her hands disappearing into the fog where her sister had been standing just a moment before. "I'll keep you safe this time. Traci, I promise. I won't let him hurt you."

Traci didn't answer.

And when Lindsey looked down at her hands, they were covered with blood.

"No!" She jolted violently awake.

Footsteps sounded nearby. A hard punch of fear sent her bolt upright. She stared into the darkness, listening, adrenaline streaking through her. Another noise to her right, and she scrambled across the bed on her hands and knees, reached for the light, almost knocked it over as she fumbled for the switch. Light flooded the area.

"Easy. It's just me."

Striker stood next to the bed, his expression sharp with concern. Vaguely, she was aware that his hair was mussed, that he wasn't wearing a shirt, and she knew she'd wakened him.

"You cried out," he said. "You okay?"

She held up her hands, studied them, saw that they were shaking. "There was blood," she said. "On my hands."

His gaze skimmed over her, stopped on her hands. "It was just a dream."

"It wasn't a dream," she snapped.

He didn't say anything.

Feeling like an idiot, she looked down at her hands again. "I don't dream like that. Not like that."

He sat down on the bed, took her hands in his, and held them so that they were visible to both of them. "No blood. Just the abrasions from earlier, when you fell." His gaze met hers, held it. "See?"

She stared at her hands locked within his, feeling foolish because she found herself actually looking for traces of red. Intellectually she knew it had only been a dream. But it had seemed so *real*.

"Jesus, you're shaking." He squeezed her hands, carefully avoiding the abraded areas.

"I'm okay," she said automatically, but she could feel the tremors ripping through her. She could feel the slick of sweat at the back of her neck. She could hear her labored breaths in the silence of the loft. She stared at her hands, remembering the blood. Traci's blood, she thought, and tried not to think about what her subconscious had been telling her.

"I didn't mean to wake you." She tried to laugh, but her throat was too tight.

"I'm not a great sleeper these days, anyway."

She looked around, needing to orient herself, trying to calm down and reassure some small corner of her mind that she wasn't lost in a foggy shipyard. That her sister wasn't twelve years old again. That Jerry Thorpe wasn't alive to make their lives a living hell. That she didn't have her sister's blood on her hands . . .

Slowly, the nightmare began to recede. The accompanying terror slithered back into the compartment where she kept it locked away.

Next to her, Striker watched her, his dark eyes cautious and awash with concern. "Better?"

"Yeah." A breath shuddered out of her, and she finally managed a chuckle. "You probably think I'm a nutcase."

"Our minds can play cruel tricks on us sometimes when we're under stress." He smiled, but she could tell by something in his eyes that he was speaking from experience.

She wondered if he had any idea how badly she'd needed to hear those words. How much they meant to her. That they made her feel connected in a way she hadn't for a very long time.

For a moment she had a difficult time meeting his gaze. She could only imagine how she looked. Her hair sticking up in disarray. The wetness of tears on her cheeks. The T-shirt she wore was damp with sweat and clung to her. She looked down, remembered belatedly that she wasn't wearing a bra. Her bare legs were exposed, and she thought she should probably cover herself up. Only Striker hadn't let go of her hands.

A new awareness crept over her. An awareness that had

nothing to do with the nightmare and everything to do with the man who'd come to her side in the middle of the night. He was sitting on the bed, facing her with his knee touching her thigh. He wasn't wearing a shirt, only a pair of faded drawstring pants he hadn't bothered to tie. Her eyes skimmed over his chest, taking in the thatch of black hair and well-developed pectoral muscles. The flat plane of his belly. The thickening of hair just below his navel where his pants rode low on lean hips . . .

Thunder crashed, and she jumped. His hands tightened on hers, but he didn't say anything. She could hear the rain pounding the skylight above them. The wind tearing around the roof of the old building. The drip of water into the pail a few feet away. For the first time, Lindsey realized the moment had become intimate. She risked a look at him, found his eyes already on her, his expression taut and slightly perplexed. A heavy five o'clock shadow shaded his jaw. His mouth was pulled into a thin line. And he was watching her with those cop's eyes.

"The dream," he said thickly, "was it about what we saw on the disk?"

She shook her head, wondering when he was going to let go of her hands. "It was just . . . jumbled and didn't really make any sense."

"Do you want to talk about it?"

She contemplated him, trying to gauge his sincerity. He didn't seem like the kind of man who would offer comfort over a bad dream. But he returned her gaze levelly. And within the depths of his eyes she saw the understanding of a man who'd experienced his own share of nightmares.

"I don't really want to talk about it," she managed after a moment. "It was just a dream."

"A dream that terrified you." He brushed her knuckles with the pad of his thumb. "It's not the first, is it?"

She looked away, didn't answer.

"Sometimes it helps to talk about it," he said.

"Sometimes talking about it just makes you remember." Her voice broke with the last word and to her horror and surprise, Lindsey realized she was going to cry.

"Shh. It's okay," he said.

But it wasn't okay. Her sister was missing. The old guilt was churning inside her. The ghosts of her past were back and haunting her with renewed ferocity.

"I think something terrible happened to her," she whispered.

"It's just the dream spooking you."

"No, Striker. It's more than a dream."

"What do you mean?"

"I've been having these dreams since before I left Ohio. Nightmares, really. They're vivid and violent and . . . jumbled with other things. I know you're going to think I'm nuts, but I saw the man in the mask in my dreams before I ever left Ohio."

His eyes narrowed. "The man on the disk?"

She nodded. "Not exactly the same, but . . . similar enough to creep me out."

"Are you sure you have the timing of it right? I mean sometimes, dreams can be confusing."

"I'm sure."

He made a skeptical sound in his throat. "Lindsey . . ."

"I don't blame you if you don't believe me."

"I didn't say I don't believe you."

"It's like I have this connection to her. This has been going on for years, Striker. I've never told anyone because it sounds so . . . crazy. But I swear, I've always known when she was in trouble. I mean, since we were kids. I would always know—" She caught herself just in time.

"Know what?"

Because she didn't know how to answer that, because she didn't want to answer, she looked away.

Surprising her, Striker let it go. "You think she's in trouble now?"

"I know she is. I feel it very strongly. That's the reason why I had the police do a welfare/concern check before I left Columbus. That's why I came to Seattle. Why I filed a missing persons report." She looked at him. "That's why I hired you."

"Lindsey, you're too grounded in reality to believe in premonitions."

"Maybe it isn't a premonition," she said. "Maybe it's intuition. I mean, we're sisters. We were close." At his skeptical look, she choked out a laugh. "I know it sounds crazy."

"It's a little out there." Tempering the words with a smile, he lifted his hand and touched her hair. "But you're not crazy. Not by a long shot."

Lindsey had never been much of a crier. She'd learned at an early age that tears never helped. Her mother had produced buckets, but it hadn't been enough to protect her two little girls from the monster she'd married.

She tried to tug her hands from Striker's, but he gripped them firmly. Mortified that she was going to cry, she bent her head. She closed her eyes tightly, but it wasn't enough to keep the tears from squeezing through her lashes. It didn't keep the pain from twisting brutally inside her. It didn't keep the guilt from tearing at a place that had already been hollowed out.

It didn't keep Striker from reaching for her. "Come here."

She wasn't used to being held. She'd never allowed herself to get close enough to anyone to accept that kind of comfort, no matter how badly she'd needed it. But when he put his arms around her, the pain receded so that she could at least bear it.

He felt solid and warm against her. When he pulled her closer, it seemed only natural that she would turn to him and loop her arms around his neck. For just a little while she could lean against him, draw from his strength, let the world go away.

Thunder crashed, and she jolted.

"I've got you," he said softly.

The light beside the bed flickered and went out.

Lindsey could hear the drum of her heartbeat in her ears, feel the pound of it throughout her body. They were sitting on the bed, facing each other, arms looped around shoulders, touching but not too close. She knew better than to get caught up in the moment. She'd spent her entire adult life avoiding situations like this. Situations where her emotions or her hormones overrode her good judgment. She'd learned at a formative age that mistakes could be costly, that they could be messy, and that most times they couldn't be taken back.

Striker pulled away slightly. She jolted when his fingertips brushed her cheek. A flash of lightning illuminated his face. She saw intent in his eyes. She saw tension in the set of his jaw, felt it in the way his shoulder muscles coiled beneath her hands. And in the murky depths of his gaze she saw the mistake they were about to make. And she knew she wasn't going to stop it.

His mouth came down on hers with the same violence as the storm outside. The initial contact jolted her, like a bolt of lightning coming through the skylight and running the length of her body. Every nerve ending snapped and began to sizzle, like a thousand live wires surging with electricity. For several heartbeats, she couldn't move, couldn't even respond. She simply absorbed the essence of him, the sensation of his mouth against hers, the quick shock of pleasure.

She told herself it was just a kiss. A moment of comfort that had turned into something neither of them wanted. A mistake that could still be corrected if she put a stop to it in the next five seconds.

Striker didn't give her the chance. He devoured her mouth like a predator consuming its prey. His lips moved rapidly over hers, hard and hungry and relentless. Lindsey's heart stumbled and then jumped into a rapid fire staccato. She could feel the beat of it throughout her body, hot blood engorging her breasts, the drumming pound of it deep in her womb, the wet pulse between her legs.

Her reaction stunned her, belied everything she'd ever believed about herself. She wanted to tell him she wasn't what he thought she was, that she would disappoint him. In the back of her mind she knew the moment would end disastrously. She knew it would complicate a relationship she wanted to keep simple. But there wasn't anything simple about what was happening between them. And for the first time in her life, she didn't heed the warning blaring inside her head. She didn't use the good judgment she'd always prided herself on possessing. She forgot all about the lessons Fate had taught her. Instead, she kissed him back with everything she had to offer and hoped it didn't cost her more than she was willing to pay.

Striker had made plenty of mistakes in his lifetime. Some were long forgotten. Others, he would be dealing with for a long time to come. He'd been born with an early warning system when it came to screwing up. A sort of internal alarm the school of hard knocks had taught him to recognize and respect.

But life had also taught him that some mistakes were worth the consequences. As the pleasure clamped down and held him in its powerful grip, he knew this was one of those times. And he knew he wasn't going to be smart about it.

He wanted to believe he'd given in to impulse because he'd been alone for a long time. Because his life was in turmoil and he needed a diversion. He wanted to believe he'd fallen for the oldest temptation in the book because he was facing ten years in prison, and didn't have a clue how he was going to deal with it. How he was going to endure having his freedom and dignity stripped away.

But deep inside Striker knew this moment had more to do with the woman than the situation or his frame of mind. He knew it had more to do with the way she looked at him than

the way she touched him. And he knew this moment had
been inevitable from the start. He'd felt the need churning
and augmenting inside him since the day she'd walked into
his office.

In the midst of personal and professional ruin, he was in
no position to partake in a relationship. This woman was a
client with a missing sister and a boatload of personal baggage. He didn't even want to consider the possibility that in
all likelihood she was probably in some very real danger.

But it was need driving him, not logic. And that need
was like a flash flood gaining momentum and barreling
down the side of a mountain. He wanted his tongue in her
mouth. His body inside hers. He wanted soft, wet heat
wrapped around him. And he wanted all of those things
right now.

She stiffened slightly when he slid his tongue between
her lips. He'd had enough experience with women to know
she was telling him to slow down. But the urgency burning
him from the inside out wouldn't let him. He plundered her
mouth. Anticipation tangled with a sharp-edged longing
when she opened to him. He went in deep, exploring the
silky darkness, reveling in the texture and warmth and flavor
of her. She tasted as rich and exotic as dark chocolate. Sweet
tempered with bitter. The combination was heady and tested
his control. He wanted to consume every inch of her.

It nearly undid him when her tongue slid tentatively
against his. Need coiled inside him, a hot wire tightening
to an inevitable snap. He was aware of her arms around his
neck. Her body brushing against his. Soft against hard.
Heat against cold stone. He cupped the back of her head
with his right hand, angled her mouth to his and deepened
the kiss. He ran his left hand down her side, marveling at
the soft curves of her body.

He breathed in her scent, filled his lungs with the
essence of her, let it fill his mind. She smelled like she
tasted. Bittersweet. He shifted closer, and the hardened

peaks of her nipples against his chest maddened him. She gasped when he ran his hands up her sides to cup her breasts. She was slightly built, but her flesh filled his hands perfectly. He molded her, marveling at the weight and sheer perfection of her. She started to pull away, but he brushed his thumbs over her nipples, urging her to stay. A tremor ran the length of her. He heard her quick intake of breath when he took her nipples between his thumbs and forefingers and gently, gently squeezed.

Then she sighed, and all he could think was that he wanted more. That he wanted it here and now and with this woman.

Never taking his mouth from hers, he took her shoulders and pushed her back so he could get on top of her. Her tongue warred with his, but it wasn't enough. He used his knee and wedged himself between her legs. Blood pounded in his groin when her legs opened to him, and he moved against her. The anticipation was like a living thing inside him. His pulse hammered out of control. He closed his eyes against a wave of dizziness.

He broke the kiss to whisper her name, but she found his mouth and kissed him again. He skimmed his right hand down her side, over the taut flesh of her belly. She stiffened slightly when he slipped his hand beneath the waistband of her panties.

"Striker," she whispered.

He cupped her mound, marveling at her softness, the way she moved against him.

"Wait . . ."

But her voice was breathless, and he barely heard it over the blood raging in his veins. He caressed her, moved his hand lower, over the crisp curls at her vee and then lower. He groaned when wet heat met his fingertips.

"Lindsey," he whispered. "Let me touch you."

Her body began to quiver. She made a small sound when he separated her folds. Then she opened to him. Her body jolted when he slicked two fingers over her. He dipped his fingers inside her, and she cried out.

Striker kissed her and stroked her, and the pleasure of touching her hammered at him like relentless waves in a wild sea. It had been a long time since he'd been intimate with a woman, and he'd almost forgotten how powerful the need could be. That it could make a man crazy if he didn't know how to keep things in perspective.

Striker had always been good at keeping things in perspective.

Light flooded the room. Her eyes were closed, her head thrown back. Her mouth was partially open and wet, and he thought he'd never seen a woman look more beautiful.

An instant later she opened her eyes. Her gaze met his. Her eyes widened. Her body went stiff. "Striker . . ."

One instant he was kissing her and stroking her and his body was jumping with the anticipation of getting inside her. The next she was pulling away and scrambling across the bed so fast he thought maybe he'd been struck by lightning.

"I can't . . . do this," she said in a ragged voice.

He stared at her, realizing with some surprise that he was breathless. That he'd broken a sweat. That his heart was beating so fast he thought he might have a heart attack. What the hell had gotten into him? What the holy hell was he thinking?

He had no right to be angry with her, but frustration made his voice harsher than he intended. "I wish you'd thought of that before . . ." Because he didn't know how to finish the sentence, he let his voice trail.

"I'm sorry. It's just that . . . I don't, you know, do this sort of thing."

He wondered if "this sort of thing" was a euphemism for sex. "Yeah, well, it's not like I do, either."

She tugged the blanket to her chest in a protective gesture. Breathing hard, she stared at him as if half expecting him to come across the bed and take what he wanted. That

chapter
18

"ARE YOU EXPECTING COMPANY?"

Striker knew better than to make eye contact with her, but figured one more mistake piled on top of a couple dozen others wasn't going to make much difference at this point. He stopped at the sofa and turned to look at her. She was staring at him, her eyes wide. Color rode high in her cheeks. Her hair tangled wildly around her shoulders. Her mouth was red from the chafe of his beard. She looked good enough to eat . . .

He cut the thought short, took a moment to get himself under control. "I'm a popular guy. What can I say?"

Her eyes widened when he started toward her. He rounded the bed, yanked open the nightstand drawer, and tugged the Heckler & Koch .45 from its leather holster.

"What are you doing?" she whispered.

"Just taking out a little insurance."

Keenly aware that he was still aroused—and that it was obvious—he crossed to the mobile closet unit and yanked a flannel shirt off a hanger. "Stay put." Holding the gun low and at his side, he crossed to the front door.

Surprise rippled through him when the peephole revealed Shep standing in the foyer area looking like he'd been violently ripped from his bed and was none too happy about it.

"Who is it?" Lindsey asked.

Striker looked over at her to see her step into her jeans. Something inside him jumped at the sight of her bare thighs and silky panties. His body responded, and he groaned inwardly, knowing how this was going to look to Shep.

Striker opened the door halfway. "You get lost on your way to the precinct?"

Shep didn't smile. He didn't even look happy to see him. "We need to talk."

Uneasiness rippled through Striker. When he hesitated, Shep's eyes flicked past him to Lindsey, and he sighed. "It's important."

Striker opened the door the rest of the way and stepped aside. "What's going on?"

Shaking the rain from his trench, Shep entered, his eyes going from Striker to Lindsey, then back to Striker. "You want the bad news first? Or shall I start with the totally fucked up shit?"

Striker got a bad feeling in his gut. "It's early, why don't you start with the bad news and we'll work our way up from there?"

"A couple days ago you had me do some digging on some names."

"What did you get?"

"I got a body. Call came in about forty-five minutes ago. Dockworker discovered a female body down by Terminal 46. We don't have a positive ID yet, but we're pretty sure it's Jamie Mills."

Striker almost couldn't believe it. Almost. "Are you sure?"

Shep nodded. "We'll verify with NOK, but we're pretty sure it's her. She had a driver's license on her. Pic matched the face—what was left of it. I thought you might want to know."

"Murder? What?"

"Someone shot her through the windshield. Two shots in the face. Mills had a business card on her. Lindsey Metcalf from Columbus Ohio. I thought it was interesting that those are two of the names you had been digging around on."

Striker cursed.

Shep's gaze flicked to Lindsey. Realization entered his expression. Then he lowered his head, pinched the bridge of his nose between his thumb and forefinger. "Tell me the chick standing next to your bed looking like someone just fucked her brains out is not Lindsey Metcalf."

Something protective and male and very mean snaked through Striker. "You asking as a friend, Shep?"

"I'm asking you as a cop who's risking his fucking job by coming here and telling you all this shit. I don't know how you're involved, but I'd appreciate it if you'd give me the goddamn courtesy of telling me what you know."

Striker sighed. "Her sister is missing. Jamie Mills works with her sister. At Club Tribeca."

"Did she plug Jamie Mills?"

"No way."

Shep didn't look convinced.

Striker scrubbed a hand over his face. "She's been with me all night."

"I gotta hand it to you, Striker. When you fuck up you don't mess around."

"Yeah, it's a gift."

"You know the primary is going to want to talk to her."

"Yeah." He looked over his shoulder at Lindsey, then turned his attention back to Shep. "Who's the primary?"

"Landreth."

Striker cursed. Hal Landreth was a decent detective. But he'd been there that day in the interview room. The day Striker lost his cool and put a man in a coma. The statement

Landreth had given later to the prosecutor's office had been damning. Because it had been the truth, Striker had tried not to hold it against him. But deep down inside, he had.

"I want you downtown today." Shep jabbed a thumb in Lindsey's direction. "Her, too. And bring that damn disk you were telling me about."

"If that's the bad news I'm not sure I want to hear the totally fucked up shit," Striker said dryly.

"I figured it would be better if you heard it from me as opposed to some jackass reporter." Shep sighed unhappily. "Someone gave up the interview room video. You're all over the news this morning."

Striker's stomach went queasy. "What the hell are you talking about?"

"Try Channel 53. They've been playing it since I got dragged out of bed. I'm not sure if you've made national yet. You will by noon. You're a hot commodity, Striker." Frowning, Shep reached out and patted his shoulder. "I got a murder to solve."

Striker closed the door. Without looking at Lindsey, he strode to the coffee table, snatched up the remote, and turned on the television set. Vaguely he was aware of Lindsey moving around in the kitchen. Of the coffeemaker bumping and grinding. He sat through the local weather, traffic, and several annoying commercials before finding what he was looking for.

A female reporter from Channel 53 stood in front of the august portals of the Seattle Justice Center in the predawn darkness. Though the morning was cold and rainy, she wore a fitted jacket and short skirt with no coat. Her expertly colored hair and glossy mouth made her look more like a model from a Victoria's Secret catalog than a journalist. Striker had met her twice in the last year. Both times she'd rubbed him the wrong way. Plastic face. Plastic personality. Just another shark in an ocean that seemed to be teeming with them. He had the feeling that a feeding frenzy was about to begin.

She put the mike to her mouth. Her eyes intensified. "Four months ago, Seattle homicide detective Michael Striker was at the top of his game. He had one of the highest solve rates in the department. He made a decent salary and had earned three weeks of vacation a year. Then came the case of a lifetime and a slow downward spiral for this decorated detective that ended in a very ugly scene right here at police headquarters.

"Detective Striker and his partner, Trisha King, were working the infamous waterfront killer case. Six women were brutally raped and murdered over a period of two years. A little over four months ago, Norman Schroeder was arrested in connection with those slayings and taken to the Seattle Justice Center and held without bond. The details about his arrest are still sketchy, but from what little information News 53 has been able to obtain, Striker's partner, Trisha King, also a detective with the Seattle PD, was somehow abducted by Norman Schroeder in the course of the investigation. King, a twelve-year veteran of the force, was raped and brutally murdered, purportedly while Michael Striker listened in on his cell phone and tried frantically to reach her."

The reporter looked appropriately solemn for a moment. "Two weeks later, Norman Schroeder was arrested for one of the waterfront murders as well as Detective King's murder, and detained at the King County Correctional Facility here at the Justice Center. Because of the circumstances of his partner's death, Striker was put on administrative leave.

"Two days after his arrest, thirty-one-year-old Norman Schroeder was taken to a room at the Seattle Justice Center for an interview with homicide detectives. His lawyer was present as well. From what News 53 has learned from witnesses at the scene, Detective Striker—even though he was on administrative leave—entered the interrogation room where Schroeder was being questioned and, according to one witness, 'went ballistic.'"

She looked down at her notes, then posed for the camera. "News 53 was able to obtain an exclusive police videotape of what happened in that room. I must warn you that the tape you are about to see is shocking and violent and could be disturbing for some individuals. Viewer discretion is strongly advised." Frowning she stepped back, and the camera cut to the video.

Striker had relived that scene a thousand times in the last four months, but he'd never seen it from the cruel perspective of a camera. He watched as the camera cut to interview room number 3. Detective Ricardo Cardona sat at the scarred wooden table opposite Schroeder. He wore a rumpled suit, a sour expression, and had a notebook and pad on the table in front of him. Detective Hal Landreth stood behind Schroeder and slightly to one side. He was hovering, pacing on occasion, classic bad cop psych-out. Schroeder didn't look affected by either man. He was leaning back in the uncomfortable wooden chair with his legs stretched out, looking bored. Schroeder's attorney, a hungry little shrew by the name of Chuck Greenblatt, sat beside him taking notes.

In the next instant, the door flew open and banged against the wall. Striker felt an odd sense of déjà vu when he saw himself burst into the room. His lips were peeled back in a snarl. He didn't even look at the two detectives or the lawyer. His eyes were wild when they landed on Schroeder. Cardona had time to turn and ask, "What the hell are you doing?"

Striker rounded the table, grabbed Schroeder by the lapels of his prison issue jumpsuit, and yanked him to his feet. Schroeder shouted, "Get this crazy son of a bitch off me!"

Striker slammed him against the wall, shook him twice, then slammed him against the wall again. "You're not going to get away with what you did to her, you sick little motherfucker!"

The sound of his own voice shocked him. He didn't

remember saying that. He didn't remember any of what happened next. Just a blur of fury. The knowledge that he was crossing a line. Too much rage to pull himself back.

He drew back and punched Schroeder in the face, hard, with his fist, putting his weight behind it. The kind of punch that broke bones. Schroeder's head bounced against the wall. He raised his hands, but he wasn't fast enough to protect himself. Striker hit him again. Schroeder's head hit the wall, then his body went slack.

Striker stared at the television screen, sick dread climbing into his throat as he watched himself punch the other man repeatedly. Right jaw. Stomach. Upper cut to the chin.

Jesus Christ.

Cardona had jumped up at this point and called for officers. "What the fuck! Striker! What the fuck!"

Landreth, who weighed in at a good three hundred pounds, came up behind Striker, locked his arms around him, tried to pull him back. But Striker twisted away and lunged at Schroeder, who was now slumped on the floor.

Striker picked him up by the scruff of his neck, slammed him head first into the wall. The sheetrock gave way, and Schroeder's head went through. Striker pulled the unconscious man's head from the hole and would have continued punching him, but two uniformed officers rushed him from behind.

Landreth went in low, rammed Striker with his shoulder, and managed to shove him away from Schroeder. One of the other officers administered pepper spray. Another officer grabbed his arms, twisted them behind his back in an effort to get him cuffed.

Striker watched the video roll in utter disgust, disbelieving that the man on the screen was him. He couldn't believe he'd lost it so completely. Couldn't believe it had taken four cops and the administration of pepper spray to get him off of a suspect. He couldn't believe he'd thrown his life away for the likes of a scumbag like Schroeder.

Dropping onto the sofa, Striker leaned forward and put his elbows on his knees. But he couldn't take his eyes off the television. He watched Schroeder hit the floor, blood gushing from his broken nose to form a pool the size of a saucer.

Shame welled inside him as the four cops fought to subdue him. He watched as he was hit repeatedly with the pepper spray and noted he had responded much the same way a junkie high on PCP would. Numb to pain. Oblivious to logic or reason or common sense. What in the name of God had happened to him?

The camera cut back to the reporter. Striker didn't miss the gleam in her eye. She knew this was the hottest story of the year. Maybe even the story of her career. He wondered how she'd gotten a copy of the tape. Who inside the PD or the prosecutor's office had seen fit to give it to her. He wondered what they'd gotten in return.

"Norman Schroeder was in a coma for two days," she said. "He sustained a broken jaw, a ruptured spleen, a broken clavicle, several broken ribs, a serious head injury, and multiple bruises and contusions. Detective Striker was arrested and later charged with first-degree felony assault. He was immediately fired from the Seattle PD and is currently out on bail, awaiting trial.

"Norman Schroeder awaits trial from inside the King County Correctional Facility. Some would say it's ironic that these two men may very well end up in the same place: prison.

"Reporting from the Seattle Justice Center, Deena Ticer, Channel 53 News."

chapter
19

LINDSEY DIDN'T KNOW WHAT TO SAY, AND THE silence was excruciating. She knew Michael Striker had some hard edges. A lot of hard edges if she wanted to be honest about it. But she simply couldn't reconcile the violence she'd just seen on the television to the man she'd come to know in the last few days.

Taking a deep breath to steady herself, she picked up the two cups of coffee she'd poured and carried them to the living area. Striker was sitting on the sofa with his elbows on his knees, staring at the floor. When he heard her approach, he raised his head and met her gaze.

His smile was sardonic. "If you want to fire me, now is probably a prime opportunity."

"I'm not going to fire you."

"I can recommend another P.I. I know a couple of guys—"

"I don't want anyone else." She shoved a cup of coffee at him. "You agreed to help me find my sister. I still want you to do that."

His eyes revealed a measure of surprise as he took the cup. "I shouldn't be taking on clients, Lindsey. I should be getting my life in order. I need to sell the jeep. Move out of the loft, put a few things in storage. My trial is in two weeks. I don't know what I was thinking when I told you I would work for you."

"Maybe you were thinking that I needed your help. Maybe you knew you could help me find Traci. Maybe you agreed to take on the job because you knew it was the right thing to do."

He set down the coffee. "I'm not very good at doing the right thing." His hand was shaking when he scrubbed it over his face, and only then did she realize how profoundly the video had upset him.

"Is this the first time you've seen that?" she asked.

"Yeah."

She chose her next words carefully. "What you did to that suspect. It was bad, Striker. Brutal, even. There's no way around that. But in the short period of time I've known you, I just don't see you snapping like that."

"Yeah, well, I did. And I don't have an excuse that's going to pretty it up for you."

"Were you drinking or—"

"Hell no," he snapped. "I was . . . furious. Out of control I . . ." Shaking his head, he let his words trail off. "It doesn't matter."

"It matters," she said.

"The tape says it all, Lindsey. For God's sake, I don't even remember half of what I did. It was like watching a madman on a rampage."

"What's going to happen?"

"I'm going to trial in two weeks. There's not a jury in the country that won't convict based on that tape."

"Even if you get convicted, you could get probation, couldn't you?"

"Not bloody likely." He rubbed at the deep grooves between his brows.

She thought about what the reporter had said about his partner. A female detective. Raped and murdered. She knew how close partners could get. "Were you . . . involved with your partner?"

He looked at her over his fingertips. "We slept together a couple of times. I mean, we were both single. But the sparks just weren't there. We figured we were better cops than lovers, so we cut it out." Sighing he leaned back. "I liked her as a person. I respected her as a cop. For God's sake, she didn't deserve what that animal did to her."

Lindsey drank some of her coffee, not sure how hard to prod. "Those are extenuating circumstances. Won't the jury take that into consideration?"

"Maybe. But juries are infinitely unpredictable."

"You were a cop. That's got to mean something."

His mouth curved, but his expression was bitter. "I used to think so, too."

"What made you snap?" That was the one question she wanted answered above and beyond all others. She wanted to know what had thrown him into a murderous rage.

He looked at her, his eyes cutting into her with the proficiency of a blade. For several uncomfortable moments he searched her face. He looked at her so long and hard that her pulse jumped and began to race.

"I don't want to get into that with you." Snagging his cup off the coffee table, he walked to the kitchen.

Lindsey sat on the sofa for several minutes, willing herself to calm down, telling herself it didn't matter that he wouldn't talk to her about it. She might have come to care for him, but she couldn't let herself get caught up in his plight. First and foremost, she needed to concentrate on finding Traci.

"The tape wasn't the only reason Shep came by this morning," he said.

She looked up to see him standing on the other side of the sofa, his expression grim. "Jamie Mills was found murdered about an hour ago."

It took several heartbeats for the words to register. "Murdered?" She stood up, felt the floor tilt beneath her feet. "My God. Are you sure?"

"The primary will cross ID using next of kin, but she had ID on her. There's no mistake."

For a moment, all she could do was stare at him while her mind tried to absorb the meaning of the words. Jamie Mills dead. She couldn't believe it. "Did the police catch the killer?"

He shook his head. "They don't even have a suspect at this point."

"Where did it happen?"

"Terminal 46. She was shot. Close range."

The words hit her like a punch, hard enough to take her breath. "My God. When?"

"M.E. will be able to narrow it down, but I'll bet the farm you were the last person to talk to her." His eyes hardened. "Besides the killer, anyway."

She pressed her hand to her stomach, feeling sick. But her mind was already going over her last moments with Jamie Mills.

Maybe I know something I shouldn't.

Jamie's words came back to her, and Lindsey shivered. "This is about the disk," she said hollowly.

"The bad news is if Jamie knew who killed that girl, she's not going to be a hell of a lot of help to us now."

Lindsey could see the wheels turning in his mind, but she didn't know what he was thinking.

"This changes everything," he said.

She swallowed hard, but it wasn't enough to keep the fear from climbing up her throat. "All I care about is finding Traci," she said. "That has to be my first priority."

"Your priorities have just changed."

"What are you talking about?"

"Someone came after you last night. If they think Jamie told you something, they're going to try again."

That stopped her, but only for an instant. Because suddenly she knew what he was thinking, and it frightened her. "You think I'm in danger."

He gave her a hard look. "I think a lot of things right now, Lindsey. I think that disk isn't the only one like it. I think someone has killed before. I think they'll kill again. I think Jamie Mills knew the killers, and that's why she's on her way to the morgue. And I think your sister either knows the killers, or she was a victim. Take your pick."

Lindsey felt herself recoil, denial welling like a bruise on flesh. "You don't know any of those things as fact."

"Tell me those scenarios haven't crossed your mind."

"Traci would never be involved in anything so heinous."

"You've been saying that a lot about her lately."

"You're being purposefully cruel."

"I'm saying out loud what both of us have been thinking for quite some time," he said. "There are some very dangerous people out there who've murdered at least two young women. We know Traci is a friend of at least one of those women. We know she is involved in pornography. We know she recently came upon some large sums of cash."

She raised her gaze to his, wondering how he could be so cold about this. "You think they murdered her."

"I think it's a possibility we've got to consider at this point." When she didn't respond, he added, "We need to start calling hospitals, check for Jane Does. We can check with the morgues for females who fit her description."

Morgues. She didn't want to think about her sister in those terms. Traci was too vivacious. Too full of life.

Lindsey stalked away from him. Halfway to the kitchen area, she whirled, strode back to him, got in his face. She could feel the denial rising in a flood. The sharp spurt of anger. "She's not dead, damn it. Traci is a survivor."

"I hope you're right."

Pressing her hand to her stomach, she turned away from him. "I'll never forgive myself if something has happened to her."

"None of this is your fault," he growled.

"Not directly. But . . . I should have kept in touch with her. I should have . . ."

"Should have what?" When she didn't respond, he crossed to her.

She jolted when he set his hands on her shoulders. A small part of her wanted to take comfort in the contact, but she was too raw inside, couldn't allow it.

"Traci is a big girl," he said. "There is no reason for you to be taking on any guilt."

"She wouldn't even be in Seattle if it weren't for me."

"What are you talking about?"

"She wouldn't have run away if I hadn't . . ."

His gaze searched hers. "If you hadn't what?"

She knew he was trying to read between the lines and make sense of what she was saying. There was a part of her that wanted to tell him everything. But Lindsey didn't want to go down that path. She didn't want Striker to know about Jerry Thorpe. She didn't want him to look at her and see the girl she'd been.

"Traci was a runaway?" he asked.

She nodded. "She left Columbus when she was fourteen."

"What makes that your fault?"

"I know her running away wasn't directly my fault. But in a very big way, it was."

"This isn't the first time I've gotten the impression that you feel responsible for at least part of this. You want to tell me what the hell is going on? What is it you think you did to her, Lindsey?"

"It happened a long time ago." She started to turn away, but he stopped her.

"The things that happened to us a long time ago are the things that made us who we are today," he said. "Those things have an impact on us whether we want to see it or not."

"I know. I just . . . don't want to discuss it."

"Now is not the time to be keeping secrets, Lindsey." When she only continued to stare at him, he grimaced. "Talk to me, damn it. What is it you think you did to her?"

Lindsey had thought she could handle telling him. Jerry Thorpe was ancient history. He'd been dead going on five years now. She was a grown woman with a full life and a successful business. She was happy and well adjusted. She'd made amends with her past and moved on.

But while Lindsey might have healed, she knew there were still scars. Scars that would always be a part of her. She knew that in some small corner of her heart, the pain and the shame of what she'd endured were still locked inside her. Like a dormant cancer, waiting to come out of remission to ravage her. Deep inside, she was still that scared little girl, terrified he would come into her room . . .

"When I was seventeen, I received a full scholarship to Ohio State University." Remembering the elation of the girl she'd been, she laughed. "It was the most exciting day of my life. I was going to the big city to start my life. I was so incredibly happy. All that hard work had finally paid off. I could hardly believe it was real."

"Most teenagers want to get away from home and go to college," he said. "There's nothing wrong with that."

"I didn't work so hard for that scholarship because I wanted to go to college, Striker. I didn't care about getting an education. I didn't even do it because I wanted to strike out on my own."

He waited.

"I worked for that scholarship because I wanted to . . . get away from him."

"Who? Your father?"

A breath shuddered out of her. "My stepfather."

Striker's expression changed, hardened. His fingers tightened around her arms. "Did he hurt you?"

She forced a smile, but there were tears on her cheeks. "Yeah. He did. Lots of times."

"Aw, Lindsey. I'm sorry."

"I'm okay. Honest, I am. I mean, yes, it was devastating, but I was an amazingly resilient kid. It was a long time ago. I've come to terms, as much as anybody can, and I put it behind me." She drew a breath, let it shudder out. "The hardest thing about what happened is that when I went off to college, I left my little sister behind."

"Lindsey . . ."

"She was only fourteen years old, Striker. I'd noticed the way he looked at her. I knew what he was capable of. She was so pretty and vivacious. I knew he'd . . . touched her inappropriately. But I didn't think he'd . . . he'd never . . ." Even after all this time, she couldn't bring herself to say the word. "I left for college knowing fully what he would do to her." She raised her eyes to his. "How could I do that to my little sister? What kind of person does that make me? I left her with a predator. My God, I didn't tell anyone what he had done to me."

For an instant he just stood there, looking shell-shocked. Big, bad Michael Striker. Shocked speechless. If she hadn't been going to pieces inside, she might have laughed at the irony of that.

He put his hands on either side of her face. His palms were warm and slightly rough against her cheeks. He looked deeply into her eyes. "Lindsey, what happened to you wasn't your fault. You understand that, don't you?"

Because her throat was locked up tight, she nodded.

"What happened to Traci wasn't your fault, either."

She closed her eyes, felt hot tears squeeze between her lashes. "I knew he would . . . rape her. The way he had raped me. But, Striker, I left anyway. I left her with him, and I didn't tell anyone. In my mind, that makes it my fault."

"You were a kid yourself. You were facing something no kid should have to face. At the hands of someone you should have been able to trust. You were probably in denial that it had even happened, Lindsey. It's a protective mechanism and probably one of the reasons you got through it."

She could feel her emotions winding up, beginning to spiral, and shook her head. "I can't talk about this anymore," she said. "I just want you to understand . . . some of the things that Traci has done. It's not her fault. It's because of what happened to her. She's a good person, Striker, with a good heart. I want you to know that."

His eyes were gentle and fierce at once when he looked down at her. "That's why you've been so determined to find her."

"I want to find her because she's my sister, and I love her."

He slid his hands over her shoulders and down her arms to her hands. Taking them in his, he squeezed gently. "Have you talked to anyone about what happened to you?"

"Some of it. After college, I went to see a psychologist for a few months. She helped me put some things into perspective." She shrugged. "Then I got busy with my catering business. You know how it goes."

"You've been holding this inside for a long time."

"It's incredibly difficult to talk about."

"I'm sure it is, but you can't lock something like that inside and expect it to go away." He studied her for a moment. "What happened to your stepfather?"

"He died of cancer five years ago."

"You never told anyone what happened?"

She shook her head. "I wanted to, but couldn't. My

mom was pretty broken up over his death. I think her finding out . . . something like that would have killed her."

He nodded. "You know it wasn't your fault, don't you?"

"I know what he did to us wasn't my fault." She felt tears begin to well and blinked furiously to ward them off. "I wish I hadn't left her with him. I wish I'd told someone."

"Like you said, it's a hard thing to talk about, especially when you're a kid. Kids just aren't equipped to deal with stuff like that alone."

"Thanks for letting me off the hook."

"That's a heavy load you've been carrying around." He brushed at her tears with the pad of his thumb and smiled at her. "Come here."

"I'm going to bawl if you don't stop being so nice."

"That's what everyone says to me."

She laughed in earnest then, a tension-releasing laugh she felt all the way to her belly. Leaning close, she put her arms around him. He must have been waiting for a signal from her because he hesitated before wrapping his arms around her.

"Promise me you'll help me find her," she whispered.

"I promise," he said and just held her.

chapter 20

STRIKER KNEW BETTER THAN TO MAKE PROMISES HE couldn't keep. He knew better than to do a lot of things when it came to Lindsey Metcalf. But the good judgment he'd once prided himself on possessing wasn't enough to keep him from wanting her. He knew he was digging a hole; he knew that hole was getting deeper with every line he crossed. He only hoped he had the strength to climb out of it when this was over and done.

They spent the morning calling every topless club in King County on the outside chance that Traci had needed some quick cash and taken a job. When that turned up zilch, Lindsey started calling hospitals, contacting every major medical facility in Seattle and Tacoma to see if Traci—or a female matching her description—had been admitted.

No one had seen or heard from Traci Metcalf.

By noon Lindsey seemed ready to snap. "It's almost as if she's dropped off the face of the earth. Damn it. Where could she *be?*"

Striker looked at her over the screen of his laptop.

"We'll try some of the clubs in Los Angeles when we get back."

"The airline ticket to LA. I'd almost forgotten about it." She shot him a questioning look. "When we get back from where?"

"From the police department for one. Landreth wants to talk to you."

"Yeah." She bit her lip. "Where else are we going?"

"I found an address for Jason Blow, a.k.a. Jace Bledsoe. I thought we might pay him a visit."

"Jace Bledsoe? That's his real name?" She gaped at him. "How did you figure that out?"

"I did a search on Jason Blow and hit on several Web sites photographers use to post their work. Some of his photographs were listed under both names on different sites."

"And the address?"

"Give me a break, Lindsey. I used to be a cop." He rolled his shoulder. "I figure we can swing by his place on the way to police headquarters."

Her gaze went wary at the mention of the cops. "They don't think I had anything to do with what happened to Jamie, do they?"

"If that was the case, Landreth would have hauled you in first thing this morning." When she only continued to stare at him, he added, "Landreth just has a few questions for you about your meeting with her."

"What do I tell him?"

"Since he's a cop, you probably ought to tell him the truth."

Half an hour later Striker parked the jeep across the street from a three-story, red-brick building in a neighborhood that had been on the downslide for a decade. He checked the address, then spotted the street number above a wooden door with peeling green paint and a missing doorknob. The apartment building sat between a pseudo-shabby coffee-house and a funky art gallery with dirty storefront windows.

Striker reached for the door handle and got out without speaking. Lindsey pulled up the collar of her jacket as she stepped into the cold drizzle. They crossed the street and stopped on the sidewalk. "You got the photograph of Traci?" he asked.

She patted her purse. "Right here."

"Keep it handy." He opened the door, stepped inside first. "Stay behind me. If anything happens, I want you to go next door and call 911."

"Are you expecting trouble?"

"No, but it never hurts to be prepared. This place looks like it's full of rats."

The stairs creaked beneath their weight as they went up. The stairwell was dimly lit and smelled of cigarette smoke and mildew. They passed two doors on the second level. Lindsey could hear a baby crying from inside one of the apartments. The steel guitar of rock and roll. The clang of dishes. Laughter.

The third level was darker, and Lindsey noticed the bulb had been removed from the ceiling fixture. There were two doors, but one of them had been removed from its hinges and sat just inside a vacant apartment that was littered with trash. Striker strode to the other door and rapped hard with his knuckles.

He looked over at her as they waited, his eyes lingering on hers, dropping to her mouth and then skittering away. He knocked again, harder this time. An instant later the door swung open. A pale young man with a dark goatee and a pierced eyebrow glared at them. "Who the fuck are you?"

"Jace Bledsoe?" Striker said.

The younger man's eyes widened. His gaze flicked from Striker to Lindsey. In the instant his eyes met hers, Lindsey felt a flicker of recognition, but she couldn't place where she'd seen him before.

"What do you want?" he asked.

"Just a minute of your time."

She knew an instant before he moved that he was going to try to slam the door. Striker must have foreseen the move, because he lunged forward, rammed his forearm into the smaller man's chest, and sent him reeling backward into the apartment.

The door flew open, slammed hard against the wall.

"Hey! You can't do this!"

Striker muscled him against the wall, used his other hand to pat him down, then glanced quickly around the room. "Don't move or I'll break every bone in your body, you got that?"

Bledsoe didn't even move his eyeballs as Striker left him and began checking rooms.

The apartment was small and reeked of incense with an underlying redolence of some kind of chemical. The kitchen was dirty and cluttered with pizza boxes and Chinese take-out containers.

Striker's face was dark with anger when he came out of the bedroom with a stack of what looked like photographs in his hand. Lindsey's pulse leapt into a sprint when he started toward the younger man. She didn't know if that look in his eye was an act designed to intimidate or if he were truly furious, but it was a frightening thing to behold.

"What the hell are these?" Striker held the photos close to Bledsoe's face, shuffling them like cards.

Bledsoe looked like he wanted to run. His gaze darted to the door, to the phone, to the window, and then finally landed on Lindsey as if in a silent plea to protect him.

"If I were you, I'd answer the question," she said.

"N—nothing, man."

"Nothing, huh?" Striker left Bledsoe, crossed the room, and disappeared into the bedroom. A moment later he walked out with a camera in one hand, an expensive-looking flash in the other.

Bledsoe eyed him warily. "Wh—what are you doing with my things?"

Striker slammed the camera against the wall hard enough to knock a hole in the sheetrock. "You really ought to be more careful with your equipment."

Bledsoe leapt forward. "Hey! You can't fuckin' do that!"

Striker pinned him against the wall. "How do you get those young women to pose for you? Do you promise them stardom? Or maybe you just give them heroin."

"I don't do that shit, man."

"Yeah. Right. That's why there's a syringe in the ashtray next to your bed." Striker made an ugly, dangerous sound. Lindsey could see him reeling himself in, working to control his temper, pulling himself back. "I'm in a charitable mood today, so I'm going to give you a chance to redeem yourself."

"You ain't no fuckin' cop." Bledsoe's eyes narrowed. "Who are you?"

"I'm the man who can ruin your life, so I suggest you shut your mouth and listen. Are you following me so far?"

"Yeah. I got it."

"Good. Because now you're going to talk to us." Taking the younger man by his lapels, Striker swung him around and shoved him into a dining room chair. "Have a seat."

Bledsoe sat down hard, a tuft of hair falling onto his forehead. "What do you want?"

Lindsey quickly removed Traci's photograph from her bag and held it out for Bledsoe to see. "Do you know who this is?" she asked.

Bledsoe glanced at the photo, then looked down at the tabletop. "Never seen her before in my life."

Striker slapped him on the back of the head. "Look again."

She held the photo closer to his face. Bledsoe looked from the photograph to Lindsey then back at the photograph and lifted his shoulder. "I coulda taken some pictures of her."

Striker sighed as if his patience were stretched wire thin. "If I go back into your bedroom, am I going to find more video equipment?" he asked. "I'll bet it cost you a pretty penny, didn't it? Do you have any idea how much it would cost to replace it if some pissed-off psycho walked into your bedroom and wigged out?"

"Don't break any more of my shit!" Bledsoe cried.

"Then you'd better start talking, junior, because I'm running out of patience."

"Her name's Traci. Okay? She did a couple of movies."

"What kind of movies?"

"Porn stuff. She liked to take off her clothes in front of people. She had sex with a couple of guys and got paid a ton of money to do it. All I did was the camera work and lights."

Striker make a sound of disgust. "Who financed it?"

"I don't know. Some production company."

"You know, Bledsoe, I'm dying to go back into that ratty bedroom of yours and start breaking things."

"Rendezvous Productions!"

"You got a check stub? Anything with a number or address?"

"No, man. They paid me in cash." When Striker only continued to stare at him, he added. "I swear. Cash under the table. No taxes, you know?"

"Why did Traci have your initials tattooed on her shoulder?" Lindsey asked. "Were you involved with her?"

Bledsoe looked like a rabbit whose leg had just been snared in a trap. "I wasn't. I swear!"

"You know, Bledsoe, for a scumbag, you're not a very good liar." Striker left the dining area and stalked to the bedroom. Lindsey saw Bledsoe's head snap around, his thin chest heaving. He stood when Striker reappeared with a video camera in his hand. In his other he held a five-by-seven-inch black and white photo. Lindsey stared at the photo, familiarity punching her like a fist.

"Sit the hell down," Striker said with deadly calm.

Bledsoe dropped into the chair, looking like he was going to cry. Lindsey crossed to Striker and reached for the photo. He made a halfhearted attempt to keep it from her, but she snatched it from him, found herself staring down at a stark black and white nude of Traci.

"Jesus," she whispered.

"Come on." Striker eased the photo from her hand and turned it so Bledsoe could see it. "Did you take this?"

The younger man looked as if he were about to choke on his own Adam's apple. "I don't remember."

Striker's lips pulled back in a snarl. "You had better start talking to me you little son of a bitch, or I swear to Christ I won't be responsible for what happens to you."

Bledsoe raised his hands as if to fend him off. "I took the shot, okay? W—we went out a few times! We had some drinks. Got high. Had a good time."

"Did you have a relationship with her?"

"I guess. We hung out together."

"Were you intimate?"

"Yeah. She was like . . ." He glanced at Lindsey and actually had the decency to look embarrassed. "Insatiable, you know? Wild as shit. I didn't know what she wanted with me. I mean, she's good to look at, and I'm just a regular guy. I figured it was because of . . . you know, the drugs."

"Heroin?" Striker asked.

Bledsoe hung his head. "Coke. Heroin. Ex. You name it, she was into it."

"When did you last see her?" Striker asked.

"A couple of months ago. Then she dumped me."

"If she dumped you, why would she have your initials tattooed on her shoulder?"

"I don't know! She was . . . a freak. Irrational half the time. She got high and did shit like that."

"Did you shoot any other movies?" Striker asked.

"We did porn, man. I mean, some of it was pretty hard-core stuff. Double penetration. S & M. Traci was into that shit. Like I said, I just did the camera work and lights."

"Where did you do the filming?"

Bledsoe turned green. "Aw, come on, man. These people are discreet, you know?"

Striker looked down at the video camera in his hand. He unscrewed the intricate-looking lens, dropped it to the floor and placed his boot on top of it, ready to crush it.

"Don't!" Bledsoe jumped to his feet.

Striker shoved him back into the chair. "Where?"

"Some rich guy's place." Bledsoe's voice rose with each word. "He's got a mansion in Kirkland. There's a pool and hot tub, and he pays cash."

"His name," Striker said.

"I swear. I don't know! I didn't ask. Traci set up the gig. I didn't ask any questions."

"You got an address?"

"I don't know. It's been a while." Bledsoe looked around wildly. "It's a big place over in the Marsh Commons area, off of Lake Washington Boulevard."

"If you're lying to me . . ."

"I'm not! I swear. Give me a break!"

Striker scraped a hand over his jaw, then shot Bledsoe a knowing look. "What about the other movies?"

"What other movies?" Bledsoe's eyes narrowed. "What are you talking about?"

"I think you know exactly what I'm talking about." Striker stared him down.

Bledsoe's eyes flicked to the video camera Striker held in his hand. "I shot some gay porn a couple of years ago for some guy down in San Francisco. But I swear, all I did was shoot the tape. I'm no homophobe, but I'm not fuckin' gay, either."

Striker let the camera drop to the floor.

"Hey!" Bledsoe's body jerked, but he didn't leave the chair.

"Where did you meet Traci?" Lindsey asked.

"On her first shoot."

"Did she have any other male friends?"

Bledsoe laughed. "Every man she met was her friend."

Lindsey winced, hating it that this perverse excuse for a human being would talk about her sister that way. "Was there someone in particular she was close to?"

"She liked to hang out with some club owner. Guy with the slick hair and fancy suits. He used to pick her up from shoots and they'd go and get high."

Lindsey looked over at Striker, then back at Bledsoe. "Mason Treece?" she asked.

"Yeah, that's him."

"Do you know anyone else who has the same initials as yours?" Striker asked. "Anyone in the business?"

Bledsoe seemed to consider the question for a moment, then looked over at his broken video camera and shook his head. "I wish I did."

Two minutes later, Lindsey and Striker were back in the jeep. "That little shit is into something," Striker said.

"You mean about Traci?"

"I don't know. Something. I could see it in his face."

Lindsey thought about that for a moment. "Striker, when he opened the door and I saw his face, I felt very strongly that I'd seen him before."

Striker cut her a sharp look. "Are you sure?"

She shook her head. "Not a hundred percent. But I swear I think I've seen him before."

"Any idea where?"

"No."

"The club, maybe?"

She thought about the night she'd been drugged, but the memory was too hazy and disjointed for her to be sure about anything that had happened that night. "Maybe. I don't know."

"Keep thinking about it. If we can tie him to Club Tribeca, it could be significant."

Lindsey was about to ask him in what way when his cell phone chirped.

Hal Landreth's voice blasted over the line. "I thought you might want to know we're about to haul in Mason Treece."

Surprise hit him like a slap. "Treece? What do you have?"

"We did some checking and found out Metcalf and Treece were an item. He was paying her rent. Bought her the car. I got two witnesses telling me they had a big brawl a couple of days before she went missing. Real knock-down-drag-out. Turns out he also had a thing going with Jamie Mills. Could be this is a love triangle thing."

Striker worked that over in his mind, but he didn't like the way it fit. "You going to arrest him?"

"We don't have enough. We're just going to haul him in for questioning, rattle his cage a little."

Striker wished like hell he were there to do the rattling. "You going to search his house? The club?"

Landreth didn't answer. Striker knew the detective had already told him more than he should have, but it didn't lessen the surge of anger he felt at being shut out.

"You know I've been expecting you and Lindsey Metcalf all morning, don't you, Striker? You going to bring her in or are you going to make me send someone to pick her up?"

"We're en route." Striker paused, took a moment to gather himself. "I need you to run Rendezvous Productions through the computer for me."

"That's not going to happen."

"I'm looking for a guy. He finances porn. Has a big mansion in the Marsh Commons area, off of Lake Washington Boulevard."

"Damn you, Striker. You know better than to ask for shit like that."

"I almost forgot to mention that you might want to reserve an interview room with audiovisual capabilities. We're going to need a DVD player and a decent monitor or television."

"What the hell for?"

"Guess I forgot to mention Jamie Mills left us a big fucking clue."

"Striker, if you're holding out on me, I swear to Christ I'll bust you."

"The name of that company is Rendezvous Productions. That's R-E-N-D-E-Z-V-O-U-S."

"I know how to spell it," Landreth snapped.

"I owe you one, Hal." Striker disconnected, then looked over at Lindsey. "They're going to pick up Treece."

She sat up straighter, turned to him. "What do they have on him?"

"Circumstantial crap, but Landreth will put him through the paces. Get his attention. Make him sweat a little."

Her eyes were large and dark when they met his. "Do you think Treece murdered Jamie Mills?"

"I think he's a piece of slime, but I never had him pegged as a killer."

"Striker, if he murdered that girl . . . If he and Traci were . . . involved. If she was blackmailing him . . ."

He didn't like seeing her go pale, but he wasn't going to offer false reassurances. He figured they both knew that the longer Traci was gone, the more likely it was that she'd met with foul play.

The Seattle Justice Center was located in the business district at Fifth Avenue and Cherry. Striker almost pulled into the city employee parking area out of habit, then realized what he was doing and put the jeep in a public lot across the street.

He hadn't been to police headquarters since the day
he'd walked out of the King County corrections facility after spending two hellish days in a ten-by-ten-foot cell. As
he crossed the street toward police headquarters, he could
feel the tension creeping up on him.

The thought of facing the men and women he'd once
worked with sent a quiver through his gut. Striker wasn't
proud of what he'd done. He'd dishonored the department,
dishonored his fellow cops, dishonored himself. It wasn't
going to be easy going back. But like a lot of other things
in his life right now, he didn't have a choice. Neither did
Lindsey.

They entered the lobby and asked the information officer for Hal Landreth. After a security check, they were es-
corted to the seventh floor.

Landreth was a huge man with a puffy face and piggish
eyes. He was waiting for them when the elevator doors slid
open. His gaze flicked from Striker to Lindsey and then
back to Striker. "How's it going?" he asked.

"Not bad, all things considered." Landreth didn't offer a
handshake. Striker figured he was still pissed about his asking for information on Rendezvous Productions. Hoping
Landreth came through for him, Striker motioned toward
Lindsey, introduced her.

Landreth showed his teeth in a bad imitation of a smile.
"This shouldn't take too long. I've got a few questions for
you about last night."

She extended her hand. "I'll help any way I can."

He took her hand, shook it gently, then frowned at
Striker. "I've got an interview room set up."

"Let's get it done," Striker said.

He broke a sweat as they passed the wide double doorway of the homicide division. He glanced into the large
room and wasn't surprised to find every eye watching him.
And for the first time in his life he knew what it was like to
be an outsider in the only place he'd ever fit in.

At the end of the hall, Landreth opened the interview room door and they went inside. Striker was surprised to see Assistant Chief of Police Bob Baker, some pencil-necked suit from Internal Affairs, a female detective from the crimes against persons unit, and an anemic-looking guy with a receding hairline.

"I was expecting this to be an informal interview," Striker said.

Assistant Chief Baker spoke up. "Detectives Landreth and Murray consulted with me earlier. They told me you believe the murder of Jamie Mills could be related to a missing person case you're working on."

"That's right."

"Even though this is only an information-sharing interview, I felt that in light of the unusual circumstances—namely your recent termination from the department and your upcoming trial—it would be best if we made this as official as possible."

"In that case, I'd like the record to reflect I've been retained by Ms. Metcalf to find her sister, Traci Metcalf, who is missing. We believe Jamie Mills's death may be related to Traci Metcalf's disappearance. There are several items I'd like to bring to the attention of the Seattle PD."

"Duly noted. The rest of us are here merely to observe the interview." Assistant Chief Baker looked at Landreth. "Hal?"

Striker pulled out a chair for Lindsey then took the one next to her.

Landreth cleared his throat. "All participants please be advised that this interview is being recorded." He recited the names and titles of each person present and ended with the date. Then he turned his attention to Lindsey. "Ms. Metcalf, can you tell me why you're here in Seattle?"

"I'm here looking for my sister, Traci Metcalf. I couldn't reach her from Ohio. I became worried and flew out here. You already know that."

"I just want to get some preliminary facts on the record, so bear with me." He looked down at his notes. "Are you aware that Jamie Mills was found murdered last night?"

"Yes."

"Are you aware that your business card was found on her body?"

"I gave it to her."

"When?"

"Last night."

"What time?"

"Eight-fifteen or so. She'd called and asked me to meet her."

"Tell me about your meeting with her."

Striker listened carefully as she described her meeting with Jamie. He watched the expressions of the people in the room as she told them about Jamie giving her the disk, about the man chasing her through the fog. He looked for nuances in their expressions that would tell him they thought she was lying, but saw nothing to indicate anything but interest.

When Lindsey had finished, Landreth leaned back in his chair and looked at Striker. "You got the disk?"

Striker removed the disk from his coat pocket and held it up. Landreth nodded at the anemic-looking young man. The kid jumped up, and Striker handed him the disk. People shifted in their chairs, and throats were cleared while the technician dropped the disk into the DVD player, tested it, then left.

The room fell silent when the video screen blinked to life. Striker watched as the young woman was brought into the room. He watched the faces around him as the man in the mask appeared. As the woman was tied down, sexually assaulted, and brutally murdered. He was aware of Lindsey lowering her face into her hands. Of Landreth leaning forward in his chair with his mouth open. Assistant Chief Baker clearing his throat repeatedly. The female detective shifting uncomfortably in her chair.

When the DVD had played out, Landreth scooted back in his chair and ran his hand over his forehead. "Holy shit."

The female detective looked tough. Steady. Like she'd seen it all and nothing fazed her. But Striker didn't miss the fact that she was gripping her notebook so hard her knuckles were white. "I've worked vice for sixteen years. I've been part of a pornography task force for the last two. I've seen several purported 'snuff' films, and not one of them has been authentic."

"Yeah, but did they look like *that?*" Landreth asked.

She frowned. "In the last twenty-five years of investigating purported snuff films, the FBI has never found one to be real." She shrugged. "I'll send it to the lab for some testing. It may look real, but my experience is telling me it's been doctored. Backroom photographers can do a lot with computer imaging."

"No credits," Landreth pointed out.

"Like someone's going to put their name on that shit anyway," Striker said.

"A production company or something would have been nice."

"Stupid criminals make things way too easy for us," the female detective said, and everyone nodded.

"You going to send it to the FBI?" Striker asked.

Landreth's eyes narrowed. "You keep a copy?"

Striker lifted his lip. "I asked you first."

Bob Baker cleared his throat again. "We'll have a copy made here. We'll send it to the FBI. But we'll have a couple of experts at the State Patrol lab look at it simultaneously." Leaning forward, he turned off the recorder and looked at Striker. "If you kept a copy—and I'm sure you did—I'd appreciate it if you'd keep it under your hat. We don't want the media getting their hands on this. The department doesn't need another shit storm."

Striker frowned, irritated that Baker felt the need to tell him that when Striker was the one in the eye of the first shit storm. "You keep me in the loop, and I'll see what I can do about keeping this under wraps."

"You're a civilian now, Striker," Baker said. "You know as well as I do that we don't work with civilians."

"I'm a licensed private detective, and I'm asking you to keep me apprised of anything that might affect my missing person case." When Baker balked, he added, "There's a certain female reporter from Channel 53 who would love to get her hands on that disk. Imagine the fun the media would have filling up the airwaves with that one."

Landreth made a sound of exasperation. The female detective smirked. Baker looked like he wanted to come across the table and strangle him.

It was the most fun Striker had had in a week.

When the interview was over, Landreth told his peers he was going down for a smoke and followed Lindsey and Striker to the elevator. They rode to the lobby in silence, crossed the marble floor, and went through the revolving door and into a light rain.

On the sidewalk, Landreth pulled a pack of Camel cigarettes from his jacket pocket along with a folded piece of paper. He put the cigarette between his lips and passed the paper to Striker. "Everything you ever wanted to know about Rendezvous Productions." He lit up and puffed hard. "There's stuff in there Joe Public isn't privy to, so keep it zipped."

Striker took the paper, shoved it into his jacket pocket without looking at it. "Thanks."

"Don't do anything stupid, Striker. That son of a bitch is very high on the food chain."

"Yeah? How high?"

"High enough so that he could step on a bug like you and not even get his wingtips dirty."

"I'll try to remember that."

"What you need to remember is that there's no one on the

force to bail you out if you get into shit with this guy. You're officially poison to the department. No one will touch you with a ten-foot pole. You screw up, and they'll burn you at the stake."

"Yeah, well, tell Baker I appreciate the send-off."

Landreth gave him a hard look, then dropped the cigarette onto the sidewalk and snuffed it out with his shoe. "See you around."

chapter
21

THE RIDE BACK TO THE LOFT WAS A SILENT AFFAIR. Striker seemed preoccupied and drove aggressively through rush-hour traffic. Lindsey sensed the darkness of his mood as keenly as she'd sensed the tension between him and the other detectives back at police headquarters.

Even the sky seemed to be in turmoil. Ominous black clouds billowed on the western horizon as another storm barreled in off the Pacific. The wind had picked up and blew paper and small debris along the sidewalks and through the downtown canyons. On the radio, the weatherman promised torrential downpours, gale-force winds, and heavy snow in the Cascades to the east.

By the time she stepped into the loft, the tension was getting to her. She couldn't get a handle on Striker's frame of mind. It was as if he'd gone inside himself. She knew from experience that bottling things up wasn't healthy, no matter how private or unemotional or tough-minded the individual. Sooner or later all of those bottled up emotions came pouring out. The longer they were capped, the more explosive the release. She wasn't sure she wanted to be around when Michael Striker broke.

His frame of mind aside, Lindsey had questions that needed to be answered. She needed to know how the murder of Jamie Mills and the added police involvement would affect her search for Traci. She wanted to know what information Detective Landreth had given him about Rendezvous Productions. If Striker had a name or address or even a place to start.

"So where does this put us?" she asked as she draped her jacket over the back of a chair.

He barely spared her a glance as he worked off his coat and headed toward the living area. "That disk put Traci at the top of the cops' priority list. Before she was just a topless dancer with a warrant who'd skipped town. Nobody gave a damn because she didn't count for shit. Now she's connected to a murder—maybe two murders if you count the one on the disk—and the cops are actively looking for her. With a little luck the lab will lift some latent prints off the DVD or the case. Depending on how the disk was created, they might be able to find the sick sons of a bitches who killed that girl."

"Did Landreth give you anything on Rendezvous Productions?"

Without answering, Striker pulled the folded piece of paper from his coat. Lindsey came up beside him and looked down at the computer-generated report. "Titus Cross."

Striker read aloud. "He owns Full Circle Media, which is a parent company of Rendezvous Productions."

"Looks like he keeps his dirty little secret well hidden." Lindsey glanced down at the address. "I think we need to talk to him as soon as possible."

"Yeah, well, I think you need to sit this one out."

"I went with you to see Bledsoe."

"Bledsoe is a stupid junkie. Cross will cut your throat."

A dark wave of uneasiness skittered up her spine. "Don't shut me out, Striker. I need to do this."

He cut her a dark look. "Do what exactly?"

"Be involved." She met his gaze levelly. "Get this done."

Muttering a curse, he turned away from her and walked to the kitchen area. Lindsey watched as he bent and retrieved a glass and a bottle of scotch from a shelf. "Want some?" he asked.

"I don't drink."

"Yeah, well, I do some of my best thinking when I'm killing brain cells." He poured a generous amount, and with his back to her, drank deeply.

Realizing she was losing him, that he was angry and unsettled, Lindsey crossed to him. "Striker . . ."

He set the empty glass on the counter and slowly turned to her. She contemplated him, taking in the tight set of his broad shoulders. His world-weary eyes. The perpetual frown. The lines on his face seemed deeper today. It was as if the trip to police headquarters had aged him, wounded him.

"Are you okay?" she asked.

He gave her a look that told her in no uncertain terms not to dig, then walked into the living area and dropped onto the sofa. "I'm peachy."

"You seem upset."

He stared at her for an interminable moment, then he surprised her by laughing. But it was a harsh sound in the silence of the loft, and his hardened expression held no hint of humor. "That's not quite the right word, but for the sake of simplicity we'll go with it."

"You've been upset since we left police headquarters."

"Yeah, well, I've got a lot on my mind these days, Lindsey."

"I know it wasn't easy for you to walk in there."

"I think it would be best if you just let it go."

"Thank you for doing that."

"As much as I'd like to take credit for being gallant, I didn't really have a choice."

Lindsey watched him lean back then rest his head against the sofa back. She walked over to him and took the cushion beside him. He frowned at her as if anticipating what she was going to say next and knowing it was something he didn't want to hear.

"You've never talked to me about that day in the interview room," she said.

"You know what happened. You saw the video."

"I want to hear your side," she said quietly.

"I don't want to get into this with you."

"Maybe you don't get to pick and choose what we get into. As much as you'd like to try, you can't control what other people think or feel. You can't control what I think or feel. I don't know what you're going through. To be perfectly honest, I can't imagine. But I can see that it's tearing you up inside."

"What happened that day has nothing to do with you or Traci or this case," he said. "It's about me, and it's off limits, so drop it."

"Your frame of mind has everything to do with me and the case, and a hell of a lot to do with Traci, too. In case you've forgotten, I hired you to find her. I've given you my trust. I've given you my faith."

"I don't want your trust." He reached for his coat and started to rise. "I sure as hell don't want your faith."

She stopped him by putting her hand on his arm. "You accepted both of those things the day you agreed to help me find her."

"Then maybe you ought to do both of us a favor and fire me."

"I need your help," she said. "Can't you see that?"

Striker shook off her hand and surged to his feet. "Yeah, well, the clock is ticking. In a couple of weeks I'm off the case, whether you like it or not."

Lindsey watched him pace to the television and stand there with his back to her. She knew pressing him about what had happened that day was like prodding an injured beast with a stick. She knew his reaction would be volatile. She wanted to believe she was doing it because she needed to know he was going to continue working for her. But Lindsey was honest enough with herself to admit there was more to it. That her motivation was as murky and tangled and complex as the case had become.

"I know the mechanics of what happened that day," she said. "I saw the video clip this morning. I noticed the way the cops looked at you today."

He didn't react, didn't even turn to face her.

"But I have yet to hear you say a single word to me about what was going on inside you."

"You don't want to know my demons, Lindsey."

"You haven't even tried to defend yourself."

"I nearly killed a man with my bare hands." When he turned to her, his face was as cold and hard as granite. "How do you defend something like that?"

"By admitting you're human?"

"For chrissake, Lindsey, just because I'm a human being doesn't mean I'm not accountable for what I do."

"He raped and murdered your partner." He flinched, and she knew she'd struck a nerve. A nerve that was exposed and scraped raw. "I can't imagine the horror of that."

For several minutes the only sound came from the patter of rain against the skylight. Then he raised his head and looked at her with those dark, tortured eyes. "When I walked into police headquarters this afternoon, it hit home that my career is over. Until today, there's always been a part of me that believed I would be going back. That I would be able to resume my life." He turned abruptly, pressed the heels of his hands to his eyes. "It's not going to happen."

"I'm sorry," she said after a moment.

"Don't feel sorry for me, goddamn it," he snapped. "That's the one thing I do not need, now or ever."

It was the most emotion he'd shown since she'd known him, and it shocked her. She stared at him, not sure how to approach him and wondered, now that she'd pried open this Pandora's box of pain, if she could handle what would fly out of it.

After a moment, he lowered his hands and blinked at her as if waking from a dream, his eyes revealing something deeper than pain, something more profound than grief. They were ancient eyes, she thought. Eyes that knew the pain of a hundred generations. A thousand hearts that had been shattered. Souls that had had the hope ripped from them.

"For the last four months, I've been looking for someone to blame," he said. "Schroeder. The department. The legal system. My lawyer. Hell, I've even tried to lay the blame on my dead partner for getting herself into the situation that got her killed. The truth of the matter is, I have no one to blame but myself."

He turned, took several steps away from her and just stood there as if trying to pull himself together.

His shoulders tensed as she crossed to him. He jolted when she touched his arm. "I don't feel sorry for you. But I am sorry you have to go through this."

"If you're smart, you'll walk away before things get any more complicated."

She didn't know if he was talking about the case or whatever it was that was happening between them. The only thing she knew for certain at that moment was that she wasn't going to turn her back on him.

"Things are already pretty complicated," she said.

Slowly, he turned toward her. The anger was gone from his expression, but it had been replaced with something else that was every bit as powerful and infinitely more difficult to understand. "I'm not someone you want to get close to, Lindsey. It would be a profound understatement for me to tell you things are not going well in my life. I'm about to face trial for first-degree felony assault. I've been in self-destruct mode for four months. I don't have anything to offer you except a boatload of grief." He raised his hand as if to touch her face, then lowered it without making contact.

She offered him a smile, but it felt sad on her face. "Is that why you're trying so hard to keep me away?"

"I'm trying to keep you away, because we both know this could turn into something neither of us wants."

She struggled to stay calm, but her pulse was zinging. She didn't know where this would lead in terms of their relationship, or in terms of the case that had brought them together. All she knew for certain was that he was a good man who'd made a terrible mistake. A man who'd been driven to violence because something inside him had snapped in the face of unspeakable evil.

He stepped back, then walked over to the sofa, and sat down. For an interminable moment, neither of them spoke. Then he said, "Come here."

Lindsey's legs were trembling when she crossed to the sofa and sat down next to him. Leaning forward, he put his elbows on his thighs, let his hands dangle between his knees. "My partner's name was Trisha King. She was a good cop and a friend. Just over two years ago we were assigned the waterfront killer case."

"I remember hearing about the case on the news," Lindsey said. "Six women were killed."

"It was a tough case. The vics weren't just murdered. They were tortured. Butchered."

"Working on something like that must have been terrible."

"I've been a cop for eighteen years, and I swear I'd never seen anything like what this guy did to those women."

"Striker, I'm sorry . . ."

When she reached out to touch him, he stopped her by taking her wrist and moving her hand away. "We didn't realize we were dealing with a serial killer right away. He was atypical. He changed his methodology. Killed in different ways. Strangulation. Stabbing. Suffocation. He found different types of women. Prostitutes, mostly, but he also killed an elementary school teacher. He was an organized killer, but twice he killed in a very disorganized, frenzied way.

"One thing that remained consistent, however, was that he always left the body in a place where it would be found, usually near the waterfront. We soon came to understand that it was important to him for the police to find the body while it was still in relatively good condition. He wanted that because he was proud of his handiwork. He wanted to horrify us.

"There were other characteristics he never veered from. For example, all of his vics were tortured before they were murdered. That's how we finally realized we were dealing with a serial killer. We had five bodies in two years and the guy was escalating. The media were in a frenzy. It was an election year, and the mayor was taking a lot of heat. The feds were called in, but the chief of police kept Trisha and me on the case locally to assist."

He blew out a sigh. Lindsey looked down at his hands as he clasped them and saw that those strong, scarred hands were shaking.

"I know it sounds like a cliché," he said. "But some cases really do become personal. You see the kinds of horrific things this guy does to human beings, and it does something to you. I don't care how professional or tough a cop is, Lindsey, he feels it when he looks down at a body and can't tell what the hell he's looking at. He feels it when he has to tell the parents their girl won't ever be coming home.

"Trisha and I were working around the clock. We were beyond exhaustion. We'd seen things in the course of the investigation that had fundamentally changed us. Things we knew would haunt us for the rest of our lives. She talked about quitting a couple of times, but she wanted retirement. And we wanted this guy so bad we could taste it. We worked under the pretense of assisting the feds, but we had our own agenda. We shared information with them, but we basically worked our own case. A lot of it was done after hours, but we didn't give a shit. Neither of us had personal lives at that point. Trisha was divorced." He smiled. "There wasn't a woman breathing who was dumb enough to get involved with me. And so we worked. We had sources on the street. Snitches. We had a rapport with some of the prostitutes in the area where the killer had picked up at least two of the vics. They talked to us, agreed to let us know if anything unusual happened or if any of the johns were unusual or violent.

"One night Trisha and I had had a couple of drinks with some of the other cops down at a local cop bar. I was dead tired, half drunk, and on my way home, and I get a call on my cell . . ."

He didn't say anything for so long, Lindsey thought he was going to stop speaking. Then a breath shuddered out of him, and he continued. "Trisha's number came up on the display. I figured she'd had car trouble, or she'd forgotten to tell me something important about the case."

Striker raised his head, steepled his fingers, and rested his forehead against them. "It was the killer calling from Trisha's cell phone. I remember staring at the number and wondering how the hell he could be on the line. For a moment, I thought it was . . . I don't know, some kind of a fucking prank. Like maybe she'd left her phone at the bar. Then I heard her scream. And I knew he had her."

"Oh, God, Striker . . ."

"A hundred thoughts went through my brain in a fraction of a second. I wanted this guy. God, I wanted to get my hands on him . . ." Striker broke off for a moment, then continued. "I needed to call the feds. I needed to call the command center. But I had to keep this motherfucker on the phone. But . . . Christ . . ."

He rose from the sofa and strode from the living area, to a part of the loft where the light was dim. "I kept him talking. I drove like a maniac to the command center at police headquarters. I kept thinking if I could get the phone company involved, they would be able to narrow down the killer's location by a process called triangulation. But the entire time, Schroeder taunted me, telling me all the terrible things he was doing to Trisha. I was screaming at him, threatening him. I was at the end of my rope, and he knew it. He *enjoyed* it. Every time he set down the phone, Trisha would start screaming. I could hear her cursing him. I could hear her crying out my name. Begging me to stop him. I didn't know what Schroeder was doing to her, but I knew what he'd done to those other women. I had a picture of that branded into my brain. And her screams were unbearable to hear, because I knew he was hurting her. Really fucking hurting her. Doing things to her that were worse than death. I knew he was going to kill her. And I knew there wasn't a damn thing I could do about it.

"Trisha had been a cop a long time. She was savvy as hell, knew the ropes. She was tough and courageous, and she didn't take any shit off of anyone. To hear him break her down like that did something to me, Lindsey. It changed something inside me that will never be the same. I kept thinking about the things that must have been going through her mind while he was . . ." His voice broke, but he gathered himself and continued. "I kept thinking about her kids, what this was going to do to them.

"By the time I reached the command center twenty minutes later, Trisha was no longer screaming. The second I walked in the door, the son of a bitch disconnected. The feds used every bit of technology they had, but it took almost four hours to locate the tower and then narrow down the location of where the call had come from. It took another two hours to search all the warehouses in the area. It was dawn by the time we found the one where he'd taken her. He was long gone. The only sign that Trisha had ever been there was the blood."

Lindsey couldn't speak. Even if she could have found her voice, she knew there were no words to console him. She couldn't imagine the horror of what he'd been through. She couldn't imagine the helplessness or the outrage or fury he must have felt.

"The next day," he continued, "a guy walking his dog near Duwamish Head in West Seattle found what was left of her body. She'd been dismembered. Autopsy later revealed she'd been . . . tortured. He'd shot her up with amphetamines to keep her from passing out. He'd used tourniquets and started the dismemberment while she was still conscious."

He turned to her, lifted ravaged eyes to hers. "Trisha had two kids. She was a decent person. A damn good detective and the best partner I ever had. She didn't deserve to die like that.

"When I heard what he'd done to her, I forgot who I was. It no longer mattered that I was a cop. I wanted to fucking hurt him. I swear to God, if it hadn't been for the other cops in the interview room, I'd be facing a murder charge right now because I would have killed him."

chapter
22

STRIKER HAD RELIVED THAT HELLISH NIGHT A thousand times in the last four months, but he hadn't spoken of it. Not to the cops, who'd had plenty of questions. Not the FBI or his lawyer or the poor excuse for a shrink the department had forced him to see. The truth of the matter was he couldn't bear to even think of that night, though his mind seldom gave him respite. He wasn't sure why he was dredging it up now, laying the horror of it on Lindsey. But once he'd started talking, the words had come pouring out, like poison from a festering wound that had been lanced.

He didn't remember crossing to the entertainment center, but the next thing he knew he was leaning against it. He could feel the cold slick of sweat on his back, chilling him, and he felt cold all the way to his marrow. His hands were shaking, and somehow that shaking had moved up his arms and throughout his body until his legs no longer felt steady.

Vaguely, he was aware of the rain beating against the skylight. The flicker of lightning in his peripheral vision. He knew Lindsey was nearby. Even on the edge of a very steep precipice, he sensed her presence, the goodness of her heart, and the depth of her concern for him.

"Striker . . ."

He jolted when she put her hand on his arm. Every nerve in his body zinged at the unexpected contact, then zinged again with the sudden need for more. He wanted to pull her close. He wanted to take comfort in the warm softness of her body. The understanding in her eyes. The kindness he sensed in her soul. But he knew if he did any of those things, the situation would spiral out of control. He knew it would change things. Change his focus. Change the way he felt about her. Facing ten years in prison, he did not want that to happen. He did not want to walk into Walla Walla knowing he'd left something precious behind.

"How did they finally get Schroeder?" she asked quietly.

He struggled to regain his composure for an uncomfortable moment, then forced his mind back to that black moment in time. "The deputy chief took me off the case after Trisha was murdered. I wasn't fit to be working, so he put me on administrative leave." He pressed his fingers into his temples where a headache throbbed. "Six weeks later, the feds nailed Schroeder. Caught him in the act with a female agent posing as a hooker and wearing a wire. He picked her up. Took her to a warehouse. Feds got there just in time to keep him from cutting her. But it was worth the risk. There was trace evidence at this warehouse. He'd killed there before. Feds got DNA. We had him by the balls.

"I thought the moment would be satisfying. I thought knowing he was behind bars would make things better. Bring some closure. Justice for Trisha. But it didn't, Lindsey. Trisha was still dead. Her kids were still without a mother. And I could still hear her screaming my name that night."

He pulled in a deep breath, let it out slowly. "I kept in contact with the detectives while I was on leave. A few days after Schroeder was arrested, Hal Landreth mentioned he would be interviewing Schroeder at police headquarters. I found an excuse to drive to the Justice Center. I was standing in the hall when they brought that little son of a bitch up to the interview room. It was the first time I'd seen him face-to-face, and I couldn't get over how harmless he looked. Like somebody's kid brother, for chrissake.

"But when he looked at me, I saw something I recognized in his eyes. Something I'd seen before, in the eyes of other killers. I saw a capacity for unspeakable cruelty. Evil, if you believe in that sort of thing. I was standing in the corridor just outside the interview room. He passed right in front of me, so close I could smell the stench of cigarette smoke coming off his jumpsuit. He looked at me and said, "She died wondering why you never came." Then he smiled, and they took him into the interview room.

"I couldn't move for the longest time. I just stood there, feeling like I was going to explode. His words kept replaying in my head. What happened next is sketchy. I remember walking into the interview room. I remember Landreth and Cardona looking at me oddly. Schroeder's lawyer telling them to get me out of there. Then I went after Schroeder. I don't remember punching him. I don't remember hitting him so hard I broke two of my fingers. The next thing I know, I'm on the floor with a couple of cops on top of me, cuffing me.

"It took me less than two minutes to end a career that had taken me eighteen years to build." He shook his head, still disbelieving that he could have done something so self-destructive. "The cops didn't know what the hell to do with me. If Schroeder's lawyer hadn't been there, they might have tried to cover up the worst of what I'd done. But Schroeder was seriously injured. A half a dozen people had witnessed the incident. I was arrested and booked into the King County Jail on a felony assault charge. Two days later I was fired."

He lifted his shoulders, let them drop. "You know the rest of the story."

"I can't imagine how devastating this has been for you," she said.

"It's been tough. But of all the people who've been hurt by this, I have to say Trisha and her two little boys got the short end of the stick."

For the span of several heartbeats neither of them spoke. Striker listened to the rain and worked hard to pull all the broken pieces of himself back together.

"Striker?"

He didn't acknowledge her. He knew what would happen if he turned and looked into her eyes. He could feel the tension winding up inside him. He could feel the need pounding through his body. He was aware of her nearness. Her scent in his nostrils. The sharp zing of awareness between them.

She traced her fingers down his arm, and he slowly turned to face her. Her eyes were so lovely they took his breath. Within their depths he saw compassion and understanding, and he suddenly knew she was his only connection to what was good and decent and just in the world. A connection he needed desperately, because he could feel himself slipping away to a place he didn't want to go.

"I just gave you about a hundred reasons why you shouldn't get any closer to me," he said.

"I'm not going deny that what you did was wrong," she said. "But I will tell you that it doesn't make you a bad person. Maybe a good man who was pushed to the limits of his tolerance."

"I nearly killed a man with my bare hands," he said. "It was premeditated, for chrissake. Don't turn that into something heroic. It was vicious and revolting. It took me down to his level."

"He murdered your partner. Your best friend—"

"I was a cop, for God's sake. I jeopardized the investigation. Schroeder hasn't gone to trial yet. Lindsey, for God's sake, if he gets off on a tech because of what I did . . ." He couldn't finish the sentence. The thought of Schroeder roaming free to kill again was too vile. Worse,

Striker knew the responsibility for whatever Schroeder did would fall on his shoulders.

"Did the police department offer you any kind of counseling for what you went through?" she asked.

"Yeah, but I was never a big proponent of shrinks."

"Even now?"

"Now it doesn't matter."

She frowned as if she didn't agree, but she didn't argue. "What happens next? I mean, for you?"

"My trial is in two weeks. It's going to be a circus."

"Is there a chance you could be acquitted?"

"Not with the incident on tape."

"Are you looking at prison time? A fine? Probation? What?"

A tremor shook him at the mention of prison. He tried to stem it, but it was powerful and ran the length of his body like a mild electrical shock. "Ten years is the max."

"Oh, Striker . . . no."

"Because of the circumstances, I'll probably get a lesser sentence. My lawyer thinks I'll pull a three- or four-year sentence. I'll do two max."

"That's incredibly unfair," she said. "You've already paid for what you did a hundred times over."

"Life's unfair." He smiled, but it felt tight on his face, like it no longer fit. "Lindsey, I didn't want to lay this on you tonight. You've got enough to deal with trying to find your sister."

"I asked because I wanted to hear it from you, not some TV reporter. I'm glad you told me."

"Now you know I'm a certifiable nutcase."

"Yeah, well, Traci's a nut, and we get along really well." A tentative smile touched the corners of her mouth.

He looked at her lips, and all he could think was that he wanted to kiss her. That he didn't deserve her. That if he touched her he would somehow taint her. That if he didn't, he would die.

A clap of thunder caused him to jolt. Realizing the moment had gone on too long, he started to turn away. She stopped him by lifting her hand and setting it against his cheek. The intimate contact jolted him a second time. Softer, but the electricity that ran the length of his body was as powerful as any lightning bolt.

The contact shouldn't have meant anything. It damn sure shouldn't have been sexual. But it was on both counts. And he felt the simple truth of it in the deepest depths of his soul.

Turning his head slightly, he pressed a kiss to her palm. "Lindsey, you're . . . caught up in the moment."

"Maybe I am. Maybe you are, too. Maybe that's how things like this happen."

"These things are called mistakes."

"How can you know this is a mistake?"

He choked out a laugh, but it was an ugly sound that held no humor. "Because this is not going to have a fucking happy ending. You're not making this any easier."

"Life isn't about easy sometimes."

He looked into her eyes and saw all the things he didn't want to see. All the things that had drawn him to her, to this inevitable moment. And he knew that even if he couldn't have forever, he wanted the here and now. He wanted it with her. And he wanted it with the desperation of a man who knew just how fleeting the moment was.

His hands trembled when he put them on either side of her face. Leaning close, he brushed his lips across hers. Then he pulled away, stunned that such a gentle touch could rock him to his foundation.

"This is probably going to cost us something," he whispered.

"None of the good things in life are free."

Looking into her eyes, he suddenly knew that while she would not walk away from this unscathed, he would be the one to bear the scars.

chapter
23

LINDSEY KNEW SHE'D STEPPED OUT OF THE shallows and into the deep the instant his mouth made contact with hers. She knew she was in miles over her head. That the water was turbulent and deep and that no matter how well she swam, there was no way she could save herself from drowning.

He took her mouth with a barely concealed violence that stole her breath. She felt his hands in her hair, tilting her head so he could get a better angle. He didn't ask for permission to use his tongue. The intrusion startled her, stirred her, and she knew he was the kind of man who would take what he wanted and deal with the consequences later.

Lindsey opened to him, testing him, but he didn't give her a chance to change her mind. He kissed her so hard, his teeth bumped against hers. She tasted the rawness of his need, and it fed hers, turned it into something ravenous. Like dry kindling thrown onto a fire, the heat building, the flames leaping high to combust and incinerate.

The sound of the rain against the skylight reached a fever

pitch, pounding down in a relentless torrent. But Lindsey was only vaguely aware of the storm. The sensation of his mouth possessing hers consumed her. She'd been kissed by men before. But no kiss had ever burned. No kiss had ever made her heart pound so hard she could feel the hot pulse of it in her breasts, in her womb, between her legs.

She'd never considered herself a sexual being. She'd spent her early years feeling damaged and used and unattractive. She'd accepted a life without passion, knowing she would never miss what she did not know.

But deep inside she knew this man was going to change that. She knew he was going to show her something that would fundamentally change her, and that she wouldn't be able to go back to the way she was before.

A protest flitted through her brain when his hands closed over her breasts, a last-ditch effort to take control of the situation before they crossed the point of no return. He was too aggressive, too intense, overwhelming her, stealing the last of her rational thought. Already, she could feel her control slipping away . . .

He molded her flesh with his hands, and pleasure sparked and ignited in her brain. She arched, and he tugged her bra up and over her breasts. His calloused palms scraped deliciously over her nipples, then slid over her belly, then lower to the waistband of her jeans. Two seconds and the button was open, her zipper came down, and his hands were against the tender flesh of her pelvis. She felt his hands trembling against her, but she didn't know if the tremors were his or hers. The sensation of his fingers dipping into the waistband of her panties made her shiver. The power of the need unraveling inside her stunned her. She felt wild inside. Frantic for his touch. Breathless with anticipation.

All the while he kissed her, his tongue entwining with hers until she was mindless with wanting him. She should have known he would do that to her. That he would break her down to her most basic elements. That there would be no pretenses. Just Michael Striker with his troubled eyes and talented mouth and his hands on her body . . .

Lindsey had only been with one other man. A tepid relationship during college that had ended badly. Sex had never been a significant part of her life. The only reason she'd even bothered was to prove to herself that she was capable. That she was healed. That she had moved beyond the damage her stepfather had inflicted upon her.

Jerry Thorpe had stolen not only her childhood, but her ability to feel passion. Tonight, she knew Striker was going to give that back to her.

He spun her around so that they were facing the same direction, with her standing in front of him. She could feel the hard ridge of his arousal against her backside. He whispered something in her ear, but she couldn't hear the words over the roar of blood through her veins. He kissed her neck, nipped at her earlobe, trapped it between his teeth, then ran his tongue along her flesh down to her shoulder.

Lindsey could hear her breaths rushing in and out. She made a sound when he skimmed his hands over her sensitized nipples, brushed them over her belly, then lower. Another sound escaped her when his fingertips slipped beneath her panties, but it was a sound of impatience now. Something she'd never felt before. Something she'd never believed she was capable of. And for the first time in her life, she knew what it was to lust.

Desperate for him to be inside her, she grasped the waistband of her jeans and worked them down her hips. She could hear her pulse raging like a freight train. She bit her lip when he cupped her mound. She arched against his hand, opened her legs.

"Striker . . . for God's sake." She barely recognized her voice. It was raw and breathless. The voice of a woman she didn't know. A stranger who knew about secrets she'd never been able to unravel.

Her body went rigid when he parted her folds and slipped

two fingers inside her. Heat coiled, a knot in her womb that begged to be untangled and released. "Please," she whispered. Then he stroked her, and her body went liquid and hot. She opened wider, began to move with him, felt herself melting around him.

She cried out when her body began to contract. But he didn't stop, didn't give her a moment to catch her breath or think about what was happening. The orgasm sucked the oxygen from her lungs. Her legs went weak as the sensations battered her, overloaded her senses. Her vision blurred, and she closed her eyes, only to realize the world had begun to dip and spin. Still he stroked her. And she couldn't stop moving, accepting him, wanting more. "Striker . . ."

"Again," he whispered, stroking, stroking.

"I can't . . . do this."

"Yes, you can. Lindsey . . . let go."

The second orgasm shook her from the inside out. She could feel herself coming apart, every cell shattering. Her senses exploded as the stark pleasure of it overwhelmed her. Her thoughts scattered in a thousand directions, like fragile crystal thrown violently to the floor. Her control left her. She threw her head back and did nothing but feel. "Oh, God. Oh, *God!*"

Her legs buckled. She would have fallen, but he caught her, pulled her hard against him. "I've got you," he said in a low, uneven voice.

Her breaths tore raggedly from her throat as the aftershocks moved through her. Her thoughts ebbed and flowed, a tidal wave caught in the powerful grasp of a hurricane. "Striker, my God . . ." She was shaking uncontrollably. Sweat slicked her forehead, the back of her neck. She could feel the wet heat throbbing between her legs. Striker's arms around her, holding her like she'd never been held before. Too much sensation to absorb, and yet she knew it would never be enough.

"Beautiful . . ." He kissed her neck. "Lindsey . . ."

Awe mingled with disbelief that he could make her feel so profoundly. That she was capable of responding so powerfully. That a physical touch could shatter everything she'd ever known about herself.

His mouth was against her ear, and he was whispering her name. For the first time she realized how much she loved his voice. How much she loved the way he smelled. The solid feel of him against her.

The next thing she knew she was being swept into his arms and carried to the bed. A wave of embarrassment washed over her when she realized her jeans were halfway down her thighs. That her bra had been lifted over her breasts. That her hair was tangled around her shoulders.

"Striker."

He looked down at her, his expression intense. Without speaking he lifted her to him and kissed her hard on the mouth. He used his tongue and the pleasure of it drugged her into submission. She could feel the arousal stirring inside her again. Her pulse began to skitter madly. She felt as if she'd just stepped off one roller coaster and jumped onto another one that was faster and wider and higher than the first.

Turning her head slightly, she broke the kiss, sucked in a breath. "What are you doing?"

"Something I've wanted to do since the day you walked into my office."

"Carry me around?"

"Take you to bed."

"Hold on a second."

"I'm not sure I can." But he must have noticed something in her expression because he slowed his pace. "Are you okay with this?"

"I'm . . . better than okay."

He tried to kiss her again, but she turned her head and his expression became concerned. "I've got protection," he said. "I mean, if that's what you're worried about."

"It's not. I mean, of course, we should be responsible,

but that's not what . . ." She wasn't sure how to finish the sentence. She wasn't even sure what she was going to say to him. All she knew was that something magical had just happened to her. It meant something to her in ways he may not understand. And it was suddenly very important that she explain.

They reached the bed and he let her slide gently to her feet. Automatically, she reached for the waistband of her jeans to tug them up, but he stopped by touching her hand. "Please don't," he said softly. "I like seeing you. Like this."

Embarrassed, she tried to look away, but he set his fingers beneath her chin and forced her gaze to his. "If you don't want to do this . . . I'm okay with it," he said.

She looked into his eyes, found herself taken aback by the intensity of his gaze, that she was the sole focus of that intensity. "What we just did," she began. "I mean, what just happened . . . between us . . ." She struggled with words that wouldn't come, trying hard to maintain some semblance of composure. "That's never happened to me before."

A heavy brow quirked. She could see that he was trying to understand and suddenly wished she hadn't breached the subject. But there was another part of her that wanted to share this with him. Let him know he'd given her something she'd never before experienced. Something precious that proved to her beyond a shadow of a doubt that she was whole and healed.

She stared at him, aware of the heat flooding her cheeks. That he was looking at her oddly, trying to figure out what she was trying to tell him. "I mean, I've never . . . you know."

"Had an orgasm?" he asked.

She knew it was a silly reaction, considering what they'd just shared, but she blushed to her bones. "Just . . . forget it," she said and put her face in her hands.

"Don't be embarrassed," he said gently.

When she didn't raise her head, he took her wrists and

gently eased her hands from her face. Feeling foolish, she
looked up at him, realized with some surprise that he was
smiling at her. A genuine smile that softened the hard
lines of his face. Smoothed out the frown lines between his
brows, deepened the laugh lines that cupped his mouth.

She studied his less than perfect face, wondered why
she'd never realized before just how attractive he was.
"You look really good when you smile."

"It's not every day a beautiful woman tells me I just
gave her her first orgasm. That's quite a coup for a guy."

She made a halfhearted attempt to pull away, but he
stopped her by kissing her. He took it slow this time, and
the sensation of his mouth against hers eased the sting of
embarrassment and aroused her all over again.

"Don't let it go to your head," she said.

He laughed, but his expression remained intense. Never
taking his eyes from hers, he skimmed his hands over her
shoulders, along her neck, then brushed his knuckles over
her cheeks. "I don't know if I deserve something like that,
but I'm flattered as hell."

She shivered when he ran his hands down her sides to
rest on her hips. Holding her in place, he pressed against
her. A tremor ran through her when she felt the steel rod of
his erection against her belly. Arousal flared, but it was
tempered with nerves this time, and she suddenly felt vulnerable. "I'm probably not very good at this," she blurted.

"You don't really believe that, do you?"

"I don't know what to believe at the moment. You make
it difficult to think. That's scaring me because I like to
think things through before I leap."

"Probably a good policy," he said. "But sometimes I like
to take things a little more recklessly and just jump."

"How do you know it's going to be a safe landing?"

"You don't," he said. "But sometimes that's half the fun."

chapter
24

STRIKER WANTED TO RAVISH HER. HE WANTED TO plunder her mouth. Possess her in every way a man could possess a woman. He could feel the need crawling inside him. The sexual tension winding up. The urgency pushing him to recklessness. His nerves jumping with every beat of his heart.

But as he lowered her to the bed and pressed his mouth to hers, he sensed the fragility inside her. Intellectually he knew Lindsey Metcalf was not a fragile person. He knew she was strong-willed and independent and stubborn as hell. But he sensed there were things about her he didn't know. Secrets he hadn't yet unraveled. Layers he had yet to explore. And that understanding gave him the restraint he needed to take things slowly.

But the taste of her mouth maddened him. The feel of her slender body beneath his brought his pulse to a fever pitch. He couldn't remember the last time he'd been with a woman. Before the nightmare Schroeder had brought to his life. Before he'd sequestered himself away from the human race. He'd barely thought of a woman since the night his partner had died.

He desperately wanted to believe this was about sex. In a couple of weeks he was going to prison for untold months of forced celibacy. He wanted some time with a woman before he went in. He knew this could never lead to anything. Lindsey knew what he was facing; he'd been straight with her from the get-go. She knew it couldn't mean anything.

But it did, and that knowledge sent a ripple of panic up his spine. Striker didn't panic. It simply wasn't part of his persona. He was a coolheaded cop who'd seen it all. Nothing fazed him. Nothing shook him.

But when he looked into Lindsey's eyes, he knew he was only kidding himself. Lindsey Metcalf was definitely going to make him lose his cool. She was going to shake him up like he'd never been shaken before.

Her face was flushed. Her mouth was chafed from his whiskers. "Turn out the light," she whispered.

He barely heard her over the raging of his pulse. "I want to see you."

"I can't. Please, turn out the light."

He told himself it didn't matter. But it did. It mattered a lot because he wanted to see every curve and secret place of her body. He wanted to see her hair spread out on the pillow. He wanted to touch every beautiful inch of her. He wanted to see his hands trembling on her body. He wanted to see her writhing beneath his ministrations. He wanted to look into her eyes when her release came and she cried out his name.

Moving away from her he got up and walked to the nightstand beside the bed. He removed a candle he'd gotten for Christmas and never taken out of the package. He found matches, lit the candle, then switched off the light and turned to her.

Lindsey was on her knees in the center of the bed. Candlelight flickered in her eyes and cast golden highlights on her hair. Striker stared at her, taken aback by her beauty, by the feelings echoing through his body, through his heart.

"Better?" he asked.

"The candle's a nice touch, Striker. You entertain the ladies often, or are you just into aromatherapy?"

He grinned. "My sister and niece came to see me right before Christmas. My niece is twelve and thought I needed some domestic touches."

"Tea and candles, huh?" She smiled. "That's very sweet."

"I think she felt sorry for me." He smiled back at her.

"Vanilla?"

"Mocha."

"Hmmm. Nice."

He knelt on the bed, then moved toward her on his knees, and set his mouth against hers. She tasted like sin. Hot, wet, sweet, and tempting as hell. Need coiled and snapped inside him. His control teetered, but he pulled back just in time to keep himself from devouring her.

Breaking the kiss, he reached for the hem of her sweater and drew it over her head. She lifted her arms. The sweater came off in his hands, and he tossed it aside. He watched her hair cascade over her shoulders. Like silk, he thought. Then her eyes met his, and within their depths he saw emotions he didn't want to see.

Reaching out, he released the clasp of her bra. She shivered as he worked the scrap of lace down her arms. The sight of her took his breath away. Her breasts were upswept with large areola and small, pointed nipples that were puckered tightly. The need inside him burgeoned. Urgency burned him, a fever that heated with every beat of his heart. He'd wanted to take this slowly, as much for his pleasure as for hers. But he knew that wasn't going to happen.

At least not the first time.

She didn't stop him when he began to work her jeans lower. Even in the dim light from the candle he could see how beautifully she was put together. Her white skin looked golden in the glow of the candle. Her waist was incredibly small. Her hips were nicely curved. An involuntary sound escaped him when the dark curls at the juncture of her thighs came into view. He couldn't take his eyes off of her as she took off the jeans and tossed them aside.

"You're shaking," he said.

Taking his hand, she pressed it against her heart, and he could feel it beating out of control beneath his palm.

He took her hand, set it against his chest where his own heart raged. "Me, too."

He worked off his shirt then quickly did away with his jeans. He was aware of her watching him, saw her eyes widen when his swollen sex came into view.

"I don't think this is going to be slow," he said.

"I think you're right."

Taking her in his arms, he lowered her to the bed and came down on top of her. Her hair spread out behind her like auburn silk. Her body was slender and soft and warm beneath him. Arousal pounded in his groin. The urgency was like a lava flow, burning through his body, consuming everything until there was nothing but him and her and the moment between them.

He could feel her trembling beneath him as he eased her legs apart with his knees. She was already moving against him, moaning a little, driving him insane. He could hear her breaths rushing between her clenched teeth. He knew better than to look into her eyes at that moment. But he wasn't a strong enough man not to, and he knew he would be seeing her face for a very long time to come. That it would haunt him on all the lonely nights that lay ahead.

Striker could deal with his attraction to her. He could deal with wanting her. He could even deal with touching her, having sex with her. What he couldn't deal with, he realized, was caring for her. And he could already feel the pain of that leaching into his brain.

Taking her face between his hands, he kissed her hard on the mouth. A groan rumbled up inside him when she reached down and guided him to her. He closed his eyes against the explosion of ecstasy when he slid deeply into her heat and began to move within her.

"Lindsey . . . Oh, God . . ."

As the pleasure crashed down around him, he had to remind himself that this couldn't mean anything. That it couldn't mean anything to either of them no matter how much he wanted it to.

But as her cries echoed inside his head, he knew he'd made a fatal mistake. He knew being with her like this was going to cost him more than he'd bargained for. He knew it was going to cost her something, too. He only hoped that when the time came for him to do the right thing, he would be strong enough to see it through.

Striker lay awake in his bed and watched the alarm clock on the night table advance to three A.M. Beside him, Lindsey slept with a deep stillness that, he knew, was a result of total physical and emotional exhaustion. He was exhausted, too, if he wanted to be honest about it. Tired in every way a man could be tired. But he knew from experience he wouldn't sleep.

He wanted to believe it was the case that was gnawing at his brain, keeping him awake. But he knew it had more to do with the woman lying next to him. What was happening between them. Not only the sex, but the way he felt about her. Those things disturbed him in a way the case didn't. Touched him in a place he didn't want to be touched. He didn't have the slightest idea how he was going to handle that.

Restless, he rose and stepped into his jeans, then walked to the living area. For a full minute, he just stood there, uncertain what to do, trying desperately to ignore the part of him that wanted to go back to the bed and make love to her until he couldn't feel anything but the hot sheath of her body around his.

For a little while she'd made him feel human. She'd made him laugh. Made him feel like a man. And for a few precious hours he'd forgotten about Traci Metcalf and Norman Schroeder and the prison sentence hanging over his head. He'd forgotten about the eighteen years of his life he'd thrown away. But the one thing he hadn't been able to put out of his mind was the cold hard reality that no matter how right it felt to be with her, he had to make sure she walked away when the time came.

The irony that he would find someone like her at a time in his life when he couldn't open his heart was bittersweet. A man could spend a lifetime looking for what he had found with Lindsey. She was all the things Striker had ever wanted. Everything he wasn't. She was light to his darkness. Laughter to the utter silence of his heart. Goodness to the shadows of his soul.

He knew he was a son of a bitch for sleeping with her. He had no right to draw her any more deeply into his life. But he hadn't been strong enough to resist the pull to her. And he knew if she reached out to him again, he would make the same mistake all over again.

Wanting to lose himself in work, he flipped through the compact disks they'd brought from Traci's house. He'd planned on skimming through each disk on the outside chance that something useful would stand out. A familiar face. An identifiable location. A name in the credits. Anything that might give them the break they so desperately needed.

He picked up the first disk and slipped it into the DVD player, then used the remote to turn on the television. For several minutes he watched the second-rate video, the second-rate actors, the poor camera work and tried hard to keep things in perspective. When Traci came onto the screen, the outrage jumped through him with a force that

surprised him. She looked like a younger, wilder version of
Lindsey. A young woman with a pretty face that might
have looked carefree on the surface. But Striker saw the
sadness in her eyes. Eyes that were ancient for a woman
who hadn't yet seen her twenty-fifth birthday.

He thought about the things Lindsey had told him about
their stepfather, and for the first time Traci's foray into
pornography made some sort of sense. The notion of some
twisted bastard putting his hands on two innocent girls outraged him. His years in law enforcement had shown him
the ravages of that kind of abuse.

Determined to keep his mind on the case, he picked up
a pen and pad of paper, then scooped up the remote and began to skip through the tracks. But again and again his
thoughts returned to Lindsey. In his mind's eye he saw the
way she'd looked at him when he'd been inside her. He
heard the sweetness of her voice when she'd cried out his
name. The surprise and awe in her expression when he'd
brought her to peak.

She was inside his head, he realized. Much worse, she
was dangerously close to his heart. A place that, until this
moment, he'd thought was as dead as the rest of him. Lindsey had proven him wrong, proven to him that he was as
alive as he'd ever been, that he was capable of wanting, that
he was capable of hurting in ways he didn't want to hurt.

"Damn it," he muttered into the darkness.

Leaning against the sofa back, he put the heels of his
hands to his eyes and tried not to think. But Striker knew
what he had to do. Find Traci. Close the case. Send Lindsey back to Ohio. Back to her business and her wholesome
life where there wasn't some fucked up ex-cop messing
things up for her. Once she was gone, he could concentrate
on getting through the trial. On getting his life in order before he went to prison. Psyching himself up for a few years
behind bars . . .

He looked at the television, disgusted by the naked

bodies twisting on the screen. He tried to turn off his mind. Tried to lock out thoughts of Lindsey and all the things that might have been.

But as exhaustion tugged him down and into a troubled sleep, it was Lindsey he saw. It was Lindsey he wanted. And it was Lindsey who broke his heart.

chapter
25

STRIKER AWOKE WITH A START. HE SAT BOLT upright on the couch, his heart pounding, his breaths tearing from his throat. For several seconds he stared into the semi-darkness of his loft, shaking, telling himself it was just a dream.

But the nightmare clung to him. He could still hear her screams. He could still feel the terror and panic and fury clamping down on him like the jaws of some giant carnivore. He'd had the dream a hundred times in the last four months, but he never grew used to the horror of it.

Tonight, the nightmare had taken on a particularly ominous twist because it hadn't been Trisha screaming his name, but Lindsey . . .

"Striker."

He jolted at the sound of his name, spun to see her standing a few feet away. She looked rumpled and grumpy and sexy as hell standing there wrapped in his shirt. The hem fell to mid-thigh, revealing shapely legs and soft flesh. Her feet were bare, and for the first time he noticed how pretty they were. Slender. Delicate. She painted her toe-nails a deep, burgundy red.

Remembering the way she'd wrapped her legs around him when they'd made love, Striker's pulse spiked. He could actually feel the hot rush of blood to his groin. He'd made love to her twice, but already he was hard and throbbing and wanting her with an intensity that verged on madness.

"Go back to bed," he said.

She came around the sofa, her eyes flicking from the notepad to the television and back to him. "What are you doing?"

"What does it look like I'm doing?" he snapped. "I'm working."

"Oh. Well, it's just that it's five o'clock in the morning . . ."

"I know what time it is."

"You can't sleep?"

"I just want to get this done."

She craned her head to get a look at the notes he'd scribbled before falling asleep. "Did you find something?"

For an instant he wanted to tell her that in the course of skimming the credits of four DVDs, he'd discovered that Titus Cross had financed more than one pornographic movie and that Traci had been the lead in two of them. But there were too many other things going on inside him to engage her in conversation. Too much temptation. Too much anger because things weren't working out the way he'd wanted them to. He told himself things would be different come dawn. They could go back to the way things were before he'd slept with her.

But Striker knew they couldn't go back. He knew things could never be the same. And he was furious with himself for letting that happen. The only person close enough for him to strike out at was Lindsey. He went after her with both barrels.

"Don't think that just because we slept together things

are going to be different," he said. "Don't think I'm going to suddenly turn into a nice guy, because I'm not, and you'd be doing both of us a big favor if you accepted that right here and now."

Her expression turned wary. He could see her mind working, knew she was trying to read between the lines, decipher his anger, understand why he was taking it out on her. He hated doing that to her. There was a very large part of him that wanted to go to her and make promises he couldn't keep. But he knew that would only make things worse because as surely as he was falling for her, the day was going to come when he would have to walk away.

"Why are you angry?" she asked.

"Because I'm a son of a bitch. Because I don't want you getting the wrong idea about things."

"Striker, where is this coming from?"

"You want me to spell it out for you?"

"I suppose you're going to have to, because I have no idea why you're so angry."

He frowned. "What happened between us . . ." Because he didn't quite know how to describe everything that had transpired between them, he let his voice trail. "I don't want it to change things. I don't want things between us getting complicated."

"You didn't seem to mind either of those things a few hours ago," she said.

"We had sex, Lindsey. It was good. It was better than good. But that's all it was. Don't let it change your mind about me."

"I appreciate your looking out for my best interest."

She was starting to get angry; he could see it in her eyes. He told himself that was what he wanted. That in the long run, it would make things a hell of a lot easier for both of them. But he felt as if he were about to shatter something precious and fragile and good.

"I'm trying to be honest," he said.

"You're trying to push me away, and I don't understand why."

"Things got . . . intense between us. I don't want you to get good sex confused with something it's not."

For an instant she stared at him as if he'd just put a bullet in her stomach. Then she jerked the shirt more tightly about her and stepped back. "You are right about one thing, Striker. You are a son of a bitch."

Self-loathing filled him as he watched her turn away and begin to gather up her clothes from the night before. He hated hurting her. She didn't deserve to be treated like that. But when he thought of how much more difficult it would be if things got any more serious between them, he knew he didn't have a choice.

Sighing, he scrubbed a hand over his face and watched as she scooped the last of her things from the floor. He could tell from her jerky movements that she was furious. He assured himself he was doing the right thing. For her. For himself.

But it felt so damn wrong.

Once she'd gathered her clothes, she stalked to the shower room to dress. He let her go. Even though he'd seen, tasted, and touched every inch of her body, he knew she wouldn't dress in front of him now. He'd hurt her, humiliated her, and there was no way she would make herself vulnerable.

Two minutes later she reappeared, fully dressed, with her overnight bag slung over her shoulder. Without looking at him or speaking to him, she started toward the door.

Realizing her intent, Striker rose from the sofa. He hadn't meant to push her so far she would want to leave. He didn't want her alone. "Where are you going?" he asked.

Glaring at him, she twisted the deadbolt, reached for the knob, and tugged open the door. "None of your business."

"Lindsey, you can't leave."

"You can't tell me what to do," she said and stepped into the foyer.

He followed, set his hand on her shoulder. "Lindsey—"

She slapped his hand away. "Get your hands off me."

He raised his hands. "Calm down and let's talk about this rationally."

"There's nothing to discuss. Just . . . stay away from me, Striker. I mean it." She started for the main door that would take her to the street. "Bill me for the rest of your charges. In case I forgot to mention it, you're fired."

Striker went after her. "It's not safe for you to be running around Seattle half-cocked."

"You have no say in the matter."

"I'm not going to let you do this."

"You touch me, and I swear I'll call the cops and press charges against you for assault."

But he was already upon her, his hands on her shoulders, turning her to face him. He wasn't expecting her to go on the offensive, but that's exactly what she did. He managed to dodge the first blow. The second was openhanded and made contact with his jaw with a loud *crack!* His head snapped back. He saw stars, felt his left eye tear up.

Striker shook his head to clear it, reminded himself he'd deserved it, and realized he was going to have to do some very fast talking to keep the situation under control. "Wait a minute."

Belatedly he remembered her green belt in karate, but either she wasn't very good or her emotions were messing up her concentration because her next punch went wide, barely grazing his temple. She tried to kick him, but he danced aside, and she ended up losing her balance. He caught both her biceps with his hands and gave her a gentle shake.

"Calm down and listen to me," he growled.

"Let go," she snarled. "You had no right to treat me like that."

"You're right. I didn't. I'm sorry."

"Striker, I mean it. Let go of me. I want to leave." She tried to twist away, but he muscled her back into the loft.

Using his foot to close the door, he put her against the wall, locked her in with his arms. She was breathing hard. Her hair hung in her face. Fury boiled in her eyes. If she had been armed at that moment, he figured he'd be taking his last breath. But she wasn't, and he suddenly knew this moment was somehow profound, that he was about to make a decision that would affect the rest of his life.

"Lindsey, listen to me for a second. Please."

She tried to move aside, but he grabbed her shoulders and pushed her back. "I'm sorry I said those things to you."

She looked up at him, hurt shimmering in her eyes. "Sorry doesn't cut it. You were deliberately cruel."

Her gaze went right through him, cut him to his core, and the pain was so great that for a moment he couldn't get his breath. He stared at her, shamed by what he'd done, shocked by what he felt, more terrified than he'd been in a very long time, because he didn't know how to handle this. "I did it to protect you."

"You don't protect someone by hurting them."

"I'm not a man you want to get involved with right now," he said.

"That's an incredibly stupid thing to say. In case you haven't noticed, I'm already involved with you!"

"Lindsey, I'm going to prison, for chrissake. Think about that for a moment. Once I'm convicted, I will have no job. No future. My life savings has been wiped out. I have nothing to offer you."

"You're not in charge of my life, Striker. I am. However much you'd like to try, you can't dictate what I feel or what I do."

"I'm trying to keep you from making a mistake, damn it. The longer we let this continue, the harder it's going to be when I have to walk away."

"You're not being honest with me. You're not even being honest with yourself."

"Sometimes honest doesn't work."

"That is *such* a cop-out!"

"I'm trying to be smart about this. I'm trying to stop things before they go too far."

She stared at him for an infinite moment. The anger faded from her expression, and her eyes turned dark and liquid within the pale frame of her face. In their depths he saw all the things he did not want to see. Respect. Compassion. Understanding. Something else he didn't want to acknowledge. But in a small corner of his mind he knew what she was going to say next. He knew it was going to shatter him.

"Things have already gone too far," she whispered.

"Don't," he said in a ragged voice.

"If you can't handle that, go ahead and run."

He ground his teeth. "You don't know me."

"I know enough about you to know you're a good man. That you're decent and kind and that you care about all the right things."

"I almost killed a man with my bare hands!"

"You didn't."

"They stopped me."

"Did they, Striker? Did they, *really?* Do you know how far you would have taken it? Do you know for a fact you would have killed him?"

"You weren't there," he said. "You don't know how it went down."

"No, I wasn't there. But I know you wouldn't have killed him. You can spend the rest of your life punishing yourself by believing otherwise. But I know you would have stopped. Whether he deserved it or not, you would have spared him, because that's what kind of man you are."

He stared at her, his heart beating wildly, her words pounding inside his brain like a drum. He knew he should move away from her, but the inner warning came too late.

She was standing too close. So close he could smell the sweetness of her breath. He could feel the warmth coming off her body to tantalize his. The need to touch her overwhelmed him, transcended logic, did away with the last of his common sense.

And suddenly he knew he'd only been fooling himself. Deep down inside he knew there was no way he could walk away from her. Not when the need to take her into his arms was more powerful than the need to take his next breath.

He didn't remember reaching for her or pulling her to him. But the next thing he knew she was in his arms, and he was crushing her against him. Saying her name. Breathing in her scent. Memorizing every inch of her because he knew he was going to need that to sustain him in the coming months.

He devoured her mouth with a desperation he felt all the way to his bones. He fed on the sweetness of her kiss like a man deprived. His control fractured, and he accepted the reality that there was no place for control when it came to his hunger for her.

As he tumbled into the mindless oblivion of his own passion, he realized he would never get enough of her. He would never be able to stay away from her. Not until the steel bars and concrete walls of prison separated them. She had become a dangerously addictive narcotic. He was a junkie, willing to sell his soul for one more high. One more touch, one more night.

Just one more kiss . . .

chapter
26

LINDSEY DIDN'T KNOW WHAT HAD BEEN UNLEASHED within him, but it was fierce and overwhelming and quickly spiraling out of control. She tasted desperation on his mouth. She felt it in the way he ran his hands over her body, the way he held her, as if he were afraid she was slipping away. She wanted to tell him that was not the case. That she was here with him, for him, that she would be there for him when he needed her.

He didn't give her the chance to say any of those things.

He kissed her with an intensity that stole her breath, overwhelmed her senses, shattered her emotions. But while her intellect told her to take it slowly, her body didn't want to wait.

He lifted the hem of her sweater. She raised her arms, let him tug it over her head. He tossed it aside. His eyes were dark when he pulled back to look at her. The intensity of his gaze shook her inside. If she thought she'd been in control of the situation, one look into his eyes and she realized she was not.

"I want you," he said darkly. "Right now. Right here."

Never taking his eyes from hers, he quickly unfastened her bra and pulled the tiny straps down her shoulders. Without touching her, he unbuttoned her jeans, unzipped them and tugged them down her hips. Lindsey could feel the tremors rising up inside her. The heat of arousal pulsing between her legs, and the power of it shocked her. When the jeans were down to her knees she stepped out of them and kicked them aside.

She gasped when Striker cupped her mound through her panties. Vaguely, she was aware of the cold wall behind her back. The hot rush of blood through her veins. A sound tore from her throat when he bent and took her nipple into his mouth. She could feel her womb contracting in response, anticipation and tension building to a fever pitch.

He suckled her, nipping at her with his teeth, taking her to the edge of pain, but never quite there. She ran her fingers through his hair, pulling him to her, wanting his mouth on her, his body inside hers. He laved her nipple with his tongue. She arched, offering her other breast and he took it, sucking and nipping until she couldn't breathe.

The pleasure consumed her when his hands closed over her breasts and he took the hardened nubs of her nipples between his thumbs and forefingers. The rest of the world melted away when he knelt and she felt his mouth on her belly. His tongue left a wet path as he trailed kisses to her navel, then moved inexorably lower. Her knees began to shake when he snagged the waistband of her panties and tugged them down her hips. Lindsey closed her eyes, knowing what would happen next. The intellectual side of her brain told her to stop before it went too far. But she knew they had already crossed the point of no return.

She made a sound when he opened her. Then his mouth was on her and she went out of her mind. The world around her ceased to exist when he began to lap at her. The intimacy of the act shattered her. Physically. Emotionally.

She'd never made herself this vulnerable to another living soul. The need to protect herself was great. But the pleasure pounding through her refused to listen to reason.

She opened to him and he stroked her with his tongue. Her vision dimmed when the orgasm crashed over her. She could feel her body contracting. His wet mouth moving against her. Sensation pummeling her endlessly. "Striker! Oh, God. Oh, *God!*"

Vaguely she was aware of his hands working to unbutton his jeans. His mouth hot against her belly. His whiskers chafing her breasts. And she was mad for him, her body writhing, her breaths coming in short, quick bursts.

Then his hands were on her hips, lifting her, pressing her against the wall. Lindsey's gaze snapped to his. A hundred emotions boiled within the depths of his gaze. For the first time since she'd known him, his face was unshuttered. His eyes were clear, and when she looked into them, she felt as she could see all the secrets he worked so hard to hide from the rest of the world. The deep well of vulnerability. The decency and goodness in his heart. The grief and anger that shadowed his soul.

"I want more than just now, Lindsey." His voice shook as he looped his arms behind her knees and opened her legs. "I want tomorrow. I want next week. Next month. I want you a hundred years from now."

It was the most emotion he'd ever shown her, and it moved her to tears. She could feel the sobs building in her throat. The tears squeezing through her lashes. And even as her emotions unraveled, she could feel her body anticipating his.

"Wrap your legs around me," he said, kissing the tears from her cheeks.

Lindsey cried out when he entered her. The pleasure was blinding and zinged through her body like a lightning strike. He began to move within her, and her head went back against the wall. She arched, taking him deeply, and felt the waves begin to break. Bending his head, he took her nipple into his mouth, laving the sensitive tip with his tongue. A groan escaped her. It was an animalistic sound, but she could no more hold it in than she could stop the reaction of her body to his. She could feel his muscles trembling with the strain of lifting her, of holding her against the wall as he slid in and out of her with long, steady strokes.

A second orgasm built inside her with surprising speed. A storm she knew would be violent and swift and powerful when it struck. She knew it would sweep her away to a place she'd never been. That it would shatter her into a thousand pieces. That those pieces would never be put together the same way they had been before.

She rocked her hips forward and an instant later came apart in his arms. She felt herself scattering, like debris caught in a tornado. She cried out his name only to realize she was sobbing. His mouth came down on hers to swallow her sobs.

And even though no one could ever take this moment away from them, she knew fate would soon step in and steal something far more precious.

Striker brewed coffee while Lindsey showered. They'd made love twice, but it still took every ounce of self-discipline he possessed to keep himself from walking into the shower room to join her. He imagined warm water sluicing over her skin. Steam rising all around. He'd been inside her less than twenty minutes ago and already he was hard, wanting her with a ferocity that verged on insane. He wanted her in ways that went beyond physical. Beyond emotional. Beyond anything he'd ever experienced in his life.

It was scaring the living hell out of him.

He was a fool for letting himself feel so much for her when his life was in a shambles. It was time to get back to reality. Back to his screwed up life. His upcoming trial. His temporary career as a P.I. And a missing person case he needed to tie up as quickly as possible.

Sighing, Striker gathered his notes and the stills he'd printed and took them to the living area where he spread them out on the coffee table. He looked down at the report on Rendezvous Productions that Hal Landreth had given him and wondered how Titus Cross fit into the puzzle. Cross wasn't the kind of guy to get his hands dirty, but then he had the money to hire someone else to do his dirty work for him and still remain squeaky clean. He'd made millions from pornography and kept it neatly buried in a mountain of companies and subsidiaries with legitimate-sounding names. Striker wondered if he was involved in snuff. He wondered how far a man like Cross would go to protect himself.

The questions taunted him with disturbing possibilities. Possibilities made even more disturbing by the reality that in a couple of weeks he wasn't going to be around to keep Lindsey out of harm's way if someone decided she was asking too many questions. Once his trial began, his life would no longer be his own. The best thing he could do for her at this point was work the case as hard as he could. Best-case scenario, he would find Traci. Worst case, he would have to refer the case to another P.I. But no matter what the outcome, he would have to persuade Lindsey to go back to Ohio. It wouldn't be easy, but then he was no stranger to manipulation; he could be cruel if he needed to. He would do whatever it took to keep her safe.

"What are you working on?"

He looked up to see her approach the living area. She was wearing faded jeans and a fuzzy black sweater. Clunky boots. Her hair was freshly washed and still damp on the ends. She wasn't wearing any makeup, but she'd slicked something shiny on her lips.

For several seconds he just sat there, looking at her, wondering if she had any idea how much she meant to him.

He looked down at his notes. "I'm going to pay a visit to Titus Cross."

"I'm going with you." She was already reaching for her coat. She looked excited. Hopeful.

"Lindsey . . ."

She snagged her purse. Striker rose, but didn't go to her. He didn't like feeling so off kilter, but for the life of him he couldn't seem to get his feet under him. "I want you to promise me something," he said.

"You know I will, if I can."

"My trial starts in less than two weeks. In the interim, I'll do everything I can to find Traci. I'll give it my all, no holds barred. But once my trial starts, I want you to promise me you'll go back to Ohio."

She blinked at him, and a sound of disbelief broke from her lips. "How can you even ask that?"

"Because I think we're into something dangerous, and I don't want you hurt."

"Striker, I know this isn't what you want to hear, but I can't leave this unfinished. I need to be here."

"I understand your wanting to find your sister, Lindsey. But you have to see my point, too."

"I think it's unfair for you to ask me to leave this unfinished."

"It's not like you'll be giving up on her, for God's sake. I know a private detective I can refer the case to. He's a friend of mine. An ex-state trooper. A good guy. Honest and experienced with missing persons. I'll call him, brief him on the case. He can pick up where I left off. I'll pay for everything. You can run the show from Columbus."

"I'm sorry, but I can't leave until I find Traci."

Striker could feel the desperation building inside him. He hated caring so much, having so little control, feeling so utterly helpless. "Someone has tried to hurt you three times already, damn it! Someone assaulted you at Traci's house. They drugged you at Club Tribeca. Who knows what the guy at the shipyard would have done if he'd gotten his hands on you. Look what he did to Jamie Mills!"

"I'm not going to have this conversation with you."

She started to walk away, but he reached out and snagged her arm. "Don't walk away from me," he growled.

"Don't ask me to turn my back on her, damn it, because I won't."

He felt the words like a noose being placed around his throat and drawn inexorably tighter. He stared at her, wanting her with every cell in his body, furious with her because she wouldn't listen to reason.

He honestly didn't think he could handle it if something happened to her. But he knew her well enough to know she wasn't going to acquiesce. While he admired her loyalty and determination, the reality of it was killing him.

chapter
27

LINDSEY SAT IN THE PASSENGER SEAT OF THE JEEP and watched the rain slap the window. Beside her, Striker wove through morning rush-hour traffic with all the recklessness of Mad Max careening through the desert. He'd been silent and brooding since leaving the loft ten minutes earlier. She hated seeing him so angry, but there was no way she was going to go back to Ohio without seeing this through.

He snarled when a traffic light turned red, and she risked a look at him. The tight clench of his jaw and white-knuckled grip on the steering wheel revealed his frame of mind. But she didn't need to see either of those things to know the blackness of his mood. A blind man could see that Michael Striker was all shadows today. She wondered how many of those shadows had to do with her.

She'd lain herself open to him in every way a woman could open to a man. She'd stripped herself bare, inside and out, handed him her heart with no thought as to whether he would handle it with care—or shatter it into a thousand pieces.

The power of her feelings for him frightened her, thrilled her, shook her so thoroughly she had to press her hands together to keep them from shaking. In the last few days, he'd touched a part of her no one had ever been able to reach. He'd helped her find a missing piece of herself she never would have found on her own. He'd healed a hideous wound that had bled for half of her life.

She'd fallen in love with him. A man whose honor would not let him love her back. The realization terrified her. The irony broke her heart.

"This is the place."

They had stopped at the mouth of a cobblestone driveway facing a tall wrought iron gate. Beyond, nestled in a forest of conifer and cedar and hemlock was a massive Tudor style home.

"This isn't what I expected," she said.

Striker's eyes skimmed the magnificent estate stretched out like a postcard for some fancy real estate company. "Who says porn doesn't pay?" he said dryly.

He lowered his window and pressed the intercom button. A moment later a male voice asked for their names. Striker uttered his name and then added, "I'm a private detective here to see Mr. Cross. Official business."

"Do you have an appointment?"

"Tell Mr. Cross I have urgent business with him regarding Rendezvous Productions. He'll want to see me."

A lengthy pause ensued. Striker tapped his fingers on the steering wheel. Lindsey stared at the gate, willing it to open.

"The son of a bitch isn't going to talk to us," he growled.

"What do we do if he doesn't—"

Her words fell short when the gates swept open.

"I'll be damned." Striker put the jeep in gear and started through.

The driveway curved through a manicured forest of towering evergreens and the winter skeletons of maples and oaks. Near the front of the house the driveway split, forming a circular drive the center of which was dominated by a stately blue spruce. Striker parked the jeep, then turned to Lindsey, his expression grim. "Are you still determined to go through with this?"

"I'm not going to cower in the jeep while you speak to Cross, if that's what you mean."

"Then let me lay down the ground rules for you. I do the talking. You listen. Don't interject. Don't let Cross engage you in a conversation, because he will try. Don't tell him your name or anything personal. Don't mention Ohio. Above everything, don't trust him."

"I know how to handle myself," she said, but her voice was taut with nerves.

"This guy's a shark, Lindsey, with big teeth and a taste for blood. You give him an opening, and he'll rip out your throat."

"I'm not going to give him an opening."

But for all her determination, her legs were jittery with fear when she got out of the jeep. Without speaking they started down the walkway to the double mahogany doors at the front of the house. Striker punched a lighted intercom button and waited. An instant later a burly man in a custom Armani opened the door and eyed them suspiciously.

"You Striker?" he asked in a heavy Eastern European accent.

Striker flashed his PI license. "I'm here to see Cross."

The man's eyes went from Striker to Lindsey, then back to Striker. He stepped back, opening the door wider. "Who's she?"

Never taking his eyes from the man, Striker walked into the foyer. "She's with me. That's all you need to know."

Lindsey followed, trying hard to shake the feeling that they'd just walked into a monster's lair.

The man turned to Striker. "Raise your arms for me, please."

Striker laughed. "You've got to be kidding."

"House rules."

Looking none too happy about it, Striker raised his hands to shoulder level while the man ran his hands quickly and adeptly over his body. He paused on the pistol Striker carried in his shoulder holster, slid it out of its leather nest.

"I'll keep this for you until your business with Mr. Cross is finished."

"If I find so much as one bullet out of place, I'll come back and use it on you."

Lindsey stiffened her spine when the man's eyes went to her. She didn't want to jeopardize their meeting with Cross, but she did not want him putting his hands on her. As if realizing that was exactly what would happen if he didn't do something to stop it, Striker put his hand on her shoulder and moved between her and the man. "She's clean."

When the man hesitated, he added, "That means keep your hands off her. Now take us to Cross."

The man's eyes lingered on Lindsey a moment longer, then he started toward the interior of the house.

The grand foyer opened to a cavernous great room with floor-to-ceiling windows that offered a spectacular view of Lake Washington. Muted lighting rained down on a cream colored sectional sofa. Directly in front of the windows a fire flickered within a floating glass fireplace set on raised marble. Sleek contemporary sculptures sneered at them from atop equally sleek tables.

Everything was sleek and sterile and cold. The house. The art. The furniture. Lindsey wondered if the man were as cold and lifeless as the place where he lived.

"Ah, Mr. Striker, what an intriguing surprise. Please come in and sit down."

She looked toward the sound of the voice to see a man silhouetted against the black expanse of Lake Washington, smoking a cigar. He raised a remote, and the lights brightened, bringing him into view.

Lindsey wasn't sure what she'd expected Cross to look like, but the well-dressed businessman in front of her wasn't it. She'd imagined him as some sleazy pervert with greasy hair and shabby clothes. She couldn't have been more wrong.

Titus Cross looked to be in his mid-forties, with salt-and-pepper hair and a physique that spoke of daily workouts with a personal trainer. He wore an exquisitely cut charcoal suit with a Hermes tie and wingtips polished to a high sheen. His nails were manicured and buffed. His face glowed from facials delivered on a regular basis. He looked so much like a legitimate businessman, in fact, that Lindsey had to remind herself that he could very well be responsible for the disappearance of her sister.

He watched them approach, then glanced at his bodyguard. "Would you pour coffee, Dimitri?"

Wordlessly, the burly man walked to a nearby wet bar and set about pouring coffee.

Striker crossed the gleaming span of black marble floor and stopped a few feet from Cross. He didn't bother with niceties. "I'm working on a missing person case. I'd like to ask you a few questions."

"Ah yes, you've become a private detective since losing your badge. Fascinating case. I've been following the story with great interest." Cross's eyes flicked from Striker to Lindsey. He smiled warmly as he strode to her and extended his hand. "I'm Titus Cross."

Lindsey accepted the handshake. "Rachael Simms."

Cross's bodyguard interrupted them with a tray containing three cups. Leaning close to Cross, he whispered something just out of earshot. Striker ignored the proffered coffee and the bodyguard. Smiling, Cross took one of the cups then sipped delicately. A nod sent his bodyguard away.

Cross faced Striker. "A missing person case. I'll certainly help you if I can."

"I'm looking for a young woman by the name of Traci Metcalf."

Cross's brows knit as if he were drawing from a place deep inside his memory, then he shook his head. "I do not know anyone by that name. Who is she, and what has led you here?"

"She's a friend," Lindsey said, ignoring the warning look from Striker. "We believe she worked for you."

"Worked for me in what capacity?"

"We know she was involved in at least two of your movies," Striker said.

Cross's gaze sharpened on Striker. "My movies? I'm afraid you've lost me."

"Let me fill in the blanks for you so we can cut the bullshit and get to the chase." Unobtrusively, Striker set his hand on Lindsey's shoulder and eased her away from Cross. "I know you own Rendezvous Productions. I know Rendezvous financed *Hollywood Belles* and *Flesh Undercover*. And we know Traci Metcalf appeared in both of those films."

Cross's expression didn't change, but his hand tightened on the cup. It was a minute movement, but enough to tell Lindsey that Striker had surprised him—and that Cross didn't like surprises.

"I own several production companies, Mr. Striker, and have over one hundred employees. I do not have personal knowledge of every actor who has ever played a role in one of my films."

"Surely you keep some kind of record," Lindsey put in.

Cross's eyes flicked to her. She held his gaze, desperately seeking something human she could appeal to. But he had the coldest eyes of anyone she'd ever encountered.

Remembering Traci's photograph in her purse, she dug it out and held it up. "She's twenty-four years old," she said, ignoring the dark look from Striker. "She's been missing for almost a week now. Please, we just want to know when she last worked. If anyone has seen her or knows where she is."

Cross held her gaze long enough to make her fidget, then studied the photo. "You look very much like her."

Lindsey didn't know what to say to that, so she remained silent.

"I never forget a face, especially a pretty one," Cross said. "I can honestly tell you I've never met that young woman." He shrugged. "Of course, if she did, indeed, work for me—even on a contract basis—there will be records."

"Is there someone we can contact at Rendezvous Productions?" Striker asked. "Someone who handled paperwork? Insurance? Maybe payroll or your HR person?"

Cross never took his eyes off Lindsey. "Give me a few hours to make some calls, send a few E-mails to my HR people, and I'll see what I can come up with."

Striker removed his business card from its case and held it out for Cross. "You can reach me on my cell twenty-four/seven."

Cross ignored the card, his attention focused on Lindsey with an intensity that had her breaking a sweat beneath her coat. She was generally comfortable around people. She didn't shrink away from touches or handshakes. She didn't wither beneath angry looks or harsh words. But a keen sense of uneasiness rippled through her when Cross stepped closer. That uneasiness deepened when he set his hand on her shoulder and squeezed.

"You must be very close to your friend to have hired a private detective," he said quietly.

"I'm very concerned about her."

Cross nodded. "Many of my films are shot on location. Paris. Monaco. London. We keep our actors busy. Perhaps she hasn't had time to contact you."

"I don't think she's out of the country."

"Whatever the case, I should be able to have an answer

for you within the hour." His lips curved. "In fact, if Ms. Metcalf is shooting overseas, I could even arrange for her to be flown home."

Lindsey knew better than to get her hopes up, especially on the word of a man like Cross, but a sharp pang of hope jumped through her at the mention of his bringing her sister home. She stared at him, trying to gauge his sincerity, but he was as unreadable as carved stone.

He glanced at the Omega watch strapped to his wrist. "I was about to have brunch." He spread his hands disarmingly. "But I despise eating alone. Perhaps you'd like to join me. We can discuss how I might help you find your friend."

The lure of gaining his cooperation was surprisingly strong, but Lindsey knew better than to accept his invitation. Before she could respond, Striker cut in. "Ms. Simms will be returning to California later. You can deal with me."

"Mr. Striker, my security director tells me you brought a gun into my home."

"I'm a licensed private investigator."

"With a reputation for violence. I'm sure you'll understand if I prefer to deal directly with Ms. Simms."

"You can deal with me, or you can deal with the police," Striker said.

Amusement flickered in Cross's eyes. "The police?" He put his hand to his heart. "Come now. I have nothing to fear from the police."

"You sure about that? Last I heard, they had a whole slew of questions for you about all sorts of things."

Lindsey looked at Striker, wondering what he was up to.

"Really?" Cross threw his head back and laughed. "And what, may I ask, has bestowed the suspicion of Seattle's finest onto me?"

"I heard one of your sleazy friends implicated you in some pretty unsavory activities."

"You hear a lot for a man who's, shall we say, out of the loop."

"I'm a good listener. And it never ceases to amaze me what people say to the police when they're scared."

"I'm sure you know all about scaring people, don't you Mr. Striker?"

"Whatever works."

"You're beginning to bore me."

"I think I'm beginning to scare you. I don't think you like it much."

Cross smiled icily. "Does this sleazy friend of mine have a name?"

"He has several, actually. Aliases. Jason Blow. Jace Bledsoe. He sang like a canary on speed, and he had all kinds of interesting things to say about Rendezvous Productions."

"Really? That's truly fascinating."

Striker didn't even pause. "Actors using heroin on the set. Underage females. Money under the table. Imagine what would happen if Mr. D.A. or Uncle Sam got wind of that."

Cross's face darkened. "That's absurd. I'm a legitimate businessman—"

"You're no goddamn businessman," Striker snapped.

"I supply a product."

"You sell filth and misery, and I'm here to tell you it's about to catch up with you in a very big way."

"Be careful who you threaten, Mr. Striker."

"When the time comes, I won't bother with a threat. I'll just take you down. When I do, it will be so hard and fast you won't know what hit you."

"You have no idea with whom you're dealing."

"I have a nose for scum, and you reek of it. I know exactly who I'm dealing with."

Cross's mouth pulled back into snarl. "I'm not some two-bit hood you can push around, Mr. Striker. You push me, and I will push back. Only when I push, people get hurt. You see, I'm very adept at finding people's weak spots. I'm betting it wouldn't be hard to find yours." His gaze cut to Lindsey.

Striker's hands clenched into fists at his sides, and for a moment she thought he was going to lose it and go after Cross. Instead, he shook himself, took a step back, and reached for her arm. "Let's go," he said, and they started toward the foyer.

"Oh, and Mr. Striker?"

They stopped at the sound of Cross's voice and turned simultaneously. Lindsey felt a quiver of surprise go through her when Jace Bledsoe walked out of an adjacent room. He looked out of place with his shabby clothes, black goatee, and pierced eyebrow. But he walked into the living area as if he were completely at ease amid the elegance of Cross's home.

Bledsoe smiled at them. "Well, hello again, Mr. Striker." His gaze went to Lindsey. "Ms. Metcalf. Nice to see you. I take it you haven't had any luck finding your sister?"

Lindsey didn't know what to say. She stood frozen in place.

Cross's eyes flicked to Lindsey. "Ah, sisters. I should have known from the resemblance." His attention went to Striker. "What were you saying about Mr. Bledsoe? Something about his singing like a canary?"

Striker said nothing, but Lindsey could feel the anger vibrating through him and into her.

Cross turned to Bledsoe. "I think you would be doing the citizens of Seattle a huge favor if you went to the police and told them about Mr. Striker barging into your home, destroying your camera equipment, and assaulting you." He smiled at Striker. "Why don't you call them right now?"

Grinning, Bledsoe unclipped a cell phone from his belt.

Striker's hand tightened on Lindsey's arm. "Let's go."

She let him guide her toward the foyer, but her attention was on the threat Jace Bledsoe posed to Striker. She didn't think he'd been bluffing about calling the police and filing charges.

The burly man with the crew cut was waiting for them at the front door. Striker snarled when the man handed him the .45 H & K. Never taking his eyes from the man, Striker quickly and adeptly released the clip. "Where the hell are the shells?"

"In a safe place." The man opened the door. "Have a nice day."

Growling a nasty retort, Striker jammed the pistol into its holster and walked out the door. Once on the sidewalk, he released her. But Lindsey could tell he was furious.

"Bledsoe wasn't bluffing, Striker. He's going to file a report against you."

Striker's jaws flexed as they strode toward the jeep. "To hell with that little son of a bitch."

"You could get into trouble."

"I'm already in trouble." Striker yanked open the jeep's door and slid inside. "I knew better than to take you in there."

"I didn't give you a choice."

He rapped his palm hard against the steering wheel. "Cross threatened you, Lindsey."

The words sent a quiver through her as she crossed in front of the jeep and got in on the other side. Neither of them spoke as Striker put the jeep in gear and pulled onto the street.

"Do you think Cross knows anything about Traci?" she asked after a moment.

Striker shook his head. "I don't know."

For the first time since she'd arrived in Seattle, Lindsey seriously considered the possibility that she would not find her sister. That she would have to return to Ohio not knowing what had happened to her.

"What do we do now?" she asked.

"We go back to the loft and try to come up with a plan."

chapter
28

STRIKER SHOULD HAVE BEEN THINKING ABOUT THE case. He should have been concentrating on putting the pieces of the puzzle together. Focusing on the people involved in Traci's life. Narrowing down the list of players who might have had a motive to hurt her. Or worse.

Only none of the pieces fit the puzzle. He couldn't concentrate, couldn't maintain his focus. And while the case was going nowhere at a very rapid pace, his feelings for Lindsey were barreling out of control. He couldn't even keep his mind off her long enough to come up with a single, viable theory about her sister. It was a hellish mind-set for a man who hadn't wanted to get involved.

He opened the door to the loft and strode to the kitchen. The answering machine was blinking, so he hit the PLAY button. It was a message from Landreth demanding to know what had transpired between him and Bledsoe.

Snarling a curse, Striker deleted the message and crossed to the counter. He was aware of Lindsey behind him, but he didn't turn to look at her. He could feel the tension climbing up his shoulders and into his neck. He knew better than to bring her back to the loft. Being with her in such close quarters was making him crazy, because every time he looked at her, he wanted her. Every time he wanted her, it made him angry, because he knew nothing could ever come of his feelings for her.

When I push, people get hurt . . .

Striker couldn't get Cross's words out of his head. That the threat had been aimed at Lindsey infuriated him, terrified him, made him feel helpless and inept.

Working off his coat, he flung it over a bar stool and bent to retrieve the bottle of Cutty Sark from beneath the cabinet. His temper spiked when he realized he'd finished the bottle the night before. Snarling an expletive, he hurled it into the trash.

He was aware of Lindsey watching him as he strode to his desk and snatched the e-ticket from the printer tray. He'd made the reservation the night before while she'd slept, on the outside chance that he would be able to talk her into returning to Ohio without her sister. He hadn't given it to her because he'd known she would fight him. But with Cross threatening her and his own feelings for her spiraling out of control, he figured he no longer had a choice.

Without speaking, he crossed to her and thrust the ticket at her. "This is a one-way ticket from Sea-Tac to Columbus. Your flight leaves in just over two hours. That gives you about twenty minutes to pack."

She didn't take the ticket. "I'm not going anywhere."

"Cross threatened you, damn it! In a little over a week, I'm not going to be around to keep him off you!"

"How can you expect me to leave without knowing what happened to Traci?"

"Come on, Lindsey! Face it! Your sister is dead!" He hadn't meant to say that. He hadn't meant for a lot of things to happen in the last few days. But he seemed destined to keep making the same mistakes over and over again when it came to this woman.

"You can't possibly know that."

"I know that people who live their lives a certain way have higher risk factors than others. Traci is off the scale. She's a topless dancer. She does drugs. She's involved in pornography. And she whores around."

"Don't you dare talk about her that way."

"She was quite possibly blackmailing one of two powerful men. I don't think either of those men would think twice about doing away with her if she became a threat."

"You're wrong, Striker. Traci is . . . a survivor. She's smart and strong." Her voice cracked. "She's not dead."

But he saw the uncertainty in her eyes, the grief etched into her features, the way her hands had begun to tremble. Her face had gone sheet white, but she was still ready to take on the world if she had to. All to save a sister who probably didn't appreciate how much she was loved.

"She's dead," he said brutally. "She's gone. Now it's time for you to go home."

Without speaking, she turned from him and started toward the bedroom area. Striker watched her cross the room. His heart was thundering in his chest. He could feel the pulse of it drumming in his head. He knew he'd hurt her, but he steeled himself against the knowledge, because he couldn't let that keep him from doing what needed to be done.

He followed her to the bedroom area.

Glaring at him over her shoulder, she picked up her overnight bag, and slung it onto the bed. "I don't need you to finish this. I'll find her on my own." Her hands trembled when she unzipped the bag and tossed a folded pair of jeans and small toiletry case inside.

Striker watched her pack. When she was finished, he said, "I'll drive you to the airport."

"I'm not going anywhere with you."

He reached for the bag. She jerked it from him, then started for the door. Grinding his teeth in anger, he crossed to her and wrested the bag from her. "Don't fight me on this, Lindsey. You'll lose."

"I'm not going to let you do this to me, Striker."

"You don't have a choice."

Abandoning the bag, she started toward the door, set her hand on the knob, twisted. Striker reached her an instant later. He put his hand on her shoulder. Lindsey turned, shoved him hard with both hands. But Striker was ready, taking her wrists and backing her against the door. "Knock it off," he growled.

Her back banged against the wall. "Get your hands off me."

"I'm not trying to hurt you. I'm handling this the best way I know how."

"You're wrong about Traci. You're wrong about me. For God's sake, you're wrong about us!"

He looked down at her, saw anger and pain and a dozen other emotions he didn't want to see. He felt those same emotions unfurling inside him, and the power of them took his breath. He could feel his need for her like a fist clenching in his chest.

"There is no us, Lindsey." His voice was deadly calm, but he could feel himself shaking inside and he knew that calm wouldn't hold much longer.

Tears shimmered in her eyes when her gaze met his. Diamond pools that revealed to him the things that up until now he'd refused to see. Proved to him the things he hadn't wanted to believe. Made him feel things he didn't want to feel.

"You can't even admit you have feelings for me," she said in a shaking voice. "You'd rather pretend they don't exist. It's easier that way, safer, because then you don't have to hurt if things don't work out. Well, guess what, Striker? Life is full of hurt, and I think you're a coward for not being able to face it."

"You don't know what the hell you're talking about. This isn't some fucking fairy tale that's going to have a happy ending," he said.

"Thanks to you, we'll never know, will we? I go back to Ohio. You go to prison. I may or may not ever find Traci." She choked out a sound that was half laugh, half sob. "That's not the way I wanted this to end."

Striker felt the truth of her words like a punch, each one gaining momentum, hitting with a little more force. Denial rose like a violent tide inside him, but when he tried to snarl a reply, his voice refused the command. That was when he knew. *He knew.*

Dread twisted inside him at the realization of what he'd allowed to happen. The truth pummeled him like fists.

He didn't just care about her; he'd fallen in love with her. He stared down at her, keenly aware that he was breathing hard. That a cold sweat had broken out on his back. He shook himself, tried to snap out of it, but the panic simply tightened its hold and shook him back with savage force.

Concern flashed in her expression. He knew she could feel him trembling, but his hands refused to release her. Something inside him desperately needed the contact, even though on another level that need was destroying him.

"Striker . . ."

He blinked at her, grappling hard for words. But nothing came. Nothing except the startling realization that he loved her. That it was going to kill him to walk away from her.

Releasing her, he stumbled back. Somewhere in the back of his mind, a little voice told him to run. Before this went any further. Before he did something he would be sorry for. Before he said something irrevocable.

"I'm going to go get a drink," he said.

"Striker . . . wait."

Without looking at her he crossed to the door. He heard her behind him but he didn't stop. His hand shook when he reached for the knob. He knew running wasn't the answer. He could never run fast enough to get away from the truth of what he had allowed to happen.

She called out his name, but Striker didn't stop. Instead, he yanked open the door, stepped into the alcove, and walked away without looking back.

chapter
29

LINDSEY'S LEGS WERE SHAKING WHEN SHE WALKED over to her overnight bag and picked it up. She couldn't believe Striker had walked out on her. That he was quitting. That she was falling apart because of it.

For a full minute, she stood there, trying to pull herself together. But the pain churned inside her like shards of glass, inflicting a thousand tiny wounds. She knew he wouldn't be back. But she'd seen the truth in his eyes. She felt that same truth in her heart. And while she knew he loved her, she understood him well enough to know he would never admit it. Not to her. Not even to himself.

She couldn't change any of what had happened. All she could do now was pull the pieces of herself together and continue with her search for Traci.

Taking a shuddering breath, Lindsey used Striker's phone to call a taxi. A quick stop at Traci's house to check messages and E-mail and pick up the car. Then she would check in to a hotel for the night and get some rest. Tomorrow she would start fresh.

Shrugging into her coat, she dropped her cell phone into her pocket and started for the door. She was halfway to the street when her phone chirped. Striker. Without thinking, she snatched up the phone and answered, "Striker?"

The sound that met her made the hairs at her nape stand on end. She knew instantly that the blood-curdling scream on the other end of the line was her sister's. "Help me! Linnnnyyyyy! *Pleeeeease!*"

Lindsey's heart began to hammer. "Traci? *Traci!* Is that you?"

Another scream ripped through the line. A horrible sound that sent shuddering waves of fear through her. "*Traci?* Honey, where are you? What's *wrong?*"

But Traci was crying hysterically, screaming for help, calling out Lindsey's name. "Help me! Oh, God! Oh, *God!* Pleeeeease! Someone help *meeeeeee!*"

Panic zinged through her body. She felt the jolt of it all the way to her toes. "Traci! Tell me where you are!"

Abruptly, the screaming stopped. Lindsey clutched the phone, straining to hear. "Traci?"

"Hello, Lindsey."

Gooseflesh rose on her arms at the sound of the guttural male voice. "Who is this?" she asked.

"Think of me as your conscience . . . Linny."

Hearing the nickname froze her in place. "What have you done with my sister?"

"She's right here with me."

"Put her back on the phone."

"Do you want me to make her scream again?"

"I want to speak with her."

"You're in no position to be making demands."

She could hear Traci crying in the background and swallowed panic. "Please, don't hurt her. Just . . . let me talk to her."

"If you want to see your sister again, shut up and listen, you meddling little bitch."

Lindsey couldn't catch her breath. "Just . . . tell me where she is. Please, I'll come and get her. I—I can pay you. I've got money."

"Meet me at the corner of First Street and Royal Brougham Way. Five minutes, or I'm going to kill this screaming whore."

"No! Please . . . don't . . ."

"You're not going to abandon her, are you Linny? Just like you left her when your old man was slobbering all over her when she was twelve years old."

Everything inside her froze into a solid block of ice. She could feel the pieces she'd so carefully put together breaking apart. She closed her eyes against the tears, felt her cell phone tremble against her ear as she clutched it. "Who is this?" she whispered.

He laughed. "You do remember those nights, don't you, Lindsey? All those long, hot summer nights all those years ago? You. Traci. That sick old man of yours."

"What do you want?"

"I want you to meet me at First and Royal Brougham in five minutes. No cops. No private detective. Just you. Or I swear I'll slit her fuckin' throat. Got it?"

Lindsey didn't know what to do. It would be sheer insanity for her to meet him. But she couldn't let her sister die. "I'll meet you," she said in a strangled voice.

"If I so much as smell a cop, or see your private detective, your sister is dead. Then I'm going to come after you. You got that?"

"I understand."

The line went dead.

"Oh God." She hit the INCOMING CALLS button, only to find that the number was blocked. Damn. Damn. *Damn!* A sob of fear and frustration squeezed from her throat. All the while, the memory of Traci's screams rang horribly in her ears. Oh, dear God, he'd been hurting her.

Quickly, she dialed the police department and asked for

Hal Landreth. The detective had barely answered when she identified herself, then quickly summarized the call. "I have five minutes to get there."

"Don't meet with him," Landreth warned. "You can't handle this by yourself."

"I don't know what else to do! My God, I could hear her screaming. He was hurting her . . ."

"Drive over to the police department. We'll put a female undercover officer in your coat. Wire her for sound."

"There's not enough time." Lindsey looked at her watch, felt another wave of terror envelope her. "If I'm not there in four minutes he's going to kill her!"

"Where are you?"

"Striker's place."

"Take him with you."

"He's not here!"

She could hear Landreth cursing. "Call him. I'm driving over there. Don't do anything until I get there."

But Lindsey knew she couldn't wait for either man. She could only hope Landreth or Striker arrived in time.

"I have to go."

"Lindsey—"

She disconnected. Forgetting about her overnight bag, she started down the hall toward the street, punching in Striker's number as she went. Even after what had happened between them, she wanted him to know what was going on. Whether or not he chose to get involved was up to him.

His phone rang. Once. Twice. "Pick up, damn it." She shoved open the door and stepped onto the sidewalk. It was raining and the wind had picked up, but she barely felt the cold. She looked up and down the street, but the taxi hadn't arrived yet.

The sound of footsteps behind her spun her around. For an instant, she thought Striker had come back. Then she heard his voice on the phone. Confusion swirled, and then a figure rushed at her from the shadows. Lindsey shoved her phone into her coat pocket and screamed as a hand clamped around her arm and spun her around. She lunged at him, tried to ram the heel of her palm into his nose, but her aim was off, and her hand careened off his cheekbone.

"Bitch."

The blow caught her left temple. Light and pain exploded in her head. Her vision dimmed. The sidewalk beneath her feet dipped. She felt herself pitching forward. And then suddenly she was on her hands and knees.

Strong hands jerked her roughly to her feet. "Hurry up and get her into the van."

Dizzy from the blow, she stumbled as two men grabbed her arms and forced her toward the alley ten feet away. She tried to twist away, but their hands were like vices around her biceps. Knowing she would be helpless once they got her inside, she did the only thing she could and screamed.

"Shut her the hell up."

The voice was familiar. Shock rippled through her when she found herself staring at Jace Bledsoe. He was holding a roll of silver duct tape. "Hello, Lindsey. So glad you could join us."

She screamed again. "Get away from me!"

The second blow slammed into her right cheek hard enough to rock her head back. Her legs went slack, and before she could react, she felt the stickiness of tape against her lips as Bledsoe secured a large swath over her mouth and around the back of her neck.

The next thing she knew she was being dragged toward the van. She managed to slide her hand into her coat pocket. Her fingers fumbled with the phone. She had Striker's number programmed on speed dial. If she could send him a message . . .

She hit Striker's speed dial, but the blow had dazed her. Her hands were shaking, and she couldn't see the buttons on her phone. Then the second man got behind her and looped his arm over her head so that her throat was in the crook of his elbow. Using her thumb, she spelled out J-A-C-E on the dial pad.

But he had tightened his hold around her throat, cutting off her oxygen. She was able to drop the phone and kick it away before panic overwhelmed her. She clawed at his forearm with both hands. She tried to open her mouth, but the tape was sealed tightly. She tried to breathe through her nose, but his arm had closed off her bronchial tube.

Dizzy with terror and from the lack of oxygen, Lindsey lashed out with her feet. The man choking her danced aside, cursing. She felt her body bucking against his. Her eyes bulging in their sockets. Oh, God, she thought, he's going to kill me right here and now.

Her peripheral vision faded to gray. She could feel her face tingling. Her arms and legs getting weak. Her concentration waning. She tried to use her fingernails on his arm, but couldn't get to the flesh beneath his jacket. At some point her legs had buckled. He was holding her upright by her throat. She was dimly aware that he had dragged her into the van. She heard the sound of an engine idling. The van door sliding closed.

She thought of Striker and wondered if he would find the phone. She wondered if he would come for her. If he would get there in time.

And then the world faded to red.

Striker knew the alcohol wasn't going to help, but he drank anyway in the hope that at some point he would be able to close his eyes and not see her face.

You can't even admit you have feelings for me . . . I think you're a coward for not being able to face it.

Her voice rang inside his head like the final notes of a ballad. Lyrical and wrenching and utterly sad. He couldn't get her words out of his head.

He tossed back the last of the scotch and tried hard not to think about what he'd done. He wanted to believe it was the alcohol making him crazy, blowing his feelings for her out of proportion. But Striker knew he would feel exactly the same stone cold sober.

He didn't want to hurt like this, like he'd been gutted and hung out to dry. He couldn't afford to let himself get tangled up like this. He did not want any ties to her the day he walked into Walla Walla.

But he knew those ties already existed. He knew they were unbreakable. And he knew that in the endless nights he faced behind bars, it would be Lindsey he longed for even more than his freedom . . .

Striker ordered another double. He'd just taken that first, dangerous sip when his cell phone beeped. For an instant, he considered not answering. There wasn't a soul on this earth he wanted to talk to. The one person he *did* want to talk to was off limits for too many reasons to count.

He glanced down at the display. His heart rolled into a hard staccato when he recognized Lindsey's cell phone number. And suddenly he desperately needed to hear her voice. He needed to tell her he was sorry for the things he'd said, the way he'd treated her. He reached for the phone with shaking hands, caught the call on the third ring. "Lindsey—"

The sound of her scream sent a shock wave through his body. He lurched from the bar stool, clutched the phone to his ear, and listened, waiting.

"Lindsey!" He heard rustling on the other end of the line. A barely audible cry. A muffled male voice. And then nothing.

Jesus Christ.

Striker didn't think. He went with his gut and acted. Clipping the phone to his belt, he sprinted to the door, shoved it open, and stepped into the rain. He could see his building from where he stood. Even from a block away and in the pouring rain, he saw the taillights of the vehicle pulling out of the alley.

"Lindsey!"

He shot into a dead run toward the loft. His arms pumped in time with his legs. His boots pounded the sidewalk in a tempo that matched his racing heart. All the while he prayed the scream he'd heard wasn't Lindsey's. But he knew it was. And he knew his worst nightmare was about to come true.

By the time he reached his building, the vehicle was gone. He stared down the alley for a moment, then darted to the front of the building and swung open the door. He tore into the hall like an enraged bull. He spotted her suitcase and hope ripped a hole clean through him. "Lindsey!" He sprinted to his door, shoved it open and burst inside. *"Lindsey!"*

He looked around wildly, called out to her, felt the dizzying squeeze of panic snake around his chest when she didn't answer.

His watch told him only two minutes had passed since she'd called. If she'd been in the vehicle he'd seen in front of the building, she couldn't have gotten far. He crossed to the phone, snatched it up, and hit redial. A taxi service answered. He slammed it down, then left the loft, barreled down the hall, and burst through the front door. To his surprise, a Yellow Cab was parked curbside.

What the hell?

Striker strode to the taxi and yanked open the driver's side door. The cabbie yelped as Striker dragged him from the seat, muscled him to the rear of the car, and slammed him against the trunk. "Where is she?" he demanded.

The taxi driver raised his hands and shook his head so hard the cigarette fell out of his mouth. "I don't know anything," he said with a heavy Asian accent.

"Why are you here?"

"I get a call from dispatch. This is the second time I drive around block, but nobody here."

Striker stared hard at him, vaguely aware that it was

pouring rain, that they were soaked to the skin. He gave himself a hard mental shake, forced his hands to relax, and release the man's lapels. "Did you see a woman?"

The man wiped rain from his face. "I just come here to pick up a ride, Mister. Nobody show."

"Did you see anyone else? Another vehicle?"

"I see a van." He pointed toward the alley. "A white one. Maybe silver. There. Two men. Up to no good. Could have been a woman with them, but I couldn't see because of the rain. I try to mind my own business, you know?"

Striker barely heard the last of his sentence. He left the man and crossed to the alley. The tempo of the rain had increased. Water streamed into his eyes. His hair was soaked. He'd left his coat at the bar, and the wet material of his shirt stuck coldly to his back.

He looked toward the cabdriver, saw him getting back into his car. Striker darted over to him, pulled him back. "What kind of van?"

"I don't know. White or silver. That all I know."

"Make?"

The man shook his head.

"Old? New? What?"

"Old. The kind with no windows."

The kind that would provide plenty of privacy, Striker thought, and felt another layer of fear unfold inside him. "Anything else?"

"I think the van only have one headlight."

Striker let go of him and backed off. The cabbie muttered something in Chinese, then slid into his cab and sped off.

For several seconds, Striker stood on the street, trying to decide what to do next. Tugging the cell phone from his pocket, he dialed Landreth's number and got voice mail. "Call me, damn it," Striker growled. He dialed Landreth's cell phone number from memory, and Hal picked up on the first ring.

"Lindsey Metcalf is missing," Striker said.

Landreth cursed. "She was supposed to wait for me."

"What the hell's going on?"

"She got a call from her sister. Some guy wanted her to meet him."

"Aw, Jesus. Tell me she didn't go."

"I'm on my way to your place to meet her."

"She's not here." Striker paced the sidewalk, trying to make sense of what he was being told. He listened to Landreth. He looked down the alley. He was about to head back to his loft when he spotted the cell phone lying on the sidewalk near the alley. Barely aware of what Landreth was saying, he picked it up and looked at the display.

J-A-C-E.

"Holy Christ."

Landreth stopped talking. "What?"

"She's with Jace Bledsoe."

"Who's Bledsoe, and where is he?"

Striker rattled off Bledsoe's address from memory. "He forced her, Hal. There's no way she'd go with that guy."

"I'll get on the horn. See if I can get a warrant—"

"Fuck the warrant."

"Striker, you're in enough trouble as it is."

But he had already disconnected and was sprinting toward his jeep.

chapter
30

LINDSEY WOKE TO BRIGHT LIGHT AND A POUNDING head. She opened her eyes, then closed them quickly as the light drilled into her brain. She felt disoriented and confused. Her throat hurt, but she didn't know why. Then she remembered the two men. Overpowering her. Dragging her to the alley and into the van . . .

She opened her eyes, blinked at the lights, tried to get her bearings. She was in some kind of warehouse. It was cold and dank with concrete floors and a catwalk that ran along the wall to her left. She was partially reclined in a chair, like a dentist's chair. She tried to move, but couldn't. Fingers of fear slithered through her when she realized her arms were secured behind her. She tested her legs, but her ankles were bound to the chair.

Dear, God, what was going on?

Cold, hard fear gripped her. At some point, they had removed the duct tape from her mouth and she could hear her breaths rushing in and out. Adrenaline burning like fire in her gut. She could hear the roar of blood crashing through her veins. Smell the coppery stench of fear . . .

She tugged against the restraints, felt the sting of a cut at her wrists and realized her captors had bound her with wire. She tried to work the wire back and forth, hoping to weaken and break it, but it was too tight. Hysteria threatened, but she shoved it back, ordered herself to stay calm. If she was going to get out of this alive, she was going to have to keep her head and think.

She looked around, took a quick inventory of her surroundings. Two photographer's floodlights were set up on separate tripods fifteen feet away. An orange extension cord ran from the lights to a cutout in the floor. A workbench was set against the wall. Above the bench, dozens of photos were affixed to the pegboard back. Lindsey was too far away to see the details of the photos, but she could tell that most of them were of women in various stages of undress.

Another swell of terror assailed her. She could feel her entire body quaking. It took every ounce of strength she could muster, but she shoved back the fear, put it in a compartment, locked it in.

The lights were uncomfortably hot, and she could feel the sweat on her forehead and neck, dripping between her shoulder blades. She looked down at her legs, used the muscles in her thighs to tug against the wire binding her ankles to the chair. She began working it back and forth, up and down.

"Ah, you're awake."

Her head jerked up at the sound of the voice. Fear jolted her hard enough to make her dizzy. She squinted past the lights to see Jace Bledsoe approach, a cup of coffee from one of the business district coffeehouses in his hand. She saw steam rising from the cup and ascertained that they probably weren't too far from downtown.

"Why are you doing this?" she asked, hating the quiver of fear in her voice. "What do you want?"

He stopped several feet away and set the coffee on the workbench. He studied her, then brought his hands up, formed his fingers into a square then clicked as if shooting a photograph with an invisible camera. "You are going to be so perfect."

"Where's my sister?"

"Relax. I just want to shoot some pics of you." He shrugged, then smiled at her disarmingly.

"Where's Traci?" she asked. "I want to see her."

He crossed to her and knelt so that they were nearly at eye level. Lindsey stared at him, her nerves snapping.

"You sure you want to see her?" he asked.

"What have you done with her?" Lindsey didn't want to cry. But the terror was breaking down her defenses. She could feel the burn of tears in her eyes. A sob building in her throat. "Please, just . . . let me see her. I—I have money. You can have it. All of it. Just . . . take it and let us go."

He studied her, his mouth pulling into a cruel smile. "You look so much like Traci, I just about had a fucking heart attack the day you and that private dick walked into my apartment. For a second, I thought maybe she'd come back from the dead, looking for a little revenge."

She tried to get her mind around what he was saying, but the fear was clouding her thoughts. "She's not . . . dead. I heard her on the phone. Please, tell me where she is."

"You know, Lindsey, I was pretty pissed about the equipment your private detective pal smashed up. That's going to cost you."

"I'll . . . replace it."

"I played the long suffering artist, but I wanted to cut his throat. I'll have my revenge. After what happened to his partner, he ought to have quite a time dealing with what I'm going to do to you." He raised his hand to smooth the hair back from her face.

She jerked away from his touch. "Take your hands off of me!"

"You're prettier than she was, Lindsey. Not as flashy. But you have a different kind of appeal. You've got that wholesome, Midwestern thing going. Nice cheekbones. Breathtaking eyes. Sexy mouth. Have you ever been photographed? I mean, professionally?"

"Just tell me where my sister is," she said. "Let us go. I swear, I won't tell anyone."

He straightened and without answering walked over to the workbench and yanked a couple of the black and white photos off the pegboard. "Traci always wanted to be a star," he said. "Take a look at these photos, Lindsey. Tell me what you think."

She got a sick feeling in the pit of her stomach when he walked over to her and held out the photos. Fearing what she would see, Lindsey turned her face away, but Bledsoe fisted her hair and jerked her head around.

"Look at them!"

A sob tore from her throat when she opened her eyes. She saw her sister. Bound and gagged, her beautiful face streaked with tears and filled with terror. She saw naked flesh. The blue steel of a blade. The shocking red of blood . . .

"No," she choked.

"Oh, yes. And I can tell you she was magnificent all the way to the end."

Horror thrashed inside her as the reality of what she was seeing penetrated her brain. She could feel it leaching into every part of her body. Shaking her. Sickening her.

"She's not dead!" she cried. "I heard her voice. On the phone."

"Come on, Lindsey. You're not that dense, are you? Your beloved little sister has been dead for over a week. What you heard was a recording."

"I don't believe you!" She screamed again, yanked against her binds. She felt the warmth of blood running down her palms, but the pain was nothing compared to the grief and horror exploding in her brain.

Bledsoe came up behind her and leaned close. "The first time I did it for the money," he whispered. "Death on film for a cool one hundred thousand dollars. No taxes. I shot it with an 8 millimeter. Not my best work, but some rich dirtbag thought it was primo. He produced a video and sold it on the black market overseas for a filthy amount of money."

"You sick bastard," she said.

"Me? Hey, I just shoot the video, supply the product. The really sick people are the ones who get off on that crap. You know what I mean?"

"My God, you're killing people . . ."

He shrugged. "At first we were going to stage it. I mean, come on. That's what snuff is, right? A staged murder? Bad special effects. Lots of flesh and blood. I'd seen one or two snuff films and figured I could pull it off. I know a little bit about special effects. But we tried it and the quality just wasn't there. There was no intensity. No passion. No . . . artistry. It was like a bad B movie, you know?

"Then Rakestraw got this wild idea to do the real thing. I didn't want to, but we had that one-hundred-thousand-dollar incentive staring us in the face. So we drove down to San Francisco. We picked up a hooker. Some dumb bitch nobody cared about. We pumped her full of smack. Brought her back here." He shrugged his thin shoulders. "And presto, you have murder on disk."

The terror she'd been holding at bay broke free. A feral beast galloping through her, trampling her intellect, her judgment. She strained against the wire binding her to the chair, barely aware that it was cutting her. "You're insane."

"Then we delivered the disk and the buyer guy went nuts over it. I mean, he had a real hard-on for it, the sick son of a bitch. He paid us without so much as blinking. Said he wanted more, no questions asked. He offered us another hundred thou for a second disk. As long as the quality was as good or better." Bledsoe shook his head. "Do you have any idea how long it takes a guy like me to make that kind of money? I mean, come on, do I want to spend the rest of my life shooting porn on the side and working at some two-bit coffee shop?"

Lindsey tasted bile at the back of her throat, choked it back. Her hands had gone numb from lack of circulation. She worked the wires, but they remained tight. In the back of her mind, she wondered if Striker had found her phone. If he'd understood her message.

Bledsoe continued. "Then Traci found the disk and freaked. I tried to reason with her, but she threatened to go to the cops." One side of his mouth pulled into a smile. "But I knew about her weakness for heroin. Turns out she wanted her drugs a hell of a lot more than she wanted justice for some lowlife whore from San Francisco. I might have been able to live with that if she hadn't had the gall to blackmail me."

Lindsey looked at Bledsoe. Hatred welled inside her, darker, more powerful than the fear. "I don't believe you."

"Oh, yeah, sweet little sister burned herself a copy of the disk she'd found. But I got tired of paying for her expensive habits."

"No . . ."

"I made the final payment in person, Linds. I went to her place. At first she wasn't even going to let me in. She was *afraid* of me. I could see it in her eyes. She'd actually bought a gun to protect herself. But she wanted the money, and I knew about her other weakness, Linds. All I had to do was show her the smack, and her door opened like magic. Once she shot up, we were best friends again."

"You murdered her in cold blood," she said. "For money. For your own twisted entertainment."

Bledsoe raised his hands. "Hey, I didn't want to hurt her. Hell, I *liked* Traci. I liked her a lot, Linds. But I couldn't let her go to the cops. I sure as hell couldn't keep paying her. And I knew sooner or later she'd open her mouth to the wrong person and get us busted. It was either kill her or go to prison. The decision wasn't hard to make. And we got the whole thing on disk."

She choked back a sob. "No."

"If it makes it any easier for you to accept, we shot her up first, so she didn't suffer as much as the others. You don't think we're that heartless, do you?"

It was surreal, listening to him speak, as if killing another human being were as insignificant as deciding which shoes to wear. Knowing she needed to keep him talking, to buy herself time, she scrambled for words. "You're the one who broke into the bungalow that night."

"We never found the disk Traci made. We assumed it was somewhere in the house. We looked a couple of times. Then you showed up and started making things really difficult. You should have just stayed in Ohio, Linds, you know that?"

She closed her eyes. "Did you murder Jamie Mills, too?"

His mouth curved. "Jamie was in on this from the get-go. Then her conscience started bothering her, and she almost ruined everything. That was when I knew I had to get rid of her."

"She gave me the disk," Lindsey said. "I took it to the police. It's only a matter of time before they find you."

He shook his head. "We were too careful. Even if they have the disk, the cops will never figure this out. Besides, we booked a flight out of town for your sister, the outlaw. Pretty soon the cops will just accept that she skipped bail and fled those nasty drug charges."

Lindsey concentrated on working the wires back and forth. All the while, her mind scrambled for ways to keep him talking. "Is Titus Cross part of this?"

"Cross doesn't have the guts or the vision to pull this off and keep it together."

"How does Club Tribeca fit in to the picture?"

"We used several clubs, actually, but it all started at Tribeca. It went down like this. Rakestraw sits at the bar and scopes for women. I mean, come on, who can resist that face? Once he spots the perfect victim, the illustrious Jamie drops a roofie in her drink. Twenty minutes later, when the woman is good and sloshed, Rakestraw takes her out back. I put her in the van and . . . let's just say no one was ever the wiser."

"It was Jamie who drugged me that night," she said.

"You were beginning to ask too many questions." He pointed a finger at her, then laughed. "We would have had you, but that son of a bitch Striker found you before we could get you into the van. That fuckin' Striker's a loose cannon. Someone ought to put him in jail." He laughed at his own joke.

She looked into his eyes, felt another dark pang of hatred. "You're a pathetic excuse for a human being."

He crossed to her in two strides. Fisting her hair again, he yanked her head back, thrust his face close to hers. So close she could smell the coffee on his breath. His lips peeled back in a snarl. "Make no mistake, Lindsey, you and I are going to get to know each other real well tonight. I'm going to teach you how to have a little respect."

She closed her eyes, felt the tears scald her cheeks. "Striker will find you," she choked. "He won't let you get away with this."

"Striker is going to prison, Lindsey. He isn't going to be around to do shit." His mouth twisted. "Once he sees your murder on disk, once he hears you screaming his name, they'll probably have to put him in a padded cell, don't you think? I mean, how much can a guy take?"

"When he gets his hands on you, you're going to wish you were never born."

Releasing her hair, he walked over to the workbench, picked up the shears and turned to her. Lindsey spotted them and control deserted her. A cry tore from her throat.

chapter
31

STRIKER MADE THE TWENTY-MINUTE DRIVE TO
Bledsoe's apartment in ten minutes. He brought the jeep to
a screeching halt in front of the building and sprinted to the
front door. He shoved it open with both hands and took the
steps three at a time. On the first landing, a woman with an
eyebrow ring and a crack pipe in her hand took one look at
him and shrank back into her apartment.

He reached Bledsoe's door, tried the knob, and found it
secure. Backing up a step, he landed a kick next to the bolt
lock. Wood splintered, but the door held. He took another
step back and rammed it with his shoulder. The lock gave
with a *crack,* and the door swung wide. He stumbled inside, looked quickly around, ascertained that he was alone.

Aware of the seconds ticking by, he strode to the bedroom. He saw cheap furniture and an unmade bed. The
smell of cigarettes and some type of chemical hung in the
air. A high-end DVD player and television were crowded
onto a dresser top. Striker crossed to the closet and yanked
open the door. The tiny space had been converted into a

darkroom. A naked bulb hung from the ceiling. He tugged
the pull chain, and red light poured down. He noticed the
photographs first. Dozens of them suspended meticulously
from a wire that had been strung across the length of the
closet. Each photograph was of a young woman. Naked or
partially clad. Hands bound. Faces contorted in horror or
pain or a combination of both. He saw shiny pools of black
blood. The shocking white of flesh.

"Jesus . . ."

He could feel their eyes on him. The dead and dying.
Their pain immortalized. Their deaths exploited.

Striker had seen a lot in his years as a cop. Murder. Sui-
cide. He'd seen his share of crime scene photographs. But
he'd never seen anything as chilling as this.

He plucked off one of the photos and stared at it, revulsion and fury and a terrible new fear rising inside him. The
man who'd taken these photos had Lindsey . . .

The reality of that struck him so hard he had to brace his
hand against the jamb. Cold sweat broke out on the back of
his neck. His heart thudded like a fist against his ribs. He
could feel the tremors running through his body. For several long seconds he stood there, trying to get his emotions
under control, trying even harder not to think of all the terrible things that could be happening to her.

He couldn't bear the thought of her being hurt. Of losing her. And at that moment he would have given his own
life just to know she was safe.

Nauseous, he leaned forward, put his hands on his knees
and gulped air. Bile rose in his throat, but he choked it
back. He could feel himself shaking, coming apart. He was
losing it. The same way he'd lost it the night Trisha was
killed. The night he'd listened to her die and hadn't been
able to help her . . .

Striker stumbled from the makeshift darkroom and
spotted an open DVD case next to the television. The case
was empty, but the power on the DVD player had been left

on. Bracing himself for what he was about to see, he turned
on the television and pressed PLAY.

Traci Metcalf was tied to a chair. Naked except for her
panties. Her hair damp and hanging in her face. The quality of the disk was good, and Striker could see the blood at
her wrists and ankles. The scrapes on her knees. The sweat
beading on her forehead. A cut on her lip.

Slowly Traci raised her head and looked at the camera.
He saw resignation and hopelessness in her eyes, and he
felt sick because he knew what this was, knew what would
happen next.

Jace Bledsoe crossed to the table, picked up something
Striker couldn't readily identify. He walked over to Traci,
fisted her hair, then yanked her head back. He fitted some
kind of gag into her mouth and then wrapped a length of
tubing around her arm, just above her elbow. Picking up a
syringe, he injected her.

Traci's eyes glazed. She smiled through the gag, then
sagged in the chair. Bledsoe left her and crossed to a
wooden rectangular table. He lifted a tarp and uncovered a
row of what looked like crude medical instruments. Box
cutters. Scalpels. Curved scissors. Small wooden batons.
Leather straps.

"Aw, God," Striker muttered.

The scream that followed made the hairs at his nape
stand on end.

The sight of such utter brutality shook him badly. He
stared at the screen, trying to pick out clues—surroundings
or background noise—anything that would tell him where
Bledsoe was operating. But the disk ended without revealing any of its terrible secrets.

Switching off the DVD player, Striker looked around
the bedroom. He tried to get into Bledsoe's mind, realized
he couldn't fathom what would drive a human being to
such depravity. Feeling the press of time, he crossed to the
night table and started yanking open drawers. He found

photographs. Film. Disks. Drug paraphernalia. Syringes. A
pipe. A bag of dope.

On top of the nightstand was a stack of bills. He was
about to fling them aside when an envelope caught his eye.
It looked like a bill and was addressed to Brandon
Rakestraw from Seattle Acoustical Contractors.

Why the hell was Jace Bledsoe receiving mail for Brandon Rakestraw? As far as he knew there was no connection
between the two men.

Aside from Traci Metcalf.

Something clicked in his cop's mind. He tore open the
envelope. It contained an invoice dated just three days earlier. He skimmed, his attention going to the far column
where *Soundproofing* was listed under the Description of
Services. He looked at the amount, *$4,062.53*. A very large
job. Why the hell would a photographer need soundproofing?

A photographer wouldn't, he realized. But a killer would.

Striker sought the location of where the work had been
performed. *Tacoma Studios, Inc., Tacoma, Wa. Thirty-five
forty-two Norse Drive*. At the bottom of the invoice, someone had scribbled in red ink: *West Seattle Bridge. Warehouse Dist. Old Scott Machine Shop building*.

Snatching his phone from his belt, he punched Hal Landreth's number. The detective answered on the first ring.

"I'm at Jace Bledsoe's place," Striker said.

"Damn it, if you're doing something you shouldn't be
doing, I don't want to know about it."

"He's got photos of dead women all over his walls."

"Sweet Jesus."

"He's got Lindsey, Hal." Striker's voice broke when he
said her name. He could hear himself breathing hard. He
could taste the panic creeping up his throat. "He's going to
kill her if we don't find them."

"Take it easy, Striker. I'm still working on that warrant.
But I'll get it. Then I'm on my way.

"I think he took her to a warehouse down in Tacoma."

"Wait a minute. How do you know that? Where?"

Striker looked down at the invoice in his hand and recited the address. "I'm going to go get her."

"Striker, damn it. Don't do anything stupid. If you go in there without a warrant it will screw up any case we might have!"

But he'd already disconnected. As he went through the door and down the steps, he prayed to God his hunch was right.

Bledsoe walked over to the CD player on the workbench and flipped a switch. Lindsey jolted when the techno-rock boomed from sleek little Bose speakers. It was so loud she could hear the corrugated steel roof vibrating.

Her heart skittered wildly in her chest when he crossed to her. "We can't start until Brandon gets here. He went to pick up some smokes. But I thought maybe you and I could get to know each other a little better while we wait."

She looked at the shears in his hand. "Stay the hell away from me. Stay *away!*"

He bent toward her so they were at eye level, and rested his hand on her knee. "Are you ready?"

Lindsey could barely hear him over the music, over the drum of her pulse. She could feel her eyes darting from his face to the scissors in his hand. The terror percolating inside her. A scream building in her throat. "Don't touch me, you sick son of a bitch!"

Smiling, he lifted the scissors to the hem of her sweater. She closed her eyes when he began to cut the material. "Don't move, Lindsey. These scissors are sharp, and I wouldn't want to cut you."

She strained against the wires binding her wrists. The flesh was numb now, but she could feel the stickiness of blood on her fingertips.

A sound escaped her when her sweater fell open. She

glanced down, saw the lace of her bra and cringed inwardly. Oh, God. Oh, God . . .

"I'm going to cut off the sweater and jeans for now and leave the rest. Snuff is about anticipation, Lindsey. The anticipation of pain. The anticipation of death." She shrank away from him when he ran his finger across her bare stomach. "We all have a morbid curiosity about death, even if we don't have the guts to admit it, don't we? Think about it, Lindsey. Death is the greatest mystery of all time. A mystery so scary no one wants to solve it."

She could feel the cold steel of the shears against her shoulder as he cut the sleeve from her arm. Her legs were trembling so violently, she couldn't still them. At some point her teeth had begun to chatter. She was cold to the bone, shivering with it.

"Oh, yeah." He pulled the sweater from her body in three pieces. His eyes skimmed over her, and he smiled. "You're going to do very nicely."

Lindsey screamed as loud as she could. "Help me! Please! *Help me!*"

"Don't waste your strength, Lindsey." He knelt at her feet and, starting at the hem of her right leg, began to cut away her jeans. "You're going to need it for later."

She closed her eyes against the horror of what was happening. She could feel the cold steel of the shears creeping up her calf, past her knee, to her thigh. *Oh, dear God, please don't let this happen to me . . .*

The clanging of the steel door opening snapped her attention back to the situation at hand. Bledsoe stopped cutting and turned his head. For a split second hope jumped through her when she envisioned Striker coming through the door with his weapon drawn. But when she looked up, Brandon Rakestraw walked through the door and approached them.

"I told you to wait for me," Rakestraw said.

"I'm just prepping her. Getting some preliminary stuff

out of the way." Bledsoe sat back on his heels and looked at her as if she were nothing more than a window display. "I thought we'd leave the panties and bra. Work on her some. Get some anticipation going."

"That's good." Rakestraw considered her. "I brought extra lighting. We can use the black backdrop this time."

"Definitely more dramatic. I'd like to shoot some black and white stills, too."

Lindsey listened, horror and disbelief pounding through her that they could be discussing what they would do to her with such cold calculation.

"Please don't do this," she said, but her throat was so tight she could barely squeeze out the words.

"Hi, Lindsey." Rakestraw crossed to her, squatted next to the chair and grinned. Charming. Handsome. A psychopath.

"Welcome to our little studio." He made a sweeping gesture with his hand. "What do you think?"

"I think you're a couple of psychopaths."

Grinning, he reached out and smoothed back a strand of her hair. "I don't think she has any appreciation for art."

"Definitely not."

She wasn't sure how she found the saliva—her mouth was bone dry—but she spit on him.

He recoiled, wiped his face with his sleeve. Then his lips peeled back in a snarl. His hand shot out, cracked across her face so quickly she didn't have time to brace. Tears of pain and outrage blurred her vision. She tasted blood. But she didn't give him the satisfaction of hearing her cry out.

"Don't mess up her face," Bledsoe said.

"She spit on me!"

Bledsoe laughed. "So gag her."

Glaring at her, Rakestraw walked over to the workbench and picked up a leather ball gag. "I didn't want to have to do this . . ."

She wanted to tell him to go to hell, but the terror choked her. Vaguely, she was aware of Bledsoe tugging at the left leg of her jeans, the denim sliding easily from her body. Of Rakestraw standing so close she could smell the stink of burnt cloves. They were watching her, touching her, and she knew they were going to do unspeakable things to her. The horror of that was too much for her mind to absorb, and she could feel her emotions shutting down. Her body going numb.

Closing her eyes, she went to a place deep inside herself. A place where they couldn't see her. Couldn't touch her. A dark place where she was safe and alone. A place she had gone many times as a child.

Slowly, the music faded. The sensation of the shears moving over her left hip diminished. The pain in her cheekbone melted away. Her world turned to monochrome. And then she was floating. Embraced by warmth and darkness and the sensation of nothingness.

chapter
32

STRIKER HAD BEEN A PATROL OFFICER FOR TEN years before becoming a detective. He knew the streets of Seattle and the surrounding areas like the back of his hand, and it took him less than fifteen minutes to reach the West Seattle Bridge. He exited at Spokane, blew the stop sign at the service road, and entered a seedy warehouse district that banked the west side of the Duwamish River.

The jeep fishtailed on the wet asphalt when he turned onto a side street. He slowed and began looking for identifying address numbers on the myriad warehouses and vacant buildings. He cut the lights and idled down the street, looking left and right. Al's Transmissions. A shipping container storage lot. Marine engine repair. Two streets down, he hit Norse, made a left. The building wasn't marked, but even in the dim light from the streetlamp, he could make out the lettering *Scott Machine Shop*.

He pulled into a deserted lot down the street and parked. The night embraced him like a cold, wet hand when he got out. He told himself it was adrenaline that had his entire body shaking, but Striker recognized the metallic taste of fear. He knew that fear didn't have a damn thing to do with himself, and had everything to do with a woman he'd come to care about more than his own life.

He tugged the H & K .45 from his shoulder holster, checked the clip, and crossed the street at a run. A gravel lot took him to the large corrugated steel building. It was unobtrusive, relatively deserted, and blended well into the neighborhood. With soundproofing, it was the perfect place for murder.

Keeping low, Striker jogged to the front door. A NO TRESPASSING sign and a brand-new padlock greeted him. He tugged at the lock, but it held. He could hear the low rumble of rock and roll coming from inside, and his nerves squirmed. Bledsoe was there. He could feel it.

For an instant he considered shooting off the lock, but knew that with Lindsey inside, a stealthy entry would be best. He glanced left and right, looking for another place to enter. The windows were high and had been sealed with some type of storm shutter. *Damn.*

Leaving the front of the building, he jogged around to the side, spotted the steel grate stairs that led to the second level. The rain was coming down in earnest now, but he barely felt the cold or wet as he sprinted to the stairs and took the steps to the top.

On the landing, he tried the door. Panic sliced him neatly when he found it locked. He could feel the seconds ticking away and tried desperately not to think of what could be happening inside. He looked around, spotted a window several feet over. It would be a precarious climb. He would have to keep his balance by clinging to the siding that had torn away from the building and maintain a foothold on a very narrow sill, but he thought he could manage it.

Praying the window wasn't locked, he holstered the gun and stepped over the steel rail. Sliding his fingers beneath a sheet of loose siding, he set his foot on the sill and sidled toward the window a few inches at a time.

The window had been blacked out, painted from the inside. He could hear the music over the din of rain. Loud enough to rattle the walls. He continued sliding his feet along the sill until he reached the window. It was an old-fashioned push-out type. The screws had rusted off the lock, and he was able to shove it open with relative ease. He slipped his head inside. The music was deafening. He looked around, noticed the hit-or-miss overhead lights. Directly below him, a steel grate catwalk ran the length of the building. On the floor level there were steel support beams and wooden pallets stacked haphazardly. Dozens of fifty-gallon drums. Plenty of cover.

Movement on the floor and to his right caught his attention. He squinted, trying to see between the steel rails of the catwalk and the support beams, and saw the bright lights. A man with dark hair. Blue jeans. Some type of photography lighting had been set up.

Then he heard the scream. High-pitched and bloodcurdling. A scream of pain and outrage and horror. Lindsey, he thought, and for moment he couldn't move, couldn't breathe. He stood there, trembling and sick and utterly terrified because he couldn't bear the thought of her being hurt. He squeezed his eyes shut, trying to shut out the sound, fought hard for control. He took several deep breaths. Reminded himself he was her only chance, felt his nerves begin to settle.

Shoving open the window as far as it would go, keenly aware that if either man looked up he would be in plain view, Striker bent at the hip, put his left leg through the window and heaved his body inside. One of the panes of glass snapped beneath his weight. He heard the tinkle of glass as it struck the catwalk. Then his left foot made contact with the steel grating on the other side. He slid in the rest of the way, drew the H & K and went to a crouch.

Another scream shattered his nerves. He heard male laughter. He closed his eyes, tried not to think about what they were doing to her.

Hang on, Lindsey. I'm coming for you . . .

He moved silently down the catwalk, took the stairs to the floor. Lindsey and Bledsoe were to his right. He darted to a steel support beam, pressed his back to it. He was thirty feet away. Close enough to hear their voices.

Holding the pistol ready, he moved soundlessly across the floor, his every sense on alert. He spotted the revolver on the workbench a few feet away where Lindsey was tied. A sawed-off shotgun was propped against the nearest steel beam.

Not the greatest odds, but Striker figured he could take them. It was two against one, but they were distracted and Striker had the element of surprise on his side.

Raising the .45, he drew a bead on Brandon Rakestraw and stepped into view.

Lindsey didn't know how much time had passed. It seemed like an eternity, but it could have been minutes. At some point she'd lost all perception of time. But the terror brought her back. It was like a wild animal trapped inside her. Her heart was like a freight train in her chest, so loud and fast she thought it would explode. She wanted to scream and scream and scream, but they'd put a gag in her mouth, and she could do nothing but make unintelligible noises.

Brandon Rakestraw stood over her. A monster in a leather mask. Unspeakable cruelty in his eyes. A few feet away Bledsoe stood with a video camera, its red eye mocking her.

"Smile for the camera, Lindsey." Rakestraw held what looked like a box cutter in his right hand. He studied it for a moment, then smiled down at her. "I think we'll begin with this."

Lindsey threw her head back and screamed, but the

sound was muffled. Vaguely, she was aware of Rakestraw laughing at her. His laughter blended with the music to form a maniacal sound as it echoed in the warehouse.

"Don't move, or I swear to Christ I'll put a bullet in your brain!"

Shock and hope swept through her at the sound of Striker's voice. She opened her eyes, saw him step out from behind a steel support beam with his gun poised on Rakestraw, and a terrible keening sound tore from her throat.

"I'm here, Lindsey," he said.

Relief poured over her in a torrent, so powerful that she was overwhelmed. She closed her eyes, and a sob choked out of her. He'd come for her. Just as she'd known he would.

Then she remembered the shotgun, and a stark new fear crept over her. She tried to warn him, but the gag made her words indecipherable.

Striker moved quickly toward them, gun trained on Rakestraw, his eyes flicking down to the box cutter in his hand. "Put it down, you piece of shit."

Lindsey saw rage in his eyes. The kind of rage that was bottomless and black and unpredictable. She saw it in the way he moved. In the way he ground his teeth. And even though Rakestraw was a despicable human being and had done unspeakable things to countless young women, she was afraid for him.

Because she knew Striker was going to kill him.

Don't, she thought. *He's not worth it.*

Striker strode toward them, his gun on Rakestraw's chest, his gaze fixed on her. His brows rode low over eyes black with fury. She stared back at him, aware that her entire body was shaking uncontrollably.

Rakestraw stood a foot away from her. He watched Striker approach, his eyes flicking from Lindsey to the instrument in his hand.

"Give me an excuse," Striker said between clenched teeth. "Because I'm dying to put a bullet in you."

Rakestraw smiled.

Lindsey knew Rakestraw was going to move an instant before he lunged. She tried to shout a warning, but the sound died in her throat when Rakestraw raised the box cutter high above his head. The instrument came down in a perfect arc. She screamed into the gag, braced for pain.

In her peripheral vision, she saw Striker move.

Then a gunshot shattered the night.

chapter
33

STRIKER WENT FOR THE HEADSHOT, WATCHED THE slug tear a neat hole an inch above Brandon Rakestraw's right eye. His body jerked. His eyes widened, then glazed. The box cutter fell from his hand. Striker felt nothing but a vague sense of satisfaction when Rakestraw crumpled to the concrete.

Bledsoe went for the revolver on the workbench. Striker turned, brought the pistol up, and squeezed off three shots in quick succession. Bledsoe screamed. Striker saw blood on the other man's sleeve, knew he'd only winged him. Bledsoe brought up the revolver and fired.

Striker shifted his aim, fired two more times. Bledsoe returned fire. Striker knew the revolver only had six shots; he tried to count. He got to four when his pistol was violently blown from his grip. Pain zipped from his hand to his elbow. He saw the gun fall to the floor and skitter away. Stunned, he looked down, saw blood, realized a bullet had gone clean through his right palm.

Son of a bitch!

Striker dove for the fallen .45, tried to pick it up to get off a shot, but his right hand was numb and useless. Cursing, he put the weapon in his left hand, spun to face Bledsoe.

Another shot exploded. Striker heard the hot zing as a bullet flew past his ear. He raised the pistol, squeezed the trigger. The shot went wide. Bledsoe laughed maniacally, fired again. Striker heard a ricochet. Bledsoe's last shot. He lowered the pistol.

Bledsoe blinked at him, confused. Then his mouth stretched into a smile. He raised the revolver, pointed it at Striker's face. "Motherfucker," he said and pulled the trigger.

Click.

Striker smiled, but it felt like a snarl on his face. "You should have counted your bullets, Bledsoe."

The other man's hand dipped into his pocket, pulled out a switchblade, flipped it open. "This will work just as well."

"Don't count on it."

"How many shots do you have left, Striker?"

"Enough to put one between your eyes."

"Really?" His gaze flicked to Striker's hand where a small puddle of blood had formed on the concrete beside his right foot. "Do you honestly think you can aim that thing left-handed?"

"Looks like we're going to find out." Striker stepped toward him. "Put down the knife."

"And if I don't?"

"I'll tattoo your fucking forehead. And I'll enjoy doing it."

Bledsoe's eyes flicked to Lindsey. "Did you know she cried out your name when we hurt her?"

Striker said nothing, but he could feel his pulse racing. Pain pounding all the way to his shoulder. The gun felt awkward in his left hand. He measured the distance between them. If Bledsoe charged, he wondered if he could get off a shot before the other man slashed his throat . . . or cut Lindsey.

"I'll make you a deal, Striker. I win this, and you get to watch me kill her. You win, and you get the girl. Deal?"

Striker remained silent, but he was exploding inside.

"I think that would get to you, Striker. What do you think?"

"I think your sick little game is about to blow up in your face."

Bledsoe nodded, then looked around. "You know, a little bit of scrambling, and I can probably lay all of this on you. I mean, come on, everyone knows you've already flipped out once. Shouldn't be too much of a stretch for them to believe you could kill your lover."

"You have two seconds to put down the knife." Striker shifted the gun, decided to take the safer body shot.

Bledsoe charged. Striker fired, but the shot went wide. Stainless steel flashed as the blade came down. He caught a glimpse of Bledsoe's face. Lips peeled back, eyes wild with rage. Striker fired again. Bledsoe jolted, but the knife arced down. Striker dodged, but the blade slashed, pain searing across his left cheek.

Striker slammed his fist into the other man's face, but Bledsoe was already limp and falling. The switchblade clattered to the floor. Bledsoe collapsed and lay still.

For several seconds, Striker stood there and watched a dark pool of blood spread. Kneeling, he pressed his fingers against the other man's carotid. A vague sense of relief went through him when he didn't get a pulse.

Lindsey.

The sight of her bound and helpless nearly undid him. Her face was white with terror and streaked with tears. At some point her nose had bled. He was too utterly shaken to do anything but stand there and look at her and thank God she was alive.

Then the need to hold her safe and warm in his arms

consumed him. Before even realizing he was going to move, he started toward her. "Lindsey. Oh, baby . . ."

She made a sound that broke his heart.

He reached her, dropped to his knees next to her. "You're going to be all right. I'm here." Using his left hand, he unfastened the gag, gently pulled it from her mouth, flung it aside.

"Striker," she choked. "Oh, God . . . Oh, dear God . . ."

"Shh. It's okay." He worked off his jacket, draped it over her. She was cold to the touch, slicked with sweat, shaking violently. An inch away from going into shock. "Everything's going to be okay."

"You came. I knew you would."

"I'm here, baby."

"I thought . . . I thought they were going to—"

"Easy. Nobody's going to hurt you. You're going to be all right. I promise." His voice was taut. His hands were shaking. Cold sweat pooled and ran down his back. For an instant he wondered if maybe he was going into shock because of the bullet wound in his hand. Or maybe he was so overcome with relief that she was alive that he was losing it.

"Your face," she whispered.

He'd almost forgotten about the cut from the switchblade. "Nicked me with the knife. It's not bad."

Her eyes flicked to Bledsoe. "Is he dead?"

He nodded. "They're not going to hurt anyone else."

She closed her eyes. He felt her body relax marginally.

"How bad did they hurt you?" he asked, but he was already running his hands over her, checking for injuries.

"I'm . . . okay. He cut my abdomen, but I don't think it's deep. He just . . . God, Striker, just knowing what they were going to do. Knowing they were going to film it. Just like that girl. They were going to . . . they were going to . . ."

He cut the wires binding her and pulled her to him, aware that she was trembling, sobbing uncontrollably, gasping for breath. Burying his face in her hair he closed his eyes. For the first time in his adult life, he felt the burn of tears.

"Striker?

"Just let me hold you for a little while, okay?"

After a moment, she pulled back slightly, gazed into his eyes. She started to say something, but he leaned forward and kissed her. A gentle kiss that tore something open inside him. He set his hand against the back of her head. Touched her hair. Her neck and shoulders. He never wanted to stop touching her. "For what it's worth," he said. "I love you."

A tremor ran the length of her. Then she smiled at him. "It's worth a lot."

"I love you more than my own life," he said. "No matter what happens, I'll always love you. Don't forget that."

"I have a really good memory," she said and kissed him.

chapter
34

Ten months later:

Lindsey brushed periwinkle blue paint over the bland off-white that had adorned the walls of her apartment for the last four years and tried to make herself believe the change of scenery was going to make her feel better. Frank Sinatra's *Fly Me to the Moon* eased from the boom box Carissa had placed on the tarp draped over the coffee table. Outside, the first snowfall of the season powdered the naked trees and turned Columbus into a pristine wonderland.

Setting the paintbrush on a protective strip of polyurethane sheeting, Lindsey stepped back and studied her handiwork. "The periwinkle is too dark."

On the other side of the living room Carissa peeked at her over the top of the sofa where she'd been taping off the baseboard and oak flooring. "It looks great against this white woodwork, Linds."

"Maybe if I bought new lamps."

Grunting with the effort, Carissa got to her feet and

brushed her hands against her hips. "What do you mean lamps? Lindsey, this place needs an overhaul. You know, the works. New sofa. New end tables." She looked around. "That coffee table looks like something Archie Bunker had in his living room for God's sake."

"That does it. You've talked me into it." Stepping onto the ladder, Lindsey resumed applying the periwinkle over the white. Ten months had passed since her trip to Seattle. She wanted to believe she was dealing with everything that had happened. The loss of her sister. The horrors she'd endured at the hands of Jace Bledsoe and Brandon Rakestraw. The end of a relationship that had meant more to her than she'd ever dreamed possible.

She wanted to believe she was healing and moving forward with her life. For ten months she'd concentrated on staying busy, taking on new hobbies, volunteering at the local Big Sister program. She had found solace in her work, some semblance of peace in the day-to-day routine of her life. She'd even gone out on a blind date Carissa had set up.

She drove herself relentlessly, never giving herself time to reflect too much or think too deeply because she knew if she did it would all come rushing back and her heart would break all over again.

Lindsey knew what she had become. A woman whose only comfort was her job. A woman who couldn't bear the silence of her own apartment. A woman who still woke to nightmares in the middle of the night. A woman who cried out in her sleep for a man she loved with all of her heart and soul.

Her therapist had told her that time was the great healer. Everyday that passed, she diligently marked her mental calendar with a giant X. With every X, she expected the pain to lessen. She expected her sister's death to hurt a little less. The loss of a man she'd loved desperately to fade a little more. She expected the ache in her heart to diminish. The wounds left on her soul to heal.

Time, the great healer, was not living up to her expectations.

Her sister was gone forever. The grinning, blue-eyed tomboy she'd grown up with. The spirited young woman who'd run away from one monster only to find another. Traci had paid for her mistakes a thousand times over. Mistakes that, Lindsey had decided, no longer mattered in the grand scheme of things. What did matter, was that Traci had loved her. That she'd had a good heart. And Lindsey had loved her with all of hers. She would always see her as the blue-eyed girl with the toothy grin and skinny legs. She would always love her. And she would never, ever forget her.

She hadn't seen or heard from Michael Striker since that terrible last night. He'd ridden with her to the hospital, stayed with her while she'd been examined and admitted. He'd been there for her when the police had questioned her. He'd been the one to confirm Traci's death, then he'd held her while she went to pieces. And after she'd fallen asleep, he'd simply vanished.

Lindsey had been released the following day. She'd tried a dozen times to contact him via his cell phone, his home, and his office. All to no avail. Not easily deterred, she'd driven to his loft. His office. She'd even braved the police department where Detectives Landreth and Murray had sworn they hadn't seen him. After three days she'd gotten the message and flown back to Columbus.

She'd expected time and distance and the fast pace of her life to help her forget about him and move on. But they hadn't.

She'd followed his trial via the Internet and the national news. She'd even subscribed to the *Seattle Times*. Every day she scoured the pages, hoping for news, praying for a miracle, settling for the mention of his name and maybe a photo if she was lucky. The trial had lasted a little over two weeks. In the end, former police detective Michael Striker had been found guilty of first-degree felony assault and sentenced to three years in Walla Walla State Prison.

Lindsey hadn't made it to the shop that day. When Carissa had come to her door, her knowing eyes filled with empathy, all Lindsey could do was go into her arms and cry. Carissa had cried with her. Ranted with her. They'd stayed up all night. Crying. Talking. Laughing. And crying some more.

They hadn't discussed it since. Carissa had breeched the subject once or twice, but Lindsey simply couldn't bring herself to talk about it because it broke her heart to think of a good man like Striker behind bars. She would never forget the time they'd spent together. She would never forget that he'd saved her life. She wanted badly to believe he'd done the right thing by forcing her to get on with her life.

She didn't believe that for a second.

The doorbell jangled, drawing her from her reverie. She looked over her shoulder to see Carissa getting to her feet. "If they're selling something, hand them a paintbrush," Lindsey said.

She returned her attention to her painting, humming along with Frank Sinatra and trying not to feel depressed. She could get through this day, she assured herself. The painting was coming along nicely. She had karate class at 7:30. A movie at the mall at 9:30. Home at midnight. Too exhausted to dream. Another day past. One more X on the calendar.

"Lindsey?"

"Hmm?"

"Um . . . you've got company."

Something in her friend's voice made her turn. Her heart did a slow backward roll when she saw Michael Striker standing in her foyer. He was staring at her, taking her measure, and for several interminable seconds she forgot to breathe.

He wore dark slacks. A gray sweater. He looked a little leaner. A little harder. And even though the day's growth of stubble on his jaw made him look a little rough around the edges, there was a softness in his eyes that hadn't been there before.

"I like the blue," he said.

Dumbstruck, she looked down at the paintbrush in her hand. A dozen responses scrolled through her brain, but she couldn't seem to form a single, coherent word. All she could do was stand on the stepladder and stare because her knees were shaking so badly she didn't trust herself to get down.

Carissa's gaze swept from Lindsey to Striker, and she grinned like a fool. "I think this is probably a good time for me to go and pick up some Chinese takeout."

Lindsey barely heard her friend. She couldn't take her eyes off Striker. Couldn't believe he was standing so close she could smell the scent of his aftershave.

"How are you?" he asked after an awkward moment.

"I'm . . ." She looked down at her clothes and choked out a laugh. "Covered with paint."

"You look really good in blue."

Ridiculously embarrassed, exasperated with herself because she could barely speak, she set her hand against an unpainted section of the wall and stepped off the ladder. "How did you . . . I mean, why are you . . . I thought . . ."

An emotion she couldn't quite read flickered in his eyes. "The governor commuted my sentence," he said. "I was released yesterday morning."

The words were almost too much to absorb. She could feel the emotions building inside her, like water against a dam, pushing, pushing . . .

Lindsey walked over to the counter and leaned, her mind reeling. "My God, Striker, that's incredible news. I don't know what to say. I'm happy for you."

"Yeah, well, I'm still trying to get used to the idea myself."

Carissa came up beside her, eased the paintbrush from her hand. "Linds, I'll clean up when I get back, okay? Why don't you two sit in the kitchen?" Not waiting for a response, she turned to Striker and stuck out her hand. "I'm Carissa, by the way, Lindsey's best friend and business partner."

He accepted her handshake. "Michael Striker."

"Yeah, I got that." She pumped his hand. "Nice to meet you and all that, but I swear to Christ if you hurt her again, I'll rip out your heart."

He arched a brow. "I gotcha."

"Just so there's no confusion." Smiling sweetly, Carissa turned back to Lindsey and mouthed the words: "You didn't tell me he was drop-dead gorgeous."

Lindsey felt the weight of Striker's stare, but she didn't look at him. She was too flustered. Her emotions were too jumbled. And Carissa wasn't helping matters by acting like an idiot.

Determined to pull herself together, she left the bar and walked into the kitchen, trying hard not to notice how faded her jeans were, that there was a hole in the left knee, or that her sweatshirt was speckled with periwinkle blue. At the sink she washed the paint from her hands. When she ran out of things to do, she finally turned to Striker.

He was standing a few feet behind her, watching her. She knew it was impossible, but he seemed taller. Even though he was more lean than buff, he seemed to fill the entire room. His eyes were clear and dark and held her gaze so that she couldn't look away.

Vaguely she was aware of Carissa going out the front door. Nerves gripped her when she realized they were alone. That she didn't know what to say or how to feel.

Her pulse began to race when he crossed to her. "Lindsey . . ."

She started to step back, but her rear hit the sink. She knew he was going to touch her and tried hard to steel

herself against him. But she jolted when he set his hands
on her shoulders. His touch was incredibly gentle, as if he
were touching something fragile and easily broken. She
could feel the heat of his fingers coming through her
sweatshirt. One of them was shaking, but for the life of her
she couldn't tell who.

"If you had called first, I would have . . . cleaned up,"
she blurted.

"I didn't call first, because I thought you might refuse to
see me."

"I'm angry with you, Striker."

"You're entitled." He studied her face the way an artist
would study a painting, taking in every detail, appreciative
of its beauty. "But that doesn't change the way things are
between us."

"You wouldn't take my calls," she said. "You didn't
write. Not even to let me know you were okay."

"I couldn't, Lindsey. Not in the position I was in. I told
you that right off the bat."

"That you were forthcoming didn't make it hurt any
less."

"I didn't mean to hurt you." He paused, looked away,
then back at her. "Letting you go . . . Lindsey, it was the
hardest thing I've ever had to do." The muscles in his jaw
flexed. "What we had . . . was intense and incredible, and I
think that took us by surprise. I wanted to be with you,
Lindsey, more than you'll ever know. But if I'd been sentenced to ten years . . . there was no way I'd ask you to put
your life on hold for me."

She wasn't sure how she felt about that. The pain was
still too fresh. The wounds too deep. The scars not yet
healed. One thing she did know was that it was the most
selfless thing he could have done.

Even if it had broken her heart.

"I followed the trial," she said. "The day you were convicted. God, Striker, it was like part of me died. The

thought of you going to prison . . . the unjustness of it tore me up."

"I know this sounds crazy, Lindsey, but I'm a better man for the ten months I spent in prison."

"That's because you're an honorable man. You hold yourself accountable."

He looked a little embarrassed, covered it with a half smile. "Don't let the stiff upper lip fool you. Being locked up . . . it was no walk in the park. Prison was bad. But, Lindsey, not seeing you, not knowing where you were or how you were doing, or if I'd ever see you again was worse. The way I left things between us, knowing I'd hurt you . . . that wrecked me."

"You could have written me. Striker, I would have come—"

"I wrote you a hundred letters in the last ten months."

"Why didn't you send them?"

"Because I knew you would have come to the prison to see me. That was the one thing I couldn't let you do. I didn't want you to walk into that place or see me like that."

She drew a shuddery breath. "How did the commutation come about?"

"The governor's office stepped in about six weeks after I went in. My being an ex-cop helped. The circumstances behind the crime I committed were . . . extraordinary. What happened to you. The case you and I cracked. Bledsoe and Rakestraw. It's not official yet, but the man who bought at least one of the disks has been arrested. Another man working out of the Philippines has been indicted. The FBI is working on extradition as we speak. The governor took all of those things into consideration and got it done."

That justice would finally prevail for the victims and their families—for Traci—gave her a badly needed sense of closure. "I'm glad," she said.

Striker's hands tightened on her shoulders. "I thought about you every day of those ten months," he said. "I was desperate to know how you were doing. How you were handling Traci's death. How you were dealing with what happened to you. I know that kind of thing can leave scars."

"It was hard," she admitted, thinking of the nightmares. Of the countless nights she'd wakened with a scream in her throat. The other nights when she'd lain in her bed, awake and missing him so desperately she thought she would die. "But things are better. I have my catering business. I take karate."

He smiled. "Still at it, huh?"

"I'm a blue belt, now."

"Thanks for the warning."

"Carissa has been an incredible friend."

"I like your friend."

"She's . . . a little protective."

"She knows what you went through?"

Lindsey nodded, then tried to look away, but he lifted his hand to cup her chin.

His eyes burned into hers. "I did a lot of thinking while I was away. A man has that kind of time on his hands . . . it gives him perspective, you know?"

She wasn't sure where he was going with that, but she nodded.

"I needed that time to figure some things out," he said.

"So do you have everything figured out now?"

One side of his mouth curved. "I'm still working on it for the most part. But one thing I do know is that the time we spent together . . . it meant something to me." He sighed, but his breath shuddered a little. "It meant a lot."

"Is that why you're here?"

"I'm here because I couldn't stay away."

"So what do we do now?"

"I thought we might take some time. Get to know each other." He shrugged. "Go out on a date."

"A date?" She choked out a laugh. "Striker, that dating stuff . . . I'm not very good at it."

"You told me you weren't good at something else once before, and then you blew my mind."

A quiver that was part emotional, part physical, moved through her. She was keenly aware of his touch, the scent of his aftershave, that his hands were trembling slightly. "I don't know where that leaves us."

"That leaves us wherever we want to be." He ran his hands up and down her arms. "I think you know me well enough to know I'm not going to walk away from you."

"Striker, you keep shocking me."

"I want to be part of your life, Lindsey. I want you to be part of mine. I want to make you happy." He smiled a little, but his eyes remained sober. "I've been waiting ten months to say those things to you."

Tears glittered in her eyes when she turned her face up to his. "I thought it was over. I thought—"

"Honey, it's not over by a long shot." Gently, he pulled her to him. "Come here."

She stepped into his embrace. A sigh escaped her when his arms went around her. His body was as hard and sleek as steel against hers. She could feel the tremors moving through him and into her. She laid her head on his shoulder and for a moment listened to the beat of his heart.

"The future is an open door," he said. "It's new and it's ours for the taking if we want it. I want you to walk through that door with me."

Pulling back slightly, she looked into his eyes. "The future," she whispered. "I like the sound of that very much."

He slid his hands to either side of her face, marveling at her loveliness, and he was amazed that Fate would be so kind as to send her his way.

"I love you," he said and lowered his mouth to hers. She opened to him, and the sweetness of the kiss devastated him. He wanted more; he could feel the sharp edge of need moving through him. But for the first time since he'd known her, he knew they had the precious gift of time.

Pulling back slightly, he took her hand in his and brushed his lips across her knuckles. "That's one message I wanted to deliver in person," he said.

"I never stopped loving you," she whispered.

He closed his eyes briefly, and Lindsey saw clearly how much those words mean to him.

Unable to speak for the emotions crowding into her throat, she rested her head against his chest where his heart beat in perfect time with hers. "So tell me, Striker, do you know how to paint?"

"I can paint like a fiend," he said.

"Roller or brush?"

He grinned. "Both."

She smiled back at him, and together they took the first faltering step into tomorrow.

NAT JENNINGS JOLTED AWAKE TO A DEAFENING CLAP of thunder. For several seconds she lay in bed and listened for the ping of rain against the window. She watched for the quick flash of lightning, waited for the ensuing crash of thunder. But the night was silent and still. Even the usual chorus of crickets and frogs from the woods behind the house was hushed.

Stretching, she turned and reached for her husband, Ward, only to find his side of the bed empty. She ran her hand over the sheets and found them cool. Puzzled, she sat up and squinted at the alarm clock next to the bed to find it was nearly three A.M.

"Ward?"

She listened for a moment, inexplicably uneasy. When he didn't respond, she rose and slipped into her robe, then padded to the door in her bare feet and peeked into the hall.

"Hon, are you there?" she called out.

The house was dark and silent as she moved down the hall toward her son's room. Fully awake now, she pushed

open the door and peered inside. A frisson of uneasiness
went through her when she found the bed empty, the Spi-
derman coverlet turned down. A few feet away the curtains
billowed in the breeze coming in through the window. Beyond, Nat saw silvered clouds skidding past a three-quarter
moon, and the hairs at her nape stood on end. She could
have sworn she'd heard thunder. . . .

Aware that her heart was beating too fast, she took the
stairs to the darkened living room. She wanted to believe
her husband and son were in the kitchen, raiding the
freezer and indulging in the rocky road ice cream she'd
picked up at the grocery. But the lights were off. She could
see the spill of moonlight slanting in through the kitchen
door. "Ward? Kyle?"

Growing increasingly concerned, she rounded the sofa
and peered into the kitchen. She saw the outline of glossy
oak cabinets. Moonlight glinting off the polished granite
countertops. The curtains fluttering above the sink.

Her heart slammed hard against her ribs when she spotted Kyle lying motionless on the floor. For the span of several heartbeats she stared at her son's form, unable to get
her mind around the picture of her seven-year-old little boy
lying silent and still on the cold tile in his teddy bear pajamas.

"Kyle?"

She smelled the blood an instant before she saw it. Coppery and warm and as black as melted tar in the semidarkness. Horror and disbelief screamed through her. She could
feel it tearing through her body with the violence of a hollow point bullet.

Her vision tunneled on her son, so tiny and pale and
bleeding out right before her eyes. The pool of blood
seemed to cover half of the floor. In a distant corner of her
mind she wondered how such a little body could bleed so
much. . . .

"Kyle!"

Then she was rushing to her child, her breaths bursting from her throat in ragged gasps. In her peripheral vision she saw Ward sprawled near the cooking island. Another wave of horror exploded in her brain when she saw that his pajamas were covered with blood.

"Ward! Ohmigod! *Ohmigod!*"

She dropped to her knees beside her son's prone form, her brain stumbling through basic first aid, knowing deep inside that it was already too late. "Kyle! Oh, baby, talk to Mommy! What *happened?*"

She heard movement behind her. A brutal punch of terror took her breath when she realized whomever had done this was still in the house. Nat didn't know how she got to her feet, but the next thing she knew she was standing, shaking, dizzy with horror. She could hear herself breathing hard. The razor edge of panic cutting her. Her pulse roaring like a tornado in her ears. Every beat of her heart was like a fist pounding her chest.

The silhouette of a man moved toward her. She saw dark clothes. A ski mask. Moonlight from the window flittered like blue ice, and she realized he had a knife.

He's going to kill me, she thought, and the terror of that paralyzed her.

"Bitch," he snarled and lunged.

Nat snapped out of her stupor just as the blade came down. Screaming, she raised her arms to protect herself. But at the last instant he changed tactics and went in low, slashing from left to right. She tried to get out of the way, but she wasn't fast enough and the blade sliced across her belly. An animal sound tore from her throat as the shock of pain registered. The sensation of heat just below her ribs. The realization that he'd cut her.

An instant later, she crashed against the counter, realized he'd cornered her. "Get away from me!" she screamed.

The knife went up. Knowing he was going to cut her

again if she didn't get away, Nat grabbed the coffeemaker, dragged it across the counter, and slammed it into him. The carafe flew from its nest and hit the stove. Glass shattered. The coffeemaker clattered to the floor.

Then she was shoving past him, expecting at any moment for the knife to plunge into her back. She left the kitchen at a dangerous speed, tore around the corner, streaked through the darkened living room. In the study, she sprinted to the gun cabinet where Ward kept his .22 revolver. Her fingers fumbled for the key, but it was gone.

She drew back and rammed her fist through the glass front. Glass exploded. Shards bit into her knuckles, but she felt no pain. Knowing she had only a fraction of a second to get the gun, she grappled blindly.

But the gun was gone.

A sound of panic and disbelief ripped from her throat. A creak from the hall spun her around. She saw movement at the door and knew the intruder had followed her. That he was going to kill her if she let him. She wasn't going to make it easy.

She lunged toward the desk, snatched up the phone. He beat her to it and ripped the cord from the wall. Knowing her best hope was her cell phone recharging in the kitchen, she bolted past him toward the door. He tried to grab her, she felt the scrape of his fingertips on her arm, heard her robe tear as he snagged the fabric, but she broke free and raced toward the kitchen.

She blew through the doorway. Shock punched her at the sight of the revolver atop the cooking island. She pounced on the gun. The wood grip was cold and rough against her palm. She gripped it tightly, brought it up as she swung it around.

Choking out animal sounds, she pulled the trigger. Once. Twice. The only sound that came was the click of the hammer against the firing pin, and it was like a death knell in the silence.

"No!" Screaming, she threw the pistol at the intruder as hard as she could.

She darted to the phone, but before she'd gone two steps, viselike fingers closed around her right biceps, jerked her around to face him. Nat had always considered herself physically strong. But the man's strength stunned her. The violence of his touch took her breath. She didn't see the knife arc. White-hot pain flashed from her wrist to her forearm. She screamed, tried to twist away. She saw his arm go up again and she thought, *Oh, dear God, he's going to hack me to death. . . .*

The blade flickered as the knife arced. She tried to jump back but he was still holding her. Heat streaked from her left breast to her navel. There was no pain, but the knowledge that she'd been cut shocked and horrified. She felt the warmth of blood on her T-shirt. The material clinging wetly to her. The metallic stench filling her nostrils.

She tried to fight, tried to free herself so she could run, but for the first time in her life Nat was paralyzed with fear. The knife came down again, and she felt the numbing pain of a razor slash on her belly. She tried to use her knee, but her bare feet slipped in the blood. The intruder jerked her toward him, and then she was falling. . . .

Nat screamed in horror and rage as she went down. She couldn't believe this was happening to her. Couldn't believe it had happened to her family. Violent crime didn't happen in Bellerose. . . .

Then she was on her hands and knees, crawling away from her attacker. Whimpering like a beaten dog, she made it to the cooking island and used the cabinet door to pull herself to her feet. She looked around, expecting him to rush her at any moment. But the kitchen was empty and silent.

"Oh, God. Oh, *God!*" Choking back sobs, Nat stumbled to the phone and punched 911.

Taking the phone with her, she dropped to her knees at

her son's side, touched his little shoulder. "Kyle," she whispered. "Oh, my baby. Mama's here, sweetie. I'm here." Gently, she turned her son onto his back. "Please, God, oh, please let him be all right. . . ."

Kyle's eyes were open, and for a moment Nat expected her little boy to look up at her and smile the way he'd done a thousand times before. But when she pressed her fingers to the carotid artery, there was no pulse.

She heard a voice on the other end of the phone.

And then Nat Jennings began to scream.

Three years later:

Nick Bastille stepped off the Greyhound bus, hefted the duffel over his shoulder, and pulled in a deep breath of air that reeked of stagnant water, sun-baked foliage, and day-old armadillo roadkill. He'd been breathing free air for three hours and fourteen minutes, and no matter how badly it stank, he still couldn't get enough into his lungs.

The October sun beat down on him like a hot cast-iron skillet as he started down the narrow asphalt road. His shirt clung wetly to his back, but the heat didn't bother him. Prison had a way of putting things into perspective for a man. After six years in Angola State Prison, the Louisiana heat mingling with the stench of his own sweat didn't even rate.

It had been eighteen years since he'd set foot in his hometown of Bellerose, but nothing had changed. Coming back was like entering a time warp and traveling back in time. The gas station out on Parish Road 53 still had only one full-service pump, which didn't accept credit cards. Old man Pelletier still grew cotton and sugar cane and drove that rusty old John Deere tractor. The shotgun shacks that sprang out of the mud like cattails on the south side of town were still just a nail or two away from sliding into the black water of the bayou with the alligators and water moccasins.

But while the town of Bellerose hadn't changed, its wayward son had. Eighteen years ago an ambitious and idealistic Nick had left this muddy little hellhole for the dazzle of New Orleans and the promise of a better life. At seventeen, he'd been on a mission to conquer the world and willing to take on any army to do it. He might have been born the son of a cotton farmer, but Fate had cursed him with a proclivity for big dreams. He'd been just enough of a gambler to pursue those dreams with the blind ambition of a reckless fool.

For a short span of time he'd had it all: a pretty wife, a beautiful little boy, a home in the New Orleans Garden District. He'd rubbed elbows with New Orleans society; he'd earned the respect and admiration of people who didn't even know little towns like Bellerose existed in their perfect worlds.

But Nick had soon learned that Fate was a fickle bitch with a penchant for cruelty and little compassion for ambitious young fools. He'd learned that dreams didn't come without a price. That hard work and a willingness to go the distance weren't enough. That love was a fallacy and trust was an illusion believed only by those who were too naïve to see the truth.

In the end Nick's dream had cost him six years of his life. Six hellish years that had ripped the last of his humanity from his soul. It should have bothered him that he was no longer even human enough to mourn its loss. But he'd long since stopped grieving over things that could never be resurrected.

Now, Bellerose's farm-boy-turned-restaurateur had nothing to his name but the clothes on his back and a hundred dollars in the pockets of his prison issue trousers. Standing in the hot Louisiana sun with the smell of swamp mud in his nostrils and a thousand regrets in his heart, he found the irony as black and endless as the bayou itself.

At the edge of town, where the cattails and alligator grass met the crushed shell road, he stopped, wiped the sweat from his forehead, and looked up at the not-so-august portals of The Blue Gator, Bellerose's only drinking establishment. Eighteen years ago, Nick had spent many an evening sipping beer and talking about all the things he was going to do with his life. Back then, the place had been an escape from the endless work of the farm and the heavy hand of his father. A place to dream and dazzle the pretty women who drove in from all over rural Tangipahoa Parish. Back then, the one-story clapboard structure hadn't seemed quite so derelict.

But The Blue Gator was as dilapidated as a place could be and still be standing. The front porch drooped like a swayback nag. The weathered wood was warped and gray as sun-bleached bones. The neon beer on tap sign looked incongruous behind the smeared glass of the single ancient window.

It was the kind of place that wouldn't last a week in New Orleans, where the health inspectors made it their mission in life to hassle restaurant and bar owners, and maybe even make a little cash on the side from the ones who could afford to avoid the hassle of citations. But The Blue Gator was exactly the kind of place that wouldn't think twice about hiring an ex-con.

Nick stepped onto the wooden porch, swung open the door, and entered the dimly lit interior. The bar reeked of spilt whiskey, old cigarette smoke, and the musty redolence of rotting wood. Slowly, his eyes adjusted to the semidarkness and he was surprised by the quick jolt of familiarity. The same dented jukebox huddled against the wall next to the men's room door. The same scarred pool table sat at the rear of the room, its green felt surface stained by booze and cigarette burns. Mike Pequinot, a man he'd gone to high school with a lifetime ago, stood behind the bar with a broom in his hand. Pequinot was an ex-biker with a fondness for Harley Davidsons, blondes in black leather, and Saturday night specials—as long as the serial number was filed off. He'd lost a leg in a motorcycle accident right before Nick left for New Orleans. He'd never bothered with a prosthesis, but it didn't look like the missing limb had slowed him down.

Pequinot stopped sweeping and looked at Nick. *"Mais, gardez dont sa."* Well, just look at that. "If it ain't my favorite con."

"Ex-con," Nick corrected and walked over to the bar. *"Il n'a in bon boute."* It's been a good while.

"When did you get sprung?"

"Cet avant midi." This morning.

Leaning on the broom, Pequinot turned and snagged two shot glasses and a bottle of dark rum from the shelf. The good stuff he saved for special occasions. He set the glasses on the bar and proceeded to break the seal and pour.

"I've been saving this for you, Nicky." Pequinot's biceps were the size of cypress trunks and just as hard. His brown hair was receding slightly, but he'd slicked it back and pulled it into a neat ponytail that reached halfway down his back. He wore a black leather vest with silver studs, faded blue jeans with a big silver buckle, and steel-toed biker boots.

"Welcome back to bumfuck, my man." He slid a shot glass to Nick. "This one's on the house."

Nick looked down at the glass. "I'm on parole, Mike."

"Fuck the Louisiana Department of Corrections. I sure as hell ain't going to tell them."

Nick didn't mention that he would be driving down to New Orleans to piss in a cup once a week for the next five years. But he knew that by the time next week rolled around, the alcohol would be long gone from his system, so he picked up the glass. "To new beginnings."

"And old friends." Pequinot downed the double in one swallow.

Nick did the same, shuddering when the rum burned all the way to his belly. He watched a heavyset woman in tight jeans and a black halter top feed quarters into the jukebox. An instant later, an old Stevie Ray Vaughan song blared from mammoth speakers situated on either side of the bar.

"That your wife?" Nick asked.

"Rita." Pequinot refilled his glass. "We tied the knot last year. She's mean as a hornet, but keeps me out of trouble."

Not wanting to get into the subject of wives and trouble, Nick didn't comment. "You seen Dutch around?" he asked, referring to his father.

"He doesn't come in anymore. I saw him at the diner last week." Pequinot grimaced. "Damn shame about the Alzheimer's."

"Knowing Dutch, I imagine he's taking it pretty hard."

Pequinot shot him a questioning look. "He keep in touch with you? Drive up to see you?"

Nick shook his head. "I told him not to," he lied.

Stevie Ray Vaughan yielded to a lively Zydeco number and with the alcohol beginning to hum through his veins and the music pounding in his ears, the place didn't seem quite so derelict, his life not quite so bleak.

"I see that ex-wife of yours around plenty, though."

Because Nick didn't want to talk about Tanya, he shrugged. "We're divorced."

"Never should have married that one, Nicky. Pretty and crazy. That's a bad combination."

"Yeah, well, you know what they say about hindsight." Nick figured he was the consummate expert on the subject.

"Divorcing you like that. It's a fucked up thing to do to a guy when he's doin' time."

Because the divorce had had nothing to do with his being incarcerated, Nick looked away. "It was a mutual thing, Mike."

Nick had spent two years of his life married to Tanya Chantal. Back then, she'd been a pretty farm girl caught up in an abusive relationship. Like some lovesick fool, Nick had rushed in to save her. The consummate rescuer, he'd fought for her and won. In the end, he'd confused lust with love and it had cost him more than he could ever have imagined a man having to pay.

"She's in here just about every night, getting shit-faced and handing it out to whoever wants it. I swear to Christ, I'd rather stick my dick in a Tasmanian devil. She's fucking nuts. Been on a downward spiral ever since—" Pequinot cut his words short, looked down at the scarred surface of the bar. *"Le Bon Dieu mait la main."* God help.

Nick tried not to react, but he felt the recoil deep inside. He tried to cover it by sliding his glass across the bar for a refill. But his hand was shaking.

It had been three years since Nick's son drowned, but the grief still cut. Some days it cut so deep, Nick thought he might just bleed out and die.

"Look," Pequinot began, refilling his glass, "you've been away for a long time. Six years is a long time for a man to go without. I know a couple of women. I can set you up. On the house for you . . ."

Though the idea of sex appealed to him greatly, Nick figured the last thing he needed in his life was a woman. Especially a hooker—on the house or not. Nick was smart enough to know when he was better off alone, and this just happened to be one of those times.

"I was actually wondering about the job, Mike. I saw the HELP WANTED sign out front." He rolled his shoulder. "I thought I might apply."

Pequinot looked amused. "This dump's a pretty far cry from that highfalutin place you had yourself down in the Big Easy."

"Highfalutin is overrated." Nick grinned, but it felt tight on his face, as if his facial muscles no longer remembered how. "Alcohol's the same no matter what kind of glass you serve it in."

"You want the job, it's yours."

Relief shuddered through Nick. Once upon a time he would have laughed at the notion of working in a dump like The Blue Gator. It was funny what a little desperation could do to a man's pride. "Thanks."

Pequinot waved off his gratitude. "I just figured you'd want to spend some time getting the farm back into shape. I hear Dutch has pretty much let everything go to shit."

"I figure I can do both." Nick finished the last of the rum and picked up his duffel.

"Ain't you going to ask me how much the job pays?"

Nick shook his head. "It doesn't matter. When do I start?"

"How about tomorrow night? We do a good business on Fridays. Shift at the mill ends at four o'clock. Guys come in thirsty. I'll need you till we close at one A.M."

"I'll be here."

Pequinot stuck out his hand. "Welcome home, Nicky."

Nick shook the other man's hand. "Thanks," he said and wished like hell he could say he was glad to be back.

Nat Jennings was going to have to stop for gas. The Mustang had been running on fumes for the last twenty miles. She'd planned on stopping at the Citgo station on the highway only to find the windows boarded up, the pumps gone, and knee-high weeds sticking out of the cracked concrete. Unless she wanted to backtrack all the way to the interstate, she was going to have to fill up in Bellerose.

"Damn," she muttered, rapping her palm against the steering wheel.

She entered the city limits, then drove slowly down Main Street, past the courthouse on the square, Boudreaux's corner drugstore, and Jenny Lee's Five and Dime. She tried hard not to notice the double takes and shocked expressions of the people who recognized her. But then she'd known before ever coming back that the upstanding citizens of Bellerose had long memories when it came to murder.

Ray's Sunoco was located on the bayou side of town, where folks were a little less interested in other people's business. The place had only one pump and hadn't yet made the technological quantum leap of accepting credit cards. *Perfect,* she thought, and pulled up to the pump and cut the engine. To her right, inside the single service bay, a black Dodge pickup was up on jacks, the jean-clad legs of the mechanic sticking out from beneath the truck. Aside from a scuffed-up Toyota, there were no other cars in sight. Relieved, Nat slid out of the car and walked around to the rear, careful to keep her back to the highway as she pumped gas.

When the tank was full, she grabbed her purse and went inside to pay. A teenage boy wearing a dirty work shirt and a sour expression sat behind the counter, eyeing her with unconcealed curiosity. A pregnant woman in a bright green maternity top was eyeballing the candy bar display.

Nat smiled at the boy. "Take a check?"

"'Slong as you have a driver's license."

"Great." Tugging her checkbook from her bag, she crossed to the counter.

"Sixteen fifty-three," he said.

Nat leaned forward and began making out the check. She could hear the low hum of the RC Cola machine out front. The hiss of the occasional car as it passed on the highway. Behind the counter, wooden shelves with peeling white paint displayed cans of 10 W-40 motor oil and filters and various sizes of engine belts. One of the cans was rattling, blending with the buzz of a fly trapped against the window.

The dizziness struck her like a sledgehammer. Too late she realized the buzzing wasn't from the soda machine or the can of oil or even the fly. The high frequency hum was

inside her head. The vibrations jolting her body all the way
to her bones. She felt the warm shock of energy. Sensations and thoughts and images looking for a channel, finding it, coming to her in dark, undulating waves.

Dear God, not now, was all she could think.

She tried to finish writing the check, but her hands fumbled the pen. Her arms drooped as if they were paralyzed.
It was a terrifying sensation, to be trapped inside her own
body and unable to control her limbs. She was aware of her
left hand clutching the pen. Her nails cutting into her palm.
Her knuckles white as her hand swept across the check.

"Lady, are you okay?"

She heard the words as if from a great distance.
Vaguely, she was aware of the boy looking at her strangely.
She wanted to answer, to reassure him that she was fine.
But the breath had been sucked from her lungs. Words and
thoughts tumbled disjointedly inside her head. She tried to
focus, but his face kept fading in and out.

An instant later her legs buckled and her knees hit the
floor with a hollow *thump!*

"Miss? Oh, good Lord!"

Nat heard alarm in the pregnant woman's voice. She
heard the shuffle of shoes against the floor. Felt a gentle
hand against her shoulder. "Honey, are you all right?"

Slowly, she became aware of the cool wood floor
against her face. She was lying on her side, still gripping
the pen. She wanted to get up, but she was dizzy and disoriented and an inch away from throwing up all over the
woman's Nikes.

"Ma'am, are you sick?" came the boy's voice.

The room came back into focus. Bracing her hand
against the floor, Nat pushed herself to a sitting position,
and shoved her hair from her face. "I'm okay," she heard
herself say.

Her checkbook lay on the floor next to her. She picked it
up, saw that her hand was trembling violently.

"You need me to call Doc Ratcliffe for you?"

Nat shook her head. "I'm fine. Really, I just . . . got a little dizzy."

Shaken and embarrassed, she rose unsteadily to her feet and brushed at her jeans. The vibrations had quieted, but her thoughts remained fuzzy and disjointed. She felt as if she'd just stumbled off some wild amusement park ride and had yet to regain her equilibrium. She glanced at the boy behind the counter, realized he was staring fixedly at the check.

bad man gonna hurt Ricky Arnaud.
hurry. water runs red

Recognizing the dark, childlike scrawl, Nat snatched the check off the counter.

Evidently, she hadn't been fast enough because the woman shot her a wary look. "What on Earth? What's that about Ricky Arnaud?"

Unwilling to explain—not sure she could even if she knew what to say—Nat shook her head. "It's nothing."

"You wrote something about Ricky Arnaud," the woman insisted.

"I just . . . must have gotten confused for a second, right before I blacked out." Nat tried to smile, but she was still too shaken to manage. "I have epilepsy."

But the woman continued to stare. Nat could practically see the wheels turning in her mind. She knew it the instant the other woman recognized her. Her eyes widened, then she took a step back, as if she'd ventured too close to something dangerous. "You're . . . Nat Jennings." The words were more accusation than revelation.

Nat slid the ruined check into the pocket of her jeans, then began writing a second one. She had wanted anonymity for her return home. She should have known that was the one luxury she would never afford. She sure as hell wasn't going to let it keep her from doing what she'd come here to do. Nat had been waiting three unbearable years for this. Come hell or high water, she was going to hunt down the son of a bitch who'd ruined her life.

The clerk and the woman exchanged startled looks. Nat did her best to ignore them, but her hand was shaking when she tore off the check and handed it to the clerk. "Thanks for the gas," she said and started for the door.